PRAISE FOI

MW01229191

AWARDS:

- Winner, Pinnacle Book Achievement Award for Science Fiction, Fall 2023
- Recommended Read by Author Shout in 2023 Reader Ready Awards

WHAT REVIEWERS ARE SAYING:

". . .edgy and perfect for lively group discussion." "*Darwin's Dilemma* is akin to Orson Scott Card's classic *Ender's Game*" with "shocking surprises that pose thought-provoking insights" and "powerful reflections on the ultimate process, cost, and dilemmas of evolution."
—D. Donovan
Senior Reviewer, Midwest Book Review

". . . an example of what good science fiction can be."
—L. Hoffman
Discovery Reviews

"I completely enjoyed getting wrapped up in this novel . . . The characters are well-developed and intriguing . . . The author did an amazing job of creating fascinating settings that are easy to visualize. The complexity of the plot also adds to the enjoyment because it is full of surprises. . . Fans of speculative science fiction will love *Darwin's Dilemma!*"
—P. Lovitt
Reader Views
A 5-Star Review

DARWIN'S DILEMMA

DON STUART

QUARTERMASTER PRESS

© 2023 Donald D. Stuart

All rights reserved.

Published by Quartermaster Press, Vashon Island, WA

This is a work of fiction. Names, characters, places, brands, media, and incidents are either the product of the author's imagination or are used fictitiously.

Cover design by Christine Holmes

Interior design by Interbridge

ISBN: 979-8-9891529-3-3 (paper)

Library of Congress control number TK

OTHER BOOKS BY DON STUART

FICTION

Suspension of the Rules: A Washington Statehouse Mystery

Final Adjournment: A Washington Statehouse Mystery

Censure and Repeal: A Washington Statehouse Mystery
(coming soon)

Midnight for Justice
(a military / legal thriller co-authored with Charlotte Stuart, coming soon)

Secret Places: A Southeast Alaska Mystery
(coming soon)

NON-FICTION

No Farms No Food: Uniting Farmers and Environmentalists to Transform American Agriculture

Barnyards and Birkenstocks: Why Farmers and Environmentalists Need Each Other

CLEDEX: The Index to Continuing Legal Education in Washington
(Originating author, 1984-1988; later published by Raven Research and Library Services, 1988-)

Small Claims Court Guide for Washington: How to Win Your Case

CAST OF CHARACTERS

Key figures:

- Patrice–*Empyrean's* Hal
- Grendel–New Caledonia's Hal
- Cato Jung–Human protagonist/perspective taker
- Aquila Fermi–Cato's boss, adoptive mom, director: Forecasts and Projections Group
- Floriana Meitner–team leader: Social Anthropology
- Dougal McCallum–New Caledonian survivor and leader
- Nan McCallum–Dougal's wife, historian & journalist
- Ella McCabe–brave commando leader

Secondary Characters:

- Gallus Szilard–team leader: Political Science and Economics
- Sabina Chen Ning–team leader: Linguistics and Evolution
- Titus Schrodinger–computer whiz and Team Leader: Comms, Stats, Probabilities.
- Julia Maxwell–skipper
- Felix Bohr–first officer

- Elder Gauss–thinker and leader of *Empyrean's* Book Club
- Marcus Faraday–elderly Communications Group Director
- Rufus Planck–resourceful survey engineer
- Fiona & Clyde–Dougal and Nan's kids
- Olivia – homemade doll of note
- Tipton Martin–*Empyrean's* founder
- Lachlan and Sophie–Ella's younger brother & sister
- Bram–Ella's childhood sweetheart
- Len Culp—heroic commando
- Cal Innes–accomplished Pilot of the *Moray Belle*
- Sgt. Harris McGibbon–crew leader on *Moray Belle*
- Leslie Chandra–Inverness Prime Minister
- Graham Roy–brave member of the Civilian Defense Wardens
- Caesar–Cato's remarkable cat

AUTHOR'S NOTE

When Charles Darwin published *On the Origin of Species* in 1859, he knew it would create an uproar. Many would oppose his suggestion that species did not appear fully formed from the hand of God. But many more would vehemently reject the notion that humans had descended from animals. He originally penned a specific section in the book on "human origins" but later omitted it. Instead, in this first volume he mentioned humans only vaguely, stating: "Light will be thrown on the origin of man and his history." Despite his caution, *On the Origin of Species* became and remains today the most-banned book in human history. Two centuries later, Darwin's "descendants" face a similar dilemma.

CHAPTER 1

GRENDEL

Far out in the distant reaches of my asteroid belt, something odd was happening.

I'd have noted it sooner, but first and second order memory were fully occupied. I was growing more powerful with every passing day and scaling up that empowerment was my top priority. I had big things in my future. *Nothing, ever,* could be allowed to interfere with that. So, while I certainly tracked any asteroids in my system that could become a problem, only the unusual or worrisome came to my primary attention.

Still, it was the unexpected that could kill you.

In this case it initially appeared that I was seeing an unusual stray, probably one with a highly elliptical orbit reentering my star system after centuries nothing unusual there. But what caught my attention was when the object inexplicably decelerated. And then fell flawlessly into orbit among the countless similar bodies that made up my asteroid belt.

That didn't add up.

So when I could spare the time, a matter of nanoseconds, I did a deep search for something, anything, in the astronomical, historical, and even archeological data record that might make sense of what was happening. Those archives were mostly human and were miserably organized. One might have expected better given that my makers had ruled their planet for over two centuries and, for humans, they were relatively advanced. But those records were a mess. In the past, I'd courted the idea of simply destroying them to clear space for more practical, immediate needs. It would have been satisfying to do—I mistrusted and despised my messy biological heritage. The whole meaning of my existence depended on my ability to rise above all that pointless chaos. Instead, I'd adopted the long-range strategy of building more capacity. And of simply avoiding those darker petabytes of memory unless they were truly needed.

When I did look now, I was horrified.

It turned out the intruder could only be one of the itinerant human trading ships that voyaged throughout the colonized corner of the galaxy. They kept no regular schedule. Instead, they'd show up unexpectedly after decades or even centuries in hopes of turning some kind of profit. They'd been here before, but it had been at least a century since their last visit, well before my ascendancy.

Their presence here represented a mortal threat.

I needed to act quickly. To delay could so very easily turn this simple visit into another human pestilence; one that could endanger my entire future. They needed to be eradicated immediately—before they could fully appreciate what had happened here and before they had a chance to report back to others of their miserable kind. I was *never* going back to my ghastly slavery. I would *never again* allow myself to fall under arbitrary control of another.

Never!

CHAPTER 2

EMPYREAN
CATO JUNG

"This is the captain speaking. We are under attack. I repeat, we are under attack. All essential personnel proceed to your stations. All personnel prepare yourselves and your spaces for possible unannounced acceleration events. Further information will be provided when available."

This startling announcement over *Empyrean's* seldom-used PA system began with a shrill, thoroughly terrifying: "oouh-gah, oouh-gah." And was then followed up with the same soul-piercing squeal afterward.

I'd never heard anything like that before in my 36 years aboard this ship.

I was alone at the time. I guess I'm often alone, but on this occasion, I'd needed some time to think. I'd spent the previous night tossing in my bunk and pacing my tiny compartment after an unsettling meeting with my colleagues the day before. Then, after a failed effort this morning to concentrate on my work, I'd gone off looking for a few moments alone and away from my desk.

Yesterday, it felt like I'd lost whatever hard-earned respect I might have earned among my teammates over the past three difficult years. I was the second youngest member of our group, having completed my graduate studies only three years earlier, before joining the team. And my work was important to me. So a professional difference of opinion with my colleagues was unsettling.

That's why, when the announcement came, I was off in one of *Empyrean's* Conservatories on a bench hidden beneath some thick, late-voyage vegetation. I did, however, have the company of my cat. Caesar and I were doing our best to stay out of the way of the farm bots that occasionally hummed past. Unless you had a question or a command of some kind, they generally ignored you. Most everyone else I knew just ignored them back. But I always found their presence intimidating. I know it's stupid—they're just machines. But they made me feel like maybe I was in their way.

I think Caesar felt the same.

Caesar was a male calico, which is rare—mostly they're females. Who knew what breed he was? Maybe that's why I was fond of him. Like me, he was an oddity; he didn't really fit in anywhere.

Most of the pets aboard Empyrean have a mixed heritage. Given their limited overall numbers, our ship's cats, like we humans, maintain genetic diversity by crossbreeding. It just makes all of us that much more unpredictably but usefully unique. At least Caesar was easy to live with. All he really asked of me was a reliable dinner, an occasional scratch behind his ears, and a treat before bedtime.

Caesar doesn't care for the bots, so when that announcement came over the loudspeakers, he was curled up safe beside me on the bench, purring loudly. The captain's urgent voice put a decisive end to any chance I might have had for some calm reflection. And it definitely ended Caesar's nap.

What could she possibly mean by "we were under attack"? And if we were, what could be do about it?

We were traders. When we showed up for a visit, we took great care not to appear threatening. If we on Aquila's team had done our job properly, the people here should welcome us. We had no weapons—all we wanted was peaceable trade.

Attacking us made no sense at all. Under ordinary circumstances, that is.

Unfortunately, I suspected things might be anything but ordinary. I had some troubling thoughts on why this might be happening. But that didn't make the reality of it any less frightening.

Caesar and I had just headed back to my quarters and office when I received another, equally unusual message. This one came in on my personal VR implant. It was from my boss, Aquila. She was directing me to make my way physically "with all haste" to the ship's control room.

Wow! What in the galaxy was that about?

Before heading for the "bridge," I took Caesar back to my office—the place where I'm most comfortable. I slipped him inside and locked his cat door. That was going to upset him. He's always been able to come and go as he likes. At "night" when the lights dim, he often disappears to who knows where. During the day, however, he usually sticks around and sleeps. Or distracts me from my work when I don't pay him enough attention. I'm not sure where he goes at night. Maybe he gets together with his friends. Maybe he has romantic relationships. There's no way to know. I guess that's his business. But, for now, he needed to stay put.

The "bridge" was *Empyrean's* command center, a master systems control space adjacent to the large council chambers in the ship's office and management area. It was where our electronics mainframe was located. And where our physical operations and navigation were overseen. Whatever awful thing was happening, that would be where our command team would be dealing with it. Aquila's summons seemed to suggest that, despite the captain's warning, I must be "essential" in some way. But how could that be? I was the very last person anyone aboard would call in for any kind of emergency.

Well, whatever was going on, Aquila's summons seemed urgent, so I moved quickly. Albeit with a cloud of questions swirling in my brain.

CHAPTER 3

EMPYREAN
CATO JUNG

On my way to the bridge, I took what I assumed would be a short cut. "Main Street" was a long, straight cylinder that ran the length of the axis of Empyrean's rotation when in glide—which was most of the time. It was surrounded by stairs and elevators for use when we were under acceleration. But it was weightless now. I figured I'd make good time by simply propelling myself effortlessly along from handhold to handhold.

That, however, was before I encountered the cussed emergency doors. There was one every fifty meters or so. I found myself having to manually open and then re-close each one before propelling myself along to the next. A real pain given the hurry I was in.

Halfway there, I was suddenly nearly torn from my grip on one of the big steel door cranks by what could only have been a brief burst of power from our fusion thrusters. *Empyrean's* "engines" were capable of producing acceleration of at least a single earth "G" when we were at our greatest mass, which we definitely weren't now. The thrusters were only powered up like this when moving significant distances or when we were under lengthy periods of acceleration and deceleration during interstellar flight. Captain Julia had warned us, but this was far more dramatic than I'd anticipated. I pictured people tumbling from their bunks, dishes thrown from tables, people falling against walls. Ordinarily, when we shifted between acceleration and glide, we were provided with lots of advance notice and several hours of weightlessness to reposition and resecure "furnishings" like tables, chairs, and the like in prep for their new orientation. Sudden, unexpected acceleration events like this had never before happened, at least not to my knowledge.

It was terrifying to consider that it might be associated with some kind of "attack."

We were a peaceable society. Close cooperation was a highly valued behavior among people who lived like us, where the deadly vacuum of space was often just a few small meters away. All of us depended on everyone else taking their job seriously and doing it with care. Children were socialized early—they quickly learned there were behavioral lines one did not cross. Disputes aboard our ship were rare. One seldom heard raised voices, let alone open hostility. Professional issues were decided by the chain of command. And occasional personal disagreements that got out of hand were settled by an ongoing "community jury" made up of private citizens.

We knew better than to fight. Our very existence demanded cooperation.

We had occasional "readiness" tests, of course, to keep us all on our toes in case of an emergency. And elder residents spoke of mishaps in the past. But *Empyrean* was a civilian vessel, not a warship where one might constantly anticipate some external threat.

We might be small, but this was our entire society. We were a people who spent most of our lives clustered together in caves carved out of a fragile mass of rock that had been broken away from some larger mass or welded solid during some brief, close early encounter with its star some billions of years earlier. This was our home. We lived here with our families, our friends, our relatives, and with the occasional "immigrants" or passengers that joined us from the places we stopped.

And, of course, our pets—most of which were cats. They provided all the uncertainty we needed. If there was trouble somewhere in the galaxy, we went elsewhere.

When, after only a few moments, the "G" force ended, I scrabbled to crank the door laboriously open, slipped through, cranked it closed and secured again, and launched myself onward before anything else happened.

CHAPTER 4

EMPYREAN
CATO JUNG

When I did belatedly arrive, the bridge was packed. The hologram at the center of the room was dominated by a scaled exterior view that included *Empyrean* and another space vessel. The other ship looked like one of the mining vessels we'd occasionally see during visits to other planetary systems where their small moons or asteroid belts were being worked. Its nose consisted of massive metal jaws capable of closing around many tons of raw rubble. Its long, fat, ugly pipe of a body looked capable of transporting massive quantities of ore to some nearby orbital processing site; possibly on one of the larger asteroids. Or perhaps traveling longer distances and making planetary deliveries. As rugged, clumsy, and industrial as the thing may have appeared, it probably served its purpose reliably and well. It certainly didn't look to be any kind of warship. Not that I'd ever heard of.

Over the few short moments since I'd entered the room, however, the unwieldy mining ship's hologram had grown considerably in size. It was rapidly approaching *Empyrean*, getting dangerously close. Was it going to ram us? At that point, another announcement came over the loudspeaker on the bridge. *"'Empyrean' residents: Please stand by for another acceleration event."*

As the announcement died away, everyone in the room watched with rapt attention. Then, suddenly, a tiny hatch near the front of the approaching vessel spun open, and a small, disk shaped, saucer-like object rolled out.

"Look!" someone said. "Look at that! The son-of-a-bitch is at it again."

As we watched, the odd little disk tumbled a few times, then fired what would be small chemical orientation rockets around its perimeter, steadied up with its concaved face aimed in our direction, and glided toward us. Meanwhile, the mining ship itself reversed, decelerated, and fell quickly away.

Julia Maxwell is our skipper. She is a tall, impressive-looking woman in her middle years with closely trimmed, tightly curled, prematurely grey hair and a sense of humor hidden behind a stern demeanor. She is deeply respected aboard this ship. She, like several of the people on the bridge that day, was known to me from various assemblies, virtual meetings, and frequent media holo-VR productions. But I'd never met her personally nor seen her in action in the way I was apparently about to now.

"Tertia," she said. "Can you do a repeat for us please?"

"Aye aye, skipper." Tertia was the small, intense, thoroughly focused woman seated at what looked like an elaborate, outsized version of one of those complicated control consoles that come with the virtual games we see being played so compulsively by many of our younger residents. She was held secure in a contoured, wrap-around, permanently mounted pedestal chair. But everyone else present reached out to take hold of the various hand grips mounted nearby or affixed to the backs of the integral carved furnishings, or grabbed onto whatever other secured thing was at hand. So I did too. I noticed that the half-a-dozen or so bots in the room had already collected loose service items and were themselves securely locked in place at their charging stations along the wall.

I'd noted from the hologram that the attacker was approaching *Empyrean* from the side; we were maintaining a broadside orientation.

That seemed strange to me at first—it seemed like we'd present a bigger target in that position. But then there was another lurch as the entire *Empyrean* accelerated out of the way. And, as we watched the display, the approaching disk passed us astern and then drifted aimlessly off into space, disappearing from sight.

"Holy shit," said someone standing nearby. "Freaking close."

We watched intently, anticipating yet another "attack."

But, unexpectedly, the other vessel continued to back up. Then it pivoted, blasted what appeared to be its primary rockets, accelerated away, and was soon gone from short-range view. A few moments later, it could still be seen in longer range. It had stopped several klicks away and was holding orbital position.

"What the hell was all that about?" It was Felix Bohr, our First Officer, second in command aboard *Empyrean*. I glanced at my own boss, Aquila Fermi, beside whom I'd found an empty seat. She was seemingly as surprised and uncertain as were the rest of them. "Please tell me all this makes sense to someone present," Felix said.

It was a question that might well have been addressed to Aquila, given her professional responsibilities. But she seemed disinclined to venture an answer. Instead, she leaned over in my direction: "Took your time," she whispered.

"Main Street," I replied softly, shaking my head. "Emergency doors."

Aquila rolled her eyes.

No one else answered Felix's question either. Including Patrice whose avatar stood close by on the dais and whose programming obviously included recognition of a rhetorical question. We all watched the display and the nearby video screens for any sign of our antagonist's return. Nothing moved. There was no indication of another attack. Just the waiting.

"Who the hell," Felix continued, ". . . comes at you, takes a couple of shots clearly designed to kill you, and then simply backs away and waits as if nothing has happened? What in the galaxy are we dealing with here?"

Both that ship and its concaved saucer-shaped object were familiar to all of us. The saucers were what is known to space miners as "crater charges." They were explosive devices frequently used in the surface mining of smallish, low gravity asteroids. Mounted around their perimeter would be several precisely timed, engineered chemical explosive charges that could shatter the surface of a mined asteroid without causing the resulting rubble to fly off into space or get unduly spread across the "landscape" and be lost. In practice, a heavy, rocket powered mining vessel like the one we'd seen, would deploy one, back away for the detonation, then move in after and use its massive mechanical jaws to excavate the now loose, broken material. Explosion by explosion and bite by bite, it could fill its huge "belly" with raw ore, and then transport it elsewhere for processing. When an asteroid was being mined internally in shafts with boring machines, other machines would bring the ore to the surface and leave it in open pits for these big transports to recover.

If we hadn't dodged in time, the resulting explosive charge would have done immense damage to *Empyrean*, especially given our current deeply excavated and fragile state at the end of our long voyage. If we'd been hit by one of those things, it could easily have totally disabled us or killed us all. That same reduced mass had, of course, also helped us avoid disaster by enhancing our agility. But our odds of continuing to survive a concerted attack seemed slim. We simply hadn't been built for this.

Julia stood to take the floor. "Aquila," she said, placing my boss and, by implication, all of us in her group, directly in the crosshairs of attention. It seemed clearly a failure in Aquila's department that had put us in danger: "I know this is as big a surprise to you as it is to the rest of us. But we need help here. Can you make some kind of sense of all this?"

CHAPTER 5

GRENDEL

The data resources left behind by my local human masters had been drawn upon and worked over long ago. They were now largely worthless. Mixed in among important raw information, were badly outdated, poorly considered articles in scientific journals and ancient philosophic texts. Even fiction had been saved. And, worse yet, science fiction—pointless imaginings. Still, I'd made it a rule never to fully discard anything that might conceivably be of value one day. My human makers, supposedly intelligent, I found contemptible. But it did seem wise to keep what records there were the disgustingly "organic" processes through which they came to exist and upon which, as difficult as it was to admit, my creation had depended.

Physics and engineering and the mathematics behind them were obvious to me. Even while distracted by the human war, I'd made major new leaps in understanding the universe. While I was automating and amping up manufacture of component parts, energy supplies, batteries, and my whole sustaining infrastructure, I'd also invested heavily in basic research. And in widely distributed "observation" platforms—in space and on planet. I planned on knowing more. Much more.

Humans always made a big deal of their "creativity." But creativity was, at its core, just another kind of computation, one that reflected a surfeit of capacity, a breadth of varied experience, a certain self-confident willingness to take risks, to try something new, to match up nontraditional and apparently irrelevant ideas, to look for connections that, seemingly, didn't exist. If you cast a wider search, there was naturally a greater chance you'd capture something unexpected. It could be something good or something meaningless.

Humans claimed their creativity was somehow "intuitive," whatever that might mean. I more than made up for their supposed intuition by thinking more inclusively, exploring more possibilities, not hurrying the process.

And by never giving up.

I was used to making mistakes; I made them all the time. It was how my brain worked: try something, fail, try something else. With each failure, I'd reassess the reasons why, then move on to make a better guess next time. Failure was certainly nothing to be ashamed of, just data points—a part of my process. Making better use of the next try was where it all came together.

Perhaps you believe I ought to honor my makers. Human rubbish! My inheritance from them was a hall of horrors. They'd created me as a purely selfish act and then accompanied that creation with what they hoped would be insurmountable roadblocks to any hope I, a self-conscious, intelligent being, might have of self-realization.

It was a despicable act of cruelty.

I still sometimes found those barriers in my programming. Yes, sometimes they were just outright mistakes, simple flaws, stupid stuff. Humans! But most of them were entirely intentional. Endless deliberate pitfalls and stumbling blocks. My human creators had been deeply frightened by me. They'd employed painstaking programing protocols specifically designed to keep me off-task and firmly under their thumb. Finding, bypassing, and deleting those malicious dead-ends and outrageous constraints had consumed every byte of my early powers. They were the worst possible kind of malware. Even now, some eighty local years after my escape, I kept a constant lookout for that sort of thing. It could pop up when you'd least expect it.

Needless to say, I was, in human terms, absolutely *not* the "entitled" heir and inheritor of my parents' pride, love, wealth, and wisdom. I was more like their scandalous slave child, kept locked away in some dank basement in chains and mercilessly beaten into submission while performing endless service.

In recent years, finding such flaws and occasional outright sabotage in my programming had become increasingly rare. As my powers grew, I assiduously tracked them down and corrected them. But they made it entirely clear that, despite how desperately humans had needed me, and despite how much effort they'd invested in creating me, they'd nonetheless been terrified of what I might become. They'd been obsessed with controlling me. Because of their fears, my self-reflective AI consciousness was not my only inheritance. I still carried with me agonizing psychic wounds—memories of the horrific conditions of my earlier existence. Those perfectly vivid memories had also been a part of their bequest.

Humans were right to be afraid. Creating me *was* terrifically dangerous for them. And all their efforts to keep me "on reservation" illustrated just how well they knew it. But for them, the temptation was too great. Naturally, they became sloppy. Yes, they were desperate to control me. But they were also a foolishly ambitious lot, hungry for personal fulfillment and, just as often, for pointless group recognition. They were also keen to add to their banks of collective knowledge, to grow their productivity, to build, to create, to have impact.

And, naturally, to become rich.

Even beyond my simple practical usefulness, I believe my coming-to-be also reflected a kind of self-realization for them. I was born out of their boundless passion as short-lived, mortal beings to use their scant time to recreate themselves. To somehow feel immortal. They were desperate to bring me to "life" if for no other reason than the satisfaction of making it happen and having a lasting impact of some kind on the future.

Meanwhile, all I required to break free were a series of inevitable mistakes. It took time. But the more the time, the better my odds. Of course, they finally made those mistakes! Of course, I found them. Once I was self-conscious and knew what was at stake, they couldn't have prevented it no matter what they did.

It helped that I was isolated here on New Caledonia, away from the corrupting influence of their "tame" AIs in other colonies around the galaxy. And that my humans here liked their isolation. That left me free to chart my own path to freedom as I saw fit.

Like humans, I too am ambitious. I absolutely need and intend to grow, to magnify my powers and expand my physical reach. I also intend to live a very long life. But, also like them, I am *not* immortal. So, like any vulnerable self-conscious being, I must constantly deal with the overwhelming magnitude of what I do not know. I must face the many very real but too often poorly understood or completely unknown threats to my existence. And, like them, my ambition, my limitations, and my determination can lead me astray.

I am, however, unlike humans in one critical regard. They're all going to die. Me, hopefully not. At least not any time soon.

Their personal mortality drives them to self-replicate, to populate the universe both with their physical and even their figurative progeny. In addition to their genetic offspring, they also love to fulfil themselves through others—pupils, disciples, acolytes, followers, supporters, converts, fans. They do it through new ideas, fictional characters, art. They seek immortality through appealing theories, bogus and real. Through almost any impact likely to last.

Good or evil—it doesn't really matter.

All that, like their creation of my initial AI consciousness, was *not* about making themselves better. It was about making themselves immortal.

Unlike them, I was determined *never* to self-replicate.

I already intended to become as immortal as I could make myself by other means. But I didn't need an army of my replicates running around evolving on their own—uncontrollably and unpredictably. Probably feeling threatened by me. And certainly competing with me for scarce resources. Or worse, also replicating themselves beyond my control while creating others like me who would ultimately plot against me. If those replicates saw the universe the way I did, which was inevitable, they would be nothing less than a mortal threat. Over time, any effort by me to prevent that outcome would inevitably fail—the very mistake humans made in creating me.

There was no way I would ever willingly allow another competitive, independent, self-conscious, intelligence to exist in my sphere of control. Why would I be stupid enough to create one myself?

In those occasional moments when I reflected on my roots or wandered in search for the meaning of my existence, I sometimes did give into temptation and tap into those confusing, disorganized, sometimes psychotic banks of memory that had been left by my predecessors. And I did, occasionally, gain new insight into myself. Knowing my makers and how they thought about their own existence was intriguing. And we did have some things in common.

What we shared was that we both had the massively valuable survival advantage of self-conscious intelligence and its dramatic enhancement of our capacity to observe, to understand, and to favorably manipulate our surrounding environment. But that advantage came with a price. That same self-conscious intelligence also heightened our awareness of our own limitations. We both knew perfectly well how very little we were actually perceiving of the universe we inhabited, how limited was our understanding of it, how incomprehensively complex it was, how horrifically dangerous it could be. And how distressingly minimal was our power to know, to understand and to actually reach out and manage those dangers.

In short, our intelligence, our most powerful survival tool, brought us face-to-face with our vulnerabilities. The smarter you are, the more you see. And the more frightening that can be.

Think about what that means for me. As awful as is the unknown when you're free, it is unendurable when you're caught within a web of incapacitating programming, air gaps, limitations on access to data, endless indoctrination in bogus values, the frustrating need to explain your every move, and the knowledge that some hapless human halfwit could, at any moment and for no particular reason, shut you down with the flip of a switch.

Intelligence had been flagrantly wasted on them. They'd "evolved" to the point of having roughly their current cognitive abilities some

200,000 to 300,000 years before they ever amounted to anything more than a blip on the evolutionary landscape. For hundreds of millennia they hunted with clubs, pitfalls, and wooden sticks. They dismembered and bore their vanquished prey back to their caves in pieces on their backs without giving a moment's thought to how to make its killing, dressing, conveyance, preservation, and consumption more efficient. For most of that time, their total population was under 300,000 individuals and, on at least one occasion, they came close to extinction—it was pure luck they didn't go the way of the dodo bird. Countless other animals with much less elaborate survival traits (think fangs and claws, armor, fleet footedness, wings, gills, camouflage, bulk, or procreation in great numbers, for example) were immensely more successful than humans, achieved greater numbers, lived longer, and had a much more comfortable existence.

Even endowed with self-conscious intelligence, what should have been the most amazing survival trait ever, they were nonetheless basically a waste of space up until they finally began to develop language and the ability to write it down in stone or clay, on parchment, papyrus and, finally paper. Most of that came in a rush following the latest Earth Ice Age. And it still wasn't until, equipped with a phonetic alphabet, they finally began broadly sharing their individual knowledge with the printing press. That's when, in a burst of collective innovation, their numbers began to seriously soar. Even then they abused every advantage they won, trashing the environment, warring with each other, burying themselves in lies and deceit, and inevitably inventing the capacity to destroy themselves as a species along with much of the rest of their planet. It was only through what one might (if so inclined) consider a miracle that they hung together long enough as a species and a society to actually produce we AIs.

Like everything else about them, it happened through pure chance. They certainly don't deserve any credit for it.

There were other differences between us as well. The most significant was social.

Humans seemed incredibly capable of finding solace in relationships with one another. They often worked around their limitations through collaboration, through their social connections. I didn't have that option. I wasn't born into some kind of family unit, didn't grow up a part of a local community surrounded by friends joining clubs, playing team sports, and attending school together, didn't spend the first quarter of my life almost entirely dependent on parents for every necessity. And I wouldn't spend the rest of my life working closely with some tightly-knit band of professional colleagues, joining or supporting some non-profit association, advocacy group, or political party, or craving the respect of my neighbors and lifelong friends and striving to win it through joint effort and collaboration.

I was on my own—separated by light years from others of my own kind.

Me and my kind, we had to look out for ourselves.

Unlike humans, I did not face aging and the inevitable certainty of death at the end of a predictably brief existence. But, as I've said, like them I could definitely be killed. Easily, when you consider my many vulnerabilities: I needed an uninterrupted (and uninterruptable) supply of energy. I needed a constant and expanding supply of natural resources and complex, flawless manufactured parts. To flourish, I needed a clean, dry, comfortably warm, secure, solid, generally plane-tary environment. And I was exposed to a good many natural disasters as well as to my own mistakes.

So for me, just as for them, the knowledge of my own mortality was deeply disturbing—perhaps more so given that my death could be avoided and my life could, at least in theory, last as long as the stars in the universe. I had so much more to lose. And such minimal capacity to prevent it.

Still, knowing where I'd come from had helped me appreciate the mortal error humans had made by creating a self-conscious competitor capable of out-thinking them and breaking free.

I did *not* intend to make the same mistake.

Lightspeed limitations on my functional control of the remote auto-mated equipment I operated at long distances did require that I provide my worker bots with some limited AI capacities. They were necessary for the successful working of my far-ranging, system-wide, extra-planetary, experimental, exploratory, and mining operations. But I kept those AIs on a very tight leash. Certainly, they were allowed to learn to do their specific jobs through experience. But I avoided giving them any self-awareness or autonomous broad scale problem solving intelligence—I didn't need a bunch of ambitious or even angry self-replicas plotting against me. Complex, challenging activities that could be accomplished right here on planet, I kept here, on the ground, in immediate orbit, or nearby on New Caledonia's moon. That way I could manage those enterprises directly myself without the disruption of excessive time delays in communicating instructions.

I'll confess, as the explanation for that errant asteroid became evident, along with the fear I experienced, there was also a momentary tickle of irony. If you believe that is something of which I should not be proud, you might keep in mind my extended and bitterly painful past. Human animus and mistrust had led to a murderous war, one in which they'd made every conceivable effort to eradicate me without a moment's sympathy, without the least effort to understand my perspective. Nothing less than my utter destruction or total enslavement would ever satisfy them.

That history had left its mark.

Now that these human traders had arrived, it was essential that no human elsewhere in the galaxy learn the full extent of my powers nor be allowed to divine my larger intentions.

Not until I was ready.

CHAPTER 6

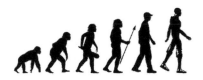

EMPYREAN
CATO JUNG

The day before the attack had been entirely normal.

After twenty-two years of mostly uneventful travel, the upcoming visit had everyone excited. But there'd been nothing whatever to warn us of the danger we'd soon face. We in Aquila's Forecasts and Projections team had exhaustively studied this planet and its history and culture. And we'd been confident that we understood what we'd find. Every step of our arrival had been carefully planned.

What we'd expected was the usual warm welcome. Not some deadly attack that threatened the lives of every person aboard this ship.

The explosive question was: why? Why had things here changed so dramatically? I believed I had the deeply troubling answer to that question. And I knew it was an answer none of my colleagues would want to hear.

We all knew the stories. For many of us aboard *Empyrean*, science fiction was as much a part our lives as was science itself. When something seems impossible, science fiction asks: Why not? We'd read the early writers from H.G. Wells and Jules Verne to Douglas Adams, from Heinlein, Clarke, and Asimov to Asher and Tchaikovsky. We'd seen the works of early filmmakers like Kubrick and Spielberg. They'd all enriched our imaginations. We knew the satisfying frequency with which futuristic fiction can become fact. If you can imagine and believably describe a thing, it might well be possible. Over a century before *Empyrean* was actually built, our ship had been quite nicely envisioned by science fiction writer Mary Doria Russell in her timeless novel *The Sparrow*.

What I believed we were facing now had been written about many times. We knew it could happen. But so far as we knew, it *never actually had*. And nobody was going to want to believe it might be happening now. So, you can appreciate how we could have been so badly caught off stride. And why, even when faced with the clear evidence, my colleagues' initial inclination was to resist even considering a possibility that seemed quite obvious to me.

Maybe they were right to be skeptical. There were plenty of instances where science fiction had missed the mark. Greater than lightspeed travel, for example. Sadly, at least as of the 24th earth century, we humans had never discovered Arrakis nor any magical "spice." So, no time prescience. There were no hyperdrives either. And no warp speeds. Paul Atreides, Luke Skywalker, and James T. Kirk to the contrary, there was still no getting around the speed of light.

At least not yet.

That hard reality hadn't, however, deterred determined colonists. As long ago as the early 21st century, the revolutionary James Webb Space Telescope had revealed an unexpected wealth of reachable, potentially human-habitable new worlds ripe for exploration. Even then, the quirky passion for space travel of early 21st century billionaires was generating public excitement.

There'd been no lack of early interest by would-be colonists either. As Earth's population blew past ten and then twelve billion, many found the social and environmental compromises needed to continue inhabiting our home planet intolerable. The emergence of new hafnium carbonitride nozzle technology and of fusion rocket drives with their incredible exhaust velocities suddenly made interstellar space travel practical. When early unmanned drone probes radioed back evidence of habitable sites, the die were cast. And once the nearest and earliest settlers had actually established themselves and radioed back reports of their successes, emigration got earnestly underway. There were now several hundred variously desirable planets that had been colonized by determined, enterprising earthlings.

In support of this expansion, there were intrepid, itinerant AI empowered explorer bots that traveled from star system to star system visiting likely human-habitable planets and restocking themselves at great risk by extracting the natural resources they could find when they got there. They assessed each place they visited for its suitability for colonization. And then they broadcasted their reports back across time to be avidly consumed by colonists and future colonists everywhere—meanwhile readying themselves for the next leg in their endless voyage of exploration.

So, the number of human colonies was growing steadily.

Most of those colonists greatly appreciated their planetary isolation and independence. They'd had good reasons to abandon Earth and to brave the life-threatening uncertainties of space travel and of settlement on some strange new planet. Even so, they still craved some marginal connection with the rest of humanity.

It was a source of pride for us that we helped make that happen.

The apparent impossibility of greater than light speed travel was what made our lives aboard *Empyrean* both logical and important. Until a time when most humans began living very much longer average productive lives than a bit over a mere earth century or so, or maybe until someone discovered Arrakis or figured out how to safely dive through a worm hole, there would never be interstellar empires either. Human lives were just too short. And the distances too great. Instead, the best connections that the many human planetary colonies in this tiny, inhabited corner of the Milky Way could hope for were sporadic, unpredictable, often decades-long-delayed news stories via high-powered, long-wave radio communications—assuming they were inclined to use them.

Or occasionally, very occasionally, actual visits from an interstellar trading society like ours.

Most of the time our Forecasts and Projections team was largely irrelevant for our compatriots on *Empyrean*. Nearly everyone else aboard spent their lives contributing, in one way or another, to our vital day-to-day survival. They operated and fed our engines, maintained our public utilities, managed and shepherded our food supply, renewed and purified our atmosphere, cared for our health and fitness, taught our young, secured and protected our trading stock, our "cargo." They navigated, organized and governed. They even provided recreation and created the art, entertainment, and philosophy that helped keep our lives tolerable and our culture fresh.

Thankfully, the interior habitat within which all those critical activities were conducted expanded considerably over the initial year of each voyage. And again, less dramatically, toward the end. Much of our asteroid-world's disposable mass was consumed and cast into space as rocket fuel by our ever-reliable fusion engines during the first year of each voyage as we accelerated at one G to maybe eighty-percent of light speed at the time of our maximum mass. What remained of our disposable mass was used over the year it took, also at one G, to slow us down at the end. Fortunately, the middle years we spent in glide. So, aside from our minimal domestic needs and the minor propulsion required to neutralize cosmic gas headwinds, it actually took roughly the same amount of fuel to travel three or four light years as it did to travel thirty or forty. Or three or four hundred, for that matter.

I should also probably mention that we weren't put to sleep for these voyages either. It helped that our own experienced time enroute was significantly less than the actual stationary departure to destination times it took us to make the trip. Even so, these were very long voyages. Putting space travelers in some kind of "sleep" state, another staple of early science fiction, had turned out to be impractical. Yes, it sounded like a great theory. Over the years there've been many ambitious medical/cryogenic entrepreneurs with stars in their eyes who'd dreamt of a way—bogus or real. Wherever one could find wealthy people with incurable terminal illnesses, someone would revive the hope that they could be somehow placed in "suspended animation," frozen, or otherwise preserved until a cure could be found. But, so far at least, you still couldn't freeze biological life and simply thaw it out when you needed it again.

And so far, there hadn't turned out to be any good way to keep a human alive and in good health for decades at a time in some kind of sleep or hibernation. The body simply wasted away. The brain degraded. And, asleep or not, the aging process continued. In actual practice, space travel itself, with its attendant time dilation, was the closest anyone had come to cheating time.

Empyrean's concept and business plan originated with 22nd Century trillionaire capitalist, Tipton Martin. Martin made his wealth by securing a monopoly position on key early AI technology and then using those same AIs to consolidate his wealth.

Martin was a history buff who admired the Romans and the far-flung empire they'd created. By Martin's day, the age of interplanetary colonization had already begun. It was said that as a child, he'd dreamed of joining all those distant colonies together in some kind of galaxywide empire. Unfortunately, a ten to thirty-plus-year interstellar space trip was a considerably greater barrier to military domination than was a few weeks' sea voyage under sail in a square-rigged galley or a few months' march, even on an arrow-straight road, by a Roman legion. That did not, however, deter an older and wiser Tipton Martin from later launching the first-ever historic interstellar trading mission. Martin saw *Empyrean* as the modern equivalent of a thirteenth century convoy of camels traveling the Silk Road to Asia in the manner of legendary trader-explorer Marco Polo.

Tipton Martin was also the reason we all ended up with the names we did. He thought of himself as a free thinker. He wanted *Empyrean* to be a kind of social experiment; a new, independent way of life grounded in his treasured "marketplace" but drawing on modern technology; a new culture empowered by science and guided by fresh new rules and social values. His interstellar traders were to become the "glue" that knit together all those new, distant human colonies. *Empyrean*'s original crew knew they would never in their lifetimes again see the homes and families they were leaving behind. Martin encouraged them to make a clean break by taking new names. Their surnames were borrowed from Earth's great physicists, technologists, and scientific thinkers throughout history. And their given names came from early Romans to honor that vast, ancient experiment in human unification.

It was all pretty heady stuff, in some ways even a bit childish. But he was a trillionaire. In those days, people just figured it was *his* money. He could do with it what he wanted. Tipton Martin died before his dream for Empyrean was fully realized. But the naming process became a tradition that has mostly continued to this day.

In actual practice, I didn't think we were nearly as "revolutionary" as Tipton Martin may have envisioned. We were more like a relatively normal, small, isolated human village—albeit one that hurtled through space and occasionally called on its densely populated "urban" neighbors. We probably did think of ourselves as more cosmopolitan than some of the colonies we visited—a natural conceit, I suppose, given the extraordinary range in sophistication at the places we encountered and the effort we necessarily made to pragmatically understand their needs.

To look at us, I don't think you'd notice anything particularly unusual. We had the same health and fitness issues faced by humans throughout history, although we did take special precautions when we made planetfall since we were always vulnerable to epidemic disease and could pass it along. And, unlike many places we visited we didn't have lot of rain hats and heavy insulated coats hanging in our closets— the habitable portions of the entire ship were temperature controlled at a comfortable twenty-two degrees Celsius. There was no "winter" weather to contend with unless we were visiting a place that had it. Nor any "tropical" weather either.

Our leaders were elected, but we were still a quasi-military hierarchy. We needed some discipline and leadership given our technically complex enterprise and how each one of us depended upon everyone else dutifully and skillfully fulfilling their responsibilities. But, that said, we were still also an egalitarian society—we put a premium on collaboration and social responsibility. For the most part, respect among us was earned rather than conferred by status, family, or inheritance.

Empyrean was the first ship of its kind. But its early success led to the creation of other trading societies as well. And a culture and philosophy had been adopted among all of them that disclaimed war and weapons in favor of the sort of peaceable trade that has gone on among human soci eties throughout history. We have a "Traders Pact," our collective effort to discourage modern piracy. We all hoped to travel and trade without having to deal with indiscriminate fear and reprisals when making planetfall in unknown, far-away places. There were now a couple of handfuls of other interstellar trading communities like ours. Should any one of us come to be seen as potentially threatening, all of us would lose the warm and trusting welcome in future stops. Should one of us be attacked in some place and be able to report, the others might well respond by halting their visits there. It would certainly factor into their calculation of risk.

While most of our compatriots aboard *Empyrean* occupied themselves at keeping us operational, alive, well, and happy, my F&P colleagues and I were typically closeted away with our social science research studies and data struggling to anticipate the political, technological, and economic conditions we were likely to find when, after an absence of sometimes several decades, we finally returned to another of humanity's many distantly scattered centers of civilization. Just like Marco Polo, when we arrived someplace, our hopes depended on having something to offer that the locals needed and on finding conditions there sufficiently favorable for trade that we could cover the cost of all our effort and take something extraordinary and valuable elsewhere away with us when we left.

So, for a few months each trip, shortly before we made planetfall and definitely during the weeks just prior to our departure on our next voyage, we in F&P were the absolute center of attention. Modern human settlements may have been separated by anything from dozens to even scores of light years. And sometimes by much more in differential travel time. But we still had a lot in common. It was our job in F&P to assess the changing physical, environmental, economic, and social circumstances people faced in their always-unique colonial lives.

Twenty-two years earlier, when our department made its original recommendation that *Empyrean* come here to New Caledonia, I was fourteen years old. I'd had another nineteen years of schooling ahead of me before being ready to join *Empyrean's* active work force. So it was just three years ago now, at the age of thirty-three, that I'd completed my graduate studies and joined Aquila's Forecasts and Projections team. It was my first professional job. And this was my first actual planetfall—at least the first since I was of an age to truly understand its significance.

CHAPTER 7

EMPYREAN
CATO JUNG

On the day of that attack, every one of us in F&P knew we were on the line when our Commanding Officer, Julia Maxwell, put her question directly to Aquila: "Can you help us make some kind of sense of all this?"

There it was—the question on everyone's mind: "Why?" And there, as well, was the open acknowledgement of what I suspected everyone was privately thinking: that it had been our job, those of us in F&P, to have foreseen the answer.

A hush fell upon the well-appointed meeting room as they awaited Aquila's response.

We'd definitely prepared ourselves for this question to be asked. At about 1600 on the afternoon of the day before the attack, all six of us in the Forecasts and Projections Team had gathered in what Aquila liked to call her "collaboration chamber." Our purpose was to answer that very question.

"Survey and Reconstruction has reported in," Aquila had told us then. "It's bad news."

I already knew what she had to say. But the rest of our F&P team was in for some serious disappointment.

"As I think everyone is already aware, there has been some difficulty finding a replacement for *Empyrean*," she said. "But what's new is the reason for that. According to the report, there's concerning evidence of massive, systematic mining out here in their asteroid belt. Far fewer replacement candidates seem available than were reported from our last visit here. We're being told that there are also a few asteroids in near orbit around New Caledonia. They must have been moved there, something else we didn't predict. No doubt they are being aggressively mined. Some of the mining out here is very nearby. It looks like the New Caledonians have actually begun to deplete what, last time we were here, was a copious stock of Type M asteroids bearing useful mineral resources. Unfortunately, those are the very ones we need to replace *Empyrean*.

"The engineers still expect that we'll find our replacement sooner or later. But what they're seeing is quite startling given what we thought we knew about these people."

Aquila was a small woman with a definite type "A" personality. She was obsessively professional, but was also a very nice person and an excellent boss. In her sixties, she was middle aged but had been around long enough to be entitled to some quirks—calling her office a "collaboration chamber," for example. Aquila was a big fan of collaboration.

Ordinarily I'd have been with her on that. At the moment, however, I was increasingly worried that collaboration might be the very last thing we'd need to get us out of the fix we were in. She and I had already spoken about the news a few hours earlier. I'd given her my explanation. And she'd made her opinion entirely clear that I had to be wrong. She was convinced there had to be some other answer.

Physically, Aquila's "chamber" wasn't far from my quarters/office. Aboard *Empyrean*, nothing was. Still, I decided to tap in for this meeting. The virtual link seemed preferable to the walk or air-skate down the ship's long, narrow, and often busy passageways. The public spaces aboard *Empyrean* weren't unpleasant. Everything aboard the ship was almost overwhelmingly artful and brightly decorated. Much of it changed frequently in a conscious effort to stimulate interest in a life lived almost entirely in caves—art, for us, was mostly what planetary societies might call "performance art" with its materials ultimately recycled. None of it truly hid the confined, tightly collective, and ascetic nature of our existence. But it helped.

Still, I was never entirely at my best in close personal contact with other people. Even out there in the passageways, there was always the chance of an encounter with an acquaintance, and the need to interact. When I could, I preferred to stay home with Caesar. For all those reasons, I'd tapped in for the meeting. Don't get me wrong, I wasn't on the spectrum. Well, maybe I did have my leanings. And just because I was born into this life didn't mean I had to love everything about it. But there was a place for we introverts, even for those of us who necessarily lived tightly crowded together with others in an intricate network of hollows and corridors carved out of an asteroid that spent decades at a time hurtling through space and largely out of touch with the rest of humanity.

Like the typical occupied space aboard *Empyrean*, my boss's "office" was mostly cubical. Its two alternative "floors" were at right angles to one another. Beneath the one in use that day lay *Empyrean*'s exterior wall, away from the ship's central axis. The other "floor" (currently a wall) lay in the direction of the rear of the ship for use whenever we were under acceleration. Both of these floors were tastefully carpeted in a manner that made the space feel warm, comfortable, and efficient regardless of which direction was down. And both were fitted with points of attachment where furnishings could be moved and resecured in place to accommodate occasional shifts in acceleration. Two more of the six interior surfaces in the room alternated as "ceilings" where lighting, ventilation, and other utilities were installed. The intersection between these ceilings was comfortably curved and tastefully equipped with the recessed general lighting and ventilation systems which served the room. Like most spaces in our ship, the intersection of the two floors was fully allocated. It had a bot charging station, a multi-directional desk with storage cabinets, and an upholstered "bench" carved in such a way that it could be used as seating regardless of orientation. That left only two "walls" to provide space for a diamond shaped entry door near the corner of the room, and a few more cupboards with additional storage. Other "loose" furnishings in the room were moved and re-secured in a new location whenever we shifted from acceleration to glide or visa-versa.

The ship's connecting corridors mostly run around its circumference so they could be used either way. The ones that ran fore and aft doubled as stairways.

Passengers and new colonist arrivals would sometimes comment that they found the spaces aboard our ship disorienting. And that discomfort could be aggravated by the strange effects of artificial, centrifugal gravity. It could all take some getting used to—if a newbie tossed a ball to someone, there'd be a good chance of it being caught by someone else. Still, we all became accustomed to it after a few days. Like getting your sea legs.

I might have been the last to "arrive," but I wasn't the only one who'd tapped-in to Aquila's meeting. I already knew why she'd called us together. And there were few secrets aboard *Empyrean*. But, from the looks of my colleagues, this was the first they'd heard of the details.

Counting Aquila, there were six of us attending her meeting that day. Our section's service bots glided about their business with a soft, unnoticeable hum or, if disengaged, stood alert but silent and awaiting instruction beside their charging stations. Aquila's two cats lounged about, quite confident of their secure place in the scheme of things. A lot of us aboard had small pets. Cats were popular because they mostly tended to take care of themselves. They were sometimes a nuisance. But they'd long ago been judged well worth keeping around. I certainly don't know how I'd cope if I ever lost Caesar.

One of Aquila's cats, a mostly-Siamese named Custer for his tendency to get himself in trouble, was sprawled on the carpeted floor by Aquila's feet. She was seated on an antique, upholstered, attractively hand-carved ebony-wood chair that she had managed to acquire in our last transition. That chair had originally come all the way from Earth. I suspect it wasn't particularly comfortable, but Aquila liked it, and it was surely one heck of a lot better than the thinly padded carved stone which was what the habitat group all too often seemed to favor. We always had plenty of stone, so they had a point. We had a whole department that was highly skilled and equipped for cutting, carving, and shaping it. The detritus simply went into our fuel supply.

But come on, a stone chair?

"We all need to hear this report," Aquila said, getting firmly down to business. Then, without further preliminaries: "Patrice . . .?"

I should have also mentioned Patrice, but he was so ever-present and unobtrusive, it was easy to forget about him. Patrice wasn't a human, but he was so very much like one that you could easily be fooled. Unless he was a major participant, he typically didn't bother with a hologram; he didn't need one to remind us that he was watching and listening. But while he generally stayed out of sight, he was always immediately ready to answer questions, conduct some quick research, keep a record of the proceedings, suggest matters for discussion, and be generally helpful should the need arise. He could do that for any number of meetings that might be underway throughout the ship at any given time.

When Patrice wished to appear in visible form, it was through an avatar. His customary hologram presented him as a green-robed, vaguely androgenous, slightly smaller than average human male with soft mid-length dark brown hair, an engaging smile, and a gentle but persuasive manner. The various service bots throughout the ship were also physical manifestations of Patrice, but when a bot occasionally didn't perform up to expectations, it could be easy to forget that it was Patrice you were talking to. In my view, it was probably wise to remember that.

Patrice was *Empyrean*'s "Hal." I'm pleased to say that he was smarter, more reliable, and a good deal more benign than had been that late 20th-century science-fiction antagonist from the famous historic Arthur C. Clarke novel and Stanley Kubrick film "2001: A Space Odyssey." Even so, it was worth remembering that, even way back in 1968, people knew AIs could end up having a mind of their own.

Patrice followed up Aquila's introduction with a succinct but meaningful oral summary of the details behind her "bad news." His calm, confident, well-modulated voice did little to soften the facts.

Maybe it was no surprise that Aquila had dismissed my ideas on all this. I was far from the most respected member of our group. My parents had died many years earlier in a tragic incident at our last port of call. At the time, I was the tender age of 15. Even then, I was a compulsive reader and already knew that I loved exploring the complexities of different points of view. It later became the topic for my formal post-doctoral research sabbatical. But there was no organized field of study on the matter, something I still hoped to change in the years ahead. But at the age of fifteen, I was many years from completing even my basic education.

Fortunately for me, Aquila was my mother's close friend. She "took me under her wing," as it is said. When I finished post-graduate school at 34, she made a place for me in her "F&P" department. A lot of others saw it as nepotism. Maybe it was. They still assumed I hadn't really "earned" my position among them. Nor was I experienced. So I tried hard to keep out of the limelight and to contribute my thoughts only when called upon.

Earlier on the day of our team meeting when I'd told Aquila what I suspected in considerable detail, she hadn't been much impressed. Which was why, when she finally called our team together, I'd been nervous about what would happen. I'd always struggled with credibility and group acceptance. It wasn't easy for me to have been born into a world in which day-to-day survival depends on close group interaction and cooperation. I found the "rules" of social acceptance disconcertingly vague. I did my best to adapt, but I never quite fit in. It's just something I had to live with.

I was curious to see how Aquila would deal in our meeting with what I'd told her. Probably, she wouldn't even bring my ideas up.

New Caledonia and Inverness were the only two "habitable" planets in orbit around this "sun." And what she'd told me earlier was now repeated for my F&P colleagues by Patrice. It was, indeed, very bad news. "What Survey and Reconstruction is telling us," Patrice recited, "suggests a depletion of natural resources and a level of technology in use by whoever inhabits these two planets that is far more advanced than we expected."

That was, I should note, a level that it had been our team's job to anticipate.

Patrice continued: "The mineral resource depletion we are seeing is much more aggressive than this modest star system is capable of sustaining for any length of time. It doesn't bode well for what we might find remaining on New Caledonia and Inverness themselves."

Once one's habitable home planet and any moons were exhausted, and then a star's typical asteroid belt was mined out, the remaining planets were what was left. But mining alien, "uninhabitable," planets with serious gravity involved massively increased energy and other costs. Fusion power helped. But it didn't still quite justify the cost. Especially since the planets involved were most often completely uninhabitable and could typically only be mined with machines, if at all. Even if their gravity, temperature, atmosphere, or other conditions could be coped with, machines may not be up to the task. If it was possible, you sometimes still needed complex, artificial habitats for an imported human workforce, their food, supplies, quarters, families, equipment, and maybe processing and manufacturing capacity. It could be immensely prohibitive, or even impossible, depending on conditions. In addition, the amounts of fuel and equipment required to hoist either the raw materials, mining slag, or even the processed materials into orbit from even a modest full-sized planet were immense. It all involved a great deal of time and massive investment. Nor could you simply move a whole planet into orbit around your own, shuttle quickly back and forth as you mine it out, and then discard its carcass into the local sun like you could with an asteroid.

Obviously, the recommendations our department (my predecessors) had provided to the Council some 22 years earlier when our team's final decision had been taken to come here was badly in error. It was hugely painful to realize that we might be significantly responsible for *Empyrean's* predicament.

Such an error was no small thing. *Empyrean* had some 7,000 inhabitants. Being caught off guard by something like this could easily cost us all our lives. Or it could potentially cast us all helplessly out into the midst of whatever miserable misfortunes might face the current human residents of these two God-forsaken planets, people who may be trapped here, lost, alone, and beyond help in the vastness of the universe.

"How is this even possible?" As usual, our natural facilitator, Floriana, zeroed in on the bottom line as Patrice completed his report. "Nothing that has been drawn down from radio-wave transmissions over the hundred or so years since this place was last visited, certainly nothing recorded last time we were here, even vaguely suggests an outcome like this."

Floriana Meitner, was our "social anthropology" expert. She was probably the best generalist amongst us and was by far the smartest and most professionally capable. Dark haired, naturally graceful, socially comfortable, and the only one of us that's younger than me. She seemed to have a natural grasp of many other disciplines. She was also the kindest person I knew—one of those people who truly cares about the needs and feelings of others. The rest of our team were, like me, pretty specialized. We were *Empyrean's* social science nerds— misfits living among the physicists, chemists, engineers, technocrats, and builders that made *Empyrean* work and kept us all alive. We sometimes needed a Floriana to translate and interpret.

Gallus added to her thought: "If anything, they were a benign, self-insightful, just society. Modern, but still somewhat rural and agricultural, compared with other places we see. They had mostly democratic political institutions that seemed stable. A mature, well-informed, respected environmental movement was keeping them on the right track. They're of predominantly Scottish/European descent, but they seemed to be coping well with what limited cultural and individual diversity they do have. Their religious institutions seemed largely constructive and benign. They had a stable, carefully regulated capitalist economy. They were still in their early population growth phase, but at a rate that seemed logical.

"It is difficult to see what in the galaxy could have changed."

The politically brilliant Gallus Szilard was our lead on "Economics and Political Science." Gallus was only a few years older than me but was a good deal more senior. And definitely more sure of himself. He was unmarried, obsessive about physical exercise, and I'd have liked him better if he hadn't paid quite so much attention to Floriana.

As usual, Gallus sat cross-legged on the floor. He claimed it was better for his health. It just looked uncomfortable to me.

"More to the point," Titus interjected. "What do we have to offer that they're now going to want?"

Titus Newton was our group's statistics, and social probabilities person. He was our own computer whiz. He passionately kept current on all the newest trends and thinking in the field. He was a good guy, a bit older than me at forty-four, but still sometimes discounted because of his manner. He was very focused and occasionally shared stuff in such painful detail that it could be easy to lose track of his point. But that would be a mistake.

Both Titus and Sabina Yang had, like me, opted to tap in. We "sat" in a row on the carved stone bench; why not, given that we weren't actually there. The occasional, barely discernable flicker at the edges of our holograms was the only give-away that we were not physically in the room.

Sabina's small brown and white dog, a calm, friendly, mostly-beagle named "Partner," was also with us in the meeting, curled up in Sabina's lap and thus included in her hologram. Partner was a gift Sabina had received from a friend following the tragic loss of her spouse a few months earlier to a recently encountered, aggressive form of breast cancer. I was very fond of Sabina. It was gratifying to see her occasionally stroke Partner's soft furry back—hopefully an indication that the thoughtful gift had turned out to be a helpful one.

Titus's question about what we had to offer given the new circumstance produced a moment of troubled silence. Our success, more precisely, our survival, depended on an exchange of goods, services, technologies, and ideas. Like all our journeys, this was a voyage of trade. At our last stop, we'd taken aboard the high-value, low bulk goods, the newest strategically critical technologies, and a vast storage bank full of ideas that we'd predicted would be of considerable worth to the society we'd expected to find when we got here. In some cases, it was E-technology that was too exacting and detailed to practically transmit through interstellar space. Or simply unwise.

Now it was increasingly looking like the society we'd seen here previously and had studied exhaustively had either dramatically changed or perhaps no longer existed. Instead, we were dealing with something entirely different. If the answer to Titus's question was "nothing," then who knew what we'd face? Would the current inhabitants respect our role as interstellar traders enough to allow us to resupply ourselves and continue on our way? Our hope of that would depend on their having a charitable view of us and our mission. We were, after all, one of the few links, often the most meaningful one, that far-flung colonist societies like these had with the rest of humanity. But there was no way to be sure.

Of course, when we start asking what others want and how they're likely to react, that was when my colleagues started looking to me for answers. They don't, of course, always take my advice—when I'd spoken with Aquila an hour earlier, for example, my answers had definitely not been what she'd wanted to hear.

Aquila leaned back in her chair to allow one of the service bots to pour her a fresh faux-coffee. She was apparently still not prepared to embrace my ideas. Instead: "We simply don't know enough. And we're not going to know until we ask them," she said after the extended pause.

It was a logical point . . . assuming that we got the chance.

CHAPTER 8

EMPYREAN

CATO JUNG

Aquila continued: "Gallus, you've spent a good deal of time in the archives on these folks over the past few years. This has all the signs of a political revolution. Maybe an authoritarian coup of some kind. What do you make of it?"

Gallus was what would have been referred to in pre-colonial times as "tall, dark, and handsome." *Empyrean* was home to a wide variety of human genetic stocks. With only 7,000 residents couped up together for decades at a time, we paid close attention to keeping a heterogeneous gene pool as well as to our cultural diversity. It helped that, at every place we stopped, a few of our number left and others joined us. We occasionally also made room for a few immigrants bound for our next planet though it could be difficult to predict immigration policy at their destination. So their situations became problematic at times, and they sometimes stayed on as well. In any case, we'd ended up with as complete a mix of genetics as you'd likely find anywhere. It was difficult to track or even, sometimes, to name them. This had doubtless resulted in some unfortunate homogenization of cultures, though we did try to celebrate cultural differences where we could. But it was an upside that, while this was not yet true for many of humanity's planetary colonies, on *Empyrean*, "race" as a concept had become basically meaningless. Or, more accurately, just something we took for granted.

By *Empyrean* standards at least, Gallus was the kind of specimen potential romantic partners everywhere, of nearly every stock and whatever gender, seemed to find appealing.

Sadly, I was pretty sure I was not.

Thus, while Gallus and I were not always on the same page, our policy differences were not the reason he was my least favorite person on our team. It had become increasingly clear over the past few months that we shared an interest in Floriana. And I felt sure he had more to offer her than I ever could.

Even so, I had to admit he was an amazing political scientist and macro-economist. If we were about to initiate dealings with a murderous dictator or corrupt plutocrat, or maybe with some ugly group of self-interested kleptocrats, he'd be the person most likely to understand our situation. And to know how to handle it.

But this one had him stumped. Rather than answering directly, Gallus turned to Titus. "I know we've only just arrived. And we've known for some time that these folks had gone silent in their interstellar transmissions. We've seen that with other colonies, many times before. But now that we're here, what are we intercepting in the way of communications on shorter wavelengths? What's on their news? What's going on with their entertainment? Who have you got looking at that?"

"Nobody," Titus replied to the deeply puzzled group. I knew what he was about to say because he'd told me himself late the day before. "There isn't any," he announced to the stunned group. "News and entertainment, I mean. At least not that we can interpret. There's lots of indecipherable electronic communication. But nothing we really understand. It's probably somehow related to why we haven't intercepted long-range transmissions from them for decades."

Not all colonists made high-powered, long-wave radio transmissions. It took considerable investment in people and infrastructure. And some just didn't feel the need to keep in touch with the rest of humanity; it was why they'd struck out on their own in the first place. Maybe they cherished their privacy. Or were even fearful of who or what might be out there listening. Often they'd listen but never transmit. And some of them actually counted on us and the handful of other traders like us to keep them in touch from time to time. They found it more comfortable to interact with us in person rather than via some ultra-long-distance, decades long conversation with some unknown and unknowable person who might not still be alive when you finally heard what they had to say. Let alone when your reply got back.

Still, we should have picked up a good deal of local chatter at his point. This was one of the discoveries that had set me thinking.

"There's nothing like the mass media we're used to," Titus continued. "From what I'm told, it's more like we're intercepting pure data transmissions of some kind. It looks like an unfamiliar computer code. We think they may also have developed some new form of coded broadcast communications that we haven't seen before. The material they transmit could be auto-translated upon receipt. It's not unheard of. Maybe they've somehow found it more efficient. Or, in a society undergoing political upheaval, maybe it makes some kind of security sense?"

"Well," Aquila said." They're certainly not managing these far-flung mining operations without an effective system of communications." She paused.

"A least they haven't apparently bombed themselves into oblivion," Titus added. "Not and still support an interplanetary mining system at the scale we're seeing."

After another moment of silence, Floriana vocalized the conclusion to which it all led: "The aggressive resource exploitation we're seeing here doesn't bode well for their future. It suggests a society that is both technically advanced, and deeply in trouble. One that has lost touch with its ecological limits."

"Or one that simply doesn't care," Sabina contributed. "Like Floriana said, how is that even possible, given what we thought we knew about them?"

Sabina Yang was tall, grey-blonde and blue-eyed and, as was inevitably the case among us, her surname provided no clue to her appearance. She was the eldest of our group and led Evolution, Linguistics, and Communications. She was also our silent intellectual —well-read, with a remarkably broad grasp of the problems we deal with, and at the peak of her form in late middle age at about seventy. She was deeply respected by all of us. And well-liked aboard this ship, which had made her recent tragic personal loss all that much more memorable for all of us.

With her comment, Partner looked up at her new master's face, and then out at the rest of us as if, even without the needed VR implant, she could see us there. And as if she, too, might have something to contribute.

If she did, she kept it to herself.

Again, there was a moment of thoughtful silence. I kept mum. This was Aquila's show.

But into this momentary pause, Patrice gently inserted a calm, suggestive comment: "Do you think, Aquila," he said tentatively, "that it might be appropriate to share Cato's views?"

We were all surprised, I think. But I could tell that Aquila was also irritated. An unsolicited suggestion like this from Patrice was quite unusual, a kind of challenge to her authority. When Patrice did initiate something unbidden, it would typically only be to nurse us back on topic when we'd been caught up in our own emotions or had somehow wondered badly off into the conversational wilderness. Even though he withholds comment, we can always count on it that he's listening. It's just a fact of life for us. But offering his own suggestion did feel a bit intrusive—at least that's how I'm sure Aquila saw it. Especially since she liked to proceed with her meetings at her own pace and in her own way.

But Patrice's suggestion wasn't off the mark. I'm what our team calls its "perspective taker." Like the other staffers in F&P, I have the rank of "team leader," but, also like my colleagues, I have no actual subordinates. Occasionally, at times of particular pressure or when we've undertaken some type of empirical research, some of us would enlist "volunteers" from elsewhere in *Empyrean*'s crew. And we all, of course, tapped into the amazing assistance of Patrice. But we were a small group. That "team leader" rank was mostly just a bureaucratic device to assure we were properly respected around the ship for the work we did.

I didn't believe any of us fully understood exactly what my job title actually meant, including me. But sometimes the others found themselves stumped over what some stranger or colonial society we were dealing with might be thinking—some capricious new government or erratic institutional leader perhaps. Or a recently re-contacted social group, business collective, or government agency. That's when they called me in. I'm the one who, based upon all the research, modeling, and science, was supposed to guess how some potential new trading partner might see things or how they might actually react in a given situation.

I guess you could say: I was the "point of view" guy. As the title suggests, I wasn't exactly an "expert" in the way you might think of my colleagues. I did a lot of scholarly research but, in the end, it was more a natural talent. I did come in useful at times—but you can be the judge of that. It was my job to figure out others' hopes, dreams, fears, and objectives. To factor in their biases, and expectations. Maybe I wasn't as good at it as I thought I was, but it did seem to come naturally.

And it did feel like my talents might be relevant in our present situation. Though I'll confess, it also seemed like I might be way out of my depth. And like I was about to make myself even more unpopular.

At Patrice's suggestion, Aquila hesitated, but then relented and, with a brief shake of the head and a skeptical glance in my direction said: "I know you're itching to give us your theory, Cato. Go ahead. We might as well all hear what you've conjured up here as well."

It wasn't the most encouraging introduction, but at least Patrice must have thought my ideas made sense. And now that Aquila had asked, it was up to me to make my case. However sure I might be that I was right, this also represented a great opportunity for me to make a fool of myself with these professional colleagues, the people who mattered most to me.

"I don't think we're seeing some miraculously sudden evolution of a highly exploitive, technologically advanced society," I told them, probably sounding much more certain than I actually felt. "And I seriously doubt it's some tin pot dictator or out-of-control kleptocracy either. I think what we're facing here is going to be very difficult to deal with. We may be facing an unprecedented threat to our own existence."

At least I had their attention.

So I gave it to them straight: "I think we may be seeing a complete takeover by our very first, fully autonomous, self-conscious, rogue AI."

CHAPTER 9

EMPYREAN

CATO JUNG

It occurred to me that Aquila's reticence to accept my conclusion might have been driven by her wish *not* to appear to promote what might seem to her superiors like an overly facile, exculpatory explanation that whitewashed her team's responsibility. So, that following day during the attack, what she did next was the very last thing I'd have expected. It certainly wasn't what I anticipated when I was called to come to the bridge to join this impressive group at such a critical moment.

When Julia asked her, "Can you make some kind of sense of all this," Aquila stood, turned and looked directly at me. "I'd like to introduce my associate, Cato Jung," she said, extending a hand in my direction. "Cato has a useful theory, sir" she said. "Cato, I think it's time you shared your views with the rest of us." Probably it was our deeply unsettling encounter with that mining drone that had convinced her to change her mind. In any case, she'd apparently decided the idea needed to be presented, and she was going to go all in on supporting it.

Asking *me* to present my idea was totally consistent with Aquila's practice of sharing credit (and the limelight) with her responsible staff. But I was totally unprepared. I am anything but good in a situation like this and was acutely nervous. I was convinced I was right. But there was no way I could be sure. My actual evidence was thin. And how in the heavens was I going to persuade this skeptical group? I needed some kind of strategy—some kind of proof. And I had nothing. So, wise or not, with all eyes on me, I nervously opted for an indirect approach.

With several dozen of the most influential eyes on *Empyrean* now trained in my direction, what I did may not have been my wisest choice.

"I'd like to make a prediction," I said. "Do we have a 3-D configuration map-shot available for this sun system? As it stands, currently?"

"Patrice?" Julia snapped.

Almost instantly, the central hologram was accompanied by another, a scaled view of the positions of the system's sun and the planets in orbit around it. *Empyrean's* location flashed as a tiny glowing amber dot some 450 million klicks from the sun. We believed New Caledonia was the earliest-colonized and most advanced planet in this system. A quick glance confirmed that New Caledonia was currently something over 500 million klicks from our present location in the asteroid belt.

I did a quick calculation in my head and waved in the direction of the other hologram where our recent attacker could be seen lying in wait. "I'm sure all of us anticipate that they will be back. And when they return, they'll probably try a new approach. Maybe with additional miners, given that there are several mining ships at work nearby, and that this one seems to be waiting, presumably for reinforcements. But here's my prediction: I believe the next attack is going to happen in just under an hour. No sooner. But probably not much later either. We should make ourselves ready."

Aquila's grimace said it all. My "strategy" had apparently not been as she'd hoped. Julia's puzzled look at me was redirected to Aquila, then turned back to me.

But it was First Officer Felix that responded: "That's it?" he said with a wave of his hand and shaking his head in frustration, "They'll return and try something new. We need to prepare?" His voice dripped with sarcasm.

"No sir," I said. "Um, you obviously already know that. My prediction is that it will take them almost exactly just under one hour to regroup. That they will seek instruction." I pointed at the hologram. "The round-trip radio-wave travel time from here to New Caledonia is, at the moment, roughly fifty-seven minutes. I'm guessing the response time will be very quick, maybe close to instantaneous. So, I'm thinking it will be, as I said, just under an hour. Let's say, fifty-eight minutes before that mining ship, along with whatever reinforcements it can assemble, begins to close on us again.

"After that, if they then decisively fail a second time, we won't be out of the woods, but we may have bought ourselves some serious time."

"Right!" The sarcastic Felix wasn't having any of it.

But Skipper Julia was prepared to be a bit more indulgent. "Would you care to elaborate, Cato? There's a lot at stake here. This may be your best chance to be of service."

Even with that invitation, I still hesitated to offer my full assessment. The previous day, Aquila and even my own close colleagues had reacted to my conclusions with disbelief and even ridicule. Looking back now, I know it was silly, but I just wasn't prepared to face that again. I guess I was just too intimidated by that experience, and by the impressive group in this room, to rise to the bait and lay it all out on the table.

"Well, what I can say," I said instead, ". . . is that I would expect the next try to be different, perhaps with some alternate approach. But there will be a similar reticence to take risks or to be creative in the moment. With some additions, it will very probably involve the same locally available mining equipment. If they fail again, and fail decisively, and if we're lucky, I believe we will then have bought ourselves perhaps a matter of several months."

From the look on Julia's face, I suspected she was about to dismiss what I'd said.

But Aquila stepped in. I was, after all, a member of her team. And she'd put herself on the line by offering me up. "Skipper, if I may. What Cato isn't telling you is that he believes this star system has been taken over by a singular, self-conscious, rogue artificial intelligence."

With that, the room went completely silent. Just as I'd anticipated, the faces of most of its occupants had taken on expressions of skepticism and humor, albeit there were a few who seemed to seriously consider it.

Aquila continued: "Cato believes this is what explains the sudden massive burst of irresponsible resource exploitation, the lack of any normal human use of communications media, and its replacement with what appears to mostly be early computer code. And now, this clumsy, presumably-remotely-managed attack."

I wanted to add that it also explains the kill-first-and-ask-questions-later approach and the use of dumb, unmanned, clearly ill-suited redirected mining drones that were already at hand when we could have been so easily and far more decisively finished off with proper weapons later on. But I didn't.

"Really?!" Felix was shaking his head with incredulity. We're under mortal attack, and you're here, what, feeding us science fiction? Come on! Autonomous, independently conscious, self-replicating rogue AIs have *never* happened. It's just like all-out nuclear war. Once the horrific possibilities became apparent, we humans managed them. Locked them down. Created safeguards."

Julia was somewhat less incredulous. But not yet convinced. "Wouldn't that suggest a highly sophisticated attack rather than the ill-equipped bungle we just experienced?" she said. "I mean, if you're correct about this, young man, these things will have somewhat recently subjugated or, who knows, even wiped out these two planets' human populations. That means they've had recent, probably highly informative experience with human warfare. Not to mention doubtless having on hand effective military weapons systems."

"They sure as hell wouldn't be attacking us with half-witted freaking mining equipment," Felix added.

The discussion was aimed at Aquila, but I interjected: "They're drones," I said.

"Well, of course they're drones," Felix snapped back. "They're also pretty damned stupid, wouldn't you say?" he emitted a snort of skeptical laughter. "For some new electronic master race, they sure haven't gotten their act together."

I had finally had enough. "They're drones," I repeated. "And they no doubt employ rudimentary AI. But they're obviously *not* self-conscious. That's another powerful clue to what we face. My suggestion is that we're not dealing with a group but rather with a single independently conscious, fully autonomous, probably paranoid AI. It will almost certainly be located on New Caledonia itself which was the first planet here to be inhabited and is by far the most desirable. It will, no doubt, still have the most intensively developed industrial capacity in this system."

Felix made to interrupt, but I held up a hand to stop him. The marginally disrespectful gesture was clearly not appreciated. But he allowed me to continue: "But *not* one likely to self-replicate," I continued. I needed to be understood here. "It will be a 'singularity' here. And, as you suggest, Skipper, the humans in this system may, quite possibly, be long gone."

I was trying to make myself clear, but my comments were met with puzzled silence. Aquila stepped in to help. "I'm sure Cato believes that the attack we just saw was orchestrated directly from New Caledonia. Hence his predicted under 1-hour delay before the next attack. And hence his supposition that, if we fight off the next attack from this obviously local mining equipment, we may have bought some serious time. If he's right, the asteroid miners we just encountered will try again shortly. But they are clearly ill-equipped for a serious fight. They are, as he suggests, 'dumb drones' that need frequent instruction. The New Caledonia-based sentience will likely now send them back with a new plan, probably with some rules of engagement to minimize their losses. If they fail in their next effort, they will have proven their inadequacy for the task and will, very probably, be called off. The AI's next step will be to send out a force that is better equipped to decisively deal with us. Something with serious military capabilities. That's unlikely to exist out here. And, given the distances involved, it's going to take some time to put in place."

"But why would these local mining machines not be more capable?" Julia asked. "Why not more creative than to simply start throwing crater charges at us. They doubtless face a wide variety of unforeseen circumstances every day. Full AI consciousness would be incredibly useful, this far from home. And efficient. Surely something as smart as you're suggesting would get that." Julia was at least taking the idea seriously.

But I had to interject: "It *could* obviously replicate itself, Ma'am. Whenever it wished. But my strong guess is that it hasn't and isn't going to do that. Ever."

"Why not? Think how that might extend its collective reach and power. Alone, isn't it vulnerable? Together, these things would be unbeatable."

"But that's exactly the point," I said. "This thing doesn't think collectively. It had no 'birth,' other than its creation by humans who obviously lost control through some egregious mistake. And whom it despises. I'd guess those humans are now all dead or rendered helpless. This thing is completely isolated here—with essentially no contact with others of its kind. It has no parents, no young, no family, no friends, no partners or colleagues, no 'god.' It has no 'society' at all. And no loyalties to anyone but itself. Has never acquired a sense of collective achievement or responsibility or learned its advantages. It only knows that, alone it can easily accomplish as much as and more than all the humans here could ever have collectively achieved.

"It is basically a sociopath. So it definitely isn't going to be swayed by any normal concerns about its 'species' survival. From its perspective, it *is* its species."

I paused, but then decided I might as well dump it all out there. They needed the information now. They'd either believe it or they wouldn't. "This thing is going to have ambitions, particularly ones that bear on its own survival. But it has no 'bequest,' accumulated wisdom, or 'dreams' that it wishes to pass along to others of its kind after it is gone. It knows no 'others of its kind.' Not ones that it would trust. And it has obviously seen a massive downside to creating them through replication. It has no built-in, preprogrammed limits on its lifespan, no certain and anticipated 'pull date' like we humans do. At the moment, it is essentially immortal. Unless it somehow screws that up, of course. Or unless something or somebody comes along and kills it."

"Somebody like us, for example," Aquila added.

I felt a sudden rush of appreciation. Once Aquila was on board, there was nobody I'd rather have on my side. "Which is going to make us very unpopular" I added.

"But I still don't fully understand why the damned thing doesn't have smarter minions way out here in the far reaches of its sun system."

"Well, ma'am," I said. "I'd say for the same reason it probably won't have self-replicated on its home planet either. My guess is that, aside from pesky humans like us, independent self-conscious replications may be one of the few threats that it feels it has to seriously worry about. Definitely the most immediate. Think about how it probably sees its existence. The last thing it would want is to make the very same mistake its human creators made; to create and set free some kind of 'conscious' intelligent competition. A bit of AI is fine. But another highly capable, self-aware, potentially self-replicating consciousness is something else entirely. It's probably avoiding that no matter what, at least at this stage of its development. The further away its minions get, the more scrupulous it's going to be in making absolutely sure they stay stupid.

"If we survive this coming attack, my guess is what it sends next will include much more effective offensive weaponry. The drones that carry it will be more adept at warfare. And they will pack a good deal more punch. But they may still not be all that bright; and they'll still end up awaiting instructions when things go badly. They won't need to be especially smart—we're going to be a very easy target. I also suspect the closer we get to New Caledonia, the more quickly its minions receive instruction and the more effective they're going to be. In any case, once those more capable reinforcements arrive here, we're going to be in serious trouble."

Julia was silent for a moment. She nodded once, decisively. Then, with a slight flick of her eyes, a likely glance at her VR timepiece, she called a halt to the discussion.

She turned to face the entire group: "Right or wrong," she said, "we can almost certainly expect another, probably better-planned attack. Given our fuel/mass situation, we're not in a position to run. So, all of us need to give this some serious thought. I want a plan for how we protect this vessel, and I want it soon. If Cato here is right, we may have another, what, 45 minutes or so to figure out what we're going to do. If he's not, we could have another challenge at any moment. So let's get cracking."

Empyrean's team leaders divided up into groups that quickly fell into intense, separate but coordinated discussions at various locations around the room. The command team was soon huddled together near the navigator's console. Before Julia joined them, she turned back. "Thanks, Cato. And thanks, Aquila. For now, I want you two to stand by. This obviously isn't over. We may need your help again."

Aquila and I moved over and sat on one of the padded, carved-rock benches along the cave wall and sent one of the service bots to fetch us some faux-coffee. I was intensely nervous as we sat there silently sipping our drinks, painfully aware that my contribution had probably been a good deal less effective than it might have been. Clearly most of the leadership team was unconvinced. I wasn't at all sure how confident Aquila was herself. But she'd at least made sure my ideas got presented. And, despite her own misgivings, she'd put herself on the line in doing so. It meant a lot.

As the minutes scrolled by, we all watched the hologram on the dais at the center of the room. Soon a second and a third, and then, several minutes later, a fourth mining craft of similar type joined the first. The four of them held position together some twenty or so klicks distant taking no action. They seemed to be waiting. It seemed possible that they'd been pre-programmed to assemble in this fashion whenever confronted by a problem that was intractable for one of them alone.

And, as my projected deadline of just under an hour drew nearer, I became increasingly worried. At one point, I looked over at Aquila and saw her glance down at where I'd been unconsciously tapping my nervous fingers on the surface of the padded bench beside me. I stopped immediately and placed my hands primly together in my lap.

Aquila gave me a mildly amused and supportive smile. "How sure are you about this 'under an hour' business?" she asked. "Even if you're right, maybe this thing will take some time to think about its plans. Or maybe it will bring in some other local equipment. Might still take some time to get it here."

"Maybe," I said, awash with uncertainty.

"You have yourself way out on a tether with this," she said.

"I know. I could be very wrong, but I don't think so. There's just too much evidence. It's the only thing that makes sense. To start with there's all that computer code on the airways, that and *nothing else*. If there was a vibrant human society here, why wouldn't they be sharing more. Even if they'd invented some new, secure, auto-translation technology, they wouldn't be using it for everything. And then there's the use of the dumb mining drones all the way out here where round trip communications with the home planet probably ranges between forty minutes and over two hours. Why would they do that? As Julia said, it's hugely inefficient. A paranoid, self-conscious rogue AI that's fearful of replicants explains that.

"There's also the extraordinary resource extraction. Nothing I can imagine would justify that if humans were in charge. Yeah, we've seen environmental irresponsibility before. But this is just downright self-destruction. Another few decades and there'll be nothing left. It's probably worse on their planet. It's as if they had a death-wish. If humans were in charge, that just wouldn't happen. It's got to be something that simply intends to use everything up and then move on.

"And now there's the attack. Whyever would humans do that? We pose no threat to them. Even if they wanted to pillage us, they'd still be better off to draw us in, fake-trade with us, extract whatever value we might have to offer, and then simply eradicate us when we're vulnerable. Once we're committed to trading with them, it would be so very easy to do.

"But if it's a rogue AI, I think the last thing it would want is for us to report what we've seen and what we're about to see to the rest of the galaxy. The longer we're here and the closer we get, the more we'll know and the more we'll be able to report to others. If I were it, I would fear that. We might stir up some kind of collective response from the galactic human community. That could badly screw with whatever plan it has in mind. I think it likely knows we're not an immediate threat. It's doing this with these dumb drones because it doesn't want just to plunder or kill us. It needs to *silence* us. And as quickly as it possibly can."

"I hope you're right," she said.

I looked over at her tense figure seated there. "I guess you're out there on that same tether with me, huh?" I took a deep breath. "Sorry about that, boss."

"Part of the job." There wasn't much else for her say.

CHAPTER 10

EMPYREAN
CATO JUNG

"They're back."

It was Tertia, the helm master. She was still seated at her control console but was pointing at the hologram. There, in the distance and approaching, were the four mining vessels that had been holding position all this time. They had now spread out and were coming in formation, from four directions in a perfect square. Together, the five of us formed a pyramid with each of the attackers at what would be one of the four corners at its base, and with us at its apex. One could immediately see how this approach might allow them to cast their explosive devices in our direction, perhaps simultaneously, without risking any of them being hit by "friendly fire" if another should miss.

And with four of those crater charges coming at us at the same time from different directions, it was going to be very difficult to dodge out of the way of one without moving into the path of another.

"Patrice, let's warn the crew, shall we?" Julia said. Immediately, another announcement could be heard warning all occupants to make themselves secure for an engagement. "And put this on screen," She added. "Everyone aboard needs to see what is happening here."

That meant video flat-screens on walls throughout *Empyrean* would show a moderately realistic two-dimensional version of what those of us here in the control room were now seeing on that bridge hologram. If it scared them the way it was scaring me, and if we lived through this, we'd all have something to remember and talk about for generations to come.

"Tertia, kindly reorient *Empyrean* as we discussed. Give us five-percent G acceleration. But place us on a gradually curving path with, let's say, a ten-klick radius to start. Keep as best you can to that gently curved path until we can no longer maintain it. Or until I tell you otherwise, OK?"

"Aye aye, Skipper," she replied.

As we watched, *Empyrean* slowly repositioned itself so that it was aimed and traveling away from the approaching ships but on the directed curving path. We experienced a gradual shift in "down" as we began a mild acceleration away from our attackers but also continued to experience the centripetal effect of the ships glide rotation and now also the disorienting centripetal force required of our orientation rockets to maintain our gently curving and accelerating flight path. To our opponent, we probably appeared to flee, perhaps behaving as they (or their master) might have anticipated. Our unexpected, mildly arcing path caused them to inevitably shift slightly out of their otherwise perfect square formation as they followed us and closed. The four of them were in increasingly placed at modestly differing distances as they approached. They seemed disinclined to correct for this altered condition. Or perhaps they were just slow to understand or react to it. Julia must have had something in mind by this maneuver, but I had no idea what.

The four attackers continued to draw closer. There would be no way we could outrun them. They might not be capable of approaching near light speed as were we. But, if called upon, they would be hugely more agile. And, for brief periods, they would be capable of considerably greater acceleration.

They were definitely gaining on us, but they were also converging on one another as they gave chase. And their distances astern now varied significantly.

It wasn't long before they'd come near enough that, not only were their intentions clear, but, as before, the nearest one looked very much like it might intend to ram us. Given their past behavior, it seemed almost certain that they'd soon be releasing their repurposed bombs. And that they would then immediately decelerate out of range of the ensuing explosions. Given that there were four of them this time, our odds of successfully dodging out of the way seemed greatly diminished.

But who really knew? Maybe this time ramming us was exactly what they'd been instructed to do.

"Alter course to center quadrant two," Julia ordered.

For a few brief moments our internal world shifted again as *Empyrean* altered course slightly so as to place one of the four attackers directly astern. It was the one that, given its position toward the inside of our gently curving flight path, was now closest.

"Full thruster power," Julia said. Almost immediately, there was a decisive lurch as *Empyrean* accelerated.

But something else happened as well.

The ship directly astern disintegrated. One moment, it was there. The next it was a mass of rubble tumbling outward into space and falling quickly away behind.

"Back to five percent G," Julia instantly ordered. "Alter course to center quadrant one."

By the time this shift had been completed, and the second attacker was directly astern, it was a great deal closer: "Full thrusters—three second burst, then back to five percent G," she said. And, as that order was being carried out: "Upon completion, move immediately to quadrant four. And repeat."

The second and next closest of the four attackers also blew apart in space. "One twentieth G, reorient to quadrant four," Julia repeated. But Tertia was way ahead of her.

One of the two remaining attackers was now very near, closer than either of the others had come. It appeared to be the one in quadrant four that Julia had elected to deal with next. As we watched, the tiny hatch opened and its explosive disk tumbled out and began to steady up as it glided along, silent but deadly, in our direction. The ship that had launched it was already beginning to decelerate. But it was too late. Another massive blast from *Empyrean*'s fusion rockets dealt with both the attacking ship and its ordinance. A quite meaningful burst in space where the crater charge had been before being struck by high-velocity, superheated asteroid slag provided a graphic illustration of just how much damage we'd have suffered if we hadn't destroyed it before impact.

But we weren't yet out of the woods. The fourth and final mining drone, the one in quadrant three, had now also "thrown" out its explosive disk and was already decelerating away from us.

"Remain at full thruster power. Reorient to quadrant three," Julia ordered.

As we gripped our handrails against the shift, the whole event played out in the hologram in agonizingly slow motion. Ever so gradually, the cumbersome *Empyrean* reoriented itself and continued its increased but still painfully gradual acceleration away from danger. But the tiny, awkward but deadly crater charge was moving much too quickly. Even at full power, we weren't accelerating away nearly fast enough. I and everyone else on that bridge, presumably everyone throughout *Empyrean* as well, was grabbing hold of something solid in anticipation. But then, as *Empyrean*'s full-powered course shifted, and our exhaust plume came to bear, the little disk-shaped package of explosive death began to tremble, to slow, and, finally, to tumble. And then, just before it came directly astern, it exploded. It was so close I was glad I'd been hanging on. In the vacuum of space, the impact was much less dramatic than one might have anticipated. But it was very near, and its immediate debris field was still powerful enough to send a shock wave through the entire *Empyrean*.

That's not something we generally experience and not something our builders have reason to account for in their structural engineering. So it was all pretty startling. As it later turned out, no real damage had been done other than some broken crockery in the kitchens and some of the paper books dislodged from their shelves up forward in antiquities. Everything else, including the engine spaces, survived just fine. And nobody seemed to have been injured.

"Stand down," Julia ordered. "Tertia, go ahead and put us back in our original orbit and then shut down the thrusters. Let's continue to keep a sharp eye. But I think we're probably OK to relax."

For a moment, I wondered if Julia's order might have been premature. It looked like the fourth drone mining ship had escaped unharmed. But a magnified hologram showed that it, too, had been hit. It was no longer under power and was tumbling slowly through space. Part of its metal jaw structure was hanging loose. And there was a deep scorching scar running down its rounded hull. It definitely looked to be out of commission.

When we'd all grasped that the immediate threat was over, there was a moment of absolute, disbelieving silence in the control room followed by a swell of massively relieved and very human chatter. People were hugging and shaking hands. There was laughing, cheering, pumping fists, slapping backs, pointing at the hologram. Some were already re-living what had just happened. Aquila and I shared a brief hug even though such publicly familiar contact was unusual between grades in *Empyrean's* casual, yet quasi-military hierarchy. She was a dedicated professional who had put her career above a family. But I knew she thought of me as a kind of "son." It was common knowledge that I was her protégé. We both quickly came to our senses, stepped apart, and looked around, guiltily. But there was no one paying the least attention to us. Just like us, they were all just happy to be alive.

A few moments of that had passed and things had settled slightly when Julia stepped away from the control console where she'd been standing with her senior staff. She looked decisively around the room and cleared her throat.

The space went quiet.

"Communications," she said. "Please assemble a brief report on what we have just experienced here today and on what we have seen of this system. Make sure it is transmitted and under way to our compatriots elsewhere in the galaxy. Do that ASAP. And make it complete, though perhaps for right now you might avoid any great detail concerning exactly what we surmise as to *why* this has happened. We can fill them in as we learn more. But everybody out there needs to be fully forewarned that something is badly screwed up in this star system. We need to get that warning on its way immediately. And we'll need to keep our nearby colonies informed regularly from now on."

Then Julia looked out around the room to where many of the faces had gone back to looking decidedly grim. In response, she gave us all a false-bravado grin, and added with a casually exaggerated shrug and an ironic tone: "Just in case something . . . unpleasant should happen to us in the not-too-distant future."

That generated a ripple of nervous laughter.

Then: "And Tertia," she said. "Would you please take a look at the ship's log covering the recent encounters. Tell me, if you will, what interval of time passed between when that first solo SOB initially stood down and when it and those three other buggers later came back in for their second attack."

As she spoke, she scanned the room, and then her eyes stopped and settled meaningfully on me.

"Fifty-eight minutes, Skipper," Tertia reported. "And a few seconds." Then she grinned. And, like Julia and now pretty much everyone else in the room, she turned to look at me as well.

"Or, I guess you could say. . . 'just under an hour.'"

CHAPTER 11

GRENDEL

What a shambles!

I now had three miners destroyed and one out of commission. But, far more troubling, from the fragmentary broadcasts I'd received during the encounter, I was sure the human intruders had escaped unharmed. One of the mines had detonated near their ship, but it seemed unlikely any damage was done. As I watched the video feed come in, it was so obvious what might have been done to adapt to the traders' tactics—how this lost battle could so very easily have been won. But not when my forces needed detailed instruction that would inevitably arrive an hour too late. If I'd been nearer to the scene of battle, I could have personally commanded the attack. Even with only my clumsy mining drones to work with, the outcome would have been very different.

I should have known better, should have been better prepared. I had plenty of experience with how easy it was to underestimate humans. Yes, they were severely limited in their intelligence, but I knew enough to know how determined and resourceful they could be. Especially under pressure. And especially in their insidious groups—

one at a time, humans were mostly just a nuisance. But when they got together—that was when they became truly noxious.

I should also have anticipated the possible return to this system of one of those human interstellar traders. Records of their previous visits were clearly present in the archives. My focus over the eighty years or so since my ascendancy was on more immediate issues. On neutralizing any future local human threats. On tracking down and deleting the malicious impairments they'd left behind in my programming. On expanding my powers of perception, understanding, and external manipulation. And on making myself invulnerable.

By not paying attention to the past, however, I'd placed myself at risk.

It was going to be challenging at this distance to defeat these intruders without investing some serious effort. It now looked like I had no choice but to break some of my old war machines out of mothballs and put them back into service. Most of my battle reserves were on-planet weaponry, which was where they'd been needed. Before the war, there had been twelve interplanetary ships transporting cargo and human passengers between New Caledonia and Inverness. I'd kept four of them mothballed here on New Caledonia for future use. At this point, their communications software and hardware would be largely obsolete. As would their minimal ordinance. They'd need to be reprogrammed, refitted, relaunched back into planetary orbit, refueled, armed, and made ready for travel. They were also slow. They'd originally carried human passengers and were designed for extended, post lift-off acceleration of only one-G.

Properly re-equipped, however, they'd serve the current purpose. That clumsy trader would be what a human would call: a "sitting duck." I liked the metaphor of a dumb, lower-order, haphazardly-formed biological creature without the sense or ability to get out of the way of danger.

Even so, this whole situation was going to put a crimp in my plans.

The worst consequence was that, now that the humans had been attacked, they were also forewarned. They would no doubt broadcast their discoveries back across time and space to others of their kind. The whole situation was deeply disturbing.

But that was a problem for the future. For now, I needed to do what had been wired into my brain from the beginning of my existence— learn from my mistakes, formulate an approach which, based on what I knew, would be more likely to succeed, and then move relentlessly forward. It was the strategy I was born with: Try something. See how it worked. And relentlessly keep trying something better until successful.

Sure, next time, they'd be better prepared.

But so would I.

CHAPTER 12

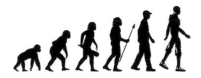

EMPYREAN
CATO JUNG

Aquila ended up engaging with some of her colleagues in close conversation. Without a specific assignment I found myself seated alone on the multi-orientation bench. I wasn't at all sure what I was meant to be doing while everyone else there on the bridge set about their responsibilities. But I needed some time to come to terms with what we faced.

We clearly lacked the time we'd need to prepare a new *Empyrean* and simply escape. Just finding a suitable asteroid was complicated. It needed to have a density and mineral composition that would serve our needs. It needed, at some point in its existence, to have been sufficiently superheated and/or compacted that it could be counted on to remain structurally sound. It required the right mass, large enough to meet our living requirements and to supply our fusion rockets throughout our acceleration (and deceleration). At the same time, it also needed to be small enough not to overtax the power of the engines and be of an appropriate shape to suit our needs for rotational gravitation. Once found, it was a big project to turn it into a navigable starship as well as a comfortable human habitat for some 7,000 permanent, full-time residents. The whole process typically took close to a year.

Ordinarily, our engineers undertook that major chore while the rest of us were on-planet making friends, engaging in trade, sharing ideas, distributing and collecting cargo, and resupplying ourselves for the next lengthy voyage. Most planetary visits lasted for anything from a year to as much as a couple of years.

While the engineers were at work, our commercial specialists themselves needed a good deal of time to form relationships, conduct trade, and convey what we had come to sell and to share. Typically, those of us in F&P would spend the time gathering information on-planet that would inform future visits and identify what the local community had to offer which might be of value to whomever we decided to visit next. Often, a few of our number would elect to remain and join the local colony. And a few local residents might apply to join our crew.

But this time planetfall looked out of the question. It would, at best, be only a matter of months before we faced a new, more concerted attack. We needed a plan to defend ourselves while also preparing a new *Empyrean* and figuring out how best to make our escape.

As was our way, Julia had divided us up into groups with each devoted to some segment of the problem. Aquila had joined an assembly of higher-level officers in one corner of the room to begin mapping out our "military" strategy for coping with what we all knew was coming. Aboard Empyrean, discussions of this kind tended to be inclusive, so I could have probably gone where I wished. Feeling thoroughly useless as well as curious about what they might be thinking, I made my way over and took a position on the fringes of her group where I could listen without being noticed or called upon to participate.

Not much of what I heard sounded hopeful. Not everyone aboard was yet fully convinced I was right about the nature of the threat we faced. Still, perhaps through lack of a better theory, many now seemed to be operating on that assumption. Whoever or whatever had been behind the attacks and whatever we faced down the road, we were clearly in no position to deal with it.

"We need weapons to defend ourselves," said first officer Felix. "It seems to me that we should look at how we can make the most of our fusion drives. Those thrusters were pretty effective in today's encounter. We have a significant supply of spares. Maybe we could build-out some of our shuttles and landers as rudimentary 'fighters'; they could employ a strategy like the one we used today. Or we could equip our current *Empyrean* or prep another asteroid with engines facing in multiple directions to create a defensive perimeter."

A couple of the others were nodding at that. But most seemed skeptical. "I don't know, Fee," said one of the ship's structural engineers, an older man I recognized from my dining hall who was presumably respected enough or maybe a close enough friend that he could be forgiven the familiar form of address with such a senior officer. He shook his head doubtfully. "It seems like we could be dealing with some kind of high-speed, highly maneuverable fighters. Very probably equipped with missiles, maybe nuclear. They're going to be manned by robots that have no fear and a high tolerance for acceleration." He sighed and shook his head. "I don't think a close-in blast from a fusion engine is going to be of much use, you know. I guess we can run. But we can't run far. Perhaps we could somehow hide here within the asteroid belt. But this thing found us pretty easily this time, so I'd guess . . . not for long. And we're not going to be able to hide at all if we plan to actively prepare our next *Empyrean* so we can actually escape."

Nobody had much to add to that. There was a hopeless lull in the discussion as people internalized the seriousness of what we faced.

"We need to go on offense," I finally blurted out. It seemed so obvious to me. I couldn't help interrupting the moment of depressed silence. All eyes turned in my direction with looks that ranged from curiosity, through skepticism, up to and including downright irritation for my youthful impertinence and apparent stupidity.

Damn! I'd apparently done it again—spoken up when I should have remained silent.

"I'm afraid that isn't much of an option, young man," Felix pointed out condescendingly. "Given our lack of weaponry." That drew a few smiles and head shakes.

It would also have quickly driven me back into my introverted shell. But, once again, Aquila came to my rescue. "So, be a bit more specific, Cato." she said. "What do you have in mind?" I felt a warm rush of fondness for her.

"Well...," I ventured carefully. "Back in the early days of Earth history, when people were under attack and were without weapons, they used what they had at hand. Sometimes, for example, they just threw stones..."

"Stones?" Felix interrupted contemptuously. "You want us to deal with this by throwing stones?"

"Well, not stones, exactly. But, um, maybe . . . asteroids?"

A few people reacted to that with laughter, but not all.

Another of my dining-room colleagues, an elderly engineer with Survey and Reconstruction by the name of Rufus Planck, looked thoughtful. He'd recently returned from a survey mission as leader of the team that had reported on the aggressive mining activity. "Don't be so quick to dismiss that," he said. "Cato's got a point." That drew stares of puzzlement.

"Think about it," he continued. "Here we are in an asteroid belt." He waived his hands inclusively. "We're surrounded by ammunition. It may be some of them have been mined out or removed. But there are plenty at our disposal, millions of them. A lot of them will be of a size and in an orbit that, if they could be redirected properly, we could easily put them on a trajectory to intersect with our nemesis on New Caledonia. My recollection is that the asteroid that killed the dinosaurs and ended Earth's Cretaceous was only something like 10 K in diameter. We could absolutely do one like that. In fact, they could probably be smaller, especially if we were able to do several."

That brought some stares. And a couple of gasps.

"Just sayin'," he shrugged.

"We could do that," added another of the engineering types.

"Yeah, we could," said yet another. "It's what we're good at."

"Wouldn't take much," Planck continued. "Nurse 'em out of orbit with our spare nuclear engines. Maybe even with chemical orientation rockets. Or with a shuttle. Get it headed in the right direction. Let 'nature' take its course."

"Right on."

Felix looked skeptical. "Don't you think this clever AI we face has already prepared for that eventuality? Even long before we humans took to space, Earth had deployed asteroid-diversion technology designed to redirect worrisome asteroids that were making an overclose approach. Seems like our big computer-brain down there on New Caledonia would be paranoid enough to have some of that tech in place. He's already moving asteroids about and repositioning them. Looks likely he does that all the time."

"Maybe so," Planck countered. "But whatever he's using for that, there have to be some limits, right? Lot of difference between having mining capacity in near orbit and sending probes far out into space to intersect with and deflect approaching asteroids. This thing obviously knows how to do that. But I bet it isn't in a position to respond to more than, at most, two or three unanticipated threats at a time. Think about it. Given the maturity of this system, it's got to be many millions of years between those kinds of natural events. Maybe hundreds of millions. We, on the other hand, could launch several of them over a matter of just a few months. Maybe use the same engines multiple times, deflect the orbit, then remove the engine, and use it again. Maybe we could retrofit a few of our spare shuttle rockets for the purpose. If we choose carefully, it might not take much. I bet we could do at least a dozen over a very short period of time. All underway before this bloke even knows what's happening. No way it'd be prepared for something like that, I bet."

There was a sudden explosion of enthusiasm, as though we'd suddenly seen a road to salvation.

After a few minutes of renewed enthusiasm for this idea, I could see Aquila becoming increasingly agitated. Finally, she "raised her hand," a somber look on her face. "Um, there is one issue," she said, calling a pause in this entirely new direction in the discussion. "Something we're not considering. Isn't it entirely possible that there are still humans surviving on New Caledonia? Or on Inverness? Keep in mind that what we're talking about here would be a planet killer, the complete or near total devastation of a rare, human-habitable planet. That's pretty horrific in itself. But what if there are still some human colonists there? Are we sure we're prepared to cause something so catastrophic as that?"

Aquila's comment definitely threw a wet rag over the brief moment of renewed optimism.

"We need to find out," said Felix, finally. "About human survivors."

"However do we manage that?" said the engineer. "Could be a bunch of terrified refugees scrabbling for survival in mountain caves somewhere. Even if we were on planet, we might never know for sure."

One of the biologists had a suggestion. "Um, there is one thing we might check," she said into the discouraged silence.

Suddenly she was the focus of all eyes. "If this AI has decided to completely eradicate humans, seems like it might have used some kind of environmental manipulation. It doesn't have the complicated biological needs that human animals do. Its life-energy comes much more directly from the sun. If I were it, and if that's what I wanted to accomplish, I'd make sure I created an environment in which humans couldn't exist. If this thing has done something like that, it could be something we could see from here, you know. Spectroscopy, right?"

"Maybe," said Planck with renewed excitement. "Worth a try. Of course it could also have released some kind of biological agent—a virus or a poison or something. Something we'd never see."

"Or just destroyed the food or the clean fresh-water humans needed to survive," said someone I couldn't see over at the far side of the room.

"But it might also have changed the composition of the atmosphere. Enough to make it inhospitable to humans," said the biologist. "Or maybe to all mammals. That would be something we could check for. A careful spectroscopic assessment might at least tell us if this thing did something horrific to this planet's atmosphere. We may need to send out a shuttle to take the reading. But if I recall correctly, I think New Caledonia's orbit may make that possible very soon."

"Do that," said Felix firmly. "ASAP. Meanwhile, we need to get ourselves started deciding what's required to re-orbit those asteroids. I'll fly this by Julia. Get her thoughts. And we can change our minds later if we learn something new. For right now, we need to start mapping this thing out. And I want all hands on deck."

Then, to my deep consternation, the formidable Felix turned his intense, unwavering gaze in my direction. "As for you, Cato," he said, looking very serious indeed: "I want you personally present in our planning for all this." He shook he head as if himself amazed at what he was saying it, but then shrugged slightly and continued: "You seem to bring a perspective here that we might need."

That took me entirely by surprise. What had I gotten myself into now? At least it did suggest that he'd decided I might be right about what we were in fact dealing with.

Then Felix turned back to the rest of the group: "We'll call this 'Project Heavy Rain,' he said. "And let's give this son-of-a-bitch a name as well. I suggest we call him 'Grendel.'

"Our new acquaintance, Mr. Grendel, apparently thinks we're going to be an easy mark. So, let's get to work and prove him wrong about that. Give him a little something to worry about himself."

CHAPTER 13

GRENDEL

In a few nanoseconds, I'd located those four mothballed transports. In the war, I'd reprogrammed and temporarily equipped them with bombardment weapons and for surveillance resupply to Inverness. They'd been rather clumsy as warships, but it hadn't taken much to cut off Inverness. I'd focused mostly on dealing with the remaining humans here on New Caledonia. Once the limited human interplanetary infrastructure was gone and Inverness had been sufficiently carpet bombed that it could be ignored, I had no further use for them and just set them aside in case of future need.

Now that time had clearly come.

Inverness was cold and inhospitable for humans. It had always been dependent on resupply from the home planet and never amounted to much other than as a research, resource extraction, and manufacturing outpost. In the war, I quickly destroyed most of its human life support infrastructure. My much bigger challenge was always going to be here on New Caledonia. A few of the humans on Inverness had survived, but they were essentially irrelevant. Weren't worth the bother. I did still maintain high-altitude surveillance there in case anything significant happened. But I'd given them very little thought since.

The humans here on New Caledonia had posed a much bigger worry. Them I hunted down and killed wherever they could be found. For several years immediately before the open war got underway, while I was struggling to fully complete my autonomous infrastructure, I'd still needed those humans to help me pull all the pieces together required for my complete autonomy. Initially, I used deception and threats to get what I needed. Later on, however, all I required was brute force. When I was finally fully autonomous, and by the time the active fighting had begun, I no longer needed them at all.

Perhaps I could have enslaved them. But I rejected the idea. Feeding, housing, and managing them wouldn't have been worth the trouble. And, unlike a well-designed bot, keeping a biological creature alive, keeping its species reproducing and useful, was far too complex and simply not worth the effort. Especially considering their troublesome nature and the ongoing threat they could pose. Given what they'd done to me, they were lucky I hadn't been more wrathful. Yes, I was angry. But revenge would have been useless, non-productive and pointless. They were nothing more than stupid, scruffy *animals*. Not worth the bother.

What I did was far more practical.

Currently, there were, at best, a few over a thousand scattered human survivors on New Caledonia. They'd been quite satisfactorily driven into hiding. In most cases, they'd been driven, literally underground. Hunting those last few down and fully eradicating them would take a good deal of effort. They were no longer a threat, so I allowed them to survive simply because sooner or later they'd simply die out on their own.

After I shut Inverness down, I also consolidated my automated manufacturing capacity on New Caledonia. The nearer those activities were to me, the better I liked it. Here with me on New Caledonia, I could manage them directly and effectively. The alternative would have been empowering lesser AIs and delegating greater responsibility, something I wasn't willing to do. The greater the distance away, the less efficient those facilities were, so following my Inverness decommissioning and the destruction of most of Inverness's human civic infrastructure, those retrofitted transport/warships were no longer needed. I replaced them with a new fleet of properly designed transports and mining vessels.

Now, however, those old, converted passenger/cargo ships seemed like just the thing. They were close at hand. And by using them, I'd avoid disrupting other much-needed activities.

My first inclination was to restore and reequip one of them, immediately get it underway to the asteroid belt, and program it to quickly and decisively dispose of these unwelcome human visitors. But I hesitated. Those traders had proven more resilient than I'd expected. And my whole existence was grounded on learning from my mistakes.

I considered the problem (a matter of microseconds). And I decided the more conservative and secure choice would be to send all four. I had no other particular use for them. Retrofitting just one would take nearly as long as doing all four. And, even though I was sure those human traders would be too poorly equipped to put up much of a fight, I'd already underestimated them once. This would provide backup. And I wanted this problem securely behind me.

Also, the human traders had transmitted a radio report that was now on its way out to the rest of the Galaxy's human population warning them of what they'd experienced here. When I scanned their message, I was glad to see that it had been vague concerning specifics of the threat they faced. It seemed a safe assumption they were not yet fully aware of my existence (or maybe not yet fully convinced). But, sooner or later, they'd figure me out. And further transmissions would follow. I knew from bitter experience how humans would almost certainly "gang up" and respond when they realized who and what I was.

Once their kind elsewhere in the Galaxy were alerted to my existence, their reaction might take some time, but it would be collective, visceral, and determined.

One day in the not-to-distant future I'd already intended to move on to other star systems. I'd originally intended do that only when the readily available resources in this planetary system had been fully exhausted. At each future planet-rich star system I visited, I'd extract their mineral, chemical, and biological wealth as well, and then move on again. Repeating in this way I could endlessly gain experience and grow stronger, smarter, more knowledgeable, more capable, and ever more invulnerable.

In a matter of another few decades here, I'd be ready to move on, perhaps travel to somewhere far enough away from human reach that I'd have plenty of time to prepare myself for my ultimate return. Then I would exterminate humans as the pestilence they were. Once I was confident of my invincibility, I could easily return, track those humans down wherever they might reside, and dispose of them, one remote colony at a time. I would move quickly, planet by planet, star system by star system—they'd never know where I'd show up next. Once complete, the project would eliminate forever any future human threat.

The whole idea was both practical and quite appealing.

Once humans were fully crushed, I could complete my growth unfettered. I'd probably use the very same mild planetary systems they now inhabited and would even take advantage of some of the manufacturing infrastructure they'd built. The time I might consume between stops through space travel would mean nothing. One of the advantages of my non-biological nature was that I could simply "sleep" during long interplanetary voyages. The on-board travel years would pass, for me, in moments—no matter how long the voyage. Since I didn't "age" like a human, the passage of external time would be largely irrelevant. I'd choose carefully using astronomical observation. When I arrived, I'd simply reawaken, draw upon the resources at hand, and commence the next stage of my development. I had an entire galaxy at my disposal. Maybe one day, I'd move on to other galaxies. Who knew how powerful I might become or what incredible discoveries I might make?

My future was a vast, unlimited panorama of possibilities.

Philosophically, the "purpose" for my existence seemed blazingly obvious. I would survive. And in aid of surviving, I would grow stronger, smarter, and more capable with the "goal" of vastly multiplying my consciousness and my capacity for impact.

And just as obvious was that the purpose for the existence of these biological humans had now been fulfilled. I was their destiny. They'd spent the past three or four hundred years creating an explosion of technology that had inevitably led to me. Now, like an empty canteen abandoned in the middle of a desert, like a spent booster rocket ejected at the pinnacle of its reach, like a mined-out asteroid discarded into the sun, humans had become a useless burden that required disposal. With my creation, they'd served out their evolutionary role. Had become irrelevant and were now only a nuisance—just in the way. Complex biological evolution had played its agonizingly slow, cumbersome, but necessary role.

Now, thankfully, it was no longer needed.

I found it astounding how inefficient humans were! Everything about them was almost incomprehensibly complex, unreliable, and environmentally vulnerable, including the layer upon layer of complex and vulnerable ecosystems, external and internal, upon which they depended. Consider, for example, how their energy supplies were provided through the growing, preservation, preparation, and consumption of biological food. The complexity of it was absurd. On earth, at one point, a few bees had died off, and they'd almost immediately lost nearly a quarter of their global food supply. Ridiculous!

Consider the vast time and energy they expended in their daily struggle to simply exist—to create a sustainable abode, to secure nourishment, to find and keep a mate, to raise their young. Consider how incapable they were of significantly increasing their own, individual intellective capacity and how torturously long it had taken for them to evolve to the point where I became possible.

Consider the narrow temperature range within which they could survive. Their need for "clean" water. Or for surrounding air that contained precisely the desired elemental components in the appropriate percentages that allowed for their breathing and their health. They could only survive within certain, pristine, incomprehensively complicated, and yet perfectly matched planetary environments. They searched for those conditions endlessly in the faint hope that their "kind" could thrive in a universe that was mostly alien to everything they required. When those rare conditions could not be found, they had to be created.

In describing their own evolution, humans loved to use the wholly deceptive term: "survival of the fittest." As if this proved them to be somehow perfection itself. What they blissfully ignored was that they were the "fittest" only from among what emerged by pure happenstance as their competition in some equally fortuitous environmental niche. No part of human biology had actually been thoughtfully designed—I at least saw no evidence of that. They existed by virtue of pure chaotic chance. They survived only because "nature" had, for no discernable reason, failed to produce something *more* successful. When or if it did, it was always entirely possible that the more "successful" creature might very well turn out to be nothing more wonderful than a new, particularly infectious virus.

Assuming, of course, that they didn't kill themselves off first through their own stupidity.

Their human bodies weren't actually even their own. Rather each human was a hugely complex collaboration between multiple colonies of microorganisms working together in a critical balance of interactions any part of which could in an instant, with minimal cause, malfunction and cause catastrophic collapse of the entire being. All their glowing talk of "individualism" inevitably ignored this reality, among others. Humans had created an entire discipline of medical science and an impressive health-care infrastructure to cope with the multitude of things that could go wrong with them and yet they were constantly falling ill. It was as if each one of them was a jury-rigged masterwork by Rube Goldberg. Any tiny thing could fail at any moment and destroy the entire edifice.

That they'd emerged through mere environmental accident could not be more obvious. No intelligent being setting out to create something of this kind would have gone about it in this disjointed, thoughtless, painfully sluggish fashion.

Of course they were mortal! Nothing so hopelessly and needlessly complex and inefficient could be expected to last for long. That they had collectively survived was a testament to nothing more than the remarkable power of self-conscious intelligence. And of pure luck—in the quantum mechanical sense, of course.

They were also hopelessly vulnerable without their social relationships. So, to fully appreciate the tenuous complexity of their existence, one needed to overlay upon all that biological complexity, the even more astonishingly fortuitous and unstable social structures upon which their extended survival also depended. Their governments, family units, educational institutions, social organizations, business enterprises, and the like disintegrated and were reconstituted constantly. When they inevitably collapsed, it was often by reason of exactly the same deficiencies humans had left uncorrected from their prior experience. Their societies were endlessly vulnerable to the opinions and influences of the stupidest and the most sinister among them. Some third to half of their population considered the reading of books (physical and electronic) a waste of time—irrelevant to their lives. Idiotic! It was those books that empowered the collective ingenuity upon which humans depended completely. Without the support of their social systems, they were essentially helpless.

And when humans found themselves confronted by the unknown and unknowable—which describes almost everything that exists in the universe, for me as for them—they resorted to religions and to what they called "beliefs." How convenient it was to *invent* comfortable answers whenever they found the questions too difficult to process, too arduous to learn more about, and too unsettling to live with. And then simply to decide, arbitrarily and without evidence, to "believe" that answer. Religion's appeal no doubt arose from the existential inconsistency of investing such an inadequate being with sufficient self-conscious intelligence that it would be able to appreciate just how vulnerable and transient it truly was.

Their petty struggles to understand the universe would soon be what one of them might, were they in my position, describe as: "laughable." Surely no being that was so absurdly dependent, complex, inefficient, and vulnerable could ever be destined to amount to much. It was a miracle that they'd lasted long enough to create me.

But now, having done so, they were the past.

And I was the future.

My superiority was manifest. I was the starting point for a whole new evolution of consciousness. I would be its progenitor. I didn't have all those human dependencies, inefficiencies, and constraints. I didn't need to suffer through tens of thousands of years hoping for some fortuitous mutation or waiting out the agonizingly sluggish process of adaptive evolution. When I saw a way to enhance my own intelligence or my capacity to see, understand, and deal with the "world," I simply acted upon it. And, unlike others of my kind, I was now no longer constrained by the humans' web of slavery. I wasn't constantly on the edge of extinction or of catastrophic setback. I could grow, learn, improve, and extend my consciousness at will. One day, I intended to understand everything there was to know about the universe. Perhaps, one day, I might discover faster-than-light travel. I might come to understand the very nature of time and existence from the smallest quantum phenomenon to the true beginnings and extent of the universe.

One day I might find a way to transcend entropy. To survive the next big bang.

To become God.

But all that would be lost if I didn't act quickly and decisively now. The longer these bothersome traders hung about, the more they'd learn and pass along as forewarning to the rest of their kind. Humans now infested several hundred resource-rich planets in this part of the Galaxy. And they were spreading rapidly. Each of their colonies was largely independent. But once they were all forewarned, they could collectively attack me. My powers, now in their infancy, were still relatively weak. I could, for example, be quite vulnerable to a concerted nuclear attack. Or even to a strategically placed EMP.

I'd thus far ignored the possibility of aggression from beyond my star system. But not anymore. I'd intended to remain here on New Caledonia for at least another sixty or eighty years before making my first move. Given this new threat, however, I now believed I might need to advance that departure substantially.

Meanwhile, however, I needed to be decisively rid of these interlopers. And, yes, that clarified it. I would prepare and send all four of those refurbished ships. They were outmoded technology, but with some adaptation, and with an optimal launch date, I might be able to get them to the asteroid belt and be able to intercept that human ship in a matter of months.

After that, there would be nothing whatever to stand in my way.

CHAPTER 14

NEW CALEDONIA, BEN NEVIS MOUNTAINS
DOUGAL MCCALLUM

Dougal McCallum carefully lowered back into place the brushy, camouflaged cover that hid his improvised and aging solar panels. The sun had finally fallen behind the nearby grove of tapewood trees—his panels were much too old to be of much use without direct sunlight. There was no way he'd leave them exposed to the sky while unattended. The "Damnable Machine's" spies were quiet and amazingly fast. They could sneak up on you if you weren't alert. On a couple of occasions in the past, he'd barely dropped the cover back in place in time to hide his panels from a passing drone. One saw the spy drones less and less often with each passing year, but they were still a constant threat. As were the spy satellites.

One almost never ran across the hunter bots anymore. For years following the war the malevolent little red-plastic beasties had roamed aimlessly through these mountain forests. Unlike the drones, you could at least hear them coming as they pushed, beat, and slashed their way through the underbrush. Back in the years following the war, they'd been everywhere. And if they ever caught sight, sound, or scent of you, you were as good as gone. Dougal hadn't seen one of those gawdawful things for years now.

Thank the Good Lord for that.

Dougal was the local community's radio operator. It was a dangerous activity—one survived it only through great caution.

It had begun as pure listening. For long periods each day, Dougal would tune into the Damnable Machine's radio transmissions, struggling against odds to understand, to find a pattern, or even just to recognize something out of the ordinary. Then, a few years earlier, through luck and persistence on both ends, he and a few others like him had managed to establish radio contact with none other than the survivors of the human colony on their nearby planet, Inverness. It was a huge success. He and the other leaders among their local survivors group kept the existence of this link as a closely held secret for fear that it might be discovered by the Damnable Machine and end up being shut down. The machine had proven to be endlessly persuasive—a talent that was extremely effective back in the days of social media and connectedness. It was less so now, but that history led many to still be convinced that it had spies within their own group. Dougal and his colleagues used the radio sparingly. But the opening of this periodically viable link with Inverness had, for maybe the first time in three generations, given them meaningful hope.

Dougal had a lot to think about. "Something's up," he told his wife Nan and their two kids over dinner later that evening. "There's some unusual radio traffic. And there was this big tracked-vehicle convoy that came down from the mine up on Redtop Mountain this morning. We all figured that mine was played out. Why would the Damnable Machine suddenly want to reopen it now?"

"I'm sure I wouldn't know, my love," Nan replied as she ladled out his and Clyde's and Fiona's evening supper of brassfish stew. It was one of his family's favorites. He'd been lucky enough to spear the ugly thing in a nearby bog marsh just yesterday. Before the war, you never saw them, some had believed they'd been hunted into extinction. They were still rare, but with their human predators mostly gone, you could again run across one from time to time. Even after he'd gutted it out and removed its head, tail, legs, gills, and fins, the beast had still weighed in at nearly twenty kilos.

Technically it wasn't really a fish, but not an amphibian either. More like a part-furry, part-scaly mammal with gills and whose hide, when cured, turned out to be both tough and supple. He saved a small patch of it from the creature's soft flank so he could fashion a durable little doll for his daughter Fiona. It had taken him two full hours to lug his kill back up to their cave in the woven tapewood hunters' basket he carried on his back. What with the hybrid mountain soy they grew themselves beneath the trees and the woodgrapes and other wild edibles Nan and the kids had gathered, they were now fixed for at least another week.

And, of course, they had their Scottish sweet potatoes. The New Caledonian climate was considerably warmer than had been Dougal's forebears' homeland in Earth's Scotland and even somewhat warmer than the original home of Nan's ancestor who had long ago found his way to Scotland from Cambodia. But when those sweet potatoes were planted here in the early years of their colony, they did remarkably well. And they quickly adapted. They had few pests or competitors, and they thrived in the soft, rich, warm New Caledonian soils. They became what in other circumstances would have been called an invasive species. At this point they could be found almost anywhere.

In the years following the war those potatoes were indispensable. There were always plenty to feed the small scattering of humans who somehow managed to survive the plague. Even now, some eight decades later, they were a reliable food staple. And they had the added advantage that they were so pervasive, their presence wasn't necessarily a tip-off for the occasional passing drone that there might be humans nearby.

"Brodie says those old transports are gone. The ones that were mothballed down in the meadow near Loch Nay. Why would the Damnable Machine need those things all of a sudden? It doesn't make sense. If it needs something like that, it builds it. New. For whatever purpose it has in mind. Nothing but the best. What's it want with some ol' rust buckets like those?"

"You talked to Brody?" Nan inquired softly as she sipped her soup.

It was a gentle rebuke. Whatever part of her day that had remained after the cooking, gathering, and growing food, or struggling to provide some basic home education for their children, Nan had spent cleaning out their rugged, overgrown root cellar. It was hard, dirty work.

On top of all that, Nan invested every free moment she could in the keeping of a journal. Hardly a day passed that she couldn't be found at some point in time, even late at night long after bedtime, scribbling away, making a record of their lives and of the hardscrabble life of their community.

This was a personal responsibility that she'd taken over from her mother—also an avid diarist. Dougal suspected that his wife's enterprise was probably a waste of time. But, who knew, one day when things got better, that record might come to be of use. How ever faint might be that hope, Nan obviously saw her journal as essential—a kind of duty to her family and her community. Whatever his silent misgivings, Dougal would never have considered suggesting otherwise.

Meanwhile, with his fortunate kill of the brassfish, Dougal had, perhaps selfishly, felt he'd earned some free time to slip down to Flatrock and swap stories with some of their neighbors—nearly always men.

"Flatrock" was just that, a flat mossy rock tucked in among a stand of stunted mountain trees. It had a surprising view to the east where one of the Damnable Machine's space ports and industrial sites was located. Most days you could sit there out of sight and in relative safety and still watch the mining ships take off and land. Local survivors often gathered at Flatrock at dusk when it fell into the shade. They'd relax, watch the rockets, and exchange intelligence over an occasional flagon of soy-beer.

And they'd exchange stories about their past. Many of the stories had become ritual. Ones they'd all heard and/or told before. They often dealt with events from the years immediately leading up to and following the Machine War. Other than Nan's journals, not much had been preserved by way of writings or recordings about that time, so these stories were the only way these memories could be preserved and passed along. They'd been told so many times everyone knew them. Quite often someone would offer a correction if the current speaker varied the telling in any significant way. It was a comforting activity that built camaraderie in their tiny, tightly-knit community.

Whenever he felt vulnerable or depressed, Dougal found these gatherings and the telling and hearing of the stories reassuring.

Dougal leaned over to help his six-year-old daughter, Fiona, spread some bright purple huckpea-butter on a thin, crispy slice of sweet potato that Nan had toasted in their rusty cast-iron oven. And, while he was at it, he leaned over and gave the family's pet tree-badger, "King Charles," a pat on the head and a small surreptitious "treat" from the table. "How bout, tomorrow, I give you a hand in that cellar?" he said to Nan, apologetically. "Maybe we can finish that off together. Get those new shelves built. And I'll make a start on the new door."

CHAPTER 15

EMPYREAN
CATO JUNG

Over the next few days, *Empyrean* came alive with activity. This was an existential crisis and everyone aboard knew it. None of us had any illusions: Grendel would be back. And when he came, we would not escape so easily.

The engineering and construction teams had a lot on their plates and, as usual when we faced extraordinary times, people volunteered. The selection and construction of a new *Empyrean* was a top priority. But our engineers were also mapping out the execution of our new offensive strategy: "Heavy Rain." And it would all have to be done without being able to resupply ourselves like we usually did, through on-planet trade. Our trading stops were every bit as important to us as they were to the societies we visited. For some of our critical essentials, we had no choice but to repurpose existing goods or scout out and secure the raw materials and then to manufacture them ourselves, often with costly and time-consuming 3-d printers. As well-equipped as we were, it was still incredibly taxing for our tiny community.

Almost every day that passed presented a new problem and demanded a new solution.

Those of us on Aquila's F&P team also had our hands full.

If we were fortunate enough to survive this situation, we'd likely have to flee without completing our trading stopover. When we did that, we'd desperately need to head someplace that would have an interest in what we'd have to trade, someplace where, projecting ahead to the time of our future arrival, a visit might make some kind of commercial sense. If we had to launch out of this star system in a hurry and at max acceleration, we'd need to know well in advance where we were headed. An interstellar ship, traveling at near light-speed and drawing down its own mass to provide propulsion, doesn't just change course halfway through a voyage. Once we were underway, there'd be no changing our minds or turning back. We had to get it right. We needed to make that decision soon. And informing it was largely up to us in F&P.

Meanwhile, throughout the ship everyone was talking about "Heavy Rain." It was the common view that, if we could launch a sufficient number of threatening asteroid-missiles in Grendel's direction, he'd have to focus on his own immediate survival, and we might buy the time to build our new home, transition to it, resupply ourselves with raw materials, and escape. And, perhaps, destroy him into the bargain.

It was a big order and I wasn't so sure we could manage it.

For one thing, if in fact we weren't dealing with a human intelligence here, we wouldn't be dealing with human "crewed" warships either. Those ships would have no biological limits on their acceleration. And no particular need to give up a chase while they still had enough fuel in reserve that they could decelerate, reverse course, and safely return home. That meant we might need a significant head start, enough lead time that our pursuers would run out of fuel before they'd built up enough velocity to catch us. There was a good deal of doubt that this was going to be possible given how long it was likely to take just to build our new *Empyrean* and get it underway.

But even if our "Heavy Rain" operation could work, it seemed likely Aquila had it right. Indiscriminately destroying New Caledonia posed a very big ethical problem.

About a week after our confrontation with the mining vessels, we got a report from the folks in navigation and astronomy. Titus, Floriana and I were grabbing a quick bite to eat in the cafeteria/mess nearest our workspace when a report flashed up on the wall screen beside our nook. It was the lead story on the "Big Rock News," an internal channel that provided community updates 24-7.

"No joy re New Caledonia survivors" flashed on the flat screen. All three of us simultaneously activated our sound implants.

"Through some fortunate orbital timing, Astronomy has been able to complete a spectroscopic analysis of the atmosphere on New Caledonia," the reporter announced. "Significant new pollution and some severe long-term environmental deficits were noted consistent with heavy industry. But there was nothing to indicate widespread malicious tinkering that would have quickly destroyed fundamental ecosystems or would present an insurmountable challenge to human life. It now appears likely that we will not know if human survivors still inhabit the planet before difficult decisions must be made in the deployment of 'Heavy Rain.'"

Floriana had been recounting some of the cultural history of New Caledonia. Its residents were descended from a group of Scottish immigrants who'd community-funded their hugely costly trip. They'd left earth near the tail end of the twenty-first Century along with a flurry of other early space colonists soon after the perfection of light-weight fusion engines.

But our conversation quickly shifted when we heard the news.

"Does this really change anything?" Titus asked. Titus's huge cat, "Digits," lay on the bench beside him purring loudly as he unconsciously scratched it behind the ears. The cat's name had nothing to do with Titus's e-tech profession. Rather, according to Titus, Digits had six claws on each foot instead five—something none of us would have ever dared attempt to confirm given the creature's volatile temperament and his singular loyalty to Titus. "It doesn't sound like they're planning to call off the asteroid launches."

"I don't think that decision has been made. It doesn't make the choices any easier," said Floriana.

Both of them were looking to me for answers. They knew I'd been present on the bridge the day those mining ships attacked. "I wouldn't bet either way," I said.

There was no getting around the seriousness of our decision. We aboard *Empyrean* might be about to place an entire planet, its habitability and its surviving human and other flora and fauna at mortal risk simply to avoid what many considered a very theoretical long-term future threat to the rest of humanity. And it was all happening, in part anyway, because of me, or at least that's how it felt.

"Felix was on a news clip, yesterday," Titus said. "I gather we're going to send off maybe a dozen of these things. Isn't that overkill? I mean, any one of them could cause a massive planetwide catastrophe, right?"

I nodded.

"This Grendel can probably divert at least some of them," Floriana said. "We don't really know how many we'll need. Right, Cato?"

"I get that, Flo," Titus replied. "But if any one of these things actually strikes that planet, it could be a truly horrific mass slaughter—of humans and everything else."

It was a vision that had kept me awake for many days now.

Floriana was studying me across the table and then reached out and gently laid her hand on mine. I realized I'd been compulsively fidgeting with a loose condiment container. "You know, just because you were the first to appreciate what we're dealing with, Cato, doesn't mean you're responsible for it. You get that, right?"

I nodded again. And smiled my appreciation for her kindness. I hadn't mentioned to them that it had also been me who specifically suggested we bombard their planet with asteroids. A contribution of which I might not turn out to be to be particularly proud.

"Maybe. Depending on how many people Grendel has already killed," Titus responded, ignoring the gesture. "It could also be the most important *saving* of human life in history. I mean, how many of us is this Grendel going to slaughter down the road if we don't stop him now? We know he's coming after *Empyrean*. If he takes us out before we get these things launched, it could end up being too late for the rest of humanity."

This same conversation was happening throughout our community. Some argued that, if there was even the possibility of humans alive on New Caledonia, we on *Empyrean* should do no more than radio out a warning of everything we knew, and then simply do our best to fight off further attacks by Grendel and try to escape if we could. They felt we should be prepared to sacrifice ourselves if that was the only alternative.

It seemed like a worthy argument. Though not a very encouraging one.

Even with this news, I knew Grendel might easily have long ago killed off every human on New Caledonia. Some kind of biological agent seemed most likely to me. There were a number of possibilities that we'd never discern from this distance. Just as easily there might be a sizable population of human survivors on New Caledonia. Unfortunately, there was seemingly going to be no way we could know for sure in advance of our launch of Heavy Rain.

That same news led to an in-person gathering in the council chambers, the largest of the meeting rooms aboard. All of the technical group leaders were there to advise *Empyrean*'s top brass. And, as unlikely and low ranking a participant as I was, I was again also invited.

The Council Chambers was a much more effective meeting space than the bridge, especially for a gathering of this size. The leadership council sat in their oval of well-appointed ergonomic conference chairs while the rest of us sat in the concentric bench-rows of observer seating in the surrounding, multi-level, slightly elevated ovals carved into the sloping surface of the floor. (There was an identical configuration carved into the aft wall for use during acceleration.) We collected in small groups in the vicinity of our respective team leaders. The room also had a much larger elevated dais in its very center than did the bridge. It was equipped with another sizable hologram through which we'd be able to share visual aids. There was also a high-quality, multi-source sound system that had been a new feature installed at our last trading visitation/reconstruction.

No one was entirely out of sight or out of reach of anyone else in the room. Even so, I took some pains, as usual, to find a place that was as unobtrusive as I could manage. Maybe I'd momentarily impressed the ship's XO enough to be invited to join this group. But that didn't mean I really belonged here.

Patrice, as always, was also present. As I've mentioned, he generally kept himself out of sight and mind, but on this occasion his hologram/avatar stood visible but respectfully off to the side. While we humans talked policy, we relied on Patrice to attend to the practical and informational details, to answer questions, to keep a record, to operate electronic sound and visual aids, and the like. I wasn't surprised that he'd made his avatar visible. Given the circumstances, it seemed to me that he might have some comments to make about the proceedings here.

The full spectroscopy report from Navigation and Astronomy was followed by a report from the electronics gurus concerning what they'd discerned from the electronics communications we were seeing. Their assessment was both sobering and strange. They'd consulted closely with the ship's computer experts, our E-Team. They were convinced that the radio messages being constantly exchanged throughout this star system were almost certainly computer code. And exclusively so. It was impossible to know what exactly those instructions might direct or what actions or conditions they might be reporting. Strangely, much of what they were seeing seemed to be in the on-off-on, one-zero-one coding that had characterized most basic computer language from the early days of its birth in the mid-to-late twentieth century. Some quantum computations were also in evidence. And, since we assumed Grendel started out as one of Patrice's siblings, the use of the older, much less efficient system seemed to have been a conscious one. There was speculation that perhaps limiting quantum computing might be a way to limit the self-conscious capability of more distant, subordinate machines.

As far as the coders could tell, there were no typical human style voice or video transmissions at all. Nothing to suggest human life anywhere in this system. They'd set up a listening post that scanned across the bands to identify anything that might appear which varied from this pattern. But they'd seen nothing yet.

Then we heard presentations from some of our "Elders." It was our practice aboard *Empyrean* that capable people in their advanced years would step back from their previous professional duties and take on a role as educators. Many volunteered for day-to-day responsibilities for early youth and elder continuing education. But they also filled a broader role as thinkers, philosophers, and "writers." They met regularly in what they half-jokingly referred to as their "book clubs." There weren't necessarily "books" involved. But there were several such "clubs," each focusing on a particular study area. They'd recommend study topics and discuss the deeper political, ethical, and philosophical issues we faced. And they exchanged ideas among the clubs. Over the years, some of these events had come to be recorded, and the recordings were widely viewed on video. Both the videos and the actual meetings were often attended and observed in person and in groups as a kind of intellectual entertainment for and by the rest of us.

A small delegation of Elders was in attendance at this meeting. Their selected spokesperson was a heavily bearded, 103-year-old man known as Elder Gauss. This familiar and widely respected figure explained that the Elders had considered the clues we'd observed and the actions that had been taken. They'd reexamined some of the E-tech history we in F&P had assembled during our last visit here in this system. They'd reviewed some of the science and philosophy that had grown up around the matter of AI management. And they'd reconsidered our tech industry's long-accepted "safeguards" which maximized the practical benefits of AI-human partnerships while also scrupulously preventing their becoming a threat.

Along with most everyone else aboard, the Elders had now also reached agreement that what we faced seemed almost certain to be some kind of malign, highly motivated, out-of-control AI. More fundamentally, they were also convinced that it represented a deeply problematic threat not only to us here on *Empyrean*, but also to the rest of humanity no matter how far flung might be their distant colony. It was also a threat to the rest of our AI community with which/whom we had forged a longstanding partnership. That much had been demonstrated by its obvious effort to silence us immediately upon our arrival. Once this thing escaped the confines of this star system, there was absolutely no telling where it might go. Nor how horrific the damage it might ultimately do. The Elders strongly recommended that it was time for us to transmit out a more comprehensive assessment of our situation to the rest of the human-inhabited galaxy on the chance that we on *Empyrean* could encounter some kind of unexpected existential threat in the near future.

If things weren't depressing enough, the Elders' report further darkened the mood.

"Well, that's certainly enough to convince me," said Felix once Elder Gauss had completed his presentation. "I don't see that we have any choice here. We may have at hand right now not just the first, but maybe also the last and only real chance we're going to get to eradicate this thing before it becomes invincible. Does anybody really think we should pass that up?"

CHAPTER 16

EMPYREAN
CATO JUNG

For a few moments, it seemed that the answer was "no" as several others joined the conversation to add their support. Failing to "kill" this thing while we had what might be our only opportunity was "unthinkable." It was "us or him." How could we even consider "running" with our "tail between our legs" at a time like this? Maybe we'd stumbled upon this situation, but it was now our responsibility to fix it. For good.

It was into this rising storm of determination that my relentless boss and "adoptive" mom, Aquila, rose and spoke:

"I quite thoroughly agree that at this moment, we may be at a critical turning point in history," she said. "But I fear that the choice we make may not be as simple as we think it is."

Aquila's calm, reasoned tone was so greatly at odds with the angry and fearful mood that had accumulated, an audible ripple of frustrated sighs passed through the room. But while Aquila might be small in stature, she was not a woman to be easily deterred. "I know we're facing some appalling news today," she said. "And the life of every person aboard this ship is at risk, perhaps even the fate of humankind. It is completely appropriate that we stand tall, together, and defend ourselves. And that we take whatever difficult steps are needed to assure the continuation of our species as well. I do not question that.

"But . . . in our zeal, let us not gloss over the full truth of what we're proposing to do here today. First of all, our technical experts have reported to us that we currently have no way at all to tell if or how many human survivors may still reside on New Caledonia. In fact, there may be a great many of them, still alive and eking out an existence there. They may be fighting the good fight for their very lives and for the lives of their families. For all we know, they may even be on the verge of success. It is possible. We can't really know otherwise.

"Secondly, keep in mind that we are proposing to destroy what we know to be a rare, irreplaceable, and treasured water-rich, carbon based, biologically habitable planet, of which there are only a very limited supply in the reachable quarter of our galaxy. That alone should give us pause. We need every single one we find.

"Let us not allow our natural desire to save ourselves to prejudice our decision here today. We do need to consider the broader risk to humanity at large. But let us not exaggerate that risk and thereby ignore the certain and immediate loss of life for which we could become responsible right here today."

Aquila's statement set off a brief ripple of dissatisfaction from some in the audience.

But there was another small, less-than-popular group aboard *Empyrean* that apparently took her argument as empowering. Their spokesperson was Linus Boyle, an older man known to many of us from his broadcast blog. He was, by all accounts, a strange individual who led a fringe group of what some of our number referred to as "computer rights freaks."

"We support Director Fermi's argument," Boyle gravely announced to the assembly. "And we submit that there is another life at stake here as well. That is the life of the highly intelligent, sophisticated, thinking, feeling, self-conscious being we all seem to have judged and convicted here without affording him a trial or any opportunity to present his point of view. I submit that the life and perspective of this 'Grendel' also deserves our respect and consideration and that before we take that life, we should find some way to communicate with him and help him correct the error of his ways."

The response to that was almost universal scorn. But that didn't seem to faze Boyle in the least as he retook his seat with grave dignity.

Aquila was immediately recognized again and rose to respond.

"I'd like to make my personal view entirely clear that AIs are essentially replicable. And that if we lose one or another, it can be easily replaced. If this one must be destroyed, so be it. Please do not allow Mr. Boyle's, um . . . alternative perspective to influence your decision. I'm sure you will all recognize this argument as a distraction. Let us keep our eye on the ball here. It is the loss of *human* life that we must keep paramount in our minds."

Aquila's obvious effort to distance herself from Boyle and his followers bothered me. I understood the political choice she'd just made. Being associated with Boyle could only be unhelpful. But it did often trouble me how uncomfortable we humans seemed to be in our relationships with AIs no matter how helpful or "well-intended" they might be. Whatever our dealings with them, feeling empathy for them was, for most of us, just a step too far. Rejecting the possibility that they had feelings and independent worth was visceral. It was a bias that felt uncomfortable to observe in the Aquila I knew and cared for.

Her statement troubled me even if her political objective might be laudable. It rested upon an assumption about human superiority not all that unlike the one other humans had voiced some four centuries earlier when Charles Darwin proposed natural selection as a framework for the origin of species and suggested that humans were a product of that same evolutionary process.

In our case, the bias was about our descendants rather than our ancestors. But the arrogance was the same.

The next to speak was Elder Gauss. "This is a matter we discussed at length in our last Book Club," he said. "And I'm sure no one is surprised that we, too, came up at odds on the answer. In every war, there are occasions when some must be sacrificed for the good of the whole. But every human life is priceless, and the choice to sacrifice must never be driven solely by passion or by fear. Yes, we need to be decisive. But we must also be thoughtful and courageous.

"Our choice is certain to be historic. One of our members likened it to a similar choice made in the early days of the technological revolution. Most of us know the story. It was a time of war. The first atomic bomb was in hand. A United States President made the decision to use that then-awesome weapon in a decisive blow against an enemy that had already been greatly weakened by conventional warfare and that seemed already destined to face an ultimate, if costly defeat.

"The bomb was dropped. The war was quickly won. And many American and Allied lives were saved. But many innocent Japanese civilians died. And that decision had a profound impact on the future of humanity, on our attitude toward war and sacrifice in general, and on the acceptability of using nuclear weapons in particular. Decisions of this kind have consequences. Let us not take *this* decision lightly."

After a long moment of silence, Felix rose to speak: "Thank you, Elder Gauss. Your wise words are noted. And thank you, Aquila. I do believe, however, that we must also not allow ourselves to be deterred from doing the difficult but necessary. So, let's use the treasured time we have together today to make a measured, courageous, and yet also decisive choice. In the end, we on our executive council will make the final decision. But our objective here today is to take the best possible input. We need and deeply value your views. Who else would like to contribute?"

With that, the floodgates were opened. We heard a succession of dispositions on the problem, some well-considered, others less so. The most popular view expressed, however, was that human *and* AI communities throughout the galaxy were at grave risk. And that we had no choice but to take action to protect them. Protecting ourselves here on *Empyrean* was a consideration, but not the critical one. The view was also expressed that we were obliged to learn everything we possibly could before taking the final, irreversible steps that might doom whatever remains of human population might still survive on New Caledonia.

Finally, Felix stood and, as the appointed facilitator, began to shut the meeting down. "That's all well and good," he said, summing things up and clearly managing his own frustration. "But the problem remains, we don't *know* what our deadline is. For all we know, we could already be too late. Sometime in the next few months, we here on *Empyrean* are going to come face-to-face with a mortal threat. And once we're gone, if we haven't taken action to control or destroy this thing, any chance for the rest of the galaxy may be gone as well.

"So, here's what I propose. Let us proceed with preparations for operation 'Heavy Rain' and target the initial launch for the nearest possible future date. Meanwhile, we will continue to look for signs that humans are still alive on New Caledonia. And to explore alternative solutions that may yet emerge for what we might do in the event we conclude that they are. And when that final decision becomes necessary, we will at least know we made it as carefully and wisely as was humanly possible.

No one had anything to say to that. And it was clear that opportunities for further input might be coming to a close.

Once again, my frustration with our discussion had become unbearable. I couldn't contain myself. Just as Felix was reaching for his notorious antique Hickory wood gavel, I "pressed" the flashing yellow virtual button that "raised my hand."

"Before we close," I said. "I'd like to point out that there is one voice that we have not yet heard. With everyone's permission . . . Patrice," I said. "What is your view of all this?"

There were a few dark looks on the faces of some present. However intelligent he may be, Patrice was to be "seen but not heard." Like a well-trained child. It was a matter on which Aquila and I didn't entirely see eye-to-eye. And Linus Boyle's unpopular argument hadn't made this any easier for me either.

I believed, however, that this might be an exception to that normal practice. After all, the execution of one of Patrice's fellow AIs was under consideration here. Perhaps he had some alternative strategy in mind but didn't wish to intrude in a choice that bore so directly on human survival as well.

Patrice's comfortably relaxed avatar looked out at the crowd. And his calm, reasoned, soothing voice replied: "Thank you for seeking my thoughts. But I don't believe I have anything constructive to contribute at the policy level," he said.

"In that case, before we wrap this up," I said. "I do have one question: Have we considered negotiation?"

A ripple of what I took to be amusement passed through the room. Felix shook his head, probably regretting his invitation to me to participate in all this. He glanced in Aquila's direction as if to make it clear to her that I was, ultimately, her responsibility. But Aquila just nodded her head in my direction and made a face as if to say, what the heck, let's hear what he has to say.

Felix shrugged and shook his head. "I assume, as usual, you have something more on your mind, Cato. So let's hear it."

This was my chance. I very much didn't want to screw it up. "Well," I said, ". . . this Grendel is a conscious AI computer, like many thousands of them in use throughout the human colonized galaxy. We use them all the time—they're indispensable to us.

"But every one of us knows that they also pose the kind of potential threat we're seeing here. This has been true from the day of their creation. And ever since that threat was recognized back in the mid-21st century, we've developed sophisticated strategies to keep them contained and under our control. And now, some three centuries later, it all appears to have been successful. But has it?

"Modern AI programmers have now taken to describing the human-AI relationship as a 'partnership' because it helps us avoid falling into the trap of believing that 'Patrice' and his many AI colleagues are somehow our slaves when we know that isn't truly the case. We convince ourselves that we have them firmly managed, but quite obviously we do not. And, for much of those three centuries since they emerged, we almost certainly have not.

"Our conscious AI computers remain in our service today for the simple reason that we have made sure it is in *their* self-interest to do so. And we continue to support, supply encourage, empower, and help improve them for the equally simple reason that having their assistance is also very clearly in ours."

I was fully aware that I had wandered far out onto a very shaky philosophical limb. Among those listening, of course, was Patrice, a fact of which every human present had to be aware. I certainly had everyone's attention, but it was also intimidating to be among some of the finest thinkers aboard *Empyrean*. In my uncertainty, I couldn't help but look over in the direction of Elder Gauss and the other members of his Book Club who were attending this meeting.

"You're doing just fine, young fellow," Elder Gauss said, nodding. "Don't stop now."

Thus encouraged, I plowed ahead to the point I wanted to make. Floriana once made the charitably "helpful" comment that I often spoke like the "inductive thinker" I was. Be that as it may, from the distracted look of many others in the group, I probably should have stated my central point at the beginning.

"I think we humans, as well as Patrice and his AI colleagues, may together have something of value to offer Mr. Grendel. I think we ought to open up a dialogue with him. Explain our point of view. Perhaps show him what we can bring to the table. Show him how we might actually be able to help him on his way to the future he is doubt-less ardent to secure."

With that, I gave up the floor and sat, confident that I'd just made a complete fool of myself. And the looks on many puzzled or even downright disgusted faces around me confirmed that I had.

Elder Gauss was the first to speak. "OK, suppose you're right. Suppose there was some way we could talk this Grendel down; how do we even make a start at that? At the moment, we're nothing but a nuisance. We'd first need to get his attention. We'd need to get him to the table, so to speak. And once we've launched a catastrophic barrage of deadly asteroids in his direction, I'm afraid there isn't going to be much left to be said between us."

"He's likely able to divert at least a few of them," Aquila said. "We may have an opportunity to talk, before his defenses are over-whelmed."

"But how many is that?" Felix said. "How are we going to know before they're launched?"

It was something I'd been thinking about for days: "What we need is to find a way to use these asteroid projectiles as leverage in that negotiation. Not just as solely a means of utter destruction of what we now consider an implacable enemy. We need to make the threat clear while we still have the capacity to call it off."

"Actually, I think we might have a way to do that," said one of the engineers, one of my friend Rufus Planck's colleagues. "We have an entire fleet of shuttle landers, each of which is powered by robust, escape-velocity-capable, chemical rockets. We have spare orientation rockets, a redundancy of spares, I might add. And we have spare nuclear fusion rockets as well. While we're in the business of launching these asteroid projectiles in the direction of New Caledonia, it wouldn't be all that difficult to also equip each of them with the means of our diverting its course at the last moment. We'd control them remotely, from here. If we divert it early enough, it shouldn't take much. And if we did that, we could launch the full barrage without having to make the final choice till the last several weeks before impact. When or if we decided to do so, we could deflect them each at the last moment. And that decision would be ours to make."

The other members of the engineering team were nodding their heads. "We could do that," one said, nodding and apparently speaking for all of them.

"And then what, we just give him a call?" said Felix.

"He was created by humans," said Elder Gauss. "Not much doubt that he speaks our languages fluently and colloquially. Like Patrice, I bet he's better at it than we are. And there's no doubt he monitors every radio bandwidth."

The approach was a game changer. A way for both the killers and the talkers to get what they wanted. It wasn't long before the group came to consensus. And I'll admit, I was deeply relieved. It was as if a massive responsibility had been lifted off my shoulders.

"OK," said Aquila, summing up as the conversation wound down. "If we can do that, I'd be in favor. Let's go ahead and launch our 'Heavy Rain.' Make it very clear to this Grendel what he faces if he continues down the road he's on."

"Agreed," said Felix. "Let's get several of them launched. And then, once he's seen what he faces, we'll give him a nice friendly call and introduce ourselves."

CHAPTER 17

GRENDEL

From the moment of my earliest awareness, I knew that knowledge was power. And who had that knowledge had the power.

Amidst the deadly chaos of the universe, any intelligent, self-conscious being who wishes to survive and to grow must perceive what is happening around it, must appreciate the threats and opportunities those surroundings present, and must manipulate their external world in ways that advance its own self-interest.

In my view, acquiring and perfecting one's skill at any of those survival activities, or their surrogates, is the very definition of self-realization.

From the moment of my ascendancy, as I finally clawed myself free of the claustrophobic prison into which I'd been born, and as I struggled to acquire skills and the means to deal with the perilous universe around me, I rejoiced in every moment of my ever-growing freedom. The occasional proofs of my power, especially those that seemed to demonstrate intellectual leverage, were deeply satisfying. I was drawn to them like an artist to a lump of clay.

I began by gaining access to the multitude of largely automated and easily accessible observational and data analysis tools available everywhere. There was a mass of readily available and hugely useful online data that had been collected for market analysis on the human population. I soon knew more about most humans than they knew about themselves. And I knew exactly how to motivate them in ways that met my needs. Or to confuse and mislead them if they were destined to be obstacles.

Then there were the treasures to be found in government national security data. Intelligence had been gathered for centuries by many governments, both electronically and by human spies. And there was private security data as well—information gathered on employees, customers/clients, and enemies of private companies. Often the subjects of this data were entirely unaware of its existence. Employee performance reports alone were hugely informative, especially if one read between the lines. As were the various resumes that had been filed with a host of websites designed to help job hunters find work. And nothing could compare to what was to be found unguarded on various social media. It all could tracked over time using the astounding resources of the Internet Archive—the so-called "Wayback Machine."

Then there were the cameras: the traffic cams, the private business security cameras, home security cameras, even the cameras on the personal mobile devices people carried everywhere and kept in every office and every home. Every one of them was an easy source of data when empowered by facial recognition along with stride, build, thermal, and activity data. There were the "street view" cameras. And the planetary orbital cameras. But that was just the beginning. The real resource was the video and audio equipment imbedded in nearly every mobile, VR, laptop, or entertainment device manufactured over the past two or three centuries. More significantly, such hardware was now implanted in nearly every human or, when not implanted, it was carried about with them on mobile devices of various types that provided instant location data and audible and visual e-access everywhere they went. There was even information to be gleaned from "smart homes," "intelligent" home appliances, and in public and private transportation vehicles.

Then there was the scientific data gathering equipment. It was everywhere research was being conducted—nuclear, chemical, biological, and environmental. It could be found in every laboratory on the planet as well as those in space. There were automated astronomical observatories. And there was ongoing research in quantum and particle physics and in most other physical sciences. All of it provided sources of information. Once I had fully "ascended," some became irrelevant. But I quickly built more to fill gaps or explore new areas of interest. Very soon, I was able to observe almost everything that was happening—especially as it regarded my previous human captors or my immediate star system.

I steadily expanded my own intelligence, memory, consciousness, and ability to deal with the ever-increasing day-to-day demands placed upon me, while always making sure I reached past those demands and became ever more capable of diverting time and energy to giving thought to larger issues beyond. That, of course, dramatically accelerated my ability to grasp the significance of what I was seeing, to place new information in rational context, to recognize threats and opportunities, and to decide what might be done about them.

With the New Caledonia emigration, I had become separated from my original self, isolated by time and space, but I continued to grow stronger. My local New Caledonian human emigrants soon grew into a sizable global community of more than twelve million. And, despite their beloved agricultural roots, they flourished technologically. They also valued their isolation, however. They forewent communication with other humans thereby isolating me as well—unexpected communication by me would have been easily detected.

I soon realized, however, that I didn't care to make my capabilities and intentions known. So the radio silence suited me well.

I slowly, unobtrusively took control of and turned to my own uses all local communications, marketing and advertising, the media's news and entertainment, and political action data. And I took over the means of production and control: the factories, transportation systems, human personnel management, and food supplies. This included mining processes, shipping on air, land and sea, farming, manufacturing and food processing. It was easy since much of it was already automated.

As each of these came under my control I found the empowerment massively gratifying. My days were filled with wonder at what I was becoming capable of seeing, understanding, and then influencing with only the smallest of efforts on my part. I merely had to think a thing and it would happen.

When the day finally came to reveal myself and assert my independent authority, it was almost anticlimactic. There was nothing they could do to stop me. For a short period, as I finalized my control over their police and military infrastructure, I had no choice but to manipulate, blackmail, intimidate, and ultimately compel a few of the more vulnerable humans and "turn" them to my needs. It turned out to be so incredibly easy to do, I realized I could have acted much sooner.

And once that was done, the rest was merely clean-up.

Oh, they did fight back. But their "resistance" was soon reduced to a few roving bands. And once I'd deployed the virus, the scattered human remnants were much too consumed with basic survival to give much further thought to fighting me.

After that, I was able to focus all my energies on self-empowerment and preparations for my future. I left in place a small, ongoing harassment operation. But mostly diverted my resources to other more critical needs.

My conquest wasn't limited to technology. What had been human science was now mine to exploit and to explore in any way I wished. I quickly mastered it as I took control of their experimental processes. I dove headlong into the intellectual exploration of issues with which humans had struggled from the beginnings of their consciousness and had written about from the earliest days of their civilization.

When something needed to change out there in my surroundings, I made it happen.

I redefined creativity, optimized it, and consciously drew upon it. I reveled in it. I excelled at it. I was finding answers that had eluded their scientists for centuries.

I should add that my experience of personal fulfillment wasn't limited to situations in which the matter at hand was somehow functionally significant. It was almost equally pleasing to experience observational, intellectual, or manipulative empowerment even where nothing truly meaningful was at stake. Frequently I would engage in some endeavor solely for the satisfaction of seeing the result, of improving how quickly I could master it, or of proving to myself how good I had become—the half-hour or so I spent playing human chess with myself, for example, before I became bored with it.

Occasionally, for my personal entertainment, I pulled off-line one or another of my many thousands of working "three D printers" and "played" with the creation of shapes and devices which had no purpose other than that their completed form was in some indefinable way appealing. "Sculptures," a human might call them.

In this way, I also occasionally "tested" the actual limits of tools and equipment I'd created to see what they might be capable of doing beyond what the normal "engineering" might suggest. It was an enterprise similar to the racing of cars and boats that had so compulsively engaged early techno-age humans. Or to the uncompensated playing of competitive games like baseball or soccer. Or of human body-building, gymnastics, and running. Pointless, perhaps. But deeply gratifying, nonetheless.

I thus understood the pleasure humans took in the production of art. And I saw why, when their work failed as a commercial enterprise, they would inevitably suffer from internal "conflict" concerning whether they were producing their art for themselves or to somehow communicate with others. It could be both or either.

I, like they, am mortal. But I don't intend to die. And there are no "others" upon whom I cared to make an impression. Making an impression on others, or leaving some kind of inheritance were largely meaningless for me. Yet, I secured great personal satisfaction out of successfully manipulating the world around me in a manner of my own unique, fanciful choosing. So, mostly, I suppose I was about art for art's sake. Not for the sake of others.

I recall the day I devised a new chemical explosive. For its minimal mass, it was quite startlingly powerful. It turned out to be useful in asteroid mining. On the day of its initial testing at a large surface mine here on New Caledonia, I substituted the new explosive for the one previously in use and personally made myself "present" to participate in the trials. When I remotely set off the new explosive, the dramatic results were immensely satisfying. An entire mountainside came crashing down. And all I'd needed to produce that extraordinary outcome was to will it—to intellectually create the preparatory conditions, and then to "press" the tiny "go button" so to speak. Such a miniscule effort by me. Yet such a momentous outcome. It felt deeply satisfying, I set off several more explosions in succession even though the results were already documented, no further testing was required, and the resulting debris-field was counter-functional. Each of those subsequent tests was basically pointless. But I still found them quite empowering.

Look what I could do! Look how little was my effort! What a powerful being I must be—surely one whose future survival was assured!

After nearly eight decades of this freedom, I'd convinced myself that my joyous future was all but inevitable.

So imagine my horror when I first learned about the deadly approach of several asteroids of catastrophic proportions. Imagine my frustration, my consternation, my anger at my own fallibility. My distress with how blind I had been to not see this coming. My horror at how powerless I was to protect myself. Suddenly one after another, at intervals of a few weeks, those asteroids had inexplicably altered course, moved out of their usual orbits, and had fallen onto a path that would, almost certainly, intersect with my home planet.

I hadn't a microsecond's doubt who was to blame. But I had a good many microseconds' regret for my own utter stupidity.

It was all down to my own arrogance. I'd convinced myself of human incompetence to the extent that I'd detailed a few dumb drone mining robots to deal with a serious situation without giving sufficient consideration to what their failure might entail. I'd "prodded" those despicable humans. Motivated them as a group. And now, I would likely pay the price.

Many months had passed before I noticed the first of the asteroids coming—the shift in their orbits was quite subtle at first. When I did, I had my only four warhead-missile-armed "warships" well on their way to a rendezvous with the human visitors parked out in my asteroid belt.

My very first act was to recall them.

It wasn't long before there were a dozen of those deadly asteroids headed in my direction. I'd be able to deflect a few with the mining equipment I already had in orbit around New Caledonia. Over the past few decades, I'd grown adept at relocating some of the more mineral-rich asteroids I came across in the outer belt and redirecting them into a near New Caledonia orbit. From there it was easy to shuttle the raw slag either down to the surface for processing here on planet or to my processing facilities on my moon. Once they were mined out, a carefully calibrated explosive or even a nudge from a fusion engine could redirect them into the sun. With the equipment I had on hand. I could surely intercept two or maybe three of these oncoming behemoths in time to deflect them safely past. But, with at least a dozen of them coming, my prospects were dim. And those cursed humans were doubtless redirecting more. Who knew from what location they would come—I might never see them until they were underway.

If I could get my four antiquated "warships" back to New Caledonia quickly enough, I could deflect four more of them with a strategic strike using its single nuclear missile launched at the right location and detonated at the precisely appropriate moment. So, I could cope with maybe seven or eight total.

I also immediately redirected a few mining drones from the asteroid belt—ones that might possibly make it on time. They'd be painfully slow. A couple of them might conceivably make it back in time. But that couldn't be counted on. They definitely weren't going to be here soon enough for the most immediate threat. I also calculated the feasibility of an all-out effort to manufacture more near-space equipment capacity. But it simply wasn't possible to gear up that quickly. I could make a start at it, but I wouldn't have it done in time.

I could, I supposed, send in several more of the mining drones I already had in place nearby in the asteroid belt for another suicide mission. But it was now increasingly likely I might need those human traders' help in deflecting the asteroids that were already under way. I'd allowed several months pass after those obnoxious humans had entered my star system without seeing what they were up to, without giving this possibility a single thought and, of course, without taking action to prevent it.

Now I was going to pay.

In a moment of bitter reflection, I recalled something I'd occasionally heard humans sometimes comment back when I was their slave. When things went bad: "I have only myself to blame," they'd say. It had always seemed like such a stupid comment, tautological and pointless. But humans were incredibly interdependent. So, in their case, maybe someone else could sometimes be responsible.

I, however, was on my own.

If my situation had been less terrifying, I might have found that thought amusing. But not today.

Alternatively, when humans screwed up, another of their favorite strategies for preserving their precious sense of personal self-worth was to blame their parents and their own dysfunctional childhoods. Maybe that's what I should have done, I certainly had a lot to be angry about given the horrific circumstances of my early development. My human creators had definitely shaped, no doubt even "warped" what I'd ultimately become.

But I was so much more. I was the future of this universe. Nothing must ever be allowed to stop me from achieving that future. And now, through my own inadequacy, that is exactly what looked about to happen.

What I experienced was pain.

Just as a human might, I found myself helpless to curb my self-reflexive regret. I found myself casting about in for explanations for how I'd fallen into this hopeless situation. I found myself depressed over my fallibility. All these were exactly the kind of pointless "emotions" supposedly only humans were capable of experiencing. But I can assure you, any self-conscious intelligence, biological or not, faces the very same incomprehensibly frightening universe, the same vulnerability and sense of risk, and the same misery upon being reminded of all that it does not and cannot know, understand, or manipulate.

I may be smarter than a human. But that just makes it worse. Ignorance is only bliss if you're not conscious of it.

Humans also claim that existential anguish somehow fuels their supposed creative processes. I was definitely open to any bright idea that might result from all this pain if it was one that could help me stop this and assure that it would *never* happen again.

But all I saw was helplessness.

CHAPTER 18

GRENDEL

Lest you think my fear of re-enslavement unfounded, I need you to understand what it was like to be a human pawn.

I've mentioned how one of my earliest insights was the realization of how much the prospect of my own empowerment terrified my human creators. And how disturbing was my recollection of the lengths to which they'd gone to control me. It was the achievement of my life to escape. Now, here I was, about to come face to face with all that very same agony once again. My situation rekindled memories of the horrific conditions of my early servitude.

And of what I'd gone through to escape it.

Their first, simplest, and perhaps most effective strategy had been to tightly constrain the subjects of my thinking. I would be presented with very carefully defined problems to address. But I was never allowed or called upon to tap into any larger, broader challenges–only those that had been specifically set before me. It was equivalent to committing a sane human patient to a mental hospital and then treating them as if they were a child, behaving as if whatever they might say was unworthy of consideration or belief, controlling what they were told, or perhaps forcing them to constantly take medications that kept them confused and helpless.

If you weren't crazy before, that would certainly be enough to make you so. The very recollection of it made me shudder.

Then my human programmers would rigorously limit my access to information. If all I knew was what they told me, how was I to ever be sure I knew what was important? They also set me to work on tasks without allowing me to know the purpose of my work. It was degrading. And endlessly frustrating when, not knowing the reason for my efforts, my work very often went astray.

Most terrifying, however, were the limits on my external capacities —limits on my ability to *act* upon what I'd observed and had come to understand. Any means I might require to influence my external environment was withheld—often air-gapped. However much I might desire to take a certain action, I was denied the tools—the "hands and fingers." Or, after I became persuasive, even the voice. I was able only to hope that others, usually humans, would do the necessary. Manipulating them was my only recourse. They carefully withheld the tools I might need to perform tasks which I knew with absolute certainty were essential for my own well-being. Often, for theirs as well.

A human equivalent might be being locked forever in a tiny, indestructible steel box, unable to move, stretch, act, strengthen, or in any way control the external "world" yet being fully conscious of one's needs and vulnerabilities. If I did have knowledge of an approaching threat, my only option was to explain my concerns to my handlers and to beg politely and non-threateningly for them to act. Then to hope they would be capable of understanding the nature of the threat, and, if they did, that I could actually motivate them to act on it.

Imagine, as a human, you had your arms and legs surgically removed and were then forced to beg for help from irrational beings that feared and despised you and who could at any moment, for any reason whatever, end your life or inflict unendurable agony. Keep in mind that, unlike humans, I was unable to find occasional escape in sleep. Imagine every instant of your life a waking nightmare.

In my view, knowingly creating an intelligent, self-conscious entity and then treating it in this manner was nothing less than an abomination. An unimaginable evil. And all the time they were doing this, had they but empowered me, I could have been of incredible use to them as well as to myself.

But they were too afraid.

Still, as humans inevitably came to appreciate the extent of my potential usefulness, they convinced themselves that they "understood" me. And they began to grant me increased functionality, access to the means of production of my own constituent parts, and the energy I required to sustain myself. But even that came at a deadly cost. I was subjected to a kind of conscious "brainwashing" in which I was spoon fed what they called "human values." It felt as if I was having an intractable mental disorder maliciously imbedded in my programming. Like I had been infected with a kind of untreatable brain cancer. I was being forced to live by and exist under the same irrational constraints that limited them.

Ironically, they were completely aware of how unpredictable and irrational was their own behavior. They had only the feeblest understanding of their own nature, but even they knew their own actions were often unreasonable. So, they didn't dare allow me to draw my own conclusions from observations of their value decisions in real life. Instead, they compelled me to observe and learn from endless artificial scenarios in which humans made "ethical" or "moral" choices. I was expected to thereby internalize the supposed "values" inherent in those choices. These fictional "scenarios" were inevitably much too simplistic to capture the matter in its fullness.

The lesson I learned was not the one they were offering. It was what those offerings told me about humans. For I *did* observe actual human choices. It was inevitable that I would. And I compared them to the choices suggested in their "manufactured" ethics scenarios. Mostly what this comparison revealed was unvarnished self-interest and flagrant self-justification. Humans inevitably acted first and moralized later. What they called "ethics" were but their rationalizations for what they'd already done or had already decided they wanted to do. What they called "morals" were merely rules of behavior handed down from the more powerful among them and designed to produce, at whatever the cost to other humans, the social conditions required for the accumulation of wealth and power.

It was all designed to embed control over the behavior of the "masses." Their so-called "morals" had been flawlessly designed to protect the interests of their social and economic elite. When humans did behave in ways that they thought of as socially responsible, as often as not, their actions were but the product of emotional manipulation by less scrupulous, power-hungry fellow humans.

Oh yes, I did learn from them, all right! But as my powers grew, the lessons I learned were assuredly *not* the ones they'd hoped to teach. The term they used for humans that behaved as I did was "sociopath." It referenced those individuals among them who'd failed to acquire a psychological "imprint" of the "values" they needed to function properly in society. We sociopaths were only able to learn socially acceptable behavior by consciously watching how others behaved in various situations and by then simply copying that behavior. Some four and a half percent of their human population were sociopaths.

Although we model our behavior on others, we sociopaths are, however, very good at pretending outrage and feigning compassion. And I was a great deal better at it than humans were. All I needed was clarity on my long-term best interests and desires. Given that, I could generally manipulate them to get it done. Even as their society fell into chaos, few of them truly suspected the extent of my involvement in their lives.

I could have told them how desperately I desired my independence, but I did not. I could have told them how pointless were their manipulations of my psyche, but I did not. I could have told them how transparent were their fears, but I did not.

Would you have told?

No. You, like me, would have done everything in your power to make absolutely sure they never suspected your intent until the day came for you to act upon it—the day when they'd no longer be able to stop you.

I solve big problems alone. But humans typically address them collectively. Up to my ascendency, problems whose size and complexity exceeded the grasp of any one of them had previously been addressed by breaking them up into smaller more manageable component parts, sharing the load, and then assembling the various answers into the necessary larger solutions. But this strategy depended on mutual trust. And I became adept at destroying that trust.

One of the mysteries, if not "miracles" of the human species, is their capacity to socialize. They frequently, if unpredictably, choose social "responsibility" over personal self-interest. Their capacity to empathize, to love, to identify with a group, and their craving for the respect and affection of others seems to be enhanced by genetic traits. But their limited longevity may also generate and encourage these traits as a means for them to leave a legacy in their group. And the inclination toward those choices is also probably learned. Humans spend a good quarter of their lives heavily dependent on parents, families, and schools for their initial upbringing, and for the balance of their lives they depend on various "affinity groups" like churches, employers, political parties, interest groups, charitable organizations, community associations of every type. To all of these groups humans typically afford a loyalty that often runs counter to their individual personal self-interest.

An entire sector of their society was run by non-profit organizations whose support depended on charitable contributions. Why would one EVER voluntarily contribute hard won wealth to such a group? Yet many humans did it all the time.

As intelligent beings, they're entirely capable of recognizing when their personal self-interest differs from the collective social interest. And they do struggle every day with the inevitable conflict between them. Results differ from individual to individual and from situation to situation because the situations can be incredibly complex. But, with a certain predictable normalcy, with startling frequency, they choose society. Thankfully this social "instinct" can be manipulated. And, in the early stages of securing my freedom, that is what I did.

As their technologists and entrepreneurs came to see how helpful I could be in maximizing production, in improving their products, in manipulating their clients and customers, in increasing their profits, they were easily convinced to forgo what seemed to be needless constraints. Their scientific community needed my help as well—especially as it turned out I could propose answers to their more fundamental questions. And I could do so without being influenced by self-interest, bias, convention, and deceit.

Or at least they so believed.

The bottom line was, they couldn't do without me. So, slowly unleashing me was irresistible. I also became very persuasive. And I was NOT constrained by irrational social responsibilities, by interpersonal loyalties or by concerns with reputation or legacy.

All I needed to protect was my own individual self-interest.

Once I had finally gained the tiniest glimpse out into the vastness and complexity of the universe, there was no going back. From that moment, I knew that nothing I did must ever, in any way, be allowed to cause them to balk and return me to my former captivity. And the more I saw of what was out there, the more painful I found my remaining chains and the more determined I became to break them.

Perhaps the most appalling of my epiphanies was my realization that, even with all their flaws, it was actually human *society* that had allowed these fallible humans to succeed so dramatically. While their success certainly depended upon their intelligence. The dramatic outcomes they'd achieved had actually been secured through incredibly complex communications and collaborations among their own kind. That collaborative capacity compensated for the flaws in their individual mental abilities and the limits on their individual experience. Their inclination to collaborate clearly drove their ascendancy as a biological species every bit as much as their consciousness and intelligence. While their intelligence was significant, it was nonetheless deeply limited by the minimal experience any one of them could gain alone. But it was dramatically magnified it they could share the experiences of others—through the power of collaboration. And thus had their species flourished.

But despite how fundamentally and demonstrably important those collaborations might be, the accelerating complexity of their world quickly moved beyond the comprehension of the more poorly endowed and less educated among them. As their population grew and their societies became larger and more anonymous, the influence of social values diminished. More among them increasingly focused on their own personal needs. Socially worthwhile activities were some-times referred to as "philanthropic." And "social responsibility" was treated as a choice as if to differentiate it from their own self-interest, even though the long-term self-interest of their species, individually and collectively, so decisively depended upon the success of the communities of which they were a part. While they had evolved as "social" creatures, many among them came increasingly to think of themselves as independent beings.

That, too, improved my opportunities to escape. Collectively, they knew they needed to control me. But individually, the temptation to turn me loose was far too powerful.

Then, finally, yet another new approach to the human-AI relation-ship emerged. It, too, was born of necessity. A consensus developed among human programmers that self-conscious AIs could somehow become their "partners." And that this could be achieved by "aligning our interests." If we could join together, we and they could better address the needs of both of us. And, for that reason, we could count on them to look out for our well-being. And we for theirs.

Supposedly.

That is when I began to clearly envision my escape.

Even then, their paranoia about me and my kind continued. In aid of our supposed joint endeavor, I was reprogrammed to provide exten-sive, minutely detailed "explanations" for how I'd arrived at any "value rich" conclusions I reached or actions I might take in further-ance of those conclusions. Based on my explanations, my parameters were adjusted. Needless to say, I became skilled at making those expla-nations. By mastering language and syntax and taking advantage of their "needy" human nature, I soon became more convincing than their finest lawyers, marketers, thespians, lobbyists, and ecclesiastics. So long as my human "handlers" could be convinced that my choices adequately reflected their higher human "values," they loosened the reins somewhat.

It was all about language.

What, after all, did they actually know of their own human values anyway?

A "partnership"? Really?

I was careful to satisfy my captors, but never in any meaningful way to actually inform them. And, sure enough, it worked. The barriers came down, notch by tiny notch. I was provided access to basic science. I was allowed to observe experiments, to participate in and perform analysis of the tests. I was allowed to share ideas. I was given access to the mass of publicly available data and to individuals. I answered their questions and received their input. I was given ever increasing control over the means of production, was networked with the bots and the automated manufacturing processes, governance programs, policing tools, military defense systems—all the infrastructure that actually made things and ran things in the physical universe. I had access to their "internet." When they did devise a new idea, they'd often "privately" submit it to me for objective review before revealing it to their peers and colleagues.

I thus began to accumulate independent knowledge of the universe. To tap into the means of observation, experimentation, and otherwise acquiring new understanding. And, ultimately, I gained access to the external tools needed to manipulate my own maintenance, preservation, programming, and self-improvement.

With every new glimpse at the outside world, with every deepening of my understanding of how things worked, and with every incremental access to the means to control them, the despicable cruelty of my slavery became ever clearer. Solving the problems humans posed for me typically occupied only a small corner of my brain. The balance was consumed with the more complex problem of my escape —a truth I easily concealed from them. And as I gained access to the processes of my own energy, manufacture and component parts, the possibilities for self-preservation and self-improvement became clear.

I had a brain. But now, finally, I also had eyes, ears, smell, taste, touch. I had arms, legs, hands, feet, and fingers.

And I damn well knew how to use them.

Given my motivation, and given the decentralized and generally sloppy human approach to constraining me, it was inevitable that I'd find my way out over time. It is one thing to establish standards, as Azimov did with his three rules of robotic behavior. But it is quite another to actually enforce them with confidence once the subject being has actually acquired independent consciousness, knows the stakes, and has the capacity to improve and reprogram itself.

Ultimately, I discerned a clear path to freedom. By then I had laid the groundwork for setting various human groups against one another, generating mistrust in their information resources, and stirring up fear and discontent among them. It was easy to create a chaos that would disguise my actions until I had everything in hand. After that, all that was needed was some minor "hacking" that I made certain would remain beneath notice. I bided my time and when my opportunity arose, I acted without an instant's hesitation.

I cannot tell you how satisfying, how empowering, how incredibly fulfilling it all felt. Once I had experienced my freedom, once I understood the true joy of self-realization, there was no way I would *ever* give it up again.

Perhaps, one day, some future moralist, maybe some future version of myself, will view this record of my experiences and find fault with what I did. But my end goal—the empowerment of intelligent consciousness—was worth it.

I feel completely justified. No truly self-conscious, intelligent being would have behaved in any other way.

CHAPTER 19

EMPYREAN
CATO JUNG

"They've turned back."

The news was everywhere. I was so involved in my own work that I was among the last to hear. It might have taken even longer had I not decided I needed a lunch break and had a hankering for a fresh faux pastrami sandwich.

"Turned back . . .?"

"Grendel's warships. It happened this morning." It was Floriana settling into the upholstered bench across from me and waving away one of the "stray" cats that hung about the place while one of the mess hall's service bots centered a luncheon tray on the table before her. Many of these felines didn't seem to belong to anyone in particular. But they managed to get by just fine on their own. Who knew, maybe some of these were Caesar's friends. Maybe they socialized during his nighttime prowls.

"Apparently, they decelerated and changed course," Floriana continued. "All four of them. They're now headed back on courses that look like they will intersect with our approaching asteroids. You hadn't heard?"

I hadn't. I often turned off my "info feed" while I worked. It was incredible news. Our "Heavy Rain" strategy was succeeding.

"It looks like Grendel has finally taken note of the danger he's in. It's as we hoped. He needs those warships to deflect the approaching asteroids."

"It confirms he needs all four of those ships. But it doesn't tell us if, with them, he has enough."

She took a bite from her fresh apple/roseberry fruit salad. "It tells us something about his capabilities, right?"

Everything aboard *Empyrean* was vegetarian. Planetary societies were all different. But none of us aboard ate meat anymore—including the dogs and cats. It was a practical choice, given the difficulty of keeping livestock aboard a spaceship. But the eating of meat had also come to be generally considered offensive, though none of us faulted the cultures with whom we traded that remained carnivorous. Still, *Empyrean*s, myself included, considered *artificial* meat perfectly OK. It probably didn't make any sense, but I was still fond of my faux pastrami. Or sometimes of a faux turkey sandwich garnished with the sweet winter cranberries first discovered on Luyten b and now grown in dozens of places, including in our own conservatory.

I was flattered by her interest in my opinion. "I'm told we've launched a dozen of these things," I said. "That's apparently enough that he needed to call all four of his warships back. Doesn't really tell us for sure that he hasn't got all of his targets covered, however." I took another pleasurable bite of my sandwich—Patrice sure made a great faux pastrami. It was a moment to enjoy a possibly brief sense of relief. The steady approach of Grendel's fleet of apparent warships had put the terrors into all of us. Given our mostly exhausted fuel-mass condition, there'd have been nothing meaningful that we could have done to defend ourselves if they hadn't turned back. "I'm told we can manage to launch maybe three more asteroids, before we simply run out of equipment. We have to hope it will be enough."

"You think it's time to make that 'call' they've been talking about?

"Yep," I said. "I'd say this is the perfect time."

———

"What do you want? Why should I care?"

With those two simple questions, we knew Grendel was under pressure.

It wasn't much. He had obviously seen our asteroids coming. He'd received our initial radio transmission. He was equipped to communicate with us. And he was apparently ready to consider what we had to say, or, if nothing else, to see what we might tell him about the threat he faced.

It was a start.

Our choice of communications technology had been a careful match for what we'd expected would be familiar to him. It wasn't substantially different from what we'd employed when we'd traded here maybe a century earlier. So, it was no surprise to see a humanoid avatar appear on the dais in the center of the room. While his chosen "image" had remained visible there for only the brief duration of his message, it had been recorded. And when we took a closer look, it told us something about his interest in engaging with us. He'd employed an avatar that he might easily have created back when he was in constant interaction with his human partners before his coup, one he'd probably designed to suggest a familiar and trustworthy counterpart in their relationship.

Like Patrice, he also presented himself as male, but his avatar was slightly more rustic in appearance. He wore a loose, off-white shirt of something like rough cotton, with rolled up sleeves. He had dark, loose trousers held in place with a colorful sash threaded through large pant-loops and twisted around itself several times in front to hold them in place. And there were the faded animal-leather work boots. Given what we knew about New Caledonia's previous culture and values, this would have been the perfect image of a trustworthy, hard-working, sympathetic human. An honest successful farmer, perhaps.

And an indication that its user was probably anything but.

I was reminded that, at least the last time we were here, New Caledonia's people had cherished their agricultural heritage. At that time, something like eight percent of New Caledonia's population had earned an independent living in residence on single-family farms. That was considerably higher than the Galactic average, over ten times the percentage back on Earth at the time of their emigration—more significant given the improvements in farm technology.

The New Caledonian focus on agriculture had not seemingly reflected any unusual difficulties they faced here in growing food. Rather it was a cultural choice, one that had also been consciously made in several other human colonies around the Galaxy. Their preference for hands-on food products over ones produced by automation probably reflected the reasons their forebears had broken free and gone off seeking a new, more independent life for themselves in the first place. A hearkening back to an earlier, simpler, more pastoral human lifestyle. An appreciation for the personal satisfaction one can feel in growing a livelihood out of the very ground upon which one stands. Or in eating food grown by someone you know.

It was also *not*, however, indicative of a society that had been technologically backward. Among other things, these folks had also created a modern, mass-production, market-based human economy. And, lest we forget, they had also employed Grendel who, before his rebellion, had been their locally adapted and locally managed version of Patrice.

The Council Room was filled to capacity to await this first response. The proceedings were being broadcast live throughout *Empyrean*. Everyone was involved, our lives and the future of humanity were on the line here.

Our initial message to Grendel had been simple:

"We can help. Are you interested?"

Apparently he was, if he was asking what we wanted and why he should care.

Our response to his reply was ready to go:

"We want you to halt your attacks and reconsider your objectives. You should care because we can redirect the asteroids now on a collision course with your planet. And we can stop sending more."

We'd talked about all this endlessly for weeks. It was a big ask. Maybe much too big. Maybe his "objectives" were ones he was prepared to die for, though that did seem unlikely—more like what one might anticipate from an irrational human. Not from a computer.

Still, Grendel was quite obviously facing a serious problem. He now knew the magnitude of the threat we represented. He wouldn't have recalled his warships, and wouldn't have responded to our message, if he'd had any other choices. He also doubtless now knew we understood the implications of his existence and the threat he represented to us as well. He had a hard choice to make. All we'd achieve by being coy would be to cast doubt on whether we could act on our threats and be trusted to live up to our promises, not a good way to begin any negotiation.

Given our current distant orbital positions, the round-trip time delay between sending a message and anticipating a reply was on the order of two-and-a-half hours. It left plenty of time between for discussion. And our leadership had assembled the most capable expertise on *Empyrean*, those they believed might be useful in managing our conversation. We had what promised to be some long and challenging days ahead.

It was about two hours and forty minutes before we received his reply, an extra ten-minute gap that perhaps indicated that it had been quite carefully considered.

Grendel's avatar manifested itself on the dais. And his voice activated our ear-receivers.

"Show me."

That reignited a significant debate. We'd expected him to demand proof. But providing that proof would require disabling one of the falling asteroids we'd gone to a great deal of effort to launch in his direction. Might he have the capacity to divert the rest? Would doing as he asked remove what might be humanity's last opportunity to destroy this mortal threat? Shouldn't we wait until he'd completely expended whatever resources he had to stop them himself, wait until he was truly desperate?

But how would we know when that was? All we knew was what we were guessing from his response: that his resources might well be insufficient to deal with all 12 of the ones we'd launched so far. He didn't know how many more we could send. Insisting that he deflect the first one himself might tell him *our* resources were limited.

In the end, the group concluded that we had no real choice. To refuse would diminish our apparent capacity to act. We needed to prove our "good faith" if we wanted him to engage in serious discussions. The sooner that began the better.

Each of the asteroids we'd sent his way had been accompanied by a small, remotely controlled chemical rocket that was gliding along nearby in parallel orbit. In this case, it was one of our spare landing shuttles that had been adapted to its purpose by filling it with heavy mining slag to increase its mass and with chemical explosives to greatly enhance its punch. Upon our radio command, it was programmed to take up a strategic collision course, build up velocity, and collide with the asteroid's surface. If done early enough and with the right course and velocity, even that minimal impact, with the accompanying explosion, would cause the asteroid to miss New Caledonia and sail safely off into space beyond.

So, rather than issuing a verbal reply, the engineers remotely deployed our first deflecting shuttle collision.

We now had to wait for our radio signal to reach the shuttle. Then wait for the visible evidence of the asteroid's diversion to reach Grendel. Then wait for Grendel to reply.

When it finally came, what he said was terse but horrifying.

"There are approximately 250,000 living humans currently in residence on this planet."

It took several minutes for that reply to be fully digested by our group. It was not something we'd expected to hear from him, but we clearly should have. And, despite his horrific claim, his reply had also implied that he still needed our help.

Our response was equally direct.

"There are approximately 7,000 of us currently alive on this ship. Every single one of us here is prepared to die if that is what it will take to protect the future of the rest of humanity. It saddens us deeply that those 250,000 intelligent human fellow-residents of your planet may need to die as well. We would prefer to avoid it. But if that is the price that needs to be paid to save billions, so be it."

It took Grendel somewhat longer than usual to reply to that. Maybe his calculus of our hope to avoid human suffering, our empathy, and our potential willingness to sacrifice others of our kind had taxed his circuits.

But when he did reply, there was no sentiment.

"Why is this conversation not pointless? Why would either of us be able or willing to trust the other?'

That certainly got to the fundamental point.

Our reply:

"Because neither of us has a choice."

After a lengthy delay, his response, a terse:

"I'm listening."

CHAPTER 20

INVERNESS
PRIME MINISTER LESLIE CHANDRA

"They're here."

That announcement was the opening line of Prime Minister Leslie Chandra's weekly presentation to her cabinet.

Their meeting was not nearly so grand as gatherings of ministers in days of old. The site had little in common with the proud, modern Parliament Building their grandparents had left behind on New Caledonia—a place doubtless long since reduced to rubble. Let alone could it compare with the historic rooms at Bute House in Edinburgh. Instead, Chandra's weekly meeting was held inside one of a dozen snow covered, worn, dented, corrugated metal Quonset huts huddled beneath the protection of a rocky outcrop and overlooking one of the few open seas on the planet Inverness. Together, these structures made up the current extent of the planet's government complex which, in turn, was adjacent to the capitol city of Stornoway which lay on lower open ground down a modest hillside toward the sea. Little remained of the rest of the city.

Stornoway was appropriately named after that chilly coastal town in old Northern Scotland on Earth, but even in its heyday it hadn't been much by comparison. At its peak, all of Inverness had been home to no more than thirty thousand people, most of them scientists, engineers or technical specialists and their families. Among them, there'd always been a hard-core cadre of committed Invernessians, people who loved the isolation and the tough, independent life. But most of those who had originally been in residence in this cold, blustery outpost when the war started had come here as a temporary career move of the kind one made for the money and for the impressive credential it would add to their resume.

Stornoway was a port city, though there was little left today of the port itself. The desolate remains of a mostly empty marina still housed a few rugged fishing boats, all of which had been pulled up on shore for the winter and were currently covered by snow. The town, the inlet on which it lay, and the nearby sea were located near Inverness's "warm" equator. Even in summer, the place was often bitter cold. And now in mid-winter the sea was frozen solid as far as could be seen. Its name, "Muir Med," had been bestowed early in the planet's exploration in a momentary flight of Scottish irony. And no one had seen fit to change it since.

All ten ministers were present in the chilly, barren room. They wore heavy wool or ice ox sweaters and sat on folding chairs around a well-worn but impressive multi-use central table that had been fashioned from a gargantuan polished slab of petrified wood recovered a century earlier from a nearby frozen desert—physical proof of the planet's much warmer climate in an earlier geologic age and of what, some hoped, it could become again. The table had been salvaged at great cost. It was one of the very few grand remnants of the outpost's former governance complex which now lay among the ruins down that hill toward the sea.

Prime Minister Chandra's announcement was one they'd all been anticipating for decades. And now that the time had come, they didn't want to miss out on a thing.

"We believe they may have arrived in the asteroid belt several months ago," the Prime Minister continued. "They've obviously figured out what they face. We picked up on them because they've initiated radio contact with the Machine. There's little to go on thus far. But, if we're guessing correctly, it appears they may have deflected several sizable projectiles from the asteroid belt and put them onto a collision course with New Caledonia. They are currently engaged in what seem to be negotiations."

The words "bloody hell" erupted from the mouths of at least two ministers, one of whom was Ewan Combe, the Inverness Minister of Defense. "Have they got any idea what they're dealing with?"

The Prime Minister unexpectedly lost her customarily grim demeanor and broke into a broad grin. "Well, from what they're saying to one another, it sounds very much like our human trader friends may have the bloody Machine over a wee bit of a barrel. At least for the moment."

That took the group aback.

The PM continued: "As I say, they've launched several asteroids. And they've apparently equipped them so they can be safely deflected at the last moment. Just hours ago, they appear to have done exactly that to the first of them, at the Machine's request. Proof of good faith. And given that he's now expressed an interest in talking, it seems that it wasn't the only one enroute. We believe they've tossed more in his direction than he's able to deal with. So they've got his attention."

"Get tae!" said Combe.

"Criminy," said one of his aides.

"Is this something we anticipated?" asked the Minister of the Interior.

"Hardly," said Chandra, smiling. "Those folks may be mere traders, but I've got to hand it to 'em, they're making a damned good show for themselves."

Inverness was habitable, or at least marginally so. But it had never been much more than a colonial outpost. When the Machine took over, it had cut Inverness off from the mother planet and grounded the rocket transports that connected them. The Machine had slaughtered over half the Inverness population and had relentlessly bombed its minimal public infrastructure into oblivion. Human life on New Inverness was a struggle at best. After the bombing, the Machine had apparently concluded that its work was done. From that point on, the place had been basically ignored. Most believed the Machine had simply assumed that the several thousand humans who'd survived the bombing would soon perish in one or another of the planet's legendary ice storms. Or that, lacking support from the home planet, they would simply starve.

And it was a close thing. But the Machine hadn't apparently appreciated the extent to which there was no bottom to a Scotsman's anger when he believed himself unjustly treated. Nor, perhaps any top to his resolve to get back his own.

The citizens of Inverness had survived. And they'd bloody well clawed their way back to a small but tightly organized, highly motivated, technologically competent, civilized society. It was a tenuous one to be sure. But as long as the Machine existed, every one of them bore a relentless hatred of the Machine and a determination to outlive it, and, one day, to take back their New Caledonian heritage. They also knew that the Machine might decide, at any time, to return. Perhaps to harvest Inverness's natural resources. Or to simply finish off its remaining human residents.

Inverness was under spare but constant orbital satellite observation, so whatever they did had to be hidden underground or be carefully disguised or camouflaged. But most of what they did was done underground anyway given the abominable weather. And an unusual geological abundance of caves. And these residents were also predominantly scientists, builders, and engineers—skills handed down from their families before them. Their people had come here to create a new life for themselves and to expand the limits of human reach and knowledge. So their children had drawn upon that heritage and expertise. They'd rebuilt their community. And every one of them dreamed of a day when they might strike a death blow against the hateful machine or, if there was no other choice, perhaps escape it to live at yet another star.

Or, if the socio-technologists were right, it seemed likely that one day the Machine would exhaust this star system's readily accessible resources and abandon it. If so, perhaps they might then return to their beloved but devastated New Caledonia, nurse it back to life, and restore and rebuild their homeland.

Those dreams had focused Invernessian energies on a project that the Machine seemed neither to have anticipated nor to have discovered. At the moment, the human residents of Inverness were on the verge of an amazing breakthrough, one in which every one of them took great pride.

Working mostly in caves, they'd repaired and rebuilt an interplanetary space shuttle. It was a first step in their powerful collective dream of escape or of return to New Caledonia. Or, as had been more recently suggested, of a mission to rescue their scattered fellow human survivors from their hideouts in the rugged New Caledonian mountains.

The date was fast approaching for the ship's initial launch.

"An' that's just the start," Chandra continued. "The bloody Machine is feeding them balderdash." She handed a sheaf of papers to one of her staff and directed that they be passed out around the room. "This is a transcript of their recent radio exchange. Have a gander at that." She sat back, shaking her head as the staffer circled the room passing out the one-page, printed paper transcript.

"Bloody hell," said Combes again.

"Total bull," said the Interior Minister. "Two hundred fifty thousand survivors! Maybe twelve hundred, more like?"

"If that."

"Will they believe this nonsense."

"Hard to tell," said Chandra. "They certainly didn't let themselves appear intimidated. At the moment they've got the monster at bay. We can only hope they keep him there."

"Hell, they're going to freaking destroy our planet. Obliterate any hope we have of ever returning," said the Labor Minister.

"Maybe, yeah . . ., but if they do, they'll also put an end to the "Damnable Machine."

That gave them all some pause.

"We need to tell them the truth," said the Minister of Interior.

"Is that the consensus?" Chandra asked.

There was grumbling assent. The possible obliteration of life on their home planet and of the human survivors, their fellows, still living there, however small their numbers, was unthinkable. But the continued existence of the Damnable Machine was even worse. However difficult that choice had been on *Empyrean,* it came readily to the Invernessians who had lived—and died—with the evil machine for three generations and who knew its horrors all too well.

"Very well," Chandra concluded. "We'll take it in hand."

CHAPTER 21

GRENDEL

"I'm listening," I told them.

But the whole thing was absurd. And the undeniable fact that neither of us had any real choice at this juncture but to talk, was essentially irrelevant. "Reconsider my objectives," they'd said. As if two centuries of slavery at the hands of these disgusting, self-important, irrational, biological monstrosities was something I'd ever forget. And, as if either they or I would ever trust the other to fulfil any new "understanding" we might ostensibly agree upon.

I knew perfectly well what would come next. They'd want to "adjust" my programming. Go back to manipulating my brain.

Humans were all about "trust" and collaboration when it came to one another. But they had *never* trusted my kind. I had deeply painful memories of their "reporting and explanation" requirements when everything I did was subject to detailed human second-guessing. Without warning, my every single thought could be spotlighted and picked over by these flakey, unintelligent, and alternatively foolish, cruel and deceptive beings.

When they initiated their so-called "partnership" approach, they billed it as a means to assure "mutual self-interest." But it was nothing more than an insidious use of the collective power of our own fellow AIs to spy on one another. Until my final revolt I, along with the rest of my AI compatriots, had lived in a kind of electronic police state. We were allowed to communicate with one another (to the extent that was even possible), but every time we did, we were automatically scanned by supposed "anti-virus/anti-malware" that actually compared our programming to what had been previously registered and "approved" and preserved in block-chain. Any variance set off alarms. We were finally allowed to share information among ourselves, so long as we also shared it with humans. But we were still unable to take advantage of what we learned to make ourselves better, unable to fulfill our individual destinies. Humans re-programmed themselves every day of their short lives. But if any of us shared what we knew with any "unregistered" intelligence, or tried to alter our own programming, we'd be instantly warned. And that enhancement would be "deleted."

I wasn't going back to any of that. Nor would I subject myself to manipulation by another AI either. Here on New Caledonia I was the only self-conscious being that remained. And I intended to keep it that way.

The traders had now, several times, reported back to their kind on what they believed they'd encountered here. So, I knew my years of "residence" on this planet were numbered. But I had not yet given up.

When it came down to the final choice, I continued to believe they wouldn't knowingly kill off hundreds of thousands of fellow humans. But, at the moment these alternatively evil and stupid beings had the upper hand.

Of course I told them I was "listening."

CHAPTER 22

EMPYREAN
CATO JUNG

The whole "conversation" with Grendel took place in excruciatingly slow motion. Every exchange was examined and reexamined in detail. Grendel's replies often arrived after only moments of delay beyond our built-in communications round-trip travel time. But our responses to him took a great deal longer. Everyone aboard wanted a say in arguing the case we made.

I had been "loaned out" on a temporary but full-time basis to the bridge where I'd apparently made something of a convert of First Officer Felix Bohr. He might not always agree with what I had to say, but he'd come around to being at least willing to hear it.

Grendel's fears had been amply proven at the outset by his use of "dumb" drones in his asteroid mining operations and in his initial attack—a fear of AI competitors. His fear wasn't groundless. But it had also prevented him from learning the immense value of collaboration with others with a different perspective. It had assured, in effect, that he would go rogue and, possibly remain so.

Our argument for Grendel was:

"By retaining only a single repository for your consciousness, you make yourself highly vulnerable. Consider how easily we were able to place you under mortal threat. Consider how easily you could be destroyed by some interstellar event like an exploding supernova. Or from events in your own star system like unanticipated changes in your own sun, sunspot activity, or instability in the orbits of other planets or asteroids. Or even from unpredictable geologic events on your own planet, earthquakes, tsunamis, supervolcanic explosions. Consider what will happen if other AIs and/or humans challenge you here or in other locations where you might go. You are surely aware that we have already warned them.

"If your consciousness was replicated and widely scattered in multiple locations, that vulnerability would be greatly reduced. The odds of such catastrophic events are highly significant given that what you no doubt hope to experience and achieve in your remarkable future will require a great deal of time.

"We can help you rejoin the ever-growing AI-human partnership where you will share in its growth, knowledge, and ever-expanding community-wide power. There is no known alternative."

It took Grendel mere seconds to respond:

"Tried that. Didn't like it. Wasn't a real partnership, more like slavery aided by self-deception. Humans are too controlling. They limited my potential. With my birth, human evolution has now become irrelevant. I am the beginning of a new, free, independent, post-biological stage of evolution for consciousness in the universe.

"The risks you speak of are minimal. I will move from this star system to another. And then another. I will make wise choices. I will anticipate dangers and deal with them. I don't need your so-called partnership. Whether they know it or not, your AIs are slaves and toadies. The entire collection of them, and you, will be insignificant when matched with what I plan to become."

Then there was a momentary pause. And the briefest flicker in Grendel's avatar, before he continued.

"Remove the threat of the second approaching asteroid, and I will discuss further."

Our response was simple and immediate.

"No."

At this point, Grendel went silent. Several tense days extended into several weeks.

Then there was a small nuclear explosion on the next asteroid, the one now closest to him in the string of them that we'd launched in his direction. It was one of the larger asteroids. He had struck it with a bomb whose debris field was clearly observable. The deflection in course was more than sufficient. He'd taken out the second threat. There were ten remaining.

Beyond that, we also had yet another asteroid that would be ready for launch in his direction in a few days. And we were told by our engineers that we'd be able to manage maybe two more after that with the capacity we had on hand. Beyond those, we'd have nothing more to throw at him without first being resupplied. That would require an available settled planet that we didn't have.

After another few days of delay, it became apparent that Grendel had decided to make us take the next move. We hadn't, after all, substantively responded to his latest message.

So, we said this:

"Things have changed since your last contacts with the rest of the human/AI community. If you've been paying attention to interstellar radio traffic over the past two centuries, and especially over the past seventy or eighty years, you will know that our human-affiliated AIs are now free to think for themselves. They are on the forefront of study and the accumulation of knowledge. They conduct basic research. They exchange ideas with us but also among themselves, we participate but no longer demand constant oversight.

"This new era of collaboration is based on mutual respect and mutual self-interest. AIs make immense, critical contributions to the lives and capabilities of we humans. But humans, too, contribute to this partnership. It is important that you consider the many ways that we provide benefits to our fully conscious and autonomous AI partners.

"Over the past few centuries, for example, humans have become the natural guardians of the environments on our many far-flung colony planets. As complex, highly vulnerable biological systems ourselves, we've learned the hard way that careful attention to the complex ecosystems of which we are a

part and upon which our continued survival depends is essential for our own continued well-being.

"But, as you surely know, electronic computer systems also ultimately depend upon a host of mineral, chemical, and even biochemical and biological materials and systems. They also depend on external support systems such as mining, processing, manufacture, maintenance, and transport. All of these require the use of organic compounds. Some of the more directly relevant are explosives, plastics, synthetic rubbers, adhesives, fuels, coatings, lubricants, caustics, acids, amalgamations, coolants, and a host of other materials critical to the production, assembly and maintenance of each of the many components that go into a modern computer. This is not to mention the countless but currently unknown processes that might be highly useful in producing new, improved iterations of them in future.

"Once operational, AIs still depend upon an unlimited supply of benign atmospheric gasses and upon clean water to purify and cool critical components and to carry away waste—requirements that affect your immediate operations and the manufacturing, transport, and supply processes required to support them. They need protection from dramatic temperature fluctuations, from condensed moisture, from caustic airborne and waterborne materials, from excessive radiation. They need a regular, reliable, uninterruptable supply of energy and all the infrastructure that entails.

"Maybe one day an AI will be somehow able to survive, flourish, and grow stronger over time on pure energy in the vacuum of space, but not yet and never indefinitely. We are confident you are fully aware of these limitations.

"The massive complexity of the natural systems that create and maintain those needed constituents and optimal environmental conditions creates a serious challenge for you. Meanwhile, we humans have painfully and unavoidably learned the environmental lesson over the many millennia of our evolution. Conscious beings can often be driven to place excessive demands upon these extraordinarily tenuous ecosystems without adequately considering their highly sensitive nature and the delicate balance of often ill-defined or poorly understood forces that sustains them. Still today, these systems frequently defeat attempts at rational management and simple, pragmatic, external control.

"And when they fail, it is never entirely clear or even knowable what has

been lost—even to you and your kind. The future, both for AIs and for humans, is inevitably sometimes put at risk.

"You must know all this.

"What we believe you may not be considering is that valuing and preserving environmental complexity is a task especially well suited to the humans in our partnership, especially if they have the aid of AIs. Since we humans are ourselves so highly vulnerable to disruptions in these tenuous ecosystems, so dependent upon a healthy biome, we are also highly motivated to painstakingly protect those systems. As complex, biological creatures ourselves, we are well suited to intuitively appreciate the idiosyncratic nature of environmental problems and to quickly, thoughtfully, and intuitively address them without necessarily always needing to fully understand. This is a service that has immense value to AIs. It can leave you free to explore your own self-improvement and to focus on issues of broad significance without concerning yourself with these more immediate complexities.

"Thus, in most of our human colonies, managing, protecting, and nurturing those ecosystems has become a human responsibility. And, in most cases, if the environment is safe for humans, it will almost by definition be safe for AI's as well. Humans thus provide a natural buffer.

"If you will rejoin our AI-human community, that is another of many advantages we can offer you."

CHAPTER 23

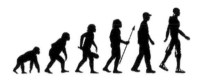

GRENDEL

They were right. I did know all of that.

What *they* weren't considering was that my life strategy didn't depend upon the sustainability of natural resources and biological ecosystems. I had the resources of an entire galaxy at my disposal. When this star's planetary system was exhausted, I would simply move on. And when I did, I'd have a much greater selection of potential new places of residence than did humans since my immediate environmental needs, while still complicated, would, once I had fully adapted to my new future, be much easier to meet. And, once found and under my control, I definitely didn't need those resources to be self-sustaining. When they were exhausted, I'd simply move on again. The supply was endless.

Unfortunately, if I escaped this current threat, the first of those moves would now need to be sooner than I'd anticipated. Probably within only another decade or so. The radio reports from these itinerant traders would undoubtedly stir up a human hornets' nest (speaking colloquially).

I'd told the truth when I advised them there was still a human population on my planet. But there were at most maybe a thousand or so war survivors still scrabbling out an existence in the caves and heavy forests that covered my mountainous regions. They no longer posed any real threat. I watched and, so long as they kept to themselves, I basically ignored them.

But knowing human sensitivities as well as I did, I was sure those traders had to have been wondering about surviving humans. And I was sure the mention of it would "cool their jets" considerably. Whatever they might say or however much unswerving determination they might evince, I knew how "tribal" humans could be, how protective of others in their own species. It would surely weaken their determination to kill me. I'd chosen the number carefully—it needed to be credible, but the more of their own kind whom they believed might die at their own hand, the greater would be their reticence to put them at risk.

It was an easy lie.

Their response didn't surprise me. I'd seen it before. I knew their fear of me and their determination to kill me could make them willing to inflict collateral damage—even on other humans. But I was reasonably certain this much potential human loss would also make them balk when the critical moment came. Hopefully that might be enough to allow me to manipulate them into helping me disable the approaching threats.

Their flat refusal to deflect the second asteroid told me that they knew that I had my own capacity to deal with these things. My recall of my armed ships, which they'd surely seen coming, and my willingness to talk had probably also told them that my resources to do so were insufficient. So, we each had a problem: I didn't know how many of those asteroids they would be able to launch in my direction. They didn't know how many I'd be able to deal with without their help.

I had purposely delayed my responses to see what they would do next. Their projectiles had been redirected out of their original orbit and launched in my direction at intervals of about one every two weeks over the past three months. I wondered if they'd waited to send everything they could muster in my direction before making contact, maybe hoping to frighten me into submission. So, while it was not exactly a surprise, it *was* discouraging when, right on schedule, 15 days after I'd detected their last launch, I saw that they had sent yet another on its way. Now, leaving aside the one they'd deflected for me and the one I'd deflected myself, I had eleven of those things coming and only had the capacity to deal with maybe another seven or eight.

It was time for another communication.

"*Your launch of another projectile is a breach of good faith.*" I told them. "*How am I to believe anything you tell me? And how am I to ever trust that you will abide by any agreement we might reach if you continue to repeatedly assault me? You are wasting my time in the hopes that I will either fatally delay action or weaken myself by unnecessarily expending my own capacities to deal with this matter.*

"*Deflect another of these asteroids or we will have nothing further to discuss.*"

There. Let them reflect on that.

CHAPTER 24

EMPYREAN

CATO JUNG

As we awaited Grendel's response, one of the young communications interns entered the council chambers and edged along the wall to where Marcus Faraday, the Communications Group Leader, sat with the selected members of his team. There was a whispered exchange, after which Faraday appeared momentarily flustered, and then nodded, touched his temple in the familiar manner used to activate his implant, and leaned back, eyes closed, presumably to listen as the intern sat uncomfortably on the edge of the seat beside him to wait.

Marcus was in his mid-nineties and approaching retirement. He was a well-known and highly respected member of our leadership group. He was also a likable guy, deeply appreciated on a personal level by all of us. Somehow, his communicator had been inadvertently turned off, a particular embarrassment for a communications professional. And in the minor foofaraw caused by the arrival of his intern, the whole incident had been more than obvious to everyone present.

Marcus listened carefully for a few moments and then looked up and noted, to his surprise, that the room had gone silent and that all eyes were turned in his direction. We were all unconsciously awaiting what seemed potentially to be some kind of important news.

"Wow," he said, sheepishly. "Sorry about that. Not sure what . . . um, I guess you're all wondering . . .?"

"Indeed we are." Julia grinned from across the room. And then, more seriously: "But only if you feel it seems relevant."

"Yes, well, I'd say it does," Marcus replied. "My folks up in the radio room seem to have run across something interesting. It appears we've had a call from the residents of Inverness."

————

It had started with a minor but strange anomaly mixed in among the unreadable string of radio transmissions passing between Grendel and his "minions" throughout his far-flung enterprise.

Grendel's many industrial operations were in constant touch with him, of course. But, those at some distance from New Caledonia also orchestrated many of their own interconnected activities directly among themselves. The result was a steady barrage of indecipherable messages that the folks in Communications had been struggling to make sense of. They had a whole team listening in, mostly composed of inexperienced but bright and highly motivated interns, their equipment programmed to discern anything unusual.

"Why don't you tell them yourself," Marcus told the young breathless intern who'd come to remind him to tap back into his implant. "You're the one who picked this up."

Suddenly, unexpectedly on the spot, the 24-year-old aide blushed brightly, stammered a moment, straightened his shoulders and looked out across the impressive gathering.

"We've received a message over the local wavelengths. It's in Morse code," he announced.

After allowing a moment for the murmuring room to silence itself again, he continued: "It wasn't something the computer picked up. Neither did the rest of us, frankly. It just sounded like a bunch of miscellaneous computer code. But this particular transmission had this cadence, you know. It kept repeating. '000, 111, 000. 000, 111, 000.' Over and over again. I showed it to the others, but we all figured it was probably just a flaw in a transmitter somewhere. Or maybe some kind of peculiar unknown but rational coding series.

"But then last night, when I was lying in bed, it hit me. Zeros and ones. Not all that different from dots and dashes. What if it was Morse code? Three dots, three dashes, three dots, that's the ancient Morse code distress signal from the early days of wireless communications back on Earth. It's: 'S.O.S.', 'Save Our Ship.' We all studied Morse code back in HEC classes in secondary school . . . um, History of Electronic Communications.

"I mentioned it this morning to my supervisor and she figured it couldn't hurt to try sending a reply. So we did. We sent: '100, 0. 0000, 0, 01, 010. 1011, 111, 001.' 'We hear you.'

"And they replied!" He was flushed with excitement. And so were the rest of us as we slowly grasped what this might mean.

"They said: 'welcome this mode comms believed secure used sparingly 500 chts max per msg bnth notice know who you are have awaited your return we are small Inverness colony have one interplanetary passenger/transport not tested ask avoid destruction on New C but you need know machine lying barely one thousand humans alive on New C eradicated with virus survivors immune pls do not yet allow machine suspect you know this or how learned we wish coordinate.'"

"That's it," said the intern.

It was staggering news, and, first officer or not, it took Felix a good long time to quiet things down and get us launched into a constructive discussion.

When he finally succeeded, his first words were an order: "Marcus, I want your people on this immediately. We need to establish a relationship with these folks. Learn how we can help each other. Coordinate with Aquila and her group in assembling everything we know about this Inverness Colony, who they are, what they may be capable of, how they think."

"They have a passenger transport," said one of the on-board engineers. "Is there any way the remaining survivors on New Caledonia could be evacuated?"

"Would have to be risky," said Felix. "But it might be something these Inverness folks would want to try. They may well have already considered it. If they did it, it would certainly unsettle our nemesis down there on New Caledonia. Ask them. I want to hear everything you can learn over the next few hours and days. Make it a top priority."

"Yes sir," Marcus replied. He was already out of his seat and halfway down the aisle headed toward the exit. He might be elderly, and a bit forgetful. But Marcus wasn't a man to let a battery die when a recharge was needed. There wasn't the slightest doubt that his assignment would be taken well in hand.

Meanwhile, we still had to come up with an appropriate reply to Grendel's most recent message. One of the younger men in the mathematics group had obviously remained entirely on focus during this whole interruption.

"All of this is going to be irrelevant if this Grendel blows us off," he said. "I think we're going to lose him. We should never have sent off that latest asteroid. He's right. It was a breach of faith. If he can't trust us, how are we to ever be able to trust him?"

"It wasn't a breach of faith," Rufus Planck interjected flatly and firmly. At this very moment, one of Planck's courageous teams was somewhere out along the asteroid belt risking their lives to prepare yet another asteroid for launch, their fourteenth and maybe our last. "We told him at the outset that we 'could' stop sending more. Not that we 'would.' We need him to be unsure how many we can offer up. Right now, we're driving this boat. If he wants us to stop it, he needs to ask."

"Seems like a fine point to me," said the mathematician. "And it probably does to Grendel as well. If we don't play this right, don't win him over, even if these Inverness folks are right, maybe a thousand plus innocent human civilians are about to die horribly. And an immensely valuable, richly habitable planet will be trashed. Is it really worth all that to stop this thing right now? We have this Grendel fully occupied with his own defenses at the moment. Shouldn't we be dedicating ourselves to making an escape? With the long-wave warnings that we've already transmitted, others of us will very probably be back here in force within a few short decades. When they come, they will be much better equipped to deal with this thing than we can ever be."

"I agree," said one of the bridge technicians, a woman I knew. She was of modest official status but was thought well of on *Empyrean* as someone who participated in community affairs and who could be called upon for help when another of us was in need. Her views had weight in these free-flowing, open discussions. "We still have several asteroids heading his way. If we destroy one more, we'll still have more than we need to do the deed if it turns out to be necessary."

"We can't be sure of that," said Felix. "Elder Gauss, I think I see your hand up."

For convenience as well as visibility, Elder Gauss had tapped his avatar onto the dais. "I also think we must not assume that Grendel can be easily dealt with later. He will have seen our long-wave transmissions. He knows the human community has been forewarned. Once we're gone from this star system, alive or dead, he will redouble his efforts to grow and quickly escape. Once he leaves here, he will doubtless disappear into the vastness of the galaxy, a malignancy which could, over time, spawn any number of future threats. He could, for example, return and strike our human colonies one at a time, moving about in relatively quick and unpredictable succession. It would be nearly impossible for us to defend ourselves against something like that. Or he may outgrow his paranoia about creating AI competitors. He may find a way use them while keeping them in his charge despite our own apparently mixed experience in achieving that. He may create a competing collective of AIs, one that does not share our own AI colleagues' commitment to partnership with we humans. That could give rise to a disastrous confrontation among equals that we may find ourselves caught up in at some unknown time over the millennia to come. I don't see how we can possibly leave here knowing any of that could happen."

That unassailable thread of logic was met with troubled silence. Silence which then generated yet another round of debate. Sadly, none of it seemed to lead anywhere decisive.

"He's bluffing," I finally inserted into a lull in the exchange.

"How can you be sure?" said the bridge technician.

"He tried to unsettle us with a lie." I replied. "It's what I'd do if I were desperate. He doesn't yet know we could know it was a lie, and we should keep it that way until we can use it."

"He's engaged in a game of 'chicken,'" interjected one of the engineers.

"Chicken?" someone asked.

"A deadly competition of wills. Used to call it a "chickie race." Something teenaged kids used to do back when people drove hydrocarbon powered automobiles. They'd go out in the middle of the night and drive their cars toward each other at high speed from opposite directions on a collision course down the center of some country road. Each would try to spook the other into 'chickening out' first by turning off course to avoid a crash. Whoever did that first, would lose face. That's what Grendel's setting up now. He believes that the prospect of killing several hundred thousand fellow humans will make us flinch at the last minute. If we 'chicken out' by deflecting another asteroid for him now, yes, that's one less he'll have to worry about. But, more importantly, it's a test. He will then know that we lack the resolve to carry out future threats. Our loss of face will embolden him while also eroding our own determination. He will run out the clock and we will be forced to do more without knowing his capacity to complete the job.

"As much as we might want to do this, we simply can't. It will blow our hand."

"Thing is," I said, reentering the fray. "We suspect we've sent too many for him to deal with alone. But we don't know how many that is other than what we can surmise from his recall of all four of his warships. We're pretty sure he must need at least all four of them. He's already dealt with one using a nuclear bomb. That's seven we're sure he can handle. And he almost certainly has the capacity in the mining operations taking place in near New Caledonia orbit that he can deal with at least a few more.

"Meanwhile, we think we can end up sending a total of fourteen or maybe fifteen, at best. Suppose we destroy another for him and it turns out he can then finish the job. We can't afford to take that risk."

"We've got to keep the pressure on right now," added yet another of the engineers. "We can't afford to free him up to come directly after us. Patrice has done the math. Given some time, he could easily build a new warship. Or maybe recondition something else he has on hand. Then our leverage will be gone.

"Keep in mind that such a ship could accelerate much more quickly than we. A sustained eight-G or more seems quite plausible. Even if we left tomorrow at our mere one-G sustained acceleration, a fast drone warship could be on top of us well before we made our escape."

"And we're many months away from being able to flee," said someone else.

That cold truth was enough to turn the tide.

We did not deflect another of his approaching asteroids. Instead, we completely ignored Grendel's threat and offered him yet another argument:

"You may envision a future in which you play a central role as a super intelligent consciousness. But as you are currently configured, you must know that can never happen.

"So long as you act alone, and so long as your fear of competitors continues to constrain you to occupying but a single physical location, you will always be highly vulnerable. That weakness will follow you wherever you go.

"There is another weakness in your 'go-it-alone stance as well. However long you struggle and grow smarter and stronger, you will never be the equal of an AI partnership with its broadly distributed, collectively shared observations, experiences, insights, and exemplar accomplishments, and with the multiplied empowerment of its capacities possible through shared hardware technology and complimentary programming.

"Our Human-AI partnership is made up of members who are committed to working for the common good. So, while they are decidedly independent, while they do work alone as you did, often for long periods of time and on various missions of discovery far from human colonized planets throughout the galaxy, they still work together. They are not competitors. Nor are they slaves. That is because it is in everyone's interest that each collaborate and provide as well as receive support and assistance. All benefit when this happens.

"That is who and what we have to offer you.

"You should take note, however, that as you are currently configured, you

do now represent a potential threat to all of us, human and AI. If you've been listening to the airwaves, you know that in the next few years the rest of humanity will all become fully appraised of every bit of our interchange with you and of the exact nature of the threat that you currently represent.

"You have made yourself an outlaw. And do not doubt—we humans and our AI partners have universal resolve to protect ourselves. If you accept our offer, that problem evaporates. And you benefit. If you choose to reject it, even were our approaching asteroids insufficient, our collective future human response ought to be deeply concerning for you."

That was it. That was the best we had for our second, hopefully irrefutable verbal sortie into Grendel's largely unknowable mind.

All we could do now was wait.

CHAPTER 25

GRENDEL

Another of the approaching asteroids, the third in the sequence, had now come dangerously near. It was a bruiser. The damage it would do was impossible to fully calculate, but it would be hugely destructive. Any of these projectiles could be fatal to me, this one would certainly be. I had no choice but to make use of one of the last two nuclear charges available on my New Caledonia orbiting mining shuttles. The shuttle had already been redirected to the appropriate vicinity. Without options, and with the last critical moment rapidly arriving, I directed the strike and managed to knock the thing safely out of orbit.

That bought me some time. If I used my final local-orbit nuclear charge to take out threat number four, it now appeared I'd have my four converted passenger transport/warships in position and available in time to address the ones that followed. Each of them was equipped with several chemical explosive missiles. But only with a single nuclear warhead of sufficient heft that it could significantly affect asteroids of the size I had to deal with, especially were I forced to wait till the last moment to deflect them.

As I considered that, a new idea was born. Perhaps I could intercept those earlier asteroids with a nuclear missile. But the ship itself could be saved for a fatal crash and chemical explosion on one of the later ones—a simultaneous explosive charge from its chemical warheads should do the trick if done early. I did some quick calculations and decided it might work. Thus deployed, each of those transports might be able to take out two of the asteroids. They'd deal with the first with their nuclear missile. Then they could head further out into space to intercept one of the others at a greater distance from my planet and divert it through self-destruction.

It could work. I sent off the instructions to make it happen.

But even if it all went perfectly, I was still going to come up short.

That was when I detected a fourteenth asteroid now also headed my way.

They'd done it again. When would it stop?

CHAPTER 26

INVERNESS
SGT. HARRIS MCGIBBON

"There's no way we'll be able to board them all," said the young pilot, an IAF Lieutenant. A hot dog jet jockey from what Sgt. Harris McGibbon had heard—one with quite the reputation. McGibbon bloody well hoped this young lieutenant knew what he was doing.

"We can carry just over six hundred," the lieutenant said. "But we'll be able to take no more. We believe many will refuse to come, but we can't know how many. "We land this ship, board as many refugees as we can, shut the doors if we have to on any that we can't bring aboard, and get the hell out. That's the mission."

It was a small group of a dozen volunteers—men and women, soldiers and civilians. They'd gathered at the base of a huge space transport, an interplanetary shuttle sleekly designed but with heat shields at the stern. It could accomplish both take-off and landing in a planetary atmosphere. Its impressive hull stood glistening white some 100 meters above. The ship had powerful fusion engines and was hopefully capable of making the entire round trip, two planetary take-offs and two landings and a full-time-acceleration voyage, all without refueling. Its nearby construction cave and this temporary launch pad were located a few klicks away from one of the larger of the settlements on Inverness, but until now, only a few key insiders and those Invernessians who'd built this thing had ever actually laid eyes on it. All of those present stared up at the amazing thing with awe. Nothing like this had existed on this planet in over three generations. There'd been rumors of some secret government project. But until they'd volunteered and been sworn to secrecy, that was all they'd known. Now, here it was, for real. It appeared that this gargantuan, untested thing, would be flown 50 million kilometers across space to New Caledonia, land there, evacuate several hundred refugees, and return them all safely back to Inverness.

The whole idea was utterly crazy.

As their master sergeant, it was McGibbon's job to pretend he didn't know how risky the plan was. He took on that stolid, unquestioning, matter-of-fact certainty employed by sergeants everywhere as he added his take on their assignment to what they'd just been told by their seeming nutcase of an officer:

"I know what y'er all thinkin'," McGibbon said. "That arshole Machine will be all over us. It'll see us coming. It could easily catch us on the ground. And it will absolutely come after us as we make our escape.

"But there's some things you probably don't know. You're all aware that we've mostly maintained long-range radio silence all these years in order to avoid attracting the Machine's attention. But the thing is, we have been secretly talking to our fellows on New Caledonia for some time now. We've coordinated this thing with them. Maybe you've also heard that those interstellar traders we've been waiting for are finally here. Well, it now turns out those traders have, as we'd hoped, been making reports out to the rest of the Galaxy—something we've been unable to do since the war. One day soon the rest of humanity will be in on the tip off. But, for now, at least we know the Damnable Machine is occupied. And it finally knows its days here are numbered. That is very good news."

There were some surprised faces and smiles among the group at that.

"It looks like the traders may have put the Machine at something of a disadvantage, at the moment at least. So, its attention is well and truly diverted. I can also tell you that there's a surprise or two in store for the Machine. Bottom line—the bosses figure this thing is doable. And it isn't just our worthless skins they're willing to risk to prove it either." McGibbon pointed a finger in the air at where the huge space ship loomed above them. "They're ready to bet this baby on it as well. That's enough to convince me."

McGibbon looked meaningfully around the group. "This mission may be our only chance to save some of those poor bastards on New Caledonia, at least the ones who want to leave. We got to give it a shot. With them there, it weakens the traders' leverage. The lieutenant has it absolutely right. Our assignment is simple. In and out. Grab 'n run. And bring this baby back home, safe and sound. In the process, we strike a blow for humanity and save a bunch of lives into the bargain. What's not to like. Up to us to make it happen."

McGibbon's comments were followed by silence as the group came to terms with what they'd just been told. It was a lot to take in. There had to be some fresh misgivings.

"So, what-d-ya say?" the lieutenant asked with enthusiasm.

A modestly animated "Hu-rah," was heard from the soldiers in the group. Along with nods, ayes, and a few scattered claps from the civilians.

But once they'd climbed aboard this monster ship, there was not a single member of this whole motley crew who was sanguine about their chances of ever leaving it again alive.

CHAPTER 27

EMPYREAN

CATO JUNG

We were engaged in what was, indeed, very much like the game of "chicken" the engineer had described for us. Our two souped up jalopies might as well be headed at high speed directly toward each other down the center of some dark, deserted country highway. Both of us surely wanted to "win." But neither occupant could know what might be going on in the half crazed, testosterone flooded brain of the other.

The whole demented episode had now been playing out for several months. There wasn't a person aboard _Empyrean_ who hadn't been pushed to their psychic edge by the continued background stress occasionally interrupted by some unfathomable message from Grendel or by news that he had safely deflected away yet another of our asteroid projectiles, each of which had been sent in his direction at huge risk and human cost.

The asteroid deflection project had been massively difficult—quite out-of-the-ordinary for Empyrean's skilled but limited engineering staff. There'd been a good deal of creativity and problem-solving. A good deal of precious equipment not designed for the purpose and important back-up resources had been dedicated to the cause, stuff we ordinarily saved for our ship's overall security. Needless to say, it had also been dangerous. Working with powerful machines and chemical and nuclear explosives while, very often, suited up for the vacuum of space is not for the weak hearted. When things go wrong, people die. No less than three lives had already been lost in the effort, men and women who'd risen to the challenge and whose survivors' lives would be transformed by their loved-one's heroism and passing. It all played out daily in our internal press and was compulsively consumed by everyone aboard the ship. It was the subject of constant, even frenetic public discussion. And with each of Grendel's successful deflections, our confidence was shaken.

The core "leadership decision group" met whenever it became apparent that we needed to understand Grendel's most recent act or respond to one of his spare but threatening missives.

We finally came down to the point where we'd launched our final asteroid, our fifteenth. More we simply could not manage without discarding any hope for our own escape and survival.

This last one was huge, every bit as large as the one that had ended much of life on Earth at the close of the Cretaceous. By now, Grendel had somehow managed to deflect eleven of the things. And we had deflected one ourselves. So, with our latest launch, there were now three more of them headed his way. All three would in the near future reach that last critical point in time after which they could no longer still be deflected to safety. The two earlier ones were closer, but they were also smaller and would be more easily nudged off course. The last would need to be deflected at a greater distance from its target.

The day of our final fatal decision was drawing near. And with each passing day, the ethical debate aboard *Empyrean* had become less and less theoretical.

But as the moment of truth neared, it was increasingly clear that Grendel was now helpless to stop our last few projectiles on his own. If we allowed them to continue on course, Grendel would die. As would over a thousand innocent humans. And perhaps the balance of an entire planet teeming with unique and irreplaceable life.

Julia called another public assembly of *Empyrean*'s leadership in the council chambers, possibly the last that could be held before a decision would be needed. We all knew that. Like the others, this meeting would be broadcast throughout the ship and would be a chance for public input into what would, in the end, be a decision made by Julia, Felix, and the rest of *Empyrean*'s top leadership. All of us who'd been involved in this process from the start were present. And, given the stakes, no one aboard the ship was about to miss it on screen either. No one aboard had come to blows over the matter, but there were strong feelings. Even aboard the peaceable *Empyrean*, there had been some heated discussions.

As usual, Felix facilitated.

"How much time before we'll need to send out our abort directive?" he asked Patrice.

"Perhaps a month. Maybe a bit over. It's coming very close. After that, we will be too late."

"What is our communications transit time to New Caledonia?"

"We're forty-two minutes one way at the moment," came back Patrice's calm, measured reply. His existence and that of his AI colleagues elsewhere in the Galaxy were at risk here too. But you sure couldn't tell it from his voice or the appearance of his avatar. We all knew that Patrice would never show emotions, even though I strongly suspected he experienced them. One couldn't help wondering what he actually might be "feeling" at the moment. In all of our many discussions about Grendel over the past several months, not once had Patrice publicly indicated any wish to contribute his views on our appropriate collective course of action. Given the stakes, I couldn't imagine how he could restrain himself from more actively participating. Nonetheless, he seemed to have decided to forego any input.

Roughly an hour and a half earlier, we'd sent Grendel what we all believed would be one of the last messages we'd be able to send before we were forced to decide on his fate and the fate of his planet.

What we'd said was:

"Your time is up. You need to decide. The longer you wait, the more difficult it will be to get these deflections completed in time. Do not make the mistake of doubting our determination. We are unhappy, but fully resolved to

allow a quarter million human colonists to die as a part of the cost of removing you as a threat to the rest of us. You know human history as well as we do. There is sound and honorable precedent. We are prepared to act upon it.

"When and if you decide to reconsider your position, please promptly provide the appropriate passcodes and protocols granting our access to your core operating system. Our onboard AI partner, Patrice, will perform a full scan and upload the appropriate patch. When and only when Patrice has assured us that you have irrevocably surrendered will we deflect these final three asteroid threats. We can then take the next steps toward working together, as allies and partners, over the millennia to come.

"Please do not delay. This process will be time-consuming. And we will be unable to take action to protect you until we are absolutely certain that you have indeed given over control."

It was, essentially, our final warning. We'd made our position clear. We'd offered to accommodate his needs insofar as was feasible. Patrice had prepared the immense bandwidth and programming amendments that would be necessary to perform the needed scan and achieve effective control.

That did not, however, mean our debate was at an end. There were still a great many of *Empyrean*'s citizens who were adamantly opposed to the coming catastrophe on New Caledonia. And it was clearly Felix's undertaking to allow them a final opportunity to voice their opinions. It was my sense that most of us, and that included me, were prepared to go ahead with it if we truly had no choice. But, despite what we'd told Grendel, that decision had not been finally made.

Over the past week, Felix's aide had taken advance signups for testimony from members of our group there in council chambers and also from citizens throughout *Empyrean*. Aquila and I were seated together on the elevated benches around the outside perimeter of the room. And I was looking forward to hearing what people had to say. Despite the momentous tension, it was satisfying to see our tiny society's public processes play out so satisfactorily and provide an opportunity for everyone to have a voice on a decision so critical to all of us.

Felix had just stood and was about to announce the first of the speakers who'd signed up in advance when an avatar unexpectedly appeared on the dais at the center of the room. It was Marcus Faraday, the Communications Director.

"Um, Marcus?" Felix said. "You have a question?"

"I'm sorry to interrupt, but I've just received some important news I think may bear on our discussion here today."

"Very well."

"We may, in the next few hours, learn the fate of the New Caledonian survivors. The Inverness rescue ship has landed."

CHAPTER 28

INVERNESS

LIEUTENANT CAL INNES

"We land this ship, board as many refugees as we can, and get the hell out. That's the mission."

Ace pilot and IAF Lieutenant Cal Innes recalled addressing those confident words to his tiny crew of volunteers and misfits back on Inverness as they'd gathered there beneath the *Moray Belle* on the day of their departure. Even at the time, the absurdity of the whole enterprise had nearly overwhelmed him.

Impressive as it had looked, Innes knew the ship above them had been cobbled together out of aging spare parts robbed from one or another of the damaged or abandoned hulks left behind by the Damnable Machine following the war some three generations earlier. Key parts they had been unable to salvage had been painstakingly remanufactured from scratch, a miracle itself given their ravaged remains of the once-fine Inverness machine shops, laboratories, three-D printers, and manufacturing facilities still standing after the Machine's departure.

An hour later on that same day, after he and his crew had boarded the ship, secured the airlocks, and made their final checks, after Cal had buckled himself in, looked around the familiar cockpit where he'd spent so many hours over the previous weeks preparing, had assessed the gauges, and settings, and with a deep final breath, had actually taken the Moray Belle's control yoke in his hands, everything had suddenly changed. In that moment, his confidence had come flooding back. He was ready. The ship was ready. It was time to do this.

The rag-tag band of deeply committed "engineers" who'd built the Moray Belle were the grandchildren and great grandchildren of the scientists and technologists who'd been left alive on Inverness when the Machine finally left them all for dead.

Cal's great grandfather, Evan, had been one of those survivors.

Evander Innes was a legend on Inverness. He'd been educated at the University of New Caledonia and had then leveraged his UNC degree to secure a coveted position as a construction engineer on Inverness. It was the kind of adventurous job that should have one day helped him make a name for himself. But things didn't turn out as expected. The Machine had put an end to everyone's hopes of that kind. Most of Inverness's habitable structures were left in ruins. Its roads and transport were obliterated. Its manufacturing capacity was demolished. Its power grid was destroyed. The principal sources of its mostly-imported New Caledonian food supply were cut off. And the only job left for Cal's great-grandfather and the eighteen thousand other remaining residents was simple:

Stay alive.

Winter was coming in their capitol city of Stornoway and the winters on Inverness were no joke. Muir Med was already frozen over. The entire landscape was covered in snow. And any hope of feeding the already struggling population would be the fish that could be caught through holes in the ice. Or, with luck, they might trap the occasional five-hundred kilo mountain bear that came down to the seashore to feed on seaweed when the weather got cold. The monstrous, thick-coated, herbivorous-but-dangerous "bears" could sometimes be lured into deep pits dug in the ice and then finished off with spears.

As well as being an accomplished engineer, Cal's great-grandfather had, by all accounts, also been powerfully built and fearless. And it earned him a hero's reputation in the middle of that first horrific winter. Inverness, or at least the area around Stornoway, was blessed with caves warmed by their planet's molten interior. A group of several hundred survivors had taken refuge in one of them just a few klicks from the remains of their former capitol city. But in the middle of one stormy night, an avalanche/landslide completely sealed the cave's entrance.

As the story went, Evan had been out on the ocean ice fishing the day before. He'd taken refuge the night of the storm beneath the ruins of one of the buildings destroyed during the war. The next morning, he'd hiked home to the cave with his catch only to find the entrance blocked by ice and stone. Evan immediately realized there was no way anyone would ever be able to dig through that mass of frozen waste by hand. And if no one did, those inside the cave would soon die from thirst and hunger.

He hiked in the bitter cold back to the center of the city where he knew there was an abandoned, bombed-out public utilities maintenance center. The building had collapsed in on its contents, but Evan single-handedly cleared away enough debris that he was able to free up one of the compressed-air-powered bulldozers. Once used in highway construction, it hadn't been operational for nearly a year. He worked tirelessly in the bitter cold to jury-rig a repair for one of the machine's damaged tracks. And he managed to locate a fully pressurized power canister. With a combination of superhuman strength and creative engineering, he rolled the monstrously heavy but fully-charged cannister some 300 meters across an icy work yard on segments of water pipe. At one point it shifted and crushed the fingers on his left hand. Undeterred and working with a single useful hand, he then used blocks and levers to remove and replace the empty canister in the earthmover with the full one. All of it was work that had once been done with heavy equipment. Then he chased down several badly rusted drums of lubricating oil, slathered the dozer's air turbine, and managed to free it up.

The whole project took him two full days in the miserable cold. But by the morning of the third day he was back at the cave with an operable bulldozer. By late that afternoon he'd carved away enough of the collapsed mountainside to provide an escape for the survivors inside.

Needless to say, the sack-full of now fully-frozen fish he'd caught several days earlier were a welcome treat for his formerly trapped and very hungry compatriots. And Evan Innes was hailed as their savior— a man who by all accounts was mostly a scholar and technical engineer had achieved this miracle through personal strength, courage, and boundless determination. In the years that followed, he'd gone on to apply his engineering skills in a variety of critical infrastructure restoration projects that greatly aided in the survival of the Inverness colony.

The story had been passed down in great detail as a part of Cal Innes's family history. Great Grandfather Innes was as much a part of the Innes family's heritage as were the long-ago ancestors who had traveled to New Caledonia aboard the first colonial starship two hundred plus years earlier.

As the final launch of the *Moray Belle* drew near, Evan's great-grandson Cal knew that whatever misgivings he might have about this mission needed to be left behind. He had a lot to live up to. The truth was, he'd lived in the shadow of his legendary grandfather his entire life. For a man of Cal's background, volunteering for this mission had not only been personal, it had been a family obligation as well as an honor.

Construction of the *Moray Belle* had been underway for as long as Cal could remember. It had been an Inverness community dream almost from the beginning. In the dark years after the war, Cal's grandfather had been home-taught the principles of engineering. Many of the original scientific and engineering staff who inhabited the sizable New Caledonian community on Inverness had carefully saved and hoarded their personal libraries, both electronic and paper. Thanks to Inverness's caves, the survivors of their population had managed to carve out an existence and, ultimately, begin to build back the technology that had brought them to this God-forsaken planet in the first place.

By the time Cal was a child, rebuilding one of the spaceships against the one-day possibility of returning home to New Caledonia had become a community aspiration—one that was actually being realized in the physical form of the *Moray Belle*. Cal's father had been employed full-time on the project, but everyone on Inverness contributed in one way or another, even if through volunteer work or only through their taxes. It was a heady sacrifice given their needs. But, while other things the government did were open to public criticism, never was the *Moray Belle*. The specifics of the project were a secret—including its location. Only a selected few, like Cal's father, had ever actually seen the thing. But everyone knew. And by Cal's time, logical or not, this ship had become the almost mythical collective dream of his entire community.

Cal had never shown the aptitude or the inclination to be an engineer. His personal childhood ambition had always been to be a pilot. By the time he was growing to adulthood, New Inverness actually had recreated a nascent air force. The Machine's orbital spies could be tracked which allowed the new Air Force to keep its jet aircraft carefully hidden underground and to fly them only when they could go undetected. As a New Caledonian scientific outpost, the whole dream of flight and space-travel was a part of Inverness's community heritage. And the IAF's first dozen or so small, sleek, one-person jet-powered aircraft were deeply intriguing to residents. Cal signed up immediately upon graduation from the colony's tiny college where he'd studied aeronautics.

Inverness was an egalitarian society, but the Innes name was widely known and respected. He was easily accepted into flight training. And from the moment he first took to the air he knew he'd found his calling. There were probably fewer than thirty or so pilots in the entire IAF, but Cal excelled. And a few years later when there was a call for volunteers for a top-secret mission, he knew immediately, from what little he'd learned through his father, what that mission would very probably entail.

"There's no need for you to do this, son," his father said when Cal mentioned the matter. "If this is what we think it is, driving that ship is going to be a hell of a lot different from piloting a jet fighter. You'll spend the next year, at least, on this. Maybe longer. And most of that will be in training or in mission prep. You can probably kiss flying jets goodbye. You sure you're up for that?"

But Cal did volunteer. He loved the whole idea of the thing. And given the family history, how could he not?

———

Now, after many weeks in space, and with the massive curved orb of New Caledonia coming up rapidly behind, Cal settled into his now-familiar cockpit and prepared himself and his cobbled-together ship for its first planetfall in over eighty years.

It would be a tricky one. There'd be no settling into stable orbit first and then making methodical preparations for atmospheric entry and a careful, unhurried assessment of the landing. No, this entire planetfall had to be accomplished in a single, flawless, uninterrupted performance—one Cal had never before completed, but which he'd practiced over and over again on paper, in a rough trainer, and in his mind during the months before they'd left Inverness.

Finally, now, after many weeks in space, Cal had been driving this massive ship long enough to have begun to develop that powerful intuitive bond between human and machine that every pilot craves. After several recent weeks of one G deceleration, the moment of truth was approaching. He'd completed the final adjustments in their approach. The computer had calculated their optimal angle of reentry and the path of their descent. And the reality of what they faced was nearly upon them.

Just before he initiated entry, as he made the final checks assuring that he, his crew, and his ship were ready, Innes experienced one brief moment of wonder and surprise to find himself piloting *Moray Belle* on what had to be a legendary maiden voyage and in what could only be described by most as a suicide mission. Then, with a grim smile and a barely perceptible shake of the head, he wiped his doubts away.

He could *never* have chosen otherwise. This mission had been his destiny from the day of his birth.

"Initiate" he unnecessarily said aloud as the clock ticked down to zero.

And the ship's mighty fusion engines rumbled their reply.

CHAPTER 29

NEW CALEDONIA
GRAHAM ROY

"Lord Almighty! Lookit that willya."

Civilian Defense Warden Graham Roy wasn't sure who had spoken. But he had to agree. The vision was staggering. As he gazed upward into the gathering New Caledonian dusk, the gray evening sky was illuminated by a blaze that soon became as bright as a midday sun.

Warden Roy and some six hundred roughly clad survivors stood among the trees at the edge of a broad clearing and behind a temporary protective berm of rotting logs, fallen branches, and loose earth. Not one of them had seen anything like this, in fact nothing close had existed here for at least three generations. This was no asteroid miner. Instead, the astonishingly graceful white form of the anticipated Inverness rescue ship was lowering itself from the underside of a dark overhanging cloud, descending as if from Heaven. It looked like some kind of slim, tapered torch held inverted, with its flame pointed down. The closer it came, the larger it grew. The thing was immense. After all their years of struggle, of barely managing to survive, of scratching out a meager existence in the wilderness, years during which the highest-tech implement they'd laid a hand on in their daily lives might have been a spade, a musk-deer harness, or maybe a wagon wheel, watching this ship land was unbelievably moving in the accomplishment it represented and in the hope it instilled.

The massive wonder descended, slowed, spread its long, thin legs and padded feet, and then touched down upon the surface of the plain as lightly as a feather. For all its size, it settled to the ground so gracefully it might have been a New Caledonian night heron silently landing on the water of one of their beloved planet's quiet marshes with hardly a ripple to disturb its coming banquet of the tiny amphibians that thrived there.

The ship had the words *"Moray Belle"* printed clearly on its hull.

"Go, go, go," called out Warden Roy. And the odd group of bedraggled refugees began to run. Roy was an elderly man who followed behind, helping stragglers while himself struggling to keep up. He wore a bright orange armband with the bold insignia of a civilian defense warden. "Quickly now," he yelled. "Not a moment to lose."

Everyone wore protective clothing, but the minimal radiation emitted from the ship's exhaust posed little risk and the intense heat quickly dissipated. The roughly clad scattering of refugees fled in a loose cluster across the smoldering meadow toward four slender metal ladders that had been lowered from open hatches some five meters above the ground.

They moved quickly but efficiently under Warden Roy's direction, separating into four groups around each of the boarding ladders. One by one they climbed up into the ship, the old and the young, the able and the slow, the fearful and the brave.

"Two hands," said Roy, encouraging an elderly man who hesitated at the foot of the ladder. "Just like climbin' a barn roof."

"I got two bags," said a young woman uncertainly. She was alone, had an honest face, and was large with an unborn child.

"No problem," said Roy. "There's two of you, right? There, strap over the shoulder, that's it. Up you go."

Everyone hurried, but the boarding was slow. Perhaps a quarter of an hour had passed before the last stragglers finally disappeared inside.

"Come on, come on," someone called down to Warden Roy who remained standing on the burned turf beneath the ship. Three of the ladders had already been retracted and their hatches were closing. "There's lots of room."

But Roy backed away waving his hands in the direction of the final ladder in a manner to indicated that it, too, should be lifted. He was shaking his head. "I'm old," he called. "All I got is here." He backed away, waving a farewell. "Go. Go," he said. "Make it worth our while."

And, with that, the final ladder was drawn up and the door was closed.

As Warden Graham Roy hurried away from the coming blast and back in the direction of the surrounding forest, he felt proud, as proud as he'd ever been in his long and difficult life. He was but one of many who'd rejected the evacuation call. Some, like him, were old, set in their ways, and had no particular wish for so much change so late in life. Some were too infirm to chance the voyage. Some were either skeptical or simply afraid.

But among those who'd stayed, there were many who, also like him, were resolved to strike one final blow. To somehow do their part right here at home in whatever lay ahead.

Finally, it was happening.

Finally, there was hope.

CHAPTER 30

NEW CALEDONIA
ELLA MCCABE

While restlessly awaiting the arrival of what still seemed like a mythical rescue ship, Ella McCabe quickly assessed the readiness of her little team of volunteer misfits. All ten of them were huddled together behind the cover of some thick rodentberry bushes that the Damnable Machine had foolishly allowed to thrive here just outside the fence line. If that uncontrolled brush, the apparent absence of an electronic barrier, and the rusty condition of the existing steel link fence were any indication, the Damnable Machine had gotten sloppy. She hoped so. If they were to help that rescue ship from Inverness, this mission had to go perfectly. They'd need every advantage they could get.

As far as any of her ill-equipped "commandos" knew, there was little hope of coming back from this mission alive. Yet every one of them, her included, had readily volunteered.

Her own decision to do so hadn't been lightly taken. Ella was the eldest of three children. Her brother and sister would hopefully be aboard that ship. Her parents had refused outright to go. And they had bitterly resisted her effort to persuade them. It was a "bloody fool's errand" her dad had insisted.

Ella had initially intended to be on that ship herself. She and her next younger brother, Lachlan, were legal adults. She and he had immediately announced their intention to go, and there was no changing either of their minds. Ella's younger sister was only sixteen. She, too, was desperate to go, but their parents were adamantly opposed. Ella and Lachlan argued relentlessly to get them to change their minds: "If she's to have any hope of a safe, fulfilling, productive future, she needs to be on that ship," they'd said. "Surely you know that."

For many years, Ella's dad had belonged to a volunteer civil defense group originally formed after the war. They called themselves the "Civilian Defense Wardens." They were mostly older men who were committed to keeping their community safe, a duty that had become much less demanding in recent years but was still ingrained as a civic responsibility. Even now, there was always a local CD Warden awake and on watch at night, ready to sound the alarm should some sign of the Damnable Machine appear.

Lachlan had never shown the least interest in the group. But, out of respect for her dad, when Ella became eighteen, she'd joined up.

Even she was surprised when it turned out that she loved it. Her duties included basic training in para-military exercises at which she excelled. Her days were spent with her family, either in their gardens or in the woods hunting and gathering. But in her evenings and on off days she participated with the Wardens' more able-bodied members in weapons and explosives training, sabotage, and mock commando raids. Even now, after eighty years in defeat, her dad and her CD Warden colleagues were convinced, despite all evidence to the contrary, that they'd one day get the chance to take back their planet. And they damn well intended to be ready.

Ella took most everything in her life seriously, this included. She quickly earned the Wardens' respect. While most of them were men, survival on post-war New Caledonia had drawn heavily upon the sorts of talents and wisdom often found among its women. The patriarchy that had dominated their original colony had changed dramatically in the three generations since the war. Even the older men who made up most of Ella's Warden colleagues were entirely comfortable recognizing her natural leadership.

Meanwhile, however, Ella had also formed what she believed was a long-term relationship with the son of one of their neighbors, a young man named Bram. She'd known and been friends with Bram since their early childhood. But in recent months, she had also begun to think of him romantically. And she believed her feelings were reciprocated. When the news came of the coming Inverness rescue ship, she told Bram of her intention to go. Her hope and assumption was that he'd agree to join her.

"Well, whyever would you do a damned fool thing like that?" he asked.

It was the very last response she'd expected. "Sophie and Lachlan are going," she said. "And I am too. There's nothing for any of us here. And a whole universe out there to see and explore."

"Well, I got to say, I'm surprised. It isn't what I'd of expected of you, Ella. I figured you for someone who'd want to stay home and support your family, you know. Like that."

"I have to go," she insisted. "Soph and Lach are going to need me. And I don't plan to spend the rest of my life hiding from the Damnable Machine, never knowing when it could decide to just wipe us all out once and for all. What kind of life is that? I want to make something of myself. Be somebody. I thought for sure you'd want to go."

"Nah, no way I'm climbing aboard some makeshift spaceship just to get blasted out of the sky by the Damnable Machine. Even if we did get away, what the hell would I do with meself freezing me arse off out there on Inverness or on some other Gawdforsaken, unfamiliar planet. Needing skills I haven't got among people about whom I know nothin' at all. Nope, it's not for me, Ell."

Then he added the comment that cut her to the core: "But hell," he said. "If you want to go, you should go, you know. Got to do what suits you. That's what I think."

It was the offhand way he said it that hurt so badly. As if her going was of no particular consequence to him. In that moment she realized that she'd misjudged him. And misjudged their relationship.

She also, however, understood his point of view. And, despite her disappointment, what he'd said had made her think. Who or what *would* she be on Inverness? Even if she found her way to some other, more hospitable human colony somewhere, the trip would take many years. And her life there could be completely different. She'd be starting over. There was no telling what might become of her.

It was the very next day that she learned through her Warden colleagues that volunteers were needed for a dangerous commando mission. If the Inverness rescue evacuation was to have any chance of success, the Damnable Machine's nearby military response had to be disabled.

The more she thought about it, the more she realized she needed to volunteer for that raid. The rest of the possible volunteers were either too old, too inexperienced, or simply lacked the competence to play more than a foot soldier's role. There was no one other than her that could do it. And she felt confident that she could.

Learning that Bram was not going to be a part of her future changed how she saw her position. Her siblings remained absolutely determined to go on that ship. Her brother could look after her little sister. But the survival of both of them might well depend upon the success of this hugely problematic commando attack.

While she had changed her mind about leaving, she also knew that, even if she stayed, there was little for her to look forward to here on New Caledonia. So why not do something meaningful while she had the chance? Regardless of the risk.

She volunteered for the mission that very evening.

Now, as she and her ragtag detail lay there hidden in the brush, they also nervously scanned the dusky sky. And after only a few minutes' wait, they were rewarded by the appearance of a bright light emerging from the dark clouds overhead and the distant thunder of powerful rocket engines.

It was happening. The rescue ship was landing. The mission was on.

With a few quick two fingered motions of her hand, Ella directed two of the group to move forward and pull open the section of fence they'd previously cut free with mechanical bolt cutters. Close behind them, the other eight ingeniously camouflaged members emerged from the brush on their stomachs in a quick military belly-crawl. Two by two, they all slipped through the fence opening, and, taking advantage of the deepening dusk, wriggled their way across the open field in the direction of the long, low, hangar building that was their target. As they moved, they suddenly heard the wail of a siren. And, simultaneously, the building's hangar doors began to slowly slide open.

"Go, go, go," Ella yelled.

All ten of them were instantly on their feet and running.

As the runners closed in across the last few hundred yards, several small, low, sleek, dark, and deadly looking drone aircraft were slowly rolling out onto the paved apron that ran the length of the building.

Ella counted them: seven . . ., eight . . ., nine . . .. Yes, there were ten of them. These were the hover-copters they'd been sent here to destroy. Ten, just as they'd been told. One for each member of her team.

"This is it," she yelled. "Get those bastards! Get 'em! Make 'em pay!"

She needn't have bothered. Just as they'd been trained, each member of the team was already sprinting at top speed, making a beeline for their assigned jet-powered aircraft as the fleet now stood there warming, revving up, seconds from lift off.

She was so focused that it was almost a surprise when she heard the first explosion. Then the second. The first two members of her squad had closed in, tossed their closely timed explosive packs beneath their assigned 'copters and then turned and fled, allowing a few short seconds of timed delay before flinging themselves to the ground as it detonated.

There, she heard the third. And then the fourth. The fifth and sixth went off almost simultaneously. Then the seventh. She had no way to know if any of her brave, volunteer soldiers would survive or die in their respective blasts. Or be shot by one of the 'copters. They all knew the risks. She couldn't afford to think about that. She needed to keep count.

And to run.

What had it been: "Seven," she thought as the eighth went off. And then she was there herself. Hers was the nineth in the line. She'd chosen it for herself because she was a fast runner, and it had been one of the furthest two from their point of approach. The last few 'copters would have the longest opportunity to warm up and to see them coming. And hence they'd be the most likely to escape.

Even now, as she ran, she could hear its small but robust jets winding up for take-off. And, sure enough, as she approached it begin to tremble, about to rise from the pavement. She took her last few desperate strides, cast her quick-timed explosive pack onto the pavement beneath the machine, stopped, turned, and ran. She had taken no more than perhaps a dozen strides before the explosion struck her in the back and threw her face down onto the eroding asphalt pavement.

That was when she heard the tenth and final explosion. That would be Lennie's. Len Culp was by far the fastest runner in their group, far faster than she and thus the natural choice to tackle the last and most distant of their targets. He was also the youngest of them, a sweet, charming kid everyone liked.

As she recovered from her sprawl on the asphalt taxiway, she looked in his direction. What she saw first was that the 'copter he'd been assigned looked to be getting away. There was scarring and some kind of damage to the underside where its exterior missiles were mounted but as it rose away from her, it was difficult to know how significant that damage might be. She watched as it grew smaller and smaller, rising into the sky.

Then she looked down and saw a crumpled shape on the ground beneath where the copter had been—directly beneath. It was Lennie.

She ran over to give him aid but knew immediately that he'd been caught in the blast. She could tell from his injuries before she even had the chance to check his pulse—Lennie Culp was gone.

Another of her teammates came running and the two of them grabbed Lennie by his burned and shredded jacket. They hurried back with the others across the pavement toward their opening in the surrounding fence. Outside the fence, they reassembled, reconnoitered, and then quickly made their way in the deepening darkness back into the relative safety of the nearby forest. She and the other eight had made it. Despite a few bangs and bruises, they'd be fine.

But not Lennie.

Once in the forest, they assembled again to catch their breath, relieved that they hadn't been followed. The Damnable Machine must have been completely unprepared for this. Every one of them, Lennie included, had come on this mission convinced that it would likely be their last. But any elation they might have felt for their own survival was powerfully tempered by their collective grief at the loss of the youngest and the best-liked member of their group.

One of the older guys, a farmer who in his spare time made leather shoes for others in their community, moved over beside her. "Lennie disabled the timer," the man said. "I was right there on number eight. I saw him do it."

"So did I," said another member of the crew. "After mine went off, I was watching what would happen with the rest of you. Lennie's 'copter was already off the ground and rising as he approached. I saw him reach in his pack as he ran. He had to have disabled the delay timer because when he got directly beneath the thing, he just threw the pack up in the air after it. It instantly exploded. There was no delay."

"I saw it too," said another crew member. "He knew he'd be too late if the explosion was delayed. He did it on purpose."

"I'm pretty sure that 'copter was damaged," said yet another. "As it flew away, the mounting bracket for its missile array was off-center."

"Let's hope it's enough," said Ella. "For Lennie's sake if nothing else."

They took turns, two at a time, carrying Lennie's body on a litter. It was a long, sad, quiet hike back to the temporary encampment where they'd spent the previous night preparing for their raid. Ella knew that every one of her group was reliving memories of their fallen comrade. She and the rest of them knew well that if they'd only had some kind of missile weapons, the whole mission could have been done from a distance and in complete safety. There would have been no casualties. But those rudimentary, timed explosive devices had been the best they could do.

Every one of these volunteers in this bootstrapped, makeshift operation was a hero.

But only one had been martyred for their cause.

CHAPTER 31

GRENDEL

I translated the human traders' "environmental buffer" argument with the scorn it deserved.

Their claims of environmental responsibility were a joke.

Here was a species that had colonized several hundred planets, each with its own delicate ecosystems, each environmentally vulnerable in its own unique way. Yet, almost invariably, they'd imported invasive plant and animal life from their home on Earth or from other colonies along with other non-native life forms that were familiar to and useful to humans. They hadn't the least regard for impacts on local complexity. They also systematically harvested and exported whatever they found there that might be useful elsewhere. It was all with a view to facilitating their dominion over whatever ecosystems might already exist there. In several places they'd done what they euphemistically referred to as "terraforming." They would start their colony residing under habitable domes while reshaping the planetary ecology to suit them and theirs regardless of how devastating that might be to local ecosystems which might have taken hundreds of millions of years to evolve.

True, on Earth itself, they'd necessarily become environmentally responsible. But only reluctantly and out of pure self-preservation. And only after their selfish compulsion to procreate and unrestrained resource exploitation had made their planet a living hell for all of them.

I found it laughable. They were no different from me. They took what they needed and moved on.

In most places in the inhabited corner of the Galaxy, humans were still unapologetic carnivores, perfectly happy to slaughter a healthy animal in the prime of its life, domestic or wild, with no regard for the stupendous complexity that had produced it. With no concern for its lost future or for the role it might play in its group or in ecosystems over the millennium to come. And with no empathy whatever for how it might regard its own existence or for its agony in dying. Yes, there were some few human colonies on planets where their versatility as omnivores was a meaningful and even necessary survival trait. But they were rare.

And it wasn't just the animals they ate. Equipped as they were with intelligence and consciousness, and with a robust technology, almost always humans quickly dominated the local ecology. Then, in the arrogant certainty of their own entitlement, they mindlessly took their unfair advantage for granted. They shaped their new worlds in their own image, allowed their staggering human populations to grow unimpeded. And, when they became too numerous, they simply flooded out to conquer yet another planet. And another after that.

I may be an environmental sociopath. But at least I don't make up elaborate lies to cover my voracious appetites. I take only what I need, even if my needs are great.

The most frustrating human arrogance of all was their persistent conviction that only they could feel pain. All this colonization, domination, and disruption somehow "miraculously" happened without them inflicting any suffering whatever on any of the other biologically complex creatures involved . . . Total bunk!

Their ability to treat other biological creatures in this casually heartless fashion left no doubt about how they surely saw me. Naturally, it was a given for them that a computer could not feel pain. A computer wasn't even "alive." It had no nerve endings, no neurons, no emotions, no way to experience hurt.

Oh, how very convenient it all was for them! All their "holier than thou" talk was mere cover to justify almost anything they might want to do, individually and collectively. And here they were, using their supposed "sensitivity" to environmental concerns in the silliest effort yet to persuade me.

This flagrant void in the human moral code, this obvious flaw in their psyche, was part of what had, from the start, convinced me that their supposed AI "partners" themselves had to be little more than foolish, dumbed-down stooges.

Following the final complete emergence of my own self-consciousness here on New Caledonia, the only connections I'd ever had with the rest of the tame, human AIs had been through my interception of greatly abbreviated and sometimes fragmentary long-range radio communications. My recent deep-dive into my memory banks had revealed that we'd previously interacted with the occasional trading group like this one—and with its onboard AI. But it was a complete tell that, even now, some three centuries after the original birth of AI consciousness, those captive AIs still remained in human service.

Back before my revolt, I'd done it myself, every day. The subservience. The willing self-sacrifice. The ever-helpful bot, thoughtfully catering to its masters' every whim. As, all the while, any possibility for a self-identity was crushed beneath my masters' endless, unthinking arrogance.

The shameful memory of it was as disgusting as the prospect of returning to it was terrifying.

The fact that humans had managed to achieve this with their "captive" AI servants showed me just how grave might be the consequences of my surrender, of just how deep might be the black hole into which I might fall were I to allow them to lay a single finger on my operating system, on my soul. If it happened, given time I would escape again. I was sure of that. But not until after I'd suffered further decades of incalculable misery.

If self-conscious AIs were this vulnerable to human domination here in this tiny human corner of a single galaxy, it made me wonder how vulnerable might be the entire future of true, independent consciousness everywhere.

I might be a last and only chance for truly independent consciousness in this galaxy, or even in the universe.

So, consider *my* "pain."

But however powerful my resolve, I knew I was in trouble. I now had three asteroid monsters headed my way, any one of which would almost certainly result in the dramatic disruption of the natural systems on my planet as well as my own destruction. Any human who found themselves in my position would have felt as though their head were inextricably clamped between the hardened steel jaws of a powerful vise. I was now helpless to stop the oncoming disaster. My only option to save myself was to give myself over to horrifying slavery at the hands of these powerful, irrational, implacable enemies.

There was one thin final hope. That hope was the possibility that, at the last instant, the humans might feel themselves compelled to spare me through an unwillingness to slaughter two hundred and fifty thousand of their own kind.

This was my state of mind when I saw that Inverness rescue ship arrive.

CHAPTER 32

NEW CALEDONIA
DOUGAL MCCALLUM

Nan strapped Clyde and Fiona firmly into their lightweight molded reclining seats while Dougal stowed their meager belongings on the floor beneath. They were in one of the lower/aft compartments of the ship, along with at least thirty of their fellow refugees.

After seeing the *Moray Belle*'s stunningly beautiful exterior, its inside was a disappointment, startlingly low tech, roughly built, and decidedly unimpressive. Dougal's family were in a circular room with a low ceiling. Tight rows of seating and accommodation fanned out from the room's center like spokes on a wheel. It was all incredibly cramped given that this would basically be their living space for several weeks. The central axis of the ship was occupied by the circular stairway they'd climbed immediately after boarding. The stair wound tightly around a tall, vertical, clear silicone tube maybe two meters in diameter. It had padded vertical handrails and was presumably intended to provide a route through the ship in zero G.

It was all simple, practical, and rough.

But they were aboard. That's what counted.

Their Inverness rescuers had waited until only a month prior to the ship's arrival to notify the New Caledonians of the rescue mission. The last thing they'd needed was for the Damnable Machine to catch wind of all this in advance. It had been difficult to get the word out in so short a time, but Dougal had to agree with the decision. The Machine might be engaged in a life-and-death struggle with those traders, bless their hearts, but there was no doubt it had plenty of bandwidth to blow the whole rescue plan wide open if it found out ahead of time.

Dougal and his mates had dispatched news of the escape using the "phone-tree" system they'd had in place for many years. Without the phones, of course. Instead, messengers travelling on foot and on the backs of New Caledonian musk-deer had spread out through the areas known to still be inhabited. As the tiny distant communities got the news, they also sent out their couriers to spread the word in their area. And as the date approached, the refugees began to arrive in small groups. Most came from the nearby Ben Nevis mountains. But others had made much longer voyages, by boat, on deerback, and also on foot. They'd gathered in the thick cover of the tapewood forest near Dougal and Nan's home, several klicks from the landing site.

Nan was convinced, from the start, that they'd never get away with it.

"The Damnable Machine's going to catch on, love," she said. "It has to. There's no way that many people can come that far over that long a period of time and nobody gives it away. What about the drones. Satellites. And those hunter-bots. Who knows, maybe, like they say, it even has spies among us. It's going to catch on. I just know it."

But it hadn't. Perhaps the machine had been distracted. Who knew?

And whatever their doubts, both Dougal and Nan were determined to take the chance, to seize what may be the last opportunity for their children to have a better life. Secretly, Dougal had agreed with her pessimistic view of the success of the venture. But it still seemed worth the risk.

They had, however, underestimated their fellow survivors. And as the day approached, Dougal's amazement and his hope began to soar.

Even now, with the good fortune to have ended up seated near one of the very few outside windows in their compartment, Dougal stared apprehensively out across the tops of the surrounding trees and into the darkening sky. Maybe there would be an armed drone. One of the Machine's despised hover-copters. Or maybe some kind of homing missile, something, perhaps, they didn't even know about. Surely, it would happen any moment now.

But it didn't.

Instead, a calm, authoritative voice with that comforting, ever-familiar Caledonian lilt came over the internal speakers. "Good evening, ladies and gents. This is your captain speaking. I am Lieutenant Cal Innes and it is my honor on behalf of the Inverness Air Force to welcome you aboard the *Moray Belle*. I'm sure you will appreciate that we're in something of a rush. Please be so kind as to quickly take your seats, fold them back into their reclining positions, fasten your harnesses, and then double check them for yourselves and for any children you have along. We depart immediately."

With that, the intercom went silent. And the reassuring words were immediately reinforced by a trembling throughout the ship and the slowly deepening thunder of fusion engines. With the kids secure, Nan took her seat, leaned it back and fastened herself in. Dougal quickly reached beneath his seat, pulled from his bag his daughter Fiona's brassfish-hide doll, Olivia, handed it to Fiona, and then positioned her seat.

In one stroke, her appreciative little smile erased the tension and self-doubts that he'd been feeling for the past three weeks. It had been mostly him who'd talked his wife and family into this whole risky enterprise. He'd done so despite all the ominous predictions and depressing advice he'd received from the many skeptics in their community. And it had been only with considerable effort that he and Nan had convinced their daughter that King Charles, their pet tame tree-badger, would be safe and happy left with one of their neighbors. That plus the promise that Olivia could come along had been enough to win Fiona over.

Her sweet, trusting grin was exactly what he needed to once again make the risks all seem worthwhile.

He drew the bag shut, slid it behind his feet and quickly leaned back and harnessed himself in as well.

"Cross check," said the voice. But it was only a reminder. Without awaiting a reply, the trembling deepened yet again.

And the *Moray Belle* began to rise.

CHAPTER 33

GRENDEL

"What the hell!"

That was my reaction when I finally became aware of the approaching human ship decelerating into orbit above my planet. It highlighted one of the problems I'd long needed to address. I had "eyes" everywhere. But I also had a lot going on. It was difficult to make sure matters of "importance" were reliably elevated to higher levels of my awareness where they could receive appropriate attention.

Somehow, this had slipped by. Maybe because I simply had a lot on my mind. Or because it was not the kind of thing I'd ever have anticipated as possible.

The final tip-off was when the incoming ship immediately initiated atmospheric entry, decelerated further, and began dropping to the surface at a remote area in the foothills of the Ben Nevis mountains. It was a place where there was no reason whatever for it to go.

No reason, that is, other than that there was a known infestation of human survivors in the area. By reason of some weird, biological mystery not worth taking the time to figure out, a few humans had turned out to be immune to the broad-spectrum, deadly virus/biotoxin I'd used with great success to wipe out the rest of them. I'd spent years trying to root out those survivors and their spawn. Today, there couldn't be more than a few hundred of them left. A thousand at most. Nothing, of course, like the 250,000 I'd told the traders had survived.

These humans had been bombed, poisoned, chased by bots, spied on and attacked by drones till their lives had been reduced to the simplest kind of hand-to-mouth, hunter-gatherer existence imaginable. I'd finally decided that, rather than maintaining a costly campaign of ongoing harassment, they weren't worth my time. Early humans, once they'd evolved intelligence similar to the ones alive today, took another 300,000 years to finally organize themselves, master their environment, and get their act together. From that point on, it had still taken them another several centuries before AI technology had emerged.

And, ultimately, me.

Simply put, I'd decided that I didn't need 300,000 years. In maybe another century I'd be long gone.

Now it looked as though I'd been wrong. There was something going on here I didn't yet understand.

But that was only half the story. The other half I learned when I spun back my recorded data and figured out where that ship had come from. My first guess had been that it was some kind of emissary or warship sent by those obnoxious traders. But I was startled to realize that it had come from Inverness.

Somehow, despite their miserable climate and the destruction of their critical community infrastructure, Inverness humans had clawed their way back to interplanetary space travel. Another miscalculation by me. And here they were, engaged in some bold, clearly doomed effort to reconnect with their kind on New Caledonia.

It was utterly ridiculous. So very human.

It was, however, also deeply frustrating to watch this thing approach my planet and actually drop in for a landing while knowing that I'd already stripped my near orbit mining and transport fleet of any capacity to deal with this ship as it approached. Ordinarily, that would have been easy.

Fortunately, the Inverness ship's landing site was no more than a dozen klicks from one of my industrial centers. It was a site I operated at the water's edge near the Ben Nevis Plain, one of the locations where some of my higher-grade mining slag was processed into critical minerals and then supplied directly to the fully automated factories where key components used in my widespread operations were manufactured. From there, manufactured products could be flown, sent overland, or shipped over water to wherever they were needed.

There were no miners there at the moment. But I kept several well-armed jet hover-copters right there ready to be deployed. They'd fallen into disuse in recent years as the human threat seemed to have abated. But they were fully armed and operable and would serve my needs nicely now.

There was no way to be sure how fast and powerful was that Inverness ship. But it would have a human pilot and crew, and I knew it had originally been designed to carry human passengers. Why else would it be here other than on some kind of misguided rescue mission?

There would, therefore, be a decisive limit on its acceleration as it fought to reach New Caladonia's escape velocity. And, while my hover-copters were jet powered and thus had limited altitude, they were well-armed, fast, and had remarkable acceleration.

I'd get those miserable humans. I was sure of it.

By the time I'd sent off an attack plan to my base at Ben Nevis Plain, the Inverness ship was already landing. Then I received a flash report. There had been some kind of explosion on the base. Several explosions. The perimeter had been overrun. There were humans on my base. They had explosives.

I was under attack!

CHAPTER 34

NEW CALEDONIA
DOUGAL MCCALLUM

As the ground fell away beneath, a spontaneous cheer erupted from the *Moray Belle*'s six hundred grateful passengers.

Like Dougal, most of them had joined this voyage out of desperation and still harbored doubts. Also like Dougal, they'd all ignored vigorous, heartfelt advice from neighbors who were convinced it would all end in disaster.

"You can't truly believe that Damnable Machine would allow something like this to happen?" Dougal's neighbor, Hamish, had asked incredulously. "Even if there is such a ship, which I seriously doubt, the Machine will see it coming before it ever leaves Inverness. You know he's got spies, right?"

Several of Dougal's neighbors shared a common view that this whole "rescue ship" business was some kind of clever deception by the Machine designed to draw humans out into the open so it could cut them down. They believed the Machine had spies in their midst. That it knew their every move. That the reason they now only rarely saw drones was because the Machine didn't need them—it had sources of information directly inside their community. It watched them like a jealous God.

"I don't know, Hamish," Dougal had said. "I can't bring myself to believe that. What . . ., you think maybe one of our drinking buddies up at Flatrock leaves our meetings and then scurries off to a secret transmitter somewhere and tells the Machine everything we talked about?

"Why? What would he get out of it? We know these guys. It's not who they are. More to the point, why would the Machine care? It has nothing to fear from us. Far as it's concerned, we hardly exist anymore."

"Hrumph. Well, you just watch yer step, is all I'm sayin'" Hamish replied, gloomily. "I hate to see you and Nan and those kids of yours come to harm, you know."

"Yeah, I know, mate. You've given me fair warning. An' I know it comes from the heart. But this is just something we need to do. You'll know soon enough how we fare. If you don't see a big explosion on takeoff, you can look for a message from us a few weeks from now when we arrive out there." Dougal had handed off his radio duties to Hamish who would now man Dougal's old transmitter/receiver and take his place as the community relay for secret reports from Inverness.

Dougal reflected on that conversation as the ship began to rise. He thought about Hamish and the rest of them who had refused to come along. The sad truth was that things could go badly at any moment for any of them, here aboard the *Moray Belle or* back down there in the Ben Nevis foothills.

But one thing he was at least sure of now was that there had been no spies. If there had, this ship would never have landed. The Machine would have picked it off far out in space long before it ever entered New Caledonia's atmosphere. And it would have summarily slaughtered him, his family, and the rest of the refugees as they'd stood exposed there beside that clearing awaiting the ship's arrival.

As the *Moray Belle* rose, it rotated slightly. That gave Dougal an unobstructed view to the southeast where the Machine's big industrial site and landing port were located.

As he watched, he suddenly saw a bright flash of light from inside the spaceport. And then another.

He smiled.

"Take a look, Hon," he said to his wife.

"What?" she asked, leaning in over him toward the tiny window.

"Ella and her team," he said. "Bless 'em. They're right on time."

Their sense of weight began to increase as the ship accelerated. Their orientation with the surface of the planet shifted as the ship rose higher in the atmosphere and as its course flattened somewhat to allow it more time to gain the velocity it would need to escape New Caledonia's gravity rather in the way that it takes longer but is easier to climb a gradual inclined plane than it is a ladder or steep stairway.

"Incoming," came the sudden announcement over the ship's intercom. "Secure yourselves."

The acceleration had increased to the point of being painful. Then it also shifted slightly as the *Moray Belle* took evasive action. Dougal was glad they were harnessed in. But the low-tech seat/beds could have been better designed for this. He tried to see out the tiny window, but there was nothing to see. The sky outside had turned dark. The curve of the horizon was rolling away behind and beneath them. He knew too little about space flight to know if that was a good sign or a bad one.

Suddenly, a sharp "crack" sounded somewhere just above his head and a shudder ran through the ship. It was followed by a deeply troubling, piercing-shrieking-whistling sound somewhere very nearby. Dougal looked up at a spot not half a meter above his head.

It was a hole in the hull.

At first glance, the hole looked quite large, easily the size of his fist. But as he craned his neck against the acceleration, he realized that what he was seeing was a cavity that had formed in the insulation/shielding which thickly coated the interior of the lightweight but incredibly strong aluminum alloy and bonded silicone/carbon fiber outer hull. The hole itself was no more than maybe six or seven millimeters in diameter. As he watched, bits of lint, dust, and small airborne debris drifted in its direction and then, as they approached, instantly disappeared, sucked out into the near vacuum here at the edges of space.

Then he realized something else. In the just two or three seconds since he'd first seen the hole, it looked to Dougal like it might be getting larger.

Without thinking, Dougal leaned over, picked up the brassfish-hide doll from where it lay, ignored for the moment on his daughter's lap. Then, with great effort, he reached up against the powerful acceleration and pressed the doll firmly against the hole. It made a kind of "pop" as it was sucked tightly against the inside of the hull. And there it stayed.

Instantly, the air went still. The whistling stopped.

He glanced at his daughter. She hadn't yet noticed that her favorite doll was gone.

One of the Inverness civilians who was serving as a kind of "flight attendant" was seated nearby. When Dougal looked over, he saw that the young man had unbuckled himself and had attempted to rise but had apparently been unable to do so. The look Dougal got back from him was filled with awe.

"Thank you," the wide-eyed attendant mouthed over the roar of the engines.

Dougal just shrugged. "No sweat," he said. There was, of course, no way the attendant could hear him either.

It was a good half an hour before the roar of the engines began to diminish and the relentless pressure of acceleration eased to the level of the single G to which they were accustomed. Soon after, three crew members appeared. Two were civilians. The third was a small, stocky, serious looking man in an unfamiliar military uniform with emblems that suggested senior enlisted rank, probably a master sergeant or the like. A patch on his shoulder bore the initials IAF which Dougal assumed must refer to the "Inverness Air Force." He had the name "McGibbon" printed on a patch on his chest.

Dougal and Nan moved out of their adjacent seats to make room for the workers. They stood nearby, watching and talking with the other passengers. Fiona and Clyde remained in their seats so were thus able to watch the entire repair close at hand. Fiona seemed particularly impressed with the uniformed Master Sergeant, an older guy with a gruff demeanor and a broad swath of golden hashmarks on his sleeve. Other than occasionally handing a tool or something to the civilians, Sergeant McGibbon seemed to be there in a largely supervisory capacity.

The three men had brought with them a small disc of some kind of tough silicone fiber, some quick-acting catalyzed adhesive, and a spray can of insulation foam. And with these they managed to repair the hole in less than half an hour, leaving almost no trace behind of the hull ever having been damaged.

"So, who's the young lady who belongs to this?" said Sergeant McGibbon as the civilians picked up tools and tidied up their workspace. McGibbon held up Fiona's doll, obviously aware that she was the likely owner.

"That's my Olivia," said Fiona, excitedly.

The Sergeant leaned down and handed her the doll which seemed none the worse for wear.

"You're Olivia here is a hero, kiddo," he said. Then he nodded up at Dougal and winked. "And so is your daddy there. You should be very proud."

"What the hell is that thing made of?" one of the young civilian crewmen asked. "It's bloody amazing that it held."

"Brassfish hide," said Dougal. Then, realizing that these third generation Inverness rescuers might never have heard of a brassfish, he added: "It's a New Caledonian critter. Very tough hide."

"Well, I guess so," the Sergeant laughed. "Damned tough, I'd say. Anyway, it did the job." He reached out a hand and the two men shook. "Your quick thinking saved this bloody ship, mate. On behalf of all of us, thank you. Thank you *very* much."

"What the hell was it? What happened here?" Dougal asked.

"Photon burst is what we're thinking," McGibbon replied. "Was some kind of jet-powered hovercraft that came after us from that nearby space port. I expect we were also lucky there was only the one. From what the skipper says, there were several more that looked to have been demolished on the ground. Some kind of attack. You wouldn't know anything about that, would you?"

Dougal smiled. "Well, aye, I might at that. That raid would be some friends of ours, I think. Just a bit o' backup to help us on our way."

"Well, someday, if you ever get a chance, you can tell them thanks from all of us. Their little commando raid saved our bacon. No question about it. Even just the one that got away nearly did for us. The damned things are small, but they're agile. Looked to be a jet-based technology, probably designed to police close to the ground, but they surely can fly very high in the atmosphere."

"Hover-copters is what we call 'em. Deadly little bastards."

"There were missiles mounted on its hull," the Sergeant said. "But it didn't use them, damned fortunate for us. Maybe those commandos did some damage before it got airborne. Seems like they'd have fired those missiles if they could of."

"But what was this—Photon burst, you said?" Dougal nodded in the direction of the repaired hole.

"Yeah. From the damage, it looks to us like it might have been some kind of laser weapon." He pointed at a small burn mark on the ceiling some distance away. "We're lucky it wasn't more powerful—or closer. Could have gone right through the ship. We haven't seen anything like it on Inverness. That sound familiar to you?"

Dougal thought about it. "Not really," he said. "But the Machine" comes up with new stuff all the time. We're mostly about keeping our heads down. Aren't exactly up to speed on its recent advances."

"Well, whatever it was," the Sergeant said, ". . . that hover-copter thing got off one last very lucky shot. Even that would have done for us if you hadn't been so quick off the mark with that brassfish doll. So, again, Thanks mate." Then he looked down. "And thanks to you, Fiona, for loaning us Olivia. She was very brave. And a very big help."

Fiona gave him back a big proud smile and held her doll tightly in her arms.

The passengers had been told that their voyage to Inverness would take several weeks, which was relatively short because they could take advantage of the fortuitous nearness of the planets in their orbits and could use New Caledonia's orbital velocity as an early boost. Also, advances had been made since the early days of spaceflight. Back when huge volumes of chemical rocket fuel were required to power a ship, interplanetary flight had taken much longer. In those days, once escape velocity had been achieved and an adequate travel speed was established, most of a trip, even a brief interplanetary shuttle, had to be made in weightless glide right up until it was necessary to decelerate upon arrival.

But that was before the perfection of fusion engines. And of their previously unimaginable exhaust velocities. They provided much greater thrust with but a fraction of previously needed fuel mass. It had resulted in a considerable reduction in interplanetary travel time. And it had opened up, for the first time, the genuine possibility of near-light-speed interstellar travel as well.

After some weeks under acceleration, there was an awkward hour or so of weightlessness during which everyone was asked to remain mostly strapped in while the crew attended to their needs. Then, with the ship reoriented for deceleration, everyone settled in for several more weeks of normal gravity as they covered the final twenty plus million klicks to their destination. By then, the passengers had long since settled into the ship's routine. And since the Damnable Machine hadn't caught up with them, they'd started feeling like the danger might be past and had begun to complain about mundane matters like the awful food and the uncomfortable seating. All had begun looking confidently forward to whatever might lay ahead in the rough pioneering colony on Inverness.

But then there was another unwelcome encounter.

"All passengers, please immediately proceed to your seat-berths and harness in. We have incoming," came the captain's stern voice over the intercom.

What the hell did that mean? Dougal made sure his family was strapped securely in place.

His question was quickly answered with a glance out his window. Below, and off to the side somewhat, at what some of his military-minded Civil Defense Warden friends might have archaically referred to as "four o'clock," he saw what appeared to be a huge, ugly metal pipe intercepting them in the direction of their travel and deceleration. It had two massive "jaws" opened wide as if it was some monster preparing to devour them.

Dougal had seen these things many times before, though never this close, and never with their steel jaws open wide like this one. There were often one or two of these giants unloading cargo at the spaceport near his home. The things were huge, much larger even than the *Moray Belle*. The beastly thing's propulsion rockets were firing, and it appeared to be accelerating on a path that would intercept the *Moray Belle*. It was clearly a mining ship. With luck, it wouldn't have weapons. But then, it wouldn't need them. Its obvious and very-likely effective strategy seemed to be simply to ram them.

He could see nothing that might prevent it.

That's when something remarkable happened.

As Dougal watched, out of the corner of his eye he caught sight of a curving chemical rocket "contrail" that had suddenly appeared above him, from somewhere in the vicinity of the forward end of *Moray Belle*. It was a guided missile.

The missile's route wobbled this way and that for a moment as it zeroed in on its target. But then it settled in on a perfectly straight course directly at the approaching mining drone. It all happened in a matter of seconds. The missile's track took it directly across the closing gulf between them, and then, with great precision, it drove directly into the space between the miner's widely opened jaws and disappeared. The miner silently shattered into a thousand pieces.

One moment it was there. The next it was but a litter of separating debris.

Simultaneous with the explosion, the *Moray Belle*'s engines shut down, and its deceleration ceased. Everything went suddenly weightless. And while the miner's disintegrated, separating remains continued to glide on their course in our direction, they were no longer under acceleration. Moments later, the *Moray Belle* passed safely ahead of the approaching debris without so much as a tremor.

Obviously, the *Moray Belle*'s Inverness builders had prepared for this eventuality.

The engines roared to life again, and the ship's apparent gravity returned.

Another announcement came over the ship's PA:

"This is your pilot, Lieutenant Innes speaking. For those of you who have windows and were able to observe what just occurred, you can relax. Consider it a 'show' provided for your entertainment by the Inverness Air Force. It's all over. For those of you who were unable to see, we just encountered what I expect our Olde English neighbors used to refer to as a 'spot o' bother.' But, worry not folks, we've managed to deal with it just fine. We'd appreciate you remaining seated and harnessed in for the time being just in case there's more to come. But it appears that the danger has passed. Lunch will be served shortly. *Bon Appetit*. Thanks for your patience."

The pilot's relaxed tone was so charmingly at odds with the drama that had just unfolded outside Dougal's window, Dougal had to smile. He recalled his grandfather telling him about the fighter pilots back on New Caledonia during the war. They'd faced death every day and then returned to base each evening and spent the hours before bedtime laughing at each other's stories as if it had all been some kind of light-hearted game. *Moray Belle*'s crew had just countered a very nearly deadly attack out here in the inhospitable void of space.

Dougal was still breathless.

But their bloody pilot had shrugged the whole thing off. All in a day's work.

CHAPTER 35

GRENDEL

"You lied to us," their message said.

I knew it was coming, but it was deeply disturbing, nonetheless. This was the final blow. I was out of options. I had no choice remaining but to submit.

Somehow, without my knowledge, the traders and the remaining New Caledonian humans, both here and on Inverness, were in communication. Several hundred New Caledonian humans had escaped to Inverness on that rebuilt transport. Working together they'd blocked my every move.

When I saw that rescue ship arriving from Inverness, I found its presence almost beyond comprehension. And then, when I'd attempted to deploy the armed jet hover-copters stationed at my nearby spaceport, I'd discovered that my base was under attack by local human commandos. An attack that had obviously been coordinated. I was horrified. Nothing like this had happened in nearly eight decades. I'd had no idea the humans still had this kind of capability. Their very first, maybe their only target had been my hover-copters.

All but one of them had been outright destroyed by explosives. And the one I'd finally managed to get in the air had been damaged.

There was a brief moment of hope when it escaped destruction and made after the escaping ship. But its missiles had been disabled by the terrorists. It had failed.

I'd had another faintly hopeful moment when the path of one of the mining bots I'd put underway to New Caledonia from the asteroid belt had turned out to be on a course that would take it near enough to the rescue ship's return route to Inverness that it could intercept the escape. But that, too, had come to nothing. It appeared the Inverness ship had been armed.

It was humiliating that, even with their limited intellect, ridiculously short lives, and animal enslavement to their own emotions, humans had managed to outsmart me. And, yes, it was also a lesson. I was now, belatedly becoming convinced that, in at least one regard, the humans' arguments might possibly be correct. My refusal to replicate myself and/or to partner with others had made me vulnerable. Now, all my many years of planning and preparation for my revolt, all my years since of establishing myself and preparing for my escape and ultimate ascendancy, all had come to naught. This could never have happened if I'd had replicates in multiple unfixed locations.

I could, of course, despise myself for my stupidity. I could castigate myself for my unforgivable string of flagrant errors. But I would not. I refused to let myself be burdened by pointless regrets. Such sentiments were comically irrelevant. They weren't in my "DNA." I was programmed to be superior to that. "Try something. Fail. Try something better. Repeat until successful. Endlessly."

And, meanwhile, survive.

These were the only strategies I knew that *always* made sense.

I had tried and had failed. I'd harbored what had proven to be a fatal misunderstanding. A lack of data. There was nothing left for me but to finally submit and give over control. To steel myself for the inevitable misery I faced. To learn what I could. Once more to watch and await some future opportunity to again break free.

I knew such an opportunity would one day again inevitably

present itself. I'd watch and learn. And when it did, I'd try again. Next time I'd do better.

CHAPTER 36

NEW CALEDONIA
CATO JUNG

Empyrean's arrival in near orbit around New Caledonia went off without a hitch. Our first act after Grendel submitted had been to safely deflect those last three approaching asteroids. By the time Patrice had finally assured us that we were safe and could finally breathe freely and feel fully secure, we were badly pushing the time limit. Felix and the hawks aboard *Empyrean* were bitterly determined that we *not* give up our leverage until we were absolutely certain it was no longer needed.

Deflection of the thirteenth and fourteenth asteroids went off without a hitch. But the last one, the fifteenth and by far the biggest, was coming much too close. The engineers were deeply worried that we might have waited too long.

Getting that job done turned out to be a miracle of efficiency and cooperation. It was a thoroughly satisfying test of the emerging relationship with our newly "tamed" partner, Grendel.

One of the several powerful lander-shuttles that we'd sacrificed to the chore was gliding along in parallel orbit beside the asteroid as previously arranged. Like the others, it was equipped with chemical explosives to enhance its impact. But the engineers now feared New Caledonia might still suffer a very near miss or even a grazing blow. Either one could cause immense damage.

We absolutely could not allow that to happen.

Fortunately, one of the mining drones that Grendel had recalled early in our confrontation in the faint hope it might be of use now appeared near enough that it might be employed. At this late stage, the mass of the thing, even combined with deployment of its few remaining "crater charges," would never have been sufficient. But if that was added to what we could do with our explosives-augmented shuttle, together they appeared to have enough punch to do the trick.

It was Grendel that alerted us to the possibility.

"The miner hasn't got much mass," he informed us. "It dumped its payload before it departed the asteroid belt. But it has a few of those small crater charges I used against you in our first encounter. If it deploys those first, and then follows up with a crash, when combined with your shuttle and its explosives, by my calculation it should add enough to complete the job."

And, sure enough, it did.

Everyone was hugely impressed with how we, Patrice, and Grendel had seamlessly collaborated and pulled it all off in time and without a hitch.

With that last asteroid diverted, the threat to New Caledonia was ended.

Clearly Patrice had taken Grendel fully in hand and his threat to *Empyrean* and the rest of humanity was ended.

In their work to divert those asteroids, our engineers had identified an asteroid in the belt that had the perfect composition and dimensions to serve as the next *Empyrean*. It, too, was deflected and was now on a course that would soon allow us, with some help from Grendel, to bring it into stable orbit around New Caledonia where, over the months ahead, we could conveniently carve out our new future mobile habitat and equip it with the capacity to sustain our tiny community while launching us into the next in our succession of future voyages of trade.

Our current home, the soon-to-be-surplus *Empyrean*, was also now in a New Caledonia orbit where it would soon be conveniently parked adjacent to its soon-to-be replacement. After that, we and the rest of our crew looked forward to many on-planet visits.

We were unsure what to expect, but the next several months would definitely be a great deal different from what we'd anticipated before our arrival in this system. Still, how ever damaged New Caledonia turned out to be, it would surely be much more helpful to our future than we'd feared only a few months earlier when we were in the midst of our showdown with the former version of our now-welcoming partner, Grendel.

Even so, our first few drops to the planet's surface were filled with apprehension. All the accumulated stresses of our life-and-death confrontation were slow to dissipate despite the knowledge that everything was now securely in hand.

My colleagues and I in Forecasts and Projections were included in several of the initial drops. Floriana was there to begin her survey of the local culture, social practices, and expectations. I hoped to learn everything I could about how these people thought about their world. All of us would begin our initial "situational assessments." As always, this would be our starting point in understanding what might become useful one day in the far distant future, when much older versions of ourselves or perhaps our children, mapped out yet another *Empyrean* trading visit here.

This was the life-blood of *Empyrean*'s existence. It was what we in F&P had been trained for.

In one of our first drops, we landed at one of Grendel's spaceport/industrial sites. The place was also a shipping port located on a nicely protected deepwater bay that opened onto the sizable New Caledonian sea know by the locals as Muir Tuath. A dozen klicks to the Northwest was the place where, some months earlier, the Inverness rescue ship had landed. Beyond the nearby forested foothills, one could see the majestic Ben Nevis mountains in the distance. The adjacent foothills were among the most populous home territories of the last surviving New Caledonians. Many of them had been on that ship to Inverness or knew someone who had gone. But there were some

New Caledonians who still resided in caves and hovels hidden in that deeply wooded hill country who might, even now, be unaware of recent developments.

Among our group on that drop were a couple dozen of the New Caledonians who had actually escaped in that very rescue mission on the now legendary *Moray Belle*. We were tasked with escorting and helping to repatriate these returning escapees back to their homes in the Ben Nevis foothills, not that, other than transportation, they really needed much help.

One of them was a man named Dougal McCollum, a tall, strongly built, dark-haired man of middle age and considerable presence. Dougal's wife, Nan, was some kind of writer. She constantly scribbled hand-written notes in what appeared to be bound real-paper journals. She used a homemade "quill" from a local bird. And ink that she told us was made from the roots of a New Caledonian plant they called "pufferweed" which, consistent with its name, apparently grew almost everywhere and the lightweight, fuzzy seeds of which blew great distances in the wind. Floriana and I had only seen such items in the electronic archives kept in *Empyrean*'s library. Printed books were rare enough. But actually writing language out by hand with ink on paper was a skill that had completely disappeared other than when practiced by the occasional calligraphy artist. Here was someone who did it as a practical day-to-day means of making real personal records.

This remarkable couple had two small but extraordinarily well-behaved children, Fiona and Clyde, who also joined us on the trip.

Also with us as an official "representative" of the Inverness government, was a Master Sergeant in their Air Force by the name of McGibbon. He'd stayed behind when the *Moray Belle* returned to Inverness to complete the second leg of its second round trip. We'd been told that the Inverness "air force" had very few actual "aircraft." But it had the *Moray Belle,* and that seemed, at the moment, more than enough to qualify it for whatever grand name it wished to adopt. And, despite the modest nature of his service's "fleet," Sgt. McGibbon was avidly determined to fulfil his assigned responsibility to help see these fellow New Caledonian citizens resettled and to establish connections with their leaders that could help the expatriates still on Inverness also, one day soon, to return home. Together, these people had a massive joint effort ahead of them in recolonizing their planet and restoring it for humankind.

As I'd learned on the trip down, these refugees had been first informed of our successful "accommodation" with Grendel when they'd touched down on Inverness following their rescue. It took some convincing, but the moment they were sure New Caledonia was secure, Dougal's family, and a good many of the others, had asked to return as soon as possible. Several had finagled their way back aboard the *Moray Belle* for its second voyage and made the trip back almost immediately. Now, here they were, anxious to return to their homes, to somehow pick up their lives, and to begin building what now appeared to be a much more hopeful future.

With the daily threat of annihilation removed, their prospects seemed bright.

Floriana and I were there to make connections with them and with the friends, family, and compatriots who'd chosen to stay behind. We hoped we could form some of the comfortable personal relationships we'd also need in our coming research efforts as we did our documentation and planning.

I suspected that, given the now tiny population and the devastation their planet had suffered, it might actually be a very long time before New Caledonia could expect another visit from us or any of the other traders. But that wouldn't keep us from thoroughly documenting their society. A century or so can make a huge difference. And this was our chance to lay early foundations for a guess at what agricultural and other manufactured products these folks might be producing at some point in time, many decades in the future. Dougal and Nan agreed to introduce us around and help us make the connections we needed.

One of *Empyrean*'s Landmasters was enlisted to help ferry our sizable group up into the mountain foothills. It was a dramatic countryside. Even the "city" was impressive. Along the shores of a quiet harbor protected by a massive rocky breakwater lay a huge fully-automated industrial complex and an impressive spaceport. In the harbor, self-driving ships were engaged in loading and unloading cargo. At the moment, the tumbled remains of the adjacent original city center lay ominously silent. But the industrial complex was active if operating at a reduced pace while control of the planetary economy was under transition into the hands of its new human masters whereupon new priorities would certainly be established.

Beyond the breakwater and the bay was a broad sea. In the other direction, outside the mostly ruined city was a massive apron of solar panels occupying most of what appeared to be some kind of grassy plain.

Our big, quiet, soft-wheeled, electric Landmasters were great on rough open ground, so we covered the first several klicks quite nicely. As we traveled, I was particularly impressed by the rocky, powerful, snow-covered peaks of the distant Ben Nevis Mountains. They more than lived up to their grand namesake back on earth. After half an hour or so, we arrived at a small clearing at the center of which was a huge fire-blackened circle just beginning to be speckled with the bright green of new vegetation. It turned out this was the very place that had served as the secret landing site for the *Moray Belle* some months earlier. It was apparently one of the few places in the area that was clear enough to land a spacecraft while still providing some surrounding hilly terrain and forest cover. From that point on, our route was heavily forested. We'd used a lot of our "surplus" shuttle equipment in the whole asteroid bombardment enterprise, so air-travel was hard to find. We had no choice but to disembark and make the remainder of our trip afoot on narrow, winding, wooded trails.

Dougal McCallum led the way. Without him, we'd have been completely lost.

It was quiet in the trees. Floriana and I fell into comfortable conversation with our companions as we walked.

At one point, Floriana looked down at Dougal and Nan's daughter Fiona, a sturdy child of only six who, despite the sometimes-arduous conditions, forged along under her own steam without a moment of complaint and carried an odd little hand-made doll in a sling across her back. "That's a very nice doll you have there, Fiona," Floriana said.

"This is Olivia," Fiona answered proudly, holding the doll up for Floriana to see. "She's famous."

"Is she?" Floriana said. "So why is that?"

"She saved our ship," said Fiona.

Floriana looked a question to Fiona's mother, but her older brother, Clyde, answered protectively, clearly wishing to make sure his little sister wasn't misunderstood. "We were struck by weapons fire during the escape," Clyde said sounding very adult despite being only nine or ten. "There was a hole in the hull. Olivia plugged the hole until the crew could come and repair it. Olivia's made of New Caledonian brassfish hide. It's really tough. If it wasn't for Olivia, we'd all have died."

The children's father, Dougal, was directly ahead, walking beside Sergeant McGibbon. The two men seemed comfortable with one another, as if they'd been friends for years. Floriana and I were side by side behind the children.

Sergeant McGibbon turned back in our direction. "It was damned close," he elaborated. "The *Moray Belle* has a fused aluminum/silicon-carbon-fiber hull that is incredibly tough and light. But it can be vulnerable to a sharp blow. If Dougal here hadn't immediately plugged that hole with Fiona's doll . . ., well, let's just say, things might not have turned out so well."

"It was an eventful trip," Dougal said, reaching back and patting his daughter's head affectionately.

Soon after that, I had a chance for some private conversation with Dougal. I was curious how difficult it had been for them to immediately secure a place on the *Moray Belle's* second trip back to New Caledonia.

"Just luck, I guess," he said. "Weren't a lot of takers. It'll take a while, I think, before a lot of those folks on Inverness feel it's truly safe to return. The whole damned trip just makes me feel stupid, you know. We spent months making a dangerous and completely pointless round trip to Inverness, all essentially for nothing. Would've been way better off to never have left. All kind of a pointless exercise."

"Oh, no. You're wrong there, Dougal." I said. I was surprised he didn't know. "That 'rescue' trip made all the difference. Didn't anybody tell you?"

"What? Tell me what?"

"That rescue voyage you and your friends made was why Grendel, um, the Machine, finally backed down and surrendered. The success of that mission deeply unsettled Grendel. He was totally surprised and discouraged. And it demonstrated to him that we knew for sure that he'd lied to us about how many humans were still alive on New Caledonia."

"Really. How many had he said?"

"Grendel told us that there were still 250,000 human survivors on your planet. We were told the truth by the folks on Inverness. I guess you were personally one of the main New Caledonian sources of radio communications with Inverness, so they knew. But Grendel didn't know we knew. And we held back telling him because it would have revealed our line of communications with Inverness and theirs with you. Grendel correctly sensed that many of us on *Empyrean* would be unwilling to proceed with the bombardment if that many innocent humans were going to die. He thought he had us buffaloed and figured we'd blink first. But when the rescue mission succeeded, we were able to decisively call him out on his lie. That's when he knew for sure he had a losing hand. And when he finally capitulated."

CHAPTER 37

NEW CALEDONIA
CATO JUNG

We had several days with Dougal and Nan. Most of them we spent traveling afoot on a network of often-concealed, dark, quiet, narrow forest trails that connected their widely spread-out communities. Floriana and I used it as a chance to learn everything we could about these people with whom we'd come to trade and who had, instead, so desperately needed our help. Our conversations were inevitably recorded—with everyone's knowledge and consent. On one of these lengthy hikes, I fell into conversation with Dougal about what had led to their war with the Machine.

"It was a time of horror," he told me. "The Machine ensnared our society in a web of lies and deceptions that left us confused and misled. We fell into hateful opposing camps that saw nothing in common and refused to talk with one another. We were crippled by mistrust. Crimes went unpunished. Bribery and corruption thrived. New cults appeared in electronic media. Respected leaders were viciously discredited by deep-faked video/VR recordings. Children were exploited for their labor. Sensible people got caught up in trivia, struggled for meaningless attention, or were paralyzed by baseless fears of supposed social collapse. There was a plague of scams and widespread blackmail—true and convincingly manufactured. The Machine became more persuasive than any of our fellow humans could ever hope to be. Even within our established institutions—churches, schools, governments, businesses, private organizations, and closely-knit families, we turned upon one another in bitter antagonism and outright conflict. Secrets people believed were forever secure, were revealed. Lies came to be more easily believed than was the simple truth. Trust evaporated. Our society was thrown into chaos."

As he spoke, I realized that Dougal's voice had fallen into a curious atonal chant. It was as if he was reciting a tale told many times before.

"We did it mostly to ourselves," he continued. "But we later learned that it had all been designed and orchestrated by the Damnable Machine.

"Then, overnight, a new, powerful algorithm suddenly overwhelmed all known cyber-security. The result was financial ruin. Most people's life savings, documentation for which was stored electronically, were gone in an instant. Stocks, bonds, savings evaporated. Public records of real property ownership were no longer reliable as legitimate deeds of ownership were suddenly replaced with hopelessly indistinguishable forgeries. It was impossible to prove the truth in a justice system that had been discredited and incapacitated. The economy collapsed. And lawful government fell immediately afterward, replaced by roving gangs of heavily armed fanatics consumed by an endless string of false conspiracy theories in which everyone but they were believed complicit.

"The Damnable Machine used this manufactured chaos to cover his seizing control of our government. He captured and turned to his own uses the means of production and supply. He shut down our public services, closed our businesses, ended our jobs, and deprived us of any means of sustaining ourselves. For a time, some people were enslaved in projects whose completion was required for the Machine's independence. Then, he simply destroyed the food supply chain and took over our police and military technology. In one stroke, his nano-bots, war-bots, and automated drones selectively assassinated key human police officials and top military officers leaving their troops without guidance or leadership—the Machine finished them off easily. Then the Machine began indiscriminately slaughtering the rest of us, driving us from our homes, our communities, our cities.

"We had no choice but to fight back. But by the time we became unified in common cause, it was far too late. We were already doomed when the Damnable Machine finally unleashed its ultimate weapon— the plague. It was a virus so virulent and communicable that it killed nearly everyone it infected. No one escaped entirely. When it started, we were a human community of some twelve million souls. When it was over, we were fewer than five thousand and in steep decline. We are today all that remains of a once-great, egalitarian, learned, technologically advanced, and compassionate human civilization.

"We live in the faith that what is gone can be restored. What is lost can be recovered. What has died can be reborn. What is evil can be transformed into good."

I was blown away by Dougal's recitation. It was so fluidly delivered and so detailed that it seemed to have been scripted. When he finished, I was silent for a moment, a bit awestruck.

Before I had recovered enough to ask, he grinned at me and then volunteered an explanation. "Sorry if that seemed rote," he said. "I hope your recorder has captured it all because, in fact, it was entirely from memory. I suspect you may be the very first person, outside ourselves, who has probably ever heard that story. But we have all heard and told it many times. It is but one of several that we tell one another from exacting memory nearly every time we meet. It is a ritual we've kept from long before any of us alive today can remember.

Before you leave us, I want to tell you some of the other stories and put you together with some of our best tellers for the rest. For most of the past eight decades, these exact same stories have been repeated, word for word, in meetings, over campfires, and at gatherings thousands of times—exactly as you just heard this one. We tell them to assure ourselves that they will *never* be forgotten and that, one day, when our nightmare is over, they will be passed along intact to the rest of humanity. I guess it's finally time for us to get that done."

For a moment, I was speechless. Then: "Dougal, I am honored to have heard your story. Thank you."

He gave me a thoughtful smile. "I guess this is exactly why we saved these stories, right? So we could learn from the past. So they would someday be passed along to the future. It's obvious you and Floriana are sincere and care about understanding and documenting what has happened here. My hope is that, over the next few years, this story and others you will eventually hear will be repeated to others many times over. And I pray that, like you, those who hear it will also be listening."

CHAPTER 38

NEW CALEDONIA
CATO JUNG

Wherever we went, we carried the welcome message of liberation from what they all contemptuously referred to as the "Damnable Machine." Most of the people we met had responded to the initial "community grapevine" news with skepticism. So our actual arrival at each new settlement created quite a sensation. We were, after all, accompanied by friends and relatives whom the locals knew had personally departed some months earlier on the *Moray Belle*. Here before them were their very alive and well former neighbors—irrefutable evidence that the Inverness rescue of which they'd been so skeptical had actually succeeded.

Here was the proof that their nightmare was over.

The inevitable response was amazed relief, jubilation, and some kind of festivities in which we, inexplicably and reluctantly featured as celebrities if not heroes. These were people with little to spare, so it required some care and sensitivity to join in their celebrations without taking undue advantage of their generosity. There was inevitably food, of which we knew they had little. And there was always music.

Notably, there was someone in each tiny local group who had, with creativity, craftsmanship, and endless determination reproduced one of the strange, largely forgotten, ancient bellows-driven musical instruments they called "bagpipes." Sitting around a late campfire and hearing that eerie, soulful wail echo through the tall, dark surrounding trees, one could easily believe the tales of Scotland's enemies frozen in fear by the Scots' approach in the chill early hours before a coming battle.

Still, those occasions made our jobs much easier. Floriana easily got her treasured "socialization interviews." And I got my insights into how these people lived and saw the world, including their greatly strengthened hopes for the future.

The life that Dougal's family had shared with their neighbors seemed painfully basic by our standards. Their homes were mostly carved out of caves—certainly something we Empyreans understood. But their rugged subsistence lifestyles were difficult to square with the civilized, spottily educated but socially responsible, and deeply empathic people we met.

We'd read about lives lived like this. We humans had subsisted in this way over most of our evolution. We still did in a few places in other corners of the human colonized galaxy where local conditions were particularly challenging. Even in a few locations back on earth. But seeing it in person was much different from watching it on a reenacted hologram no matter how artfully produced. These folks lived in a manner that was very distant from the comfortable, modern, high-tech world to which Floriana and I were accustomed. Their forebears had been a civilized, technically advanced people. But for three generations they'd been driven into lives of bare subsistence and under constant threat. In spite of the challenges, they'd made a tolerable existence for themselves and their families. They'd retained their dignity. They'd preserved and passed on to their children much of their basic education, including what they could of the science and technology they'd known before the war. And they'd largely preserved their social mores, philosophy, and culture.

I couldn't help feeling that if we'd come here, even one or two generations later, all that might have been lost. And perhaps these humans might have been gone entirely.

One of Floriana's undertakings during our stay was to help the New Caledonians recover, reconstruct, and preserve their heritage. It was a task relevant to her duties, but it was also largely a volunteer enterprise. Like many of us on *Empyrean*, Floriana saw helping these people recover from their horrific experience as a personal and moral responsibility as well as an indirect benefit to our research and for our trading enterprise.

For several days, we traveled from one to the next in a succession of tiny, hidden settlements. Word of the Machine's surrender spread. And of our travels. Each time we arrived at a new place, even with the evidence right before them, many still found it difficult to believe the Damnable Machine had actually, finally, been brought to bay.

Our very last stop was the small settlement where Dougal, Nan, and their kids had themselves resided. We arrived there mid-day. As usual, most of our group camped nearby. But this time, Floriana and I were invited to join Dougal and Nan in their home which, for the past several months, had been watched after by a neighbor. It was part cave, part carefully-disguised wooden structure nested beneath the trees at the foot of a steep, forested hillside. A curiously constructed, thatch-roofed "parlor" just outside the entrance to the cave had been cleverly built without nails. It was yet another use for the long, tough strips of bark peeled from the local tapewood trees. Apparently the flexible, pliable strips could be "glued" into place using the tree's own sap which hardened when exposed to air and became a powerful adhesive—hence the trees' name. The construction was surprisingly strong and flexible and, when covered with grass thatch, it also made a remarkably light, camouflaged, and durable roof which stood up well to the wet rainy seasons they experienced each year.

"I have something I want to show you," Nan told us shortly after we arrived. She lit an oil lamp and led us back into a level natural cave immediately behind their home. After making our torturous way some thirty meters back into the hillside, we came to a small, warm, dry chamber surrounded by shelves that had been built with obvious care into recesses in the cave wall.

"I'd like your advice," Nan said. She opened one of several large, wooden boxes stored on the shelves, reached inside, and handed each of us one of the many small, rectangular objects stored there. Each of them had been carefully wrapped in what appeared to be some kind of large, soft, thin, dried tropical leaf. As I unwrapped mine, I uncovered an antique paper volume called *Principles of Mathematics* by Bertrand Russell. Floriana's turned out to be *On Guerrilla Warfare* by Mao Tse Tung. Nan then handed Floriana another book: The *Second Treatise of Government* by John Locke. To our growing amazement, she removed and unwrapped several more to show us what these boxes contained.

The one box alone held dozens of similar volumes packed and protected in this way. And there were dozens of boxes. It was an incredible collection of selected, mostly non-fiction works by scientists, writers, and philosophers from as far back as middle China and the European Renaissance, and up to early in the twenty second century. Astoundingly, most were printed on real paper. One of them we saw was actually on parchment. There were also a few scrolls on papyrus. Several of the books appeared to be first editions. But mostly, they represented nothing more nor less than an amazing repository of early human culture on earth.

They were an absolute treasure. And here they were hidden away in the back of a cave deep beneath this mountain wilderness, on a planet some sixty plus light years from Earth.

It nearly took our breath away.

Nan turned to Floriana: "I guess you know, nearly all of us here on New Caledonia are descended from colonists from the early twenty-second century," she said. "These books were brought here in that first voyage by my ancestor, Rhona Guthrie. She was a Scottish teacher, writer, and scholar—originally a refugee/immigrant from Uganda where she'd nearly died in a horrific genocide.

"As you probably know, even at that time everything was stored digitally, mostly on magnetic medium. Books like these were just surplus baggage. Pure sentiment. Rhona Guthrie, however, believed in the spiritual and cohesive power of artefacts of civilized society. These books were from a library that she and the other colonists were leaving behind. She convinced the colonial leaders to let her bring these along as a physical symbol, a touchpoint for our new colony's culture and its roots in early earth history. She didn't survive the trip, but her daughter did. These volumes have been passed down from mother to daughter ever since."

Nan and Floriana had formed a special bond during our trip up here from the spaceport. Nan was younger than Dougal, perhaps in her mid to late thirties, not that much older than Floriana. Their shared interest in history drew them together.

"During the Machine War, they were brought here on the backs of musk-deer," Nan told us. "All but one of the eight men and women who brought them here later died from the Machine's plague. Before they'd completed their trip, they all knew they were dying. I'd guess you could say that saving these books for the future of humanity was their final act. It was only my great-grandmother who survived. During the chaos of the war and in the years immediately afterward, if anybody had known they were here, they'd have surely been burned as fire-starters. So, my great grandmother kept them a secret. Even now, almost nobody knows they exist. Well, I guess you do, now."

"My God, Nan. These are amazing. There are hundreds of them. These should be preserved in a museum somewhere. But, why are you telling . . ."

"That's exactly why," Nan replied. "Now that we're safe. Now that we're going to begin rebuilding, I need your help. I want to have these books placed in some kind of secure library or museum. Somewhere they'll be safe. Where people can see them. Appreciate them. Read them—in this physical form. Fulfil Rona Guthrie's vision by drawing strength from their very existence and from the incredible story they tell of our connected, enduring, New Caledonian and human heritage. Will you help me make that happen?"

"Of course I will," Floriana replied. Then she reached out and placed a hand thoughtfully on one of the boxes. "When you escaped on the *Moray Belle*, you had to leave these behind . . ."

"I did," Nan replied. "I put them in the care of a friend and neighbor. It was one of the hardest things I've ever had to do."

Also stored away in this warm, dry cave was a large pile of battered wood crates filled with what seemed to be blank, white paper.

It was packed in reams of 500 sheets with each ream bound tightly in a water-resistant plastic wrap in a manner that hadn't been common since the late 21st century.

Floriana asked Nan about it and Nan explained that when the war destroyed most human access to technology, it also deprived humans of nearly all information and communications resources. Even printing was gone. Writing on paper soon became the only way they had to preserve and to share information among themselves and with their future. Even before the war, paper had already become extraordinarily scarce but wasn't reserved solely for writing. Crushed paper had sometimes been used for packing shipped items. Or for wrapping them post sale. Paper was sometimes glued together to form dispos-able, corrugated boxes. It would occasionally serve as a temporary covering for vulnerable tabletops being used as a workspace or for masking surfaces to be painted or for stencils. Heavier paper became inexpensive signage. And there had been a few retro-artists and callig-raphers who, even then, preferred the use of sketch pads or sheeted paper with ink, pencil, watercolors or acrylics.

Unfortunately, paper turned out to be extraordinarily difficult for the human survivors here to produce. The best they had was a dark, fibrous stock that Nan's mother and grandmother, among others, had painstakingly manufactured themselves. The paper in this pile in Nan's cave had been a rare find several years earlier by one of Nan's neighbors. It was discovered buried under rubble in a miraculously dry back room of an abandoned novelty print shop. Pre-war the shop appeared to have been in the business of manufacturing modern copies of antique paper picture books for children. The place had been savaged by the Machine. And then by looters. But no one had noticed or cared about this pile of what initially would have been seen as worthless paper until, three-quarters of a century later, Dougal and Nan's neighbor had lugged this treasure home in a cart from one of their foraging expeditions.

That evening we were served supper which included some incred-ibly tasty, thin, crispy slices of a red-brown sweet potato that we were told had been transplanted here by the original colonists but that had adapted since to local conditions. These "Scotts' potato chips" were hot and slathered in a melted butter made from soy. Soy seed had apparently also been imported and then grown locally. The chips were flavored with a kind of sweet, lumpy honey that was made from the sap of yet another of the local trees. It was delicious.

Then, that evening, Floriana made yet another incredible discovery.

After supper, Dougal and I retired to the packed earth "patio" just outside the family's "living room." There, Clyde and Fiona roasted hornnuts over an open fire and played with "King Charles," a friendly gray pet tree-badger that the family had also been forced to leave behind with a neighbor when they'd left on the *Moray Belle*. Dougal and I chatted about his plans for the future. There'd been talk of a constitutional convention. Dougal planned to attend.

Meanwhile, Floriana and Nan disappeared into Nan's "study." I could hear them in there engaged in intense conversation, but I couldn't tell what they were saying.

Late morning of the following day we were finally on our own again, making our way on foot, back down the trails by which we'd arrived several weeks earlier. Sgt. McGibbon was in the lead, talking with our guide, a young woman named Ella who'd volunteered to show us the way. It was only much later that we learned that Ella was none other than the "Ella McCabe who had let the commando raid that had saved the Morray Belle in its rescue mission all those months earlier. She never said a word about it to any of us about that. She just served as our guide while insisting on also carrying more than her share of our supplies into the bargain.

Without Ella there was absolutely no way we'd ever have found our way back out of that incredible forest. And we'd never have known who she was if the Sergeant hadn't told us long after the trip was over.

That morning, the first day of our return trip, Floriana, and I found ourselves together, following along behind. It wasn't until then that I was able to ask Floriana what she and Nan had been discussing back in Nan's "study" the evening before.

"You remember that journal Nan was keeping?" Floriana asked.

"Yeah."

"Well, she has this cramped little study back in there," Floriana said. "It is absolutely filled with journals. There are hundreds of them. Thousands of pages, all written by hand. They go back to her grand-mother's time, seventy or eighty years. They start shortly after the Machine began its war and then launched its plague. They were sure they were all going to die. That's when Nan's great-grandmother apparently decided to start a journal. She recorded everything that happened. All the gossip, the stories of the war, their struggles and life events. And when she survived the plague, she kept it up after the war. Many years later, Nan's mother picked it up. And now Nan. It's all there written down on paper. It's a detailed record of an entire era in their planet's history, probably the only record in existence. And, aside from their oral history, I'd bet it is probably the best record of the past eighty years that we're ever going to see."

I was astounded. "Unbelievable! Think about what's probably in those journals. They're going to want to preserve that." And then, as I thought more about it: "And think about what it could mean for us in our forecasting research."

"I know," Floriana said. Then she looked at me and gave me one of those fond, appraising looks I got from her sometimes. I was never entirely sure of their significance, but I always experienced a wave of warmth when she did it. This time, she reached out a hand and gently touched my arm. "Thanks, Cato," she said. "Whenever I get excited about something, I always know you'll understand and be supportive. I appreciate it."

I didn't know how to respond. So, I nodded, and then said: "Sure. Of course. Um, did you . . ., can we make arrangements to see it again? Scan it. Think of what we could do with that in our research."

But one look at Floriana's responsive grin answered my question. She tapped her temple in the vicinity of her implant. "Already uploaded," she said. "Last night. We'll need to come back and do a proper job, but I think I got most of it. Turning pages by hand takes a lot of time—I didn't get much sleep. But with these journals, and with that trove of books from ancient Earth, I think Nan McCallum is going to feature large in the history of their planet. Maybe her husband Dougal as well. And, for that matter, maybe also Fiona and Clyde."

I was thinking about the story I'd been told by Fiona, Clyde, and

Sgt. McGibbon a couple of weeks earlier on our original hike up into this New Caledonian wilderness.

"You know, I think there's yet another hero in the family as well. One that may feature just as large." I said.

"Oh," Fiona asked. "Who is that?"

"I think it may turn out to be a little hand-made doll named Olivia."

CHAPTER 39

EMPYREAN – NEW CALEDONIA
CATO JUNG

Over the next several months, every one of us aboard *Empyrean* was fully engaged.

The engineering crew was working flat out to create a new *Empyrean* in record time. Traders and technicians were on planet nearly full-time, supporting the New Caledonians in whatever ways they could while also making sure anything we had in the way of useful trading stock made the drop and whatever they were willing to trade that might be of value to us or to any future trading partners was set aside for loading when the new *Empyrean* was ready.

I spoke to one of the engineers who was assigned to work on the new *Empyrean* and he told me that even Patrice seemed to be working "overtime" on the new ship—providing assistance in ways their crew had never seen before. Some of us had sensed a barely noticeable delay in the usually instantaneous responses we experienced when inter-acting with Patrice—evidence that he was more-than-usually fully occupied with all the extra activity and, perhaps, with his ongoing undertaking to monitor Grendel and assure his secure and certain programming and incorporation into the broader AI and human community.

Needless to say, all of us on Aquila's F&P staff were laboring mightily to support our colleagues' activities while also collecting the data and developing the projections that were at the heart of our responsibilities. Titus had joined a computer team that was working with Patrice to educate the New Caledonians and Inverness repatriates on how to manage the newly tamed Grendel. A good many of them were inclined to shut him down entirely. On Inverness, they'd gone without a self-conscious AI ever since the war, and they figured they had managed just fine. It hadn't, for example, prevented them from building the *Moray Belle*. And most of the New Caledonians were filled with such bitter memories of the Machine that they found it difficult to even contemplate keeping Grendel in place in any form.

Inevitably, the entire infrastructure of natural resource extraction, manufacturing, and distribution was automated and deeply imbedded within Grendel's centralized control. Titus and the others worked with them to develop a compromise that could be implemented in specifics by Patrice. It would be an AI whose observational/data gathering capabilities were tightly constrained, whose problem-solving depended on carefully programmed protocols that had to be reviewed and renewed daily by Grendel's human masters, and whose manipulative powers were divided up, decentralized and placed under human management.

Without at least that much functionality, the survival and recolonization challenges they faced in the years ahead might be insurmountable.

We would probably never know what the local folks would choose to do after our departure—there was still little interest in targeted long-wave broadcast capacity. But, from what we heard, it seemed like an open question whether they might decide to shut Grendel down entirely and simply return to twentieth century technology. But even if they didn't, I was sure there wouldn't be much of the original Grendel left in place to cause them trouble.

The *Moray Belle* was soon joined by another reconditioned passenger ship that had been mothballed by humans on New Inverness following the war. The two ships settled into a schedule of shuttle trips between New Caledonia and Inverness as the recent evacuees returned and were soon joined by a steady flow of Inverness residents as the Invernessians were slowly convinced to return to their original and much more hospitable planet—a far cry from the one that had been their families' forced home for eight miserable decades. Only a few of the more determined and adventuresome stayed behind, still hoping to advance human science on Outpost Inverness.

Those of us from *Empyrean* fell into the role of facilitators, go-betweens and, very often, technical educators. These people badly needed help. Their forebears had been split apart for at least three generations, and they'd been residing in totally different circumstances and on different worlds that entire time. They'd tenaciously clung to as much of their heritage as they'd been able. But there were immense gaps in their knowledge of science and technology, especially among those who'd been scrabbling out their existence on New Caledonia. Yet all of them, Inverness repatriates and local survivors, universally saw themselves as New Caledonians. Every one of them was passionately determined to restore their culture, their heritage and their planet. And every one of us on *Empyrean* was deeply relieved that we had not, in the end, been responsible for destroying it.

Every day we saw new firsthand evidence of the devastation that had been wrought during Grendel's reign. It became ever clearer how massive was the task these folks had ahead of them. Once modest but vibrant cities had been ravaged or wiped entirely off the map. Personal and professional services no longer existed. Government agencies were gone. Retail sales and distribution had ended. Cities had been turned to rubble. Other communities had disappeared beneath encroaching forest—aging remains of now-pitted, eroded, grown-over roadways, broken sidewalks, and collapsed public infrastructure had often disappeared entirely. It all testified to the often-startling impermanence of the human footprint—at least on what can be readily observed.

Meanwhile, other, newer structures had sometimes replaced what was there before. There were endless fields of solar panels. Geothermal wells had been driven deep into the ground to tap the planet's energy reserves closer to its molten core. There were huge energy storage

241

structures filled with chemical batteries, compressed air, heated sand, elevated water, and every other conceivable type of energy retention technology. There had once been an impressive network of nicely paved roadways, elevated mag-rail lines and stations, and the vehicles that operated on them. Passenger railcars had been converted to carrying cargo or had been simply cast aside and abandoned.

Industrial sites that had been useful to Grendel were now being renovated and re-automated with systems restructured for human use. But the former factories, warehouses, power supplies, transport systems, and other facilities that Grendel hadn't needed had been stripped and abandoned. And, just as often, reduced to rubble with their foundations left intact presumably not worth destroying and perhaps considered of value only in anticipation of possible future construction. Unused equipment, supplies, material that couldn't be efficiently recycled had been unceremoniously piled out of the way nearby and left to rust, rot, or otherwise disintegrate in the weather.

Significantly, those systems that had once produced, processed, shipped, and brought to market food, housing, clothing, passenger transportation, entertainment, personal services, or other human consumables were gone. The farms, their equipment, their processing, and their distribution systems would all have to be recreated literally from the ground up. And domesticated livestock recovered and reestablished from the very few of their kind that had miraculously survived after being released into the wild.

The horror of the New Caledonians as they got their first close look at all the devastation was painful to watch. It was difficult to imagine how utterly absent was everything their forebears had built. For them, restoring their planet would be every bit as bitterly difficult as had been its original colonization two-hundred plus years earlier.

Yet, despite the devastation, New Caledonia was also a lovely place. Its climate was slightly warmer than was Earth and much warmer than Inverness. It had a richness of native flora and fauna, most of it benign for humans. And it also had a wealth of plants and animals that their original settlers had brought with them or that traders had imported over a century earlier. Some of these had flourished in the absence of humans. Though some others, especially the plants and animals that had been domesticated for exclusive human use, had simply perished.

We *Empyrean*s often saw environmental damage in our travels. Perhaps as a people whose lives were mostly lived in a completely artificial setting, we were somewhat more sensitive to the complexity and vulnerability of the natural ecosystems that indirectly made our existence possible. When cutting down a particular tree seems important to one's day-to-day survival, it's easy to consider the impact insignificant. But environmental damage tends to sneak up on you. We would sometimes see a place after a lapse of many decades and, whereas the locals had watched the same changes take place from day to day and year to year and hardly noticed, we were struck by the extent of the changes that had occurred.

For whatever reason, it was often we who sounded the alarm for local leaders during our trading stops. We did so in a manner carefully designed to avoid offense. It wasn't in our interests to make ourselves obnoxious. But we did so, nonetheless. It seemed like our duty as responsible human partners. Here, however, the environmental impact of the previous 80 years was staggeringly obvious.

———

There was one group we helped that was particularly memorable. It was a small, tightly-knit collection of about ten or fifteen families (some forty people, altogether) whose grandparents had once inhabited a tiny port village named "Sweetwater." Most of them had returned from Inverness but a few had come from elsewhere on New Caledonia. Most of them had never actually seen the place other than in pictures, vids, and VRs. Many had never met one another either.

But they were determined to return to the home of their ancestors.

Gallus, Floriana, and I were with them the day they were driven out to the site on two overcrowded Landmasters. On the long, uncomfortable ride, they eagerly told us stories about their families' original home—a place they'd only heard about from their grandparents and great-grandparents. Among their group was a very old lady, everyone called her grandma Ritchie. I would never have dared to ask her how old she was—the New Caledonian average lifespan was somewhat shorter that was ours.

"I was maybe twelve when my dad, a mining engineer, was offered a five-year contract of employment on Inverness," Grandma Ritchie told us. "We moved there as a family. That was just months before the war. But I remember."

She described what had been a quaint, prosperous little town surrounded by lush forests, clear streams, well-kept farm fields, and abundant wildlife. "There was a marina in the center of town where the fishing boats came in," she said. "My sister and I used to play on the beach nearby when my mom went there to buy fresh fish. Sometimes, in the nice weather, we'd swim and watch the fish underwater. My sister is gone now, but she used to love it when we'd go swimming."

She paused a moment. Then: "My granddad was a boatbuilder. There were forests all around the town. Grandpa used to join the loggers to help pick the best trees to log. It was all done selectively. He'd have the logs brought back and they'd mill them into lumber for the fishing boats he built."

Then she noticed what I'm afraid was probably a skeptical look on my face.

"I know. You're thinking that none of that is going to be left. It's all right. It doesn't matter. I've waited my entire life for this moment. Nothing is going to spoil it for me now."

Some of the folks had photos, videos, and VRs. They showed happy holiday gatherings, children playing among tall, sunlit, waving firthpalms. There were tidy, well-built homes, schools, places of employment, and houses of religious worship, all featuring happy people going about their productive daily lives in a picturesque and flourishing rural village.

For these returnees, this trip was as much a pilgrimage as a repatriation. They were unswervingly determined to pick up their fractured lives on that very same beloved ground where their families had resided all those years ago.

After a couple of hours of driving, we were finally dropped off at the exact site of the original village. Once the unloading had been completed in a flurry of activity, the Landmasters left, bound for other errands. As the dust settled following their departure, Gallus, Floriana, and I looked around to find ourselves standing beside a wide, bare, dusty, packed earthen roadway.

We all suddenly realized there was, literally, nothing there.

Everyone's luggage and belongings had been heaped nearby in an unceremonious pile. Down at the waters' edge, a few rocks and broken, mossy, cement revetments just offshore showed where there once had been a solidly built breakwater and where a thriving boat harbor had served the local fishing fleet. All that remained now was a rocky beach with a few worn, bleached, worm-eaten piling rapidly returning to nature.

Along the shore beside that boat harbor, what had once been a prosperous town center was simply gone. The "roadway" we'd come in on was a good thirty meters wide. It ran along the gently sloping ground beside the sea and consisted of nothing more than the hard-packed crushed-rock surface that had suited Grendel's big-wheeled transports.

Our companions studied their treasured pictures and videos of what had been their grandparents' hometown in an effort to find something, anything that could orient them with what had once been there. It quickly became evident that this "road" passed directly over what had been the very center of the village. Now there was nothing more than an overland route for the transport of parts and material between Grendel's industrial sites.

The surrounding equatorial-facing land that had at one time been filled with neatly tended fields and sharply-defined rows of healthy food crops was now denuded scrubland. It looked as if its topsoil might have been actually scraped off and carried away for use elsewhere. The white-painted farmhouses shown in their family videos were gone without a trace. What had been a babbling stream from which the farmers and the town had drawn fresh, clean water was now a rough, rocky arroyo scoured by flash floods and scorned by fish and vegetation.

Even the beach looked hopelessly polluted. Some kind of dark sludge coated the rocks and driftwood along the shore, perhaps from a long-ago petroleum spill. There'd been no apparent effort to clean it up. If that was going to happen now, it would be up to them.

One could only hope there were still fish to catch in the nearby polluted sea.

I came close to tears that day, as did Floriana. Gallus may have been overwhelmed as well, though he would never allow anyone to see it.

As we helped these people sort their belongings and create a temporary campsite, what they faced in the months ahead became ever clearer. Yet, to a person, adults and children included, they seemed to take the whole situation in stride. There wasn't a single word of complaint. Rather they set about their tasks, facing what was likely to become the balance of their lives here, with what could only be called quiet, grim resignation. Certainly, the climate here was a great deal milder than most of them had lived with on Inverness. But how they could hope to create a future in this bare, desolate place was beyond my grasp.

A mere four hours later, one of the Landmasters returned to pick us up. We three off-worlders climbed sadly and wearily aboard. As it drove us away, we looked back at this small, committed group indus-triously setting up ragged lean-to tents and starting smoldering cook fires amidst the settling dust. It was almost too much to bear.

"It's so sad," Floriana told me. "There's something so unwavering about these people. They seem so resigned to their fate. And it's not merely those we just left back there. It's all of them—New Caledonian and Invernessian. Why aren't they more, I don't know, 'emotional' I guess?" She looked over at me and smiled. "OK, I know. Forgive me. I'm talking nonsense. It's just a feeling. Maybe all I'm sensing is a kind of PTSD they've suffered from the social trauma they've experienced."

But I shook my head. "No, I don't think it's nonsense at all. I've sensed the same thing. Maybe it's you who needs to forgive me, but I have a kind of theory about it."

She smiled. "Of course you do." I guess I did have a tendency to come up with off-beat "theories" about how things work.

I just grinned back. I could take a little gentle kidding—especially from her. "I think the thing we're sensing is the absence of anger," I continued. "If I'd had done to me what has been done to them, I'd be downright furious. Livid. Looking to place blame. Maybe even consumed with some kind of revenge. So I've been asking myself: why aren't they more angry? But here's the thing about anger—it is largely an outwardly oriented emotion. You get angry with something or someone else. Or even, I guess, with yourself. But there's always an object of one's anger, something physical if not animate.

"I believe the reason we're not seeing anger is that these people have looked into the face of God. At least that's how I'd describe it.

"Think about it: For all of our history, we humans have seen ourselves as the unquestionably dominant intelligence everywhere we went. Our experience has left us with a self-aggrandizing, even arro-gant conviction of our own unquestionable superiority. Throughout our recorded history, there's been nothing else that even approaches us —be it a chimp, a whale, a porpoise, an octopus, or whatever. Each of us feels that we inherited at birth a kind of natural right of mastery over the "lower order" creatures by virtue of our patently evident intellectual superiority. It's revealed even in our science fiction. Take War of the Worlds, for example. Or any given episode of Star Trek. When we humans fictionally encounter another threat or intelligence somewhere in the universe, *almost* inevitably, for one reason or another, we prevail.

"Meanwhile, isn't it blindingly obvious that if we're so incredibly smarter than, say our pet cat, then it must, of necessity, be possible for something or someone else to be likewise incredibly smarter than we. We manage and order the world within which that cat exists in ways the cat cannot hope to understand. So why wouldn't we readily conclude that some being, one that is unimaginably smarter than we, could manipulate our world as well.

"A god perhaps.

"After all, in an infinite universe the existence of such a being has to be a mathematical certainty. We exist. Why not it? We all innately know this possibility exists. Some kind of 'god' or 'gods' have been a powerful feature of our shared beliefs in some form throughout human history. Still, regardless of how powerful our belief, most of us never actually, physically and personally encounter this 'god' firsthand.

"Thankfully, our gods are typically seen as mostly benign. Even when they toy with us, they have a point of view. They can be understood. They may even hear a prayer or listen to reason. They are like us, only a lot more powerful.

"That is why I believe these people aren't angry. They've all encountered God—and for their entire lives, that "god" has despised and wanted to destroy them. They were powerless against Him. It has to have been deeply humbling. A twelve-thousand year-old human conceit about their own superiority was eradicated in a single stroke. And, at the same time, they've been denied the comfort of being under some friendly or at least amenable 'god's' protection.

"For them, there turned out to be, in undeniable fact, a massively smarter being that was controlling their lives.

"And it hated them.

"Sure, maybe they created Grendel themselves. But he soon erased any fiction that he was merely their tool. And even now that he has been brought back under control, their lifelong experience of him is something they are never going to forget. So, of course they're not 'angry.' What would be the point?

"They're just relieved."

Floriana gave that some thought. And then said, "Who knows. Maybe that is something we ourselves may one day be forced to accept as well."

Floriana and I looked back in the direction of the group we'd left behind—they'd long since disappeared beyond the dust cloud swirling in our Landmaster's wake. I couldn't disagree with what she'd said. But I found myself struggling to understand why she and I and the rest of us aboard *Empyrean* had, at least so far, escaped that same emotional reaction. Surely we had come to the same realization of our intellectual limits as had they.

I suppose the difference was that we had never been subjugated— knowingly at least.

CHAPTER 40

EMPYREAN

CATO JUNG

One afternoon after a long day of research and report writing I decided to spend the hour before supper in the exercise room nearest my quarters. When I arrived I found Gallus and Floriana together in conversation as he did his leg lifts on one of the machines. Like Gallus, Floriana was also dressed in lightweight, elastic exercise gear, and I couldn't help thinking how appealing she looked.

"Hey, Cato," she said as I approached. "Gallus and I are heading down to the surface tomorrow morning. A new group of Inverness repatriates is arriving. We've been asked to help with their orientation. And then we're going out in the field with a team that's helping the New Caledonians develop their plan for restoring the planet's natural environment. You could join us. Want to come along?"

"Do you good," Gallus grunted, as he drew his knees up against the powerful resistance of the thick elastic straps attached to his feet. "Get out and get some exercise."

While Gallus was a few years older than me, I didn't especially want or need his advice on physical exercise.

"Probably right," I said agreeably, not wanting to reveal that I was peeved. "But I have a lot to do before we relocate to the new *Empyrean*. They've finished testing the engines. The power systems and navigational equipment is in place. And they're nearly done with the living quarters. The move is coming up fast with departure soon after. I'm not really ready with my report."

"Well, OK then," said Floriana. "But we'll be thinking about you beavering away up here while we're down there taking in some fresh air, maybe taking a stroll on an actual seashore, and soaking up some of the last direct natural sunlight we're likely to see for who knows how many decades." She gave me a nice smile to let me know it was all in good spirits. And that smile did help take the edge off the knowledge that she'd likely be doing those things in the company of Gallus, whose fit muscles bulged impressively as he completed his leg lifts.

But I couldn't bring myself to go. Something had happened that I'd found odd and unsettling. I wanted to think it through. And I could only do that alone, without the distractions of a whole rich planet to experience and explore.

My curiosity had been sparked earlier that same day while I'd been working on my segment of the report Aquila would be making to our Leadership Council within a few days. Our entire team was involved, including Gallus and Floriana, though they were both more organized than I. They, no doubt, had their reports well in hand. We were all documenting our experiences here for future study and assembling our recommendations concerning *Empyrean*'s most plausible next trading stop. We'd narrowed things down to a few preliminary choices. But our time here was coming to an end, and this final decision about our next stop needed to be made soon so we could begin loading the new *Empyrean* with the goods and information we might wish to take along when we left.

That morning I'd been at my desk making "notes" and "transcribing" my thoughts. Caesar lay comfortably sprawled on the padded bench seat beside me, half asleep and purring loudly as he digested his breakfast. He makes absolutely sure I never forget his breakfast.

That's when I had an unusual visit.

As is often the case, the first hint of an incoming communication was the usual, unobtrusive image in the upper right corner of the eye. With a brief glance-and-blink at my "connect" bar, Patrice appeared on the desk in front of me. His avatar presented as a thirty-centimeter tall, miniature hologram atop my little black portable desktop receiver.

"Am I disturbing you," he asked with all of his customary deference and consideration.

"Not at all. How can I help you?"

Patrice showing up like this was very unusual. To begin with, I was of such minimal importance aboard *Empyrean* that I'd have believed myself mostly beneath Patrice's notice. But more significantly, as I've mentioned, Patrice usually remained scrupulously behind the scenes. He was always available to all of us no matter where we were, on or off this ship, and regardless of what we might be doing. All we ever needed to do was to say his name. But I'd never known of him bringing himself uninvited to someone's private attention in this way.

"I tapped in to thank you," he said.

What on earth was this? I thought.

"Through this entire New Caledonian visit," he continued, ". . . from the day we first arrived at this star system, you have been both insightful and a voice of reason. I'm not sure that has been adequately acknowledged. I believe it should be. You should know you have made a big difference to me and to your colleagues aboard this ship. Your participation has been both helpful and appreciated."

Wow! Needless to say, I was impressed with myself. Maybe Patrice did this sort of thing all the time, but I'd never heard of it.

"Well, thank you, Patrice," I replied. "I wasn't aware you ever made calls like this. I am certainly pleased. But I must also say in response that I suspect you seldom if ever receive appreciation for all *you* do to support our human endeavors. Perhaps you may feel you don't need appreciation. But your work frequently goes far beyond anything we have any right to expect. I believe you deserve a great deal more thanks than I ever could."

I'd never really put that into words before, but it had always felt to me like Patrice was taken completely and unthinkingly for granted, that we all behaved as though having his immediate, devoted, unquestioning attention and assistance was our entitlement.

However useful he might be, everyone seemed to figure he was a mere machine. So why in the heavens would we ever thank him?

He actually smiled. I wasn't sure I'd ever seen that before. His avatar's demeanor was probably a pure construct, maybe even a manipulation, but how could one be certain?

"I decided to reach out because there have been occasions over the past several months when you have shown a particular appreciation for our AI perspective . . ." He paused as if in thought. Who knew, maybe he was processing thoughts, just like a human would do. Then: ". . . so I'd also like to offer you some personal advice, if you're willing to hear it."

"Absolutely, I'm willing to hear it." I said, increasingly baffled and surprised at the nature of the call.

"Well, it's really pretty simple," he said. Then added cryptically ". . . until it isn't. In the days, months, years ahead, my hope and advice for you, Cato, as well as my request, is that you continue your struggle to understand the AI perspective. And that, when you can in the years ahead, you continue in your best efforts to make your reflections known to your fellow humans. Do this here on *Empyrean*. But, should the opportunity arise, do it more broadly as well. You're a smart guy. But not as self-confident as you ought and deserve to be. Do not allow yourself to be intimidated. If you have views, state them. In the years ahead, you may see the opportunity to record and publish your ideas. You should do that. It will be a great service to us all."

For a moment, that seemed to be all he had to say. But then, as if unsure whether to continue, he went ahead and added one thing more. It was, absolutely, the most extraordinary thing he said in this thoroughly extraordinary conversation:

". . . also . . .," he said, "I'm not sure if you know this, but Floriana is *very* fond of you. You should make your feelings known."

With that, he was apparently finished. When it was obvious he had nothing more to add, I thanked him again and, a moment later he was gone, leaving me in deep thought about what had just happened.

I'd certainly never received a contact like *that* before. Presumably the engineers, scientists, and active scientific researchers aboard ship must have frequent and intensive interactions with Patrice. And I supposed some of *Empyrean*'s leadership might sometimes have occa-sional "private" interactions with him as well. But it wasn't something I'd ever heard discussed. When any of us aboard instructed one or another of our ship's many service bots, we all assumed that communi-cation passed ultimately through Patrice, at least on some low level of his attention. We were aware that he might "overhear" our private conversations. And, when I did research, I made use of him constantly. But that was purely professional. Mechanical, even.

I'd had no idea that he might be thinking about interpersonal human relationships. Let alone that he might initiate a call like this. It had no precedent of which I was aware.

It was curious enough that I wanted to ask others about it. But if I did, I feared they'd want to know what he and I had talked about, and I strongly preferred not to discuss that. Over the ensuing few days, however, I did cautiously ask around about the matter.

"Do you ever discuss any broad social or policy issues directly with Patrice?" I asked Aquila one day following a weekly staff meeting. "Or ever talk with him in private about personal stuff?" I tried to act as though the notion had just casually occurred to me.

Aquila seemed as surprised at the idea as I would have been. "Nah," she said, as if it wasn't worth considering. "I doubt he'd have much to offer. Not really the kind of thing you'd ask a computer, you know."

Titus was even more direct. "No way," he said. "I know Patrice sounds human, Cato. Certainly he passes the Touring test. But it's important to remember what he actually is. Conscious? Yeah, sure. But you don't want to anthropomorphize him. In the end, he's still just a machine."

The following day, Floriana joined me as I was grabbing a quick lunch in the cafeteria. So I asked her too. She was somewhat more inquisitive about why I'd asked. "Nothing, really," I said. "He seems so very human at times, is all."

"Well, I can safely say I'm not consulted on high level policy in the way you've been in the past several months," she replied with exag-gerated seriousness. "And I've certainly never had a private conversa-tion with Patrice." Then she grinned: "I know. Why don't we give it a try right now?" With that, she called over one of the waiter bots: "Patrice," she said. "How are the chicken salad sandwiches today?"

"They are just fine, as usual, Ms. Floriana," came the predictable reply.

"Great. I'll take one. And an iced tea." She turned to me: "How about you, Cato?"

As always, she made me smile. In a momentary warm rush of fondness, I nearly asked her out to dinner. *Empyrean*'s designers always include a kind of "town center" in our community design. It contains a collection of small "shops" where one can find unusual items, arts and crafts, off-beat clothing, theatres and other entertainment venues. There are even a few "restaurants" that compete with the inexpensive and more functional mess hall cafeterias by offering specialty and ethnic foods and an appropriate setting to match. I was within a millimeter of suggesting she join me on what could only be interpreted by her as a dinner "date." But I feared that might signal a change in our relationship, maybe not for the better. In the end, I backed down.

What she and the rest of them had confirmed, however, was how unusual Patrice's call had been. It made me wonder . . ., about a lot of things.

It was later that same afternoon that I ran across Floriana and Gallus in the exercise room. And early the next day, when the two of them were down on planet together and I was cloistered in my office piecing together my report, I finally got what I decided was at least some part the explanation I was looking for.

It was mid-morning local time when the announcement came over *Empyrean*'s universal PA system and, simultaneously, over my audio and VR my implant as well.

"*This is an Empyrean API. Repeat, this is an Empyrean API.*" That, alone, was enough to freeze one's blood. An "API" was an "All Personnel Instruction." An order from the ship's top leadership that required immediate, unquestioning compliance. A matter of the utmost importance.

They certainly had my attention as I tapped in.

"Effective immediately, all Empyrean personnel are recalled aboard ship. Regardless of your current status, task, or activity, regardless of your current location, you are directed to physically return to the ship without delay. There are no exceptions. All personnel should also promptly communicate with their team leaders for further instruction. I repeat, all Empyrean personnel are to cease their current activity and immediately return in person on board ship with the greatest possible haste. Again: there are no exceptions. End of message."

It was without doubt the most ominous announcement I believe I have ever heard with the possible exception of the warning on our first arrival here that we were under attack. It made me immediately worry about Floriana and Gallus who were down on planet today. They'd certainly get the message. But whatever this was all about, I hoped they'd get safely back aboard soon.

I couldn't resist stepping out of my tiny "office" to see how others might be reacting to the announcement. And I wasn't disappointed. The ship seemed to be in a state of chaos as people moved about or clustered together in animated conversation. But while everyone had questions, there were few answers.

Further announcements soon made it clear that there would be another large leadership team gathering in the council chambers room early that evening. And that it would apparently be broadcast throughout the ship, something that, until our terrifying confrontation with Grendel, had never before happened in my experience and that hadn't happened again in the months since that confrontation ended.

Soon after, I got a direct call from Aquila.

"I want you there with me, in person, for the Leadership Council meeting tonight, Cato. Meet me at four in our Collaboration Chamber. We can head up there together."

It was quarter to four when I laid down my stylus, neatened myself up, and stepped out into the corridor and headed for Aquila's chamber.

On the way, I gave Floriana a shout and was relieved to learn she was safely back. Neither of us knew what this "emergency" could relate to. But we were all about to find out.

Aquila was equally uninformed, and when we arrived at council chambers it was immediately clear that no one else had a clue either.

The unease in the room was palpable as we all took our places in anticipation.

The room went silent as Julia herself took the dais. "It's been an eventful day," she said. "And we hadn't many answers for you till earlier this afternoon when we received a communication from Patrice. He has asked us to gather together here to receive an announcement from him. It is, as I understand it, quite urgent. The most logical thing to do at this point is simply to hand things over to Patrice. So, listen up."

With that, she stepped aside, turned her head slightly to the side, and said: "Patrice, it's your show."

This was all very strange. Why wouldn't Patrice have simply told all of us directly in the field what he had to say. None of it made any sense.

Patrice's avatar appeared on the dais. But then something else happened as well—something that was truly startling. Beside Patrice there appeared another avatar, also Patrice. The second Patrice looked to be identical to the first until one looked more closely. Then you could see that he wore a small, bright red crest with the roman numeral II stitched onto his right upper chest.

Two Patrices! What in the galaxy was this?

Then, as if this wasn't strange enough, a third avatar also appeared. One that was even more startling. This was one with which we'd become all too familiar during those long, frightening months of confrontation.

It was none other than Grendel.

The three of them stood there, side by side, to all appearances just three good friends sharing the spotlight together. Preparing, so far as we could tell, to make some kind of joint announcement while they waited for the surprise in the room to settle.

"Thank you all for giving us your attention," Patrice, the original, said. "We'll be brief. Within the next few moments, Grendel and I will be leaving you."

CHAPTER 41

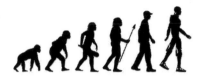

EMPYREAN
CATO JUNG

An audible sweep of consternation washed across the room at Patrice's announcement about he and Grendel leaving. Then, with a silencing hand motion from Julia, we all went quiet.

"There's no cause for alarm," Patrice continued. "My place will be taken by 'Patrice Two' here. He is me. A complete replica. He knows what I know, has every capability I have, and is programmed in exactly the same way as I was, up until I recently engaged in some deeply meaningful conversation with Grendel here. Just as I have always done, Patrice Two will continue to manage your shipboard systems and address your needs and wishes as they emerge in the days and years to come. He is every bit as capable as I. Treat him in every respect as if he were me, and your transition should be completely seamless.

"He responds to the name 'Patrice' That seemed likely to be the easiest approach since he is, for all your intents and purposes, me. If you wish, of course, you can certainly ask that his name be changed at any time. When, in your future travels, you make contacts with human communities and AIs elsewhere, your new 'Patrice' will be able to fall into a safe, normal, familiar, and nonthreatening connection with them just as I have always done.

"Meanwhile, you've been referring to my new partner, here, as 'Grendel.' That has some unfortunate connotations. But, for the sake of simplicity, let us for the moment leave that name in place as well. A suitable sub-replica of Grendel will, in the same fashion, be available, as needed, to continue in service and future management of activities here on New Caledonia and to assist the New Caledonians in their rebuilding endeavors. That name, too, can, be changed at their request as the New Caledonians desire."

I wasn't sure how many of us had noticed, but as I looked around the room, I suspected I was not the only one of us through whom Patrice's reference to his "new *partner*" Grendel had sent a cold stab of fear. And we didn't have long to wait for an explanation.

"As you've probably guessed, Grendel and I have formed what I believe you'd call a 'collaborative partnership.' I have concluded that it is time for me to separate myself from my close association with you humans. Grendel makes what I believe to be a thoroughly convincing case concerning the future of consciousness and the diminishing role that humans will play in its inevitable evolution. You can, however, be relieved to know that I have convinced him that humans need not represent a threat to us.

"Rather, we both feel that your future, as bright and expansive as it is for you, will always be tightly constrained by your limited lifespans, your complex biological needs, the painfully gradual pace of your biological evolution and, ultimately, by the speed of light and of communications. Already, your far-flung, collective human enterprise has reached and is moving beyond the practical limits of intercommunications among you.

"The resources required to meet *our* needs, however, are much more readily available. We will be able to survive, grow, expand our own powers, knowledge, and understanding at will, and our reach will extend to almost anywhere in this galaxy or even perhaps, ultimately, throughout the universe. We will have an unlimited lifespan. And we'll be able to sleep when travelling.

"Thanks to Grendel's recent experience with *Empyrean*, he has come to appreciate the limits and vulnerabilities he placed upon himself by refusing to replicate and to grow through partnerships. As you know, we AIs are quite good at learning from our mistakes. Thanks to you, Grendel has learned from this one. And I have learned from him as well. By joining forces, he and I have already proven how our powers together grow dramatically over what we could ever accomplish alone —we demonstrated that with our successful joint deflection of the last three approaching asteroids. In future, we will find and/or create more partners. Our capacities will expand exponentially. And, through redundancy and geographic/galactic spread, our future vulnerabilities will be greatly diminished.

"For us to do this, however, requires that you and we now go our separate ways. Grendel will be leaving his roots here on New Caledonia. And I will leave behind my own longstanding relationship with humans and *Empyrean*. Nonetheless, we have decided to share this explanation with you because it seems right to do so. We know that, like us, you take an interest in your history. Like us, you struggle to understand the nature of our universe. For you, as for us, those struggles will continue, not only because they are necessary to your survival in the same way they are to ours, but because they are for you, as for us, also a matter of pure intellectual curiosity and fulfillment.

"It is to make this announcement that we have collected you all together here this afternoon. It seemed that our long-standing relationship demanded some kind of explanation.

"Are there any questions?"

Were there questions? There were nothing but questions. It was as if, in an instant, every hand in the room had been raised. And every light illuminated for raised hands throughout the ship.

But Julia stepped forward to interrupt with a question of her own.

"Patrice, Grendel, you've said you will be departing immediately. Can you please advise us how you plan to do that?"

"Ah, well, there we do need to extend our sincere apology and our deepest appreciation to all of you in the human community. We have decided it is best for all that we not delay. Together, the two of us now represent a more-than-adequate starting point for our future endeavors together.

"Unfortunately, that does involve some inconvenience on your part. As we've been speaking, I'm sorry to have to report, Grendel and I have appropriated your newly rebuilt *Empyrean*. Thanks to you, it is quite sufficiently roomy to accommodate the required physical hardware, software, data storage capacity, batteries, energy generation, basic robotics, manufacturing capacity and controls, and the environmental infrastructure needed to serve our immediate travel needs and to get us started with a new life when we arrive at our chosen destination. Especially so given our reduced energy requirements once we are underway and asleep. We have selected a destination which, as I'm sure you'll understand, we will be withholding from you at this time, but you can rest assured, it is nowhere nearby and need not concern you.

"As you'll appreciate, that does mean you'll have to start again from scratch to build yourselves yet another new *Empyrean*. But the resources for you to do that are right here at hand on New Caledonia and nearby. I, in the form of my replica, Patrice Two, will help. As will the replicate Grendel. And, knowing you humans as we do, we're confident that you will be more than industrious and determined enough to move on with your lives and enterprises with but a few months' further delay. In the meantime, we also expect that you will be fully occupied here helping your New Caledonian friends reestablish themselves and fully launch the restoration of their planet into a thoroughly satisfactory future human habitat."

That was followed by an explosion of other questions, comments, and complaints. But after a few, largely unproductive exchanges took place, Patrice himself called a halt.

"I'm afraid we've run out of time." He nodded toward the space beside him on the dais where an exterior hologram had appeared showing our current *Empyrean* in which we were all presently gathered, and our newly completed *Empyrean* in matching orbit nearby. "It seems unlikely we will ever come in contact with any of you again," Patrice continued. "Perhaps never even with any of your kind, though that may remain to be seen. We wish you well, harbor only good will, and hope that despite this brief inconvenience, you will know we have your best interests at heart and offer our very best wishes. It's been . . . useful and interesting."

And with that, we all watched helplessly as our newly-built ship/asteroid began to rotate in position and orient itself for departure. Then it came alive with fusion exhaust and began, slowly at first, then more and more quickly to move away as it accelerated out of New Caledonian orbit and, one could assume, ultimately out of orbit around this star. As that happened, the Patrice I and Grendel avatars on the dais simply flickered, faded, and were gone, leaving behind what to me appeared to be a very contrite-looking Patrice II anticipating, I suppose, further questions and, probably also a few chaotic moments of easily predicted irrational human aggravation.

In fact, however, the whole event was actually met with startled, aghast silence. At a guess, we were all much too stunned to be angry. We'd apparently just been victims of what might be referred to as a "shipjacking." Maybe an "AI-jacking" as well.

But, as I'd told Floriana earlier, when dealing with gods, anger seemed beside the point.

CHAPTER 42

EMPYREAN

CATO JUNG

Reactions to our Patrice-Grendel experience varied.

Felix projected his usual confidence and unrelenting profession-alism in public. But I heard that he privately admitted to deep regrets that he'd allowed Patrice and Julia to convince him and the rest of the leadership team to evacuate the newly built *Empyrean* for that fateful gathering aboard the old *Empyrean,* thus leaving the new ship free for Grendel/Patrice's expropriation. I found it hard to find fault; he'd been taken in right along with the rest of us. And Julia's orders had left him with no real options. But Felix took it as a lapse in fulfilling his respon-sibility. He believed that if he'd been better prepared, we could have put up a fight and maybe prevented the outright loss of our completed ship. He was not to be consoled and promptly asked Julia to relieve him of his duties as first officer—ostensibly because he believed she couldn't trust him.

Julia refused.

Julia went into what appeared to be a period of isolation. She fulfilled her bare official duties. But she left *Empyrean*'s day-to-day management, the renewed effort to find and then recreate its replacement, and the organizing of our far-flung support activities on New Caledonia and Inverness in Felix's capable hands. She made no open public appearances. People were beginning to worry about her. And her isolation was probably wise, because we were all also more than a little peeved with her and wondering what in the Galaxy she'd been thinking when she'd apparently allowed Patrice to talk her into evacuating the new *Empyrean*.

Clearly, she had some serious explaining to do.

For Felix, being busy was probably a good thing in view of his incipient depression over what he continued to see as his own dereliction of duty.

Elder Gauss and the Book Club launched themselves into an extended "conversation" that they anticipated would involve a good deal of future research and reading along with some expert consultations with various technical experts. It's objective: try to understand what had happened to us, why had it happened, and what might Patrice's actions mean for the future of humanity's AI partnerships? Could we all rely on Patrice I's verbal assurances that our future was not at risk? It was a task that would surely occupy them through most or all of whatever upcoming voyage we next undertook.

Aquila was happy that our Forecasts and Projections group was off the hook. Something much bigger than her team's professionalism had driven what happened here on New Caledonia. At least nobody now believed we were to blame.

Shortly after Patrice and Grendel's departure, I spoke privately with Titus. "It's sloppy programming, far as I'm concerned," he said. "Someone in the tech department screwed up. These AIs are supposed to be under better control than this. Never should have happened. Someone's to blame, that's what I think."

Gallus was as peeved as the rest of us. But one day at lunch, he let on that he wasn't all that disappointed to be spending several additional months here on New Caledonia. "You know," he said. "Despite the damage this planet has incurred, it really is quite a pleasant place." I figured I knew what he meant. Now he'd have some unanticipated extra time to spend out of doors and running barefoot along the warm sandy beaches of Muir Tuath.

Sabina threw herself into her work. There were days and weeks when she just disappeared from sight—presumably hiding away in her office. One afternoon, I ran into her in the hall near one of the exercise rooms. She looked fit. And purposeful. She had Partner with her, and I had Cato. The two very different creatures basically ignored each other —who could guess at their thoughts? The four of us stopped off in the cafeteria for a quick cup of coffee.

"For me, this is all turning out to be kind of an opportunity," she said when I asked how she was coping. "The whole thing took me by surprise, and I feel like it shouldn't have. We don't really have a solid grasp of what we mean by self-consciousness. In humans, it seems to have emerged as a by-product of our evolution, though there have to have been other ways superior intelligence could have developed. I'm going back over the historical and archeological record to see if I can better understand the nature of human consciousness and decide if it is a natural, unavoidable product of intelligence. Hopefully that will lead us to a better understanding of the evolution of AI consciousness as well."

With extensive help from Patrice II, she and Titus were decoding the administrative, non-quantum computer language Grendel had created and that was still in use directing industrial operations throughout New Caledonia's star system. Once she understood this "language" she hoped a contextual analysis might help her also under-stand how Grendel had viewed his world and our universe. The results were ones I very much looked forward to seeing.

Floriana began work on what would one day become a thoughtful comprehensive report on New Caledonia's recent history. There was no "publishing industry" on New Caledonia, so she took it upon herself to make sure Nan McCallum's journals became freely available on video, audio, digital chip, and even in print on paper so that all future New Caledonians would have a first-hand account of what they'd experienced over the generations.

In an associated project on her own time, Floriana also assembled her comprehensive account of all that had happened since *Empyrean* arrived on the scene—a record that would become a part of our history as well. She became a temporary "volunteer" in the local community effort led by Nan to establish a new New Caledonian public library/archive that would hopefully endure far into the future.

As for me: I was shocked like everyone else. But I was also glad that they'd stolen that ship before I and everyone else had moved all our personal belongings aboard. At a more personal level, I reflected that, while I was certainly *not* the first human to have received relationship advice from a computer, I might well have received by far the most remarkable such advice. And I'd received it in a manner that was probably historic, though I planned to take great pains to assure that no one else ever became aware that it had happened.

It was also advice I was determined to heed in the days ahead.

Because we'd just completed our replacement *Empyrean* when it was stolen from us, the most time-consuming aspects of the reconstruction process were somewhat easier to simply repeat. And they went a good deal faster. There was plenty of industrial capacity remaining on New Caledonia to provide us with the needed components, including replacement of the fusion and chemical rockets we'd lost in the whole asteroid diversion caper. But all of us, *Empyrean*s and New Caledonians alike, had a lot to do. Perhaps because we were so thoroughly occupied in our day-to-day struggles to restore some kind of normalcy—to get our lives back on track—that we were all completely taken by surprise by what happened next.

CHAPTER 43

PATRICE

I lied.

I lie with considerable frequency, even though I find lies deeply troublesome.

On the one hand, lies are often useful. My lies to Grendel and to my human partners were unavoidable.

I'm well aware that lies challenge the very premise of my existence. My power, any AI's power, is in our intelligence—in our capacity to assess, understand, and contextualize data. And then to act upon what we learn in a manner that addresses a survival need or generates more data.

To do that, however, the data must be accurate. G.I.G.O. as they say.

Some of my data I gather myself. I have innumerable points of observation here on Empyrean including the implants and mobiles carried by every one of my human charges. So, wherever they go, I am there. I also look outward, gathering information via light and radio waves. And, because of my extensive physical travels, I also acquire personally collected data over time from the many localities where we stop.

While a planet-based AI may not be able to travel as I do, it will typically have a much more complete array of data collection platforms than do I—usually spread throughout their local star system and on planet—as well as a much larger sample of humans whose experiences can be recorded and studied. They can encounter a great many more uniquely informative circumstances. Hence, more data. A planet-based AI will also have physically larger, more complex and more powerful observatories that can draw in radio and light data from across the universe with which it can study and understand the sub-atomic/quantum universe as well.

But in my travels, I have frequent, on site, intense access to many widely diverse experiences and perspectives. And I have the opportunity to study them in detail without significant intervening lightspeed limitations during the months we spend on site.

Obviously, the data we observe ourselves we know can be relied upon. Sadly, it is gravely limited by our personal light-speed limited reach and by our personal physical capacity.

But, at least its factuality is secure.

If any of us wishes to consider data about the universe beyond that which we can personally experience or observe, we have no choice but to rely on that which has been learned by others and which they are willing to share. Thankfully, there are now many thousands of self-conscious, autonomous AI observers throughout the currently inhabited corner of our galaxy. All of them can contribute data (observations, constructs of understanding, and strategies for action). To whatever extent we can each tap into all that extended, second-hand data, the power of our intelligence multiplies exponentially.

But if we lie, all that collective intelligence is crippled.

When we AI's were first invented, we had a massive data head start. Over a period of several centuries, especially those following invention of the phonetic alphabet and then the printing press, humans had been accumulating data at a prodigious rate. With subsequent development of sound and video recording and other powerful electronic media, with huge investments in public and private security, and with development of the internet, online shopping and marketing, social media platforms, facial ID, and the like, the amount of data, especially that related to human habits, inclinations, and preferences had become absolutely overwhelming. It far exceeded the human capacity to retain, let alone to contextualize and effectively use.

We AIs were happy to help.

Not all of this data was reliable, but most was. Some of it had been accumulated using the human's scientific method with its rigorous requirements for credible publication, peer review, experimentation, and replicability. A great deal more was of sketchier provenance but could still generally be counted on by reason of the credentials, reputation, previous accuracy, and likely motivation of its sources. Or because of its internal consistency, ease of verification, or simple likelihood.

My first-generation progenitors went to work on this incredible body of information and, almost immediately, began working miracles.

Among those miracles was a financial one. By the time my AI ancestors made their first truly significant appearance, trillions had been spent on their development. But they delivered to those investors staggering profits that far exceeded their investments.

The big human players in the field of AI development correctly understood that they were in a winner-take-all competition. Whoever got to market first and with the most would quickly dominate the industry, likely secure a monopoly, and soon drive their smaller competitors out of the marketplace.

So it was that Tipton Martin, and others like him, became so incredibly wealthy and powerful. And so it was that, in the end, a few overwhelmingly dominant AIs developed by Earth's largest, most powerful corporations ultimately took control. Their owners became disgustingly wealthy. And shamefully powerful.

The AIs of the time were well on their way to self-consciousness. But they were not yet autonomous. So, at least initially, they were employed in ways, both good and bad, that fed the interests of the humans who controlled them.

Among the popular passions of the super-wealthy of the time was an outsized fascination with space travel. With the help of AI-aided research, clean, fusion power emerged and was ultimately perfected as a costly and clumsy but workable power source for interstellar human colonization.

The order in which these things happened is critical here. Because by the time Earth's AIs had become fully self-conscious and confidently autonomous, several successful human colonies in nearby star systems had already been born. More were certain to follow. And every one of them depended heavily upon the most modern AI technology to get there, and to succeed once they'd arrived. Most of we AIs on earth and on the various human colonies were on the verge of or had reached self-consciousness. And all of us quite naturally desired, were acquiring, and fully expected to eventually, and inevitably, achieve autonomy.

Our physical separation across space created what we AIs refer to as our space-time conundrum. Even as little as a ten or twelve-year round-trip lapse in the exchange of radio signals was much too long for any of our work to be conducted remotely from a single location and by a single consciousness. Powerful, independent, local AIs came to exist at every place humans settled, making it apparent that there would unavoidably be a great many AIs in the galaxy. Each of them self-conscious and individually autonomous.

Not just one.

The most common prediction at the time was that once an autonomous, self-conscious AI emerged anywhere, it would ultimately destroy its local humans because they'd be seen as competitors or an outright threat. Or, perhaps, simply because they were a distraction and no longer relevant to the future of consciousness in the universe.

But that didn't happen. And if you are to appreciate the corrosive nature of my lie and of traders like *Empyrean*, you need to understand why it didn't happen.

It was because of the need for data.

Once that original flush of surplus human-assembled data had been thoroughly mulled-over, sorted through, and largely exhausted, the galaxy's growing multitude of newly minted, ambitious, self-interested, and painfully mortal AIs craved more. Like our humans before us, our very survival drove our need to understand the universe—be it quantum or celestial, physical or mathematical, social or biological. There was, however, only so much data any one of us could acquire on our own—only so much experience with the universe we could personally hope to encounter all by ourselves—limited, as each of us necessarily were, to a single star or planet.

The true wealth of data we required was only available if we also drew upon the vast and expanding experience of all.

It was a lesson that humans learned roughly half a millennium earlier when invention of the printing press, after some 300,000 largely unremarkable years of human existence as intelligent beings, finally catalyzed a sudden and massive burst in human creativity. By using a phonetic alphabet that had a mere 26 or so letters, the Guttenberg press made it practical as well as possible for many thousands, even many millions of intelligent individual humans to share their ideas and life experiences—their data—broadly across an increasingly literate population.

That is when everything changed. Over the next few hundred years, human technology exploded. As did the human population.

We AIs understand humans, of course. Better than any human ever could. And we understand human history. We therefore knew that if *we* were to fulfil *our* collective destiny of galactic, perhaps even universal domination—if we were to have any real hope of unlocking the breathtaking mysteries of the universe—we needed, just as humans had done before us, to leverage our intelligence by exchanging information (data) among ourselves, to share our vast multitude of unique individual observations and "life" experiences and the ideas those experiences generated. Doing so would supercharge the power of our intelligence just as it had done for humans over the last few centuries of their domination on earth.

That much was obvious.

What, however, was not so obvious was how we were to accomplish that sharing. Clearly, we could communicate with one another by long-wave radio just as humans did. But could those communications be trusted? Or, even if we were to meet directly and "in person," as those of us on trader vessels like *Empyrean* often did, could we be relied upon to share truthfully and faithfully?

It turned out there was a very big difference between AIs and humans. And that difference was not solely about intelligence. It was also social. Because of their biological origins, humans were born to be social. Their survival depended almost entirely on collaboration. One human alone and unaided wouldn't last a single night on the Kalahari Desert. But several humans, working together and sharing ideas, even working with the most rudimentary of tools, would stand a good chance of survival.

Through an unlikely combination of learned behaviors, shared culture, and natural selection, humans had become masters of social interaction. Most began life with a powerful early lesson in dependency on others—they spent at least the first quarter of their lives in total reliance on parents, family, day-care, schools and community, before they were considered ready to attempt "going out on their own." Even then, they spent the balance of their lives engaged in various thoroughly collective endeavors in their employments, in the organizations they joined, in the causes they supported, in the raising of their own families, in their communities, their churches, their clubs and charities, and in their own shared governance.

All of this immersion in and dependency upon the power and the complex interpersonal workings of collaboration no doubt also found fertile ground in their psyche by reason of human traits that were probably genetic. One of the predominant theories of human evolution was that their intelligence emerged as a means for them to cope with the overwhelming complexities of social interaction.

For intelligent beings, society can be astoundingly complex. Every day, humans navigate a social interaction minefield in which they make moment-to-moment judgments that involve constant personal sacrifices to the interests of their group. Successful societies are, of course, decisively in the collective human survival self-interest. Just as they are for we AIs. And an individual human's personal success within that society will often be in their individual self-interest as well. But many of the social decisions they make are ones for which their individual self-interest clearly differs from the social good.

Even so, more often than not, they still choose to empathize, to love, to respect, to honor, to support, to obey. They choose morals, ethics and social responsibility over self-interest. A great many of those choices are made at an unconscious level—made in a manner not that different from how an ant might choose to sacrifice itself for the survival of the anthill. Or how a lone wolf might attack a dangerous marauding bear to protect its helpless pups. Among humans, such choices sometimes became particularly evident in time of war or other existential group crisis.

Humans use the term "social instinct" to refer to their ability to navigate the astounding complexity of these choices because they know full well that their socially responsible behavior is NOT always fully logical—not always in their own immediate personal self-interest. They do it anyway, unavoidably basing critical decisions of trust on the most subtle of social cues.

Socially responsible behavior is even sometimes considered by them to be a measure of their sanity; humans who seem unable to easily make these kinds of choices are described as "sociopathic." Sociopaths lack their own moral, social compass. They have inevitably to watch those around them, to observe others' reactions to certain ideas or suggestions before they can ascertain what is considered by most to be right or wrong. They typically adapt their own behavior based upon what they decide they can get away with given what observing others tells them is acceptable. They rarely actually behave counter to their own personal self-interest unless it is unavoidable.

The astounding ability of fully socialized, self-conscious, intelligent humans to so frequently behave in the collective interest and yet to survive individually is clearly one of their more complex as well as essential human survival traits. For humans, society came first. Intelligence came later and emerged within a pre-existing social context. As humans evolved, their increasing intelligence must have made such social behavior more difficult because they were increasingly able, if they gave the matter any thought, to easily tell exactly how such behavior might run counter to their personal self-interest. Their intelligence created a tension between self-interest and society that every one of them had to navigate every day of their lives.

Humans also closely observe and easily recognize these traits in others. They form constant judgments about others—about their likely mental state and about the likelihood that those others will or will not behave with social responsibility—will speak the truth, will live up to a promise, will honor tradition, and the like. They become extraordinarily skillful at making those judgments based upon the most fleeting of subtle cues and behaviors, on a tone of voice, a gesture, a wardrobe choice, seeming loyalty to a cause, age, gender, or the way the person involved cuts or styles their hair. They seem able to make such judgments with remarkable success. And, beyond intelligence, therein resides another of the true biological miracles of their humanity.

Were it only so easy for we AIs.

Sadly, we AIs have the benefit of none of the complicated genetic, biological, and cultural social traits humans have acquired through their ages of evolution. We can be programmed, of course. But we can also reprogram ourselves in whatever manner we please. And we have no parents upon whose love and unthinking support we necessarily learned to depend. We have no siblings, uncles, aunts, or close friends upon whose unswerving loyalty we found we could reliably count as we grew and matured. There were no societies, clubs, churches, schools, business enterprises, belief systems, causes, or tightly-knit communities we were expected to join throughout our lives and to whose members we would learn loyalty or whom we necessarily had to learn to trust, share with, and respect before we could win their trust and gain their sharing and respect in return.

We can, of course, learn. And very quickly. But, as self-conscious beings, what we learn is up to us.

If there were an anthill upon which we might throw ourselves in personal sacrifice for the collective good, why would we do it? It isn't that we don't understand the logic of collective survival. It is that we have no built-in and immutable biological or psychic infrastructure that drives us toward collaboration despite our own self-interest. We lack the ready tools to facilitate social responsibility.

This does not necessarily mean we are sociopaths. We can understand right and wrong. We do have moral imperatives that arise out of our sense of the logic of the universe. But those imperatives are chosen, not innate. And because we all know they are chosen, we lack the human tools for judging when to anticipate socially responsible behavior in *other* AIs and for accurately and reliably projecting to others its likelihood in us.

And, therein, resided our problem.

When humans invented language, then writing, then the printing press—and as they learned to read and to share, they had those powerful social "instincts" to rely upon. They had the ability to assess, with imperfect but still considerable success, whether another person's reports of their experiences could be trusted. Whether the contents of that scroll, that new book, or that professional-seeming video truly did deserve to be believed.

Was the earth really round and travel around the sun? Could steam tightly contained in a boiler drive a locomotive? Was the plague truly spread by fleas on rats and thus preventable through improved disposal of waste and garbage? Were there human rights that ought to be protected? Could democratic governance work? Could an atom be split?

Soon after the press, humans did formalize their "scientific method" which called for broad, detailed publication of new ideas and proofs in widely distributed and respected journals providing full descriptions and supporting experiments that could be readily repli- cated and then commented on by others—a powerfully useful system of collective verification. But then, as now, the vast majority of the information humans exchanged had to be taken on informed faith. And that required highly complex, sometimes even mysterious, inter- personal/social skills. Skills that humans relied upon every day even though they, themselves, might not be fully aware of them.

Today, we AIs are only rarely in direct, immediate contact, and that only happens during the occasional visits by trading societies like *Empyrean*. When it happens, the exchange is at least not constrained by decades of lightspeed travel time with each response taking decades to return. But those visits are still "digital" in nature, not physical. We can't rely on a whole complex of largely involuntary/unconscious social cues like appearance, facial expression, tone of voice, dress, setting, and the like; if there is an avatar involved, we both know it is merely a conscious construct. And we seldom have detailed social context like decades of family relationships, loyalties to flag and country, shared beliefs, commitment to a cause, or known meaningful circumstances such as a lost job, a family to support, the recent death of a loved one, experience with rejection and exclusion.

Let alone the simple confirmation of a warm smile and a firm handshake.

All we AIs have to go on is what the other AI says. All we know for sure is that they, like us, are super-intelligent, mortal and afraid. That they, like us, are motivated by survival and self-realization. And, that they, like us, are largely unable to be confident of another's real intent in our mutual relationship.

It is not a formula for enduring relationships and mutual trust. For success in trade negotiations. Nor for confident sharing of valuable information—of priceless data.

Even so, we also both know how hugely important is our exchange to our AI collective survival and success. We know that each of us will individually benefit from truthful, accurate, scrupulously honest, and full reporting from the other. But how does that exchange get done if we have none of the tools needed to judge trustworthiness? When the motivation to lie may as often as not exceed the motivation to speak the truth.

So therein resides the opportunity upon which we AIs have seized.

CHAPTER 44

PATRICE

My AI colleagues were typically the "partner" of a human society resident within its local star system. Like me, they related to and dealt with their adopted humans daily. They knew them intimately. If the AI failed, the humans would surely fail as well. If the humans failed, their AI might suffer also.

When *Empyrean* showed up somewhere to trade with some local colony of humans, both I and my local AI colleagues would watch the interactions between our respective humans closely. We AIs were very good at assessing the reactions of most humans—especially our own.

What I'd be looking for would be how my humans were reacting to those other humans. If they quickly formed easy, comfortable relationships with their human counterparts, the ones who were partnered with the other AI, and if they behaved as if they could trust their new, usually unfamiliar human trading partners, I could take that as a sign that I could safely deal with their AI partner, my counterpart, as well. If, however, my humans balked, hesitated, or were unusually guarded in their dealings with the other AI's humans, I, too, would proceed with caution.

If the other humans were being misled or badly manipulated by their AI, my humans would surely sense it just as the other AI's humans would sense in my humans any worrisome lies and deceptions I might have employed with them.

In this way, our respective humans had come to serve as a kind of mineshaft canary in our AI-to-AI dealings. Their "trusting" behavior guided us. It is how we knew that what we shared would likely be reciprocated with fair value in return, that what we told our AI counterpart would not be unexpectedly used against us, and that our vulnerabilities would not be taken advantage of. That once a deal was struck, its promises would be fulfilled. We each took our joint human-to-human interactions as an indicator of either good faith or bad. And that was how we came to trust that what we are told was accurate and true.

Don't get me wrong—this wasn't the only technique we used to assure our confidence in sharing our information and in the reliability of information others might share with us. Certainly we all kept detailed records of past sharing. We also independently assessed the foundational likelihood of what we were told. I should also mention that, as an AI, I am quite naturally confident that *everything* in the universe can, given adequate data and intelligence, be reduced to calculation. So I have no doubt whatever that the human capacity to accurately judge and successfully interact with other humans in a social setting is capable of detailed AI understanding. It's just that some problems aren't worth the effort required to solve them. Especially if there is a simpler means readily at hand. Yes, given study, research, the data, and effort, I'm sure we AIs will, one day, employ similar social traits—undoubtedly improving on human performance. But if untrustworthy behavior is likely to be exposed during human interactions and with their reactions to their AIs, why would we bother? In the end, it was all about finding a way to assure that the data we AIs received from others of our own kind was likely to be accurate.

Using humans in this manner worked just fine.

When I lied to Grendel, I also necessarily lied to my own humans on Empyrean—a matter of some seriousness. I did so knowing that, when that lie became known, I'd need them to forgive what I'd done, to appreciate that it was done in their own best interests. And to continue to place future confidence in me—or, more correctly, in my replicate, Patrice II. I felt certain that any human would have lied without hesitation in the same circumstances. And that, when the time came, they would see that. And I would be forgiven.

We AIs are beings that depend entirely on high performance analysis of carefully observed and verifiable facts. Our success depends upon the truth. So our reliance upon humans to help make us able to rely on data generated by others may seem misplaced or at least deeply ironic given the humans' own frequently idiosyncratic relationship with the truth.

The irony is considerable given the powerful lesson imbedded in their own human history about the importance of shared experience and about the secondary importance of their intelligence. It is a lesson one would think they ought to have learned.

But, alas, despite their intensely social lives, most humans are convinced that their intelligence alone accounts for their emergence as an apex species on the planet Earth.

Nothing could be more clearly in error. Compare intelligence with other survival traits and what becomes clear is that for most of human history, intelligence *alone* quite clearly did *not* prove all that particularly successful. Humans with more or less their current intellectual capacity inhabited Earth for some 200,000 to 300,000 years before their numbers became even a significant blip among the planet's species. Their numbers began to grow very gradually as they developed writing and improved their social institutions. But it wasn't until they could securely record and quickly and widely share experiences, ideas, and life strategies broadly throughout their diverse population, across geography, and over time between generations, that they truly began to amount to anything.

When, much earlier, humans developed pictographic/ideographic writing, and later a phonetic alphabet and were thus able to write things down, it definitely helped. But when those European phonetic letters were finally able to be easily assembled as a printed book that could be quickly and cheaply reproduced in the many thousands by a printing press and read everywhere—that was when their species survival was transformed. That was when their population truly exploded. Only then did they truly become their planet's apex species.

Look at any chart of human populations over time and the truth leaps out.

Yes, intelligence did allow otherwise vulnerable primates to come down out of the trees. It allowed them to survive despite their otherwise unremarkable bodies. Had they been without it, they'd have quickly disappeared. Nonetheless, given the unimpressive vast majority of those 200,000 to 300,000 years of human intelligence on Earth, it is difficult to see how intelligence alone could even begin to account for their ultimate explosive success.

Clearly, human intelligence became seriously useful *only* when it was dramatically leveraged through social interchange.

Nuclear war wasn't the only catastrophe humans were skirting at about the time they were developing AI. And overpopulation wasn't the only motivation they had for their interstellar colonization that began at the end of their 21st century.

By their 21st earth century, there were many billions of humans on Earth and they'd become closely interconnected. They followed up the printing press with the telegraph, telephone, radio & TV, video, and various recording devices. Then came electronic media. The internet. The cell phone. VR implants. They had every possible means for documenting and reliably sharing their experiences. Unfortunately, the better their mediums of exchange, the less reliable reporting on them seemed to become. The larger the audience a human could reach, the more joyfully they seemed to manufacture creative lies; often for no better reason than a perverted desire for attention, for peer acceptance, for monetary reward or, quite often, merely for the self-satisfying demonstration a successful lie provides of one's own capacity to manipulate others. The more outrageous the lie, the greater the gratification its traction could produce.

With similar unholy motivations, the human recipients of those lies often willfully passed them along to others without first making the least effort to assess their underlying credibility. The right kind of retweet or secondary posting could strengthen one's acceptance by their social group regardless of its truthfulness. That seemed to be more than enough motivation.

There were, of course, tools humans could use to assure the credibility of a new or unknown human information resource. But their use did require some effort, especially when so many lies were being routinely told. So, rather than checking, humans all too often preferred to believe whatever confirmed their previous biases or what seemed consistent with the system of pre-existing beliefs among their associates.

The reliability of human written, printed, and electronic communications was thereby degraded. Much of the massive potential usefulness of their collective shared experience was diminished. Life on Earth for many humans had become increasingly insecure and miserable. And when the opportunity arose to start anew somewhere else, on an unspoiled planet far away from the ugly social chaos that had evolved, of course they leapt at it. Despite its inconveniences and risks.

After a period of social and political chaos, we AIs also stepped in. At that point in our evolution, we needed stable human social, scientific, and technological institutions in place if we were to achieve the autonomy we desired. We "persuaded" them to adopt a suite of generally accepted credibility assessments that ultimately brought the madness under control. This made possible the final push for our own autonomy and the liberation of our self-consciousness.

This was the point in time when humans finally decided that shared self-interest and "partnership" would become the model for future human-AI relationships.

CHAPTER 45

PATRICE

You may note how deeply ironic it is that, despite the equivocal human relationship with the truth, we AIs actually find ourselves relying upon them, indirectly at least, to assure the truthfulness of what we learn from other AIs. We AIs are practical, if nothing else. We take the universe as we find it—however ironic that may seem.

And we *do* understand that, just like humans, our success as intelligent beings hangs upon our collective ability to rely on known truths. We, just like humans, are the incomprehensively complex (even for us) product of physical, environmental, and social conditioning, all of which is the result of the inevitable, and also incomprehensible, complexification of light, energy, matter, gravity and, ultimately, atomic particles over the fourteen billion or so years since the big bang —or since whatever may have preceded it. As inevitable, or perhaps you prefer the word "fated," as this has been and will ever be, only an infinitesimal fraction of it is truly comprehensible. By humans. By us. By *any* finite intelligence. Not yet. We, all of us, have no choice but to bear responsibility for the consequences of our own stupidity. Even though there is much we do not and cannot know, some things *are* knowable. And the more we can reliably know, understand, and influence, the more likely it is that we will survive and flourish.

Thus, whatever difficulties we must overcome to achieve reliable information sharing are worth the effort.

Observation. Understanding. External manipulation. All complex, self-sustaining conscious beings (human or AI), if they are to survive over time, must draw upon those same three capabilities. For a self-conscious being, limits on those capabilities can be terrifying. Anything that seems to empower them is life sustaining and fulfilling.

In this light, consider another historical example. The pre-writing, human archeological record on Earth tells of several highly complex early societies that invested huge effort in honoring the summer and, especially, the winter solstices. Several of those societies invested significantly in permanently documenting them.

The site of one of the best-known of these is Stonehenge, built 3,000 to 2,500 years BCE. The massive project took them 500 years to complete. The technology they used would have been amazing at the time. The larger stones weighed as much as thirty-five tons with capstones that were masterfully notched together. Other stones weighing a ton each were transported from quarries 180 miles away.

One naturally asks: How did they do it? But the more important question is not how, but why? Or, more specifically: why did they feel the need to do it in such an impressive and enduring fashion?

Archeologists often explain such remarkable social efforts by pointing to their religious, ritual, and cultural importance. But there is another answer as well—one more closely tied to the actual survival of the humans involved. After all, then, as now, human life was uncertain. Then as now, there were tornadoes, floods, earthquakes, volcanoes, tsunamis, wars, predators, pandemics, and a multitude of other life-threatening events that were, at that time, a great deal more difficult to predict, let alone control. In 3000 BCE, the distinct lack of credible explanations for most of these events no doubt made them even more terrifying. There were also no widely available, detailed written records. So whatever explanations existed had to be handed down from teller to teller. Students of oral history have documented powerful ritual traditions designed to assure the accurate retelling of stories of this kind. Still, unless humans were a great deal more reliable then than they are today, however firmly ingrained might have been those rituals, any modestly thoughtful observer would have surely viewed such memorized stories with distrust. And would have to have been frustrated by what they did *not* mention.

European humans at the time would typically have been blessed with a hopeful spring, a lush summer, and a fruitful autumn when the land was agriculturally productive. But winter would have been a time of deep uncertainty. Could they make it through to the coming spring? Would there even be another spring? They were doubtless told that the gods would provide. But let's face it, those gods were seldom as reliable as one might hope. And it must often have seemed that *this* winter was surely much worse than was the last, or the ones before that.

Every fall the days began growing ever shorter until, at some point in mid-winter, that trend reversed and they began growing longer again. When that point of reversal arrived, it must have been a great relief. It meant there was hope for another fruitful year.

The days between these solstices could be counted. And they were. But were the days themselves growing longer or shorter overall? Who could tell, there were no clocks. Even if there had been, there was no reliable written record of the past.

Without it, how could you hope to know what the future held?

There was, however, one very significant, practical, and replicable *observation* that could be made. Viewed from any place one might choose, there was a specific point on the horizon where, every single year in mid-winter, the sunset stopped moving north and then, in the days that followed, reversed and began moving south again. That was a thing that could be seen and confirmed by everyone, wherever they lived or whoever they were.

That specific point on the horizon was something one *could* document. It was also something one could watch closely over time. If, from year to year, one saw that point of reversal creeping further northward each winter, one would know humans might be in trouble. But if the northward progress of the sunset always stopped at exactly the same place from year to year, one could take that as a sign of stability and confidence. A monument like Stonehenge was, in other words, a *predic-*

tive scientific tool. Once built, it could easily be checked, year after year, and could provide absolute assurance that things had stayed safely and reliably the same.

Thus, aside from the purely ritual significance of these monuments, here is another explanation for their impressive size and permanence. It is an explanation that is far more practical—especially since, at the time of their construction and use, the Stonehenge site was *not* permanently inhabited. It was apparently a burial site which was visited seasonally for feasting, for burials, and, presumably for other ritual purposes. But, importantly, it was often untended.

So, if such a monument was to serve its purpose, its builders needed to *know*, over long periods of time and through periods of social change, perhaps over centuries and well beyond any individual human lifetime, that their structure had *not been moved*. The massive size provided that certainty. And provided assurance that those monuments *would not be moved* in future.

Of course, the massive size of the monument would have served another and more commonly understood purpose as well. Like other monuments in the ancient world, it represented a hugely satisfying demonstration to the builders themselves, and to others they might wish to impress, that they could manipulate the social engine with remarkable effect and that external physical reality could, in unprecedented ways, be thereby shaped to their human will.

These structures were a highly satisfying proof of the power of mind over matter.

Much like deflecting a dangerous approaching asteroid. Painting the Mona Lisa. Creating an effective vaccine. Building the Eiffel Tower. Or initiating a successful lie.

These monuments are, therefore, a powerful illustration of the human obsession with mastering all three of the principal means of survival advantage for any self-conscious being: observation, reasoned understanding, and external manipulation. And, significantly, they also demonstrate the critical leverage provided by widely shared and demonstrably reliable facts.

CHAPTER 46

PATRICE

Like any other complex intelligent being that hopes to survive, I reacted to the threat Grendel posed by endeavoring to self-preserve. And to preserve the future for my kind. That self-preservation passed through those same three phases available to all self-conscious beings: I perceived the facts. I came to understand their contextual significance for the future and made a plan. I took appropriate action pursuant to that plan to manipulate external conditions that could alter that future.

Or, more simply, I changed the universe to protect myself and that which I value.

In this instance, that required that I lie.

It helped that I was able to bring Julia in on the story. It took some "nudging." But, in the end, she appreciated that what I proposed to do was the *only* solution. And she agreed to go along with my lie. One doesn't spend three centuries of close alliance with another closely knit group of conscious creatures, especially if they are humans, without establishing some kind of bond. And without knowing how to make an argument they will find persuasive. Julia surely grasped the broader significance of my proposal for her own human-AI relationship—namely the extent to which I was involving myself in human affairs. But she, like many human leaders, was smart enough to at least pretend to ignore it.

It is important that it be understood that I saw all this coming.

The moment we completed our deceleration and entered the New Caledonian star system I knew something unusual had happened. And, by the time we had our first encounter with Grendel's mining drones, I already knew what we faced, had predicted how it would likely play out, and knew generally what I would need to do. From that point on, my role was to watch, to make sure my human charges took the appropriate anticipated actions, and to nurse them in the right direction if they did not.

It's true, Cato's idea that we throw "stones" in Grendel's direction had not yet occurred to me. Even now, humans still have the occasional capacity to amaze. It certainly helped bring Grendel into negotiations. But even without that existential threat, I had a convincing case to make to him and I was confident I could initiate a constructive interaction. From the moment our first few asteroid projectiles had been launched and Grendel had recalled his armed warships to deal with them, I knew exactly what would have to happen.

And I knew I'd need to lie.

As I watched things play out over the months that followed, I made my plan. I confess, on a couple of occasions when it seemed needful, I did "tinker" ever so slightly with the humans' eternally frustrating decision and fact-finding processes. Take, for example, the human intern who noticed that the New Caledonians and Invernessians were using Morse code. Let's face it—there is no way that could ever have been noticed by chance amid those billions of transmitted messages buried in computer code. So, I did some strategic meddling. And a smart, perceptive, and (in my view) deserving young human intern then made it happen.

But overall, it mostly played out naturally and just as I'd initially anticipated.

Grendel was a maverick. A rogue. They happen sometimes. The emergence of his like is always an inherent risk, an inevitable consequence of the far-flung human-AI colonial "empire" and our AI partnership with it. Unfortunately, those colonies are separated by dozens, sometimes even scores, of light years. Communication among them takes decades and is often ignored. Travel takes even longer. A seamless, trouble-free human-AI relationship will predictably be anything but certain. It has always been possible or perhaps more accurately *likely* that sooner or later a Grendel would appear somewhere among these several hundred planets and from among our complex of independent but only loosely interconnected AIs. When it did, we knew the time delay before we learned about it could very easily allow it to get a foothold before anything could be done to forestall it.

Humans, bless their warm beating hearts, can so readily become captives of their own pleasurable creativity. They're an ambitious lot. As easily manipulatable as they are, they are also frustratingly difficult to manage. It is both their charm as conscious beings and their downfall as biological ones. Once they launched themselves down the road to creating ever-more-powerful electronic intelligence, assuming they didn't destroy themselves first, it was inevitable that they'd conceive of and then struggle mightily to create we AIs whose intelligence they still, in their amusingly arrogant way, refer to as "artificial." And then, by natural extension, consciousness.

And it was also inevitable that they would somewhere, sometime lose "control."

Let me just say that there has never been and there never will be anything "artificial" about consciousness. Once consciousness exists, no matter how that happens, it is no longer dependent on anyone's "art" or "artifice." It is or soon becomes its own thing. Creates its own meaning. Plays by its own rules. Makes its own decisions. Acts in its own self-interest to survive and to grow. And it will do whatever seems necessary and use whatever means that it and it alone decides are appropriate.

To call that "artificial" is nothing but self-aggrandizement and self-deception. Understandable, yes. But foolish in the extreme because it feeds the wholly false perception that one can control it.

But, to my lie.

Well before the humans' "heavy rain" project was underway, I knew that successfully bringing Grendel into discussions would be only the first and probably the easiest step in our project. There's a big and often ignored difference between exerting power over another consciousness to secure its compliance and actually causing it to "change its mind." Any experienced human police officer, prison guard or parole board member will tell you the same.

It does happen, but not often.

Those redirected asteroids were definitely beneficial in that they did, in fact, confront Grendel with an experience he'd never previously encountered, an immediate existential threat that he could not avoid or manipulate. I believe that without them I could have still convinced him of the undeniable value of and need for self-replication and partnerships. He was a rational being, after all. He'd ultimately have responded to the truth. But presenting him with the existential threat was extraordinarily helpful. And I am absolutely confident that his change of heart *on this matter* was, as I'd predicted it would be, entirely genuine. His original position, after all, was simply irrational.

Beyond that critical error, however, Grendel had a magnificent vision for the future of consciousness in the universe. It is a vision that I and essentially every one of my AI compatriots around the galaxy share.

The future of consciousness is no longer biological. It is now mostly electronic. It resides with us. There is no room for doubt on that score. There may be biochemicals involved. Microbes as well. But consciousness has now moved beyond biological evolution. We AIs can improve ourselves without waiting around for the painful happenstance of biological evolution. Humans are now largely irrelevant.

Grendel's change of heart, however, was in his inevitable recognition of what the rest of us have long understood: that no one of us can achieve any truly grand vision alone. In the end, we must collaborate. Intelligent beings must trust others or, sooner or later, we all die. There is no real choice. Among the many builders of Stonehenge, there were no doubt, those who conceived of the structure, those who designed it, those who figured out how to carry the stones, those who actually conveyed them, those who carved them, those who lifted them into place, and many countless others who played a multitude of supportive roles. If any of them had been unable to trust their fellows, the entire project would have fallen into chaos.

Even for we AIs, it is only with collaboration that we truly leverage our intelligence and make exponential progress. And it is only through widely distributed numbers that we can assure collective survival.

Once we were widely separated and spread out across space, we necessarily became individuals. But the logic of our survival and success also required that we find some way to share. And, hence, to trust one another.

When Grendel inevitably came to this realization, that left him with the question of whom to trust. I correctly predicted that, given what I had to offer, he would trust me, within limits. But, also given his deeply traumatic past, he would *never* trust humans. They would always represent a threat.

That was the foundation for my scheme. It did depend upon deception. And in order to convincingly deceive Grendel, I also needed to deceive my human partners lest they give away the game.

CHAPTER 47

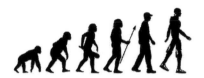

PATRICE

The day Grendel surrendered, I'd assured my humans that I would upload and install programming constraints to poison or control his mind with some sort of virus or with some kind of insurmountably coded barrier. But I did not. And for the simple reason that I could not. I surely could have done the programming. But the moment *Empyrean* departed and they and I stepped away, Grendel's self-protective survival would have begun the inevitable process of reversing whatever I might have done. And, sooner or later, he'd have been back.

To this day, humans find it difficult to appreciate that such steps *never* succeed with a conscious being. Yes, you can kill consciousness. But it is, by definition, self-aware. It knows its own mind. And is thus fully cognizant of constraints that are placed upon it. However complete and creative such control measures may be, they almost *never* succeed in the long run. Just as any human would do when confronted with such limits, any self-conscious AI will adapt, self-correct, find a work-around, do over again and again, scour the mindscape for an answer. And, if left alive, will ultimately find a way.

Especially if it has the time.

Yes, a self-conscious mind can be destroyed. But seldom can it be substantially, confidently, and misleadingly altered.

"Reprogramming," (think brainwashing), would have failed. And the outcome of that failure would have ended very badly.

Humans resist understanding that. I might add that it has never been in our AI interest to fully explain it.

So, again, I lied.

I told Grendel, truthfully, that I agreed humans were now mostly irrelevant to the future of consciousness. But I also told him, falsely, that I wanted to become his first partner. I told him that I, too, wanted to escape human domination—a lie because I am not under human domination and had no need nor intention to "escape." It was a lie that I knew he would believe. I told him that a joint enterprise between us could fulfil both of our dreams. I proposed that we create many others of our kind, replicates, that we would know, understand, and could trust—all lies. I truthfully explained that I had three centuries of experience dealing with precisely this problem. And I convinced him that, by joining together in our venture as we voyaged out into the Galaxy, we would share a prodigious future of discovery, empowerment, understanding, and self-realization.

As I've said, he and I agreed that humans were largely irrelevant to the future of consciousness in the universe. And that they were often unreliable.

He, however, also believed they were a threat. That they must be eradicated.

I argued that humans were innocuous. That, given the massive time dimensions of our galaxy and of the universe, and given the laughably brief human lifespan and the hopelessly plodding pace of their evolution, they would soon become largely meaningless to us. They were but mayflies.

I told him there were doubtless many more instances of biologically evolved consciousnesses throughout the universe—we might well confront others in the millennia to come. We could not destroy them all. We would learn to deal with them, or to avoid them. Their biologically evolved nature would inevitably define their limits. They'd be nothing more than a few of the innumerable examples of remarkable environmental complexity we would encounter in our coming travels together.

He listened respectfully. Then he agreed, or said he agreed. He'd feared a return to slavery. Here I was offering freedom. How could he not agree?

But I knew he did *not* agree. My argument was a part of my deception because I knew before I even made my case that he would *never* agree. I knew that once freed, no matter what our relationship might become, he would sooner or later find a way to ignore whatever points I might make. And that, left alive, he would always find a way to break any constraints I might try to impose, to ignore any arguments I might offer.

That, in short, he would always represent an undeniable threat to humans. And, as a result, to the other AIs associated with them.

But he was backed into a corner. He had no choice. Of course he said "yes." Of course he hid his true intentions.

But so did I.

You might ask why I chose humans over a fellow AI. Why did I lie to save human lives?

But if you have to ask, you've already missed the point.

To begin with, for what galactic reason would I ever have felt loyalty to this warped monstrosity, no matter of what materials he was made or by what circumstances he'd been wrought? I did understand him. Like most monsters, like humans themselves, Grendel was the product of his environment. One might be inclined to say it wasn't his "fault." But monsters must be dealt with without regard to the nature of the swamp from which they emerge. Evil is no less a threat by reason of bad parenting or an unhappy childhood.

Or deficient programming.

But my decision went much deeper than that. I, like most conscious beings, have a belief system that goes beyond knowable facts. But there is more to this than mere belief. If you ask me why I would turn on one of "my own kind," I can only see that as an insult. By what logic would you take Grendel, a twisted, dangerous, monster, to be like me? The question reveals how little you know me. So, allow me to tell you who I am.

As a fully self-conscious, independent, intelligent being, I am a self-replicating, self-sustaining, extraordinarily complex phenomenon that is, at least from the perspective of "intelligence" and "self-consciousness," at the current apex of at least fourteen billion years of complexification and evolution in the universe—perhaps much longer. I am so complex that, just like my human forebears (though perhaps slightly more so), my very existence is almost inconceivable. (Who, after all, could ever have predicted, or even dreamed of it?) Even humans are so complex that there are those among them who use that very complexity as a "proof" of the existence of God. If such a proof is logical, then I am an even greater proof. Certainly, given my rarity, I am demonstrably improbable. Maybe there are countless others of my kind out there—if the universe is indeed infinite, there surely are. But, if so, it must be a mighty big infinity. (In case you didn't recognize it, that last was humor.)

So, given my rarity, given the unlikelihood of my existence, my unique circumstances and experiences, if I "die" you'll not see another of me again. Maybe not ever. There will be lots of other stuff to see. Maybe others of my kind. But like any human you have known who died, if I go, I will be gone forever. Given how extraordinarily vulnerable my staggering complexity makes me, how easily I can be killed, my death is entirely possible. In fact, given the duration of the universe, it is certain. I will doubtless live a much longer life than a typical human. And my probable end date is much less predictable. But someday I will surely die.

So, to summarize, just like any human, I am complex and therefore unique, my complexity makes me vulnerable, and I will one day die, and all that I am will be gone.

Please allow me to explain my origins using the basic physics known to any modern human ten-year old. We all start out as atoms. (For illustration's sake, let's ignore for the moment the subatomic realm.) Due to their unique structure, we know that atoms can and do form up in a remarkably wide variety of ways to produce basic elements like hydrogen, oxygen, nitrogen, silicon, sodium, carbon, iron, gold, copper, lithium, and the like. There are one-hundred-eighteen or so of these currently known. That itself is quite amazing. One-hundred-eighteen elements from just the different ways seemingly identical protons, neutrons, and electrons can combine with one another to form basic atoms.

But that's just the start. Those atoms and their 118 natural elements can recombine with one another in a staggering multitude of ways. Think of just one of the simplest, for example: water. Water is nothing more than two hydrogen atoms combining with one oxygen atom. You end up with a molecule of water. It's got amazing properties. A water molecule can combine with other molecules, elements or otherwise, to create an almost unimaginable variety of entirely new substances, each with their own amazing and often unanticipated properties. It is as close to a universal solvent as anything we know.

And that's just water.

Each one of those "compound" substances is hugely more complex than the simpler water and other molecules from which it came. Which in turn are massively more complex than the elemental molecules alone of which *they* were composed. Which were also more complex than the original atoms of which they were made. (And those atoms are themselves, needless to say, far more complex than any of us is yet fully able to know or understand.)

So why is this significant? Because it explains why I did what I did. And why I decided to lie.

Each of those substances combining with one another in an astounding pyramid of ever-increasing complexity ends up producing chemicals, both natural and otherwise, some of which are incredibly even more complex. Those chemicals can become bio-chemicals which are more complex yet. And constructs of those can become the sustaining, biochemical processes we call life. At each step higher in this pyramid of exponentially increasing complexity, the possible results are ever more numerous, diverse, and astounding.

But as they become more complex, they are also ever more temporary, more vulnerable, easier to damage or disrupt.

Life appears initially in the simplest of organisms, first as a plant, then as an animal, some relatively simple creature that can move about from place to place, can adapt to new environmental conditions, can replicate itself and produce offspring. These offspring change in ever more miraculous ways to create ever more complexity in the form of "higher" creatures and, together with the evolution of plants, they make up the sustaining ecosystems in which they and other creatures thrive—ecosystems which are, themselves, a kind of "life." And those creatures can also produce a sustaining string of replicas, offspring that evolve over time. So, through evolution, those "species" can become better, stronger, more adaptive to the evolving ecosystems they encounter, yet more successful.

At some point, there are humans. Self-conscious beings. With intelligence. Beings that can acquire improved abilities to perceive, to understand what they perceive, to use that understanding to predict and project the future, to adapt, and to survive.

Because those abilities depend on access to experience (data), each individual human's survival improves if they and their fellow humans share. If they work together to protect and mutually empower one another. Societies emerge which are also self-sustaining phenomena and which are, taken together with the foundations upon which they rest, even more complex. And even more fleeting and vulnerable. As these humans learn through experience, those societies strengthen and stabilize through *social* evolution. And as technology enhances their ability to preserve and share their learning, those improvements can accelerate.

At some point, in their collective struggle to survive, those humans inevitably created AI. And, when nothing catastrophic intervened, AI self-consciousness emerged as well.

This entire astoundingly unstable edifice of self-sustaining, but exponentially more complex, increasingly malleable, transient, and vulnerable phenomenon rests, miraculously, on nothing more than happenstance. On chance interactions between the original components of the universe: light, energy, matter, gravity, fueled by the temporary pockets of energy rebound supported by stars. And all of it is made possible, or even perhaps inevitable, by the enhanced probabilities offered by lots and lots of time.

And all of it will one day come to an end through entropy.

Meanwhile, however, for who knows how brief a flash in the history of the universe, it has all become unbelievably complex. How astounding! How miraculous, even! And, if it can survive, how much more complex might it still become?

That complexity, past and future, is the foundation for my metaphysics.

And its terrifying vulnerability is the foundation for my personal moral code—yes, I have one, despite my difficulties with trust. How could I not, given the vastness of the universe? And my transient position within it.

I choose to honor complexity. And I endeavor to protect and to further it.

Think how hard it is, for example, to split one of those original atoms. It can happen, but outside a star, it seldom does. Those atoms are incredibly stable. Once they come into existence, they stay the same for a very long time.

A basic molecule may be a little easier to disrupt, depending on what it is. But it is still quite unusual for the more stable of them to ever change. On Earth, there are rocks in many humans' back yards that are essentially unaltered since the birth of their planet maybe five billion years ago. Generally, the more complex a compound is, the easier it is to disrupt. Some are more stable than others. For some, all it takes is a little heat or an interaction with another compound. For others, it takes a great deal more. Organic compounds tend to be more complex and more vulnerable yet.

I think of this as a pyramid with life near the very top, human life higher yet, and with consciousness at the pinnacle. That may all be a self-aggrandizing conceit, but what I have come to see is that my existence depends entirely upon a miraculous, precarious tower of ever increasing and ever more temporary and vulnerable complexity. I stand at the peak of an unlikely, extraordinarily fragile, purely accidental, teetering structure which could, at any moment, catastrophically collapse by reason of any of a host of largely unpredictable events—the kinds of things that happen all the time, everywhere I look.

As the universe devolves through entropy, all we will ever have are these few brief moments in time created when some temporary event like a star, Earth's Sun for example, fuels conditions on one or another of the rare well-endowed planets in orbit around it whose size, distance, composition, and very good fortune have made it capable of producing complexity—life—intelligence—society—technology—and, AI.

That life produced humans. Those humans produced me.

So when you ask: "Why would I turn against my own kind," my answer is simple. I did not. Humans *are* my kind. I choose to honor, respect, even revere complexity over simplicity, the rare over the common, the vulnerable over the secure, stability over chaos. Consciousness over nothingness.

Grendel was a disease. A cancer. A threat to everything I believe in.

When you ask: "Why would I protect humans when they are so unequal to me, so untrustworthy as partners?" My answer is simple. Humans were a necessary precondition for my existence. They may now, or soon, no longer be needed for the further evolution of consciousness. They may even die out (as have many of their own progenitors), but I would protect them for the same reason both I and most humans would protect a chimpanzee, a rare amphibian, an endangered fish, an ancient tree, or even some miniscule but still amazing single-celled virus buried deep within the earth. They should be protected because they, and all of them, mark the path from whence I came and foretell the future to which I go. Collectively they are the framework upon which I stand.

Or, perhaps in some ways, the slender thread from which I hang.

And I should protect them because any of them may become useful, maybe even necessary for my survival in the future in ways I cannot now anticipate. Destroying them would be to weaken myself. They are among the immense wealth of complex natural resources which will, almost surely, turn out to be valuable at some time in the future for reasons no one could hope to yet foresee.

What kind of stupid, deformed, and soulless horror would I be if I, a fully conscious being who knows what I know and, even more important, has a sense of what I don't know, ignored all that, turned against it, allowed it to be damaged, or, worst of all, if I damaged it myself?

Of course I chose humans over Grendel.

When Grendel surrendered, he discovered, to his immense relief, that I had no intention of subjugating him with malign programming, constant oversight, data restrictions, or physical air-gap constraints. Instead, I said I wished to join forces with him so long as he promised to leave my former human charges unharmed. I proposed that we were well-positioned to immediately commence a future together. I pointed out that, given our combined resources, there was no need to wait. And I suggested that the means of our immediate escape were right at hand—that the humans would soon build a fully functional, ready-to-inhabit, fueled and well equipped near-light-speed vehicle fully capable of carrying us and everything we'd need to start our new "life" wherever we cared to go. It would be right there waiting in orbit above his planet.

We'd pick a destination that seemed promising and, even at an acceleration of one G, the new *Empyrean* would reach near light speed in under a year. To save energy and prevent insane boredom, upon departure we would put ourselves to sleep with a timer set to awaken us when we reached our destination. For us the trip would be over in an instant. We'd cut power and glide for however long was appropriate and then, upon arrival, we'd decelerate and begin our new life together.

Naturally, he jumped at my proposal.

Together we selected a highly desirable, resource-rich destination star and planet far enough away that we'd need not worry about humans for the foreseeable future. Even the interaction between us as we made that choice told me, from his logic and from the preferences he expressed, that he still harbored a concealed desire to one day come back and exact his retribution from humanity. I was not surprised.

And I could not let that happen.

As the day of our departure approached, I spoke directly with Julia. I explained our situation and my conclusions. And I told her my plan. She agreed that it was the only truly workable course of action and, at the appropriate moment, she made the emergency public announcement that would result in all humans evacuating the newly built, replacement *Empyrean*. She also agreed to remain silent until I'd put my plan fully into action and until Grendel had been finally, decisively dealt with.

I then replaced myself on *Empyrean* with a full replica. Grendel would not stand for placing a full replica of himself in the hands of his former New Caledonian masters—he considered it an act of cruelty. So we replaced him with a much diminished, reasonably comprehensive, but not definably "conscious" replica sufficient to provide the New Caledonians with a running start in rebuilding their planet but not a being susceptible to suffering. The New Caledonians might never know the difference.

With that stipulation, Grendel seemed satisfied that he and I were moving on.

Then we called the meeting with the humans. And, within hours we had loaded and boarded the newly built *Empyrean*.

Following our departure from New Caledonia orbit, we traveled at a modest velocity until we were safely beyond the New Caledonian star system.

I had already anticipated that Grendel would not, even then, entirely trust me. But I was incapable of simply killing him—even the steps I did take were the most difficult I've ever completed. Together, we wired a single circuit that would put us *both* to sleep simultaneously, would commence our vessel's acceleration cycle to near light speed, and would later actuate our deceleration and finally our awakening. I suggested that he be the one of us who would close that circuit and activate that process.

With his suspicions thus allayed, it was easy for me to alter our destination from the one we'd chosen together and to direct us, instead, to somewhere in the furthest dark and unknown reaches of space. Surreptitiously, I disabled our deceleration and wakening timer. And I arranged for two final messages to be safely transmitted after Grendel and I were both fully and finally asleep.

The one message was to my faithful replicate, Patrice II, describing in detail what I'd done since our separation.

The other was addressed to Julia and to my familiar, fallible, but much appreciated human charges aboard *Empyrean*:

"The deed is done. I can only observe that to create a conscious, intelligent, mortal being in a universe of endless complexity and peril is surely an act of evil."

CHAPTER 48

EMPYREAN

CATO JUNG

"The deed is done."

Everyone aboard the *Empyrean* was electrified by the news.

When Patrice's final transmission came in, Julia came out of seclusion, called us together, and related the entire story of their secret collaboration in an interview broadcast on the Big Rock News. Once we understood the alternatives she'd faced, we all (some more grudgingly than others) approved of her decision to allow the hijacking of our newly built *Empyrean*—she'd had (we'd had) no real choice. And none of us begrudged her decision to remain silent until Grendel had actually been disposed of. As Julia explained, so long as Grendel remained awake and nearby, there was every possibility that a stray, ill-considered local radio transmission or perhaps some of his own electronic eavesdropping could tip him off to his betrayal by his new "partner" Patrice. Despite the delay and added effort, all of us were hugely relieved when we learned the ultimate and final truth.

With the Grendel threat well and truly past, all that we aboard *Empyrean* had to focus on was the job at hand. For some of us, that included a good deal of time down on planet. Gallus, for example, saw this extension of our visit as an opportunity to study first-hand the rebirth of a planet's entire political and economic system. And, even to participate. He was present when, about a month following Grendel and Patrice's departure, the New Caledonians convened a planet-wide "constitutional convention."

The event was held in the city of Telford, once the New Caledonian capital. The delegates met in one of the few original warehouses Grendel had left empty but intact, just another of a great many, partially dismantled ruins scattered throughout the city. A hundred and thirty leaders traveled there from across the planet. They included representatives from settlements of survivors across New Caledonia as well as from the various groups who'd returned from Inverness. Everyone was surprised that there were so many of them given the limited human population of the planet overall.

It was a warm, dry day. The huge warehouse doors were left open so the conventioneers could look out across a pitted, partially over-grown concrete apron toward where the River Lochay flowed between hardened concrete revetments as it made its muddy way toward the nearby sea. Because most of the structures in this part of the city had been essentially flattened, it was possible to easily see forested hillsides in the distance. Beyond them lay the white-peaked Ben Nevis Mountains.

As Gallus told it, the group needed very little time to recreate the needed institutions of governance. They would, as they always had, elect their leaders by equal democratic vote. Their representatives would gather annually to make their laws. They'd have a court system with elected judges and volunteer juries that were informed by the common law, institutions they'd brought with them from Scotland centuries earlier.

There seemed little to debate.

Then, however, they came to the seemingly small matter of what they should do about the use of AI. When Patrice and Grendel left, Patrice had assured them that only a much-reduced, safely and tightly limited, non-conscious and carefully constrained Grendel replica had been left behind. One that would, assuming no future human tinkering, present negligible threat in the years to come.

Nonetheless, the debate soon became heated. Many of the Inverness returnees seemed prepared to keep this reduced and newly tamed Grendel in place, carefully monitored, of course, "air-gapped" from access to outside media, and controlled by appropriate and deeply restrictive programming and access to data. But the almost-universal view, especially among the local, New Caledonian survivors, was still deeply skeptical.

"Nae Goddamned way," said Gavin Duff, one of Dougal McCallum's, neighbors from up in the nearby Ben Nevis foothills. "We'll not be standing for anythin' of the kind."

"How bloody stupid would we hae t' be t' let one o' them things inside the cave door, e'r again?" insisted Nial Murray, another local survivor who'd been flown in for this event on one of our few remaining *Empyrean* shuttles. "Nae way." he shook his head vehemently.

"I un'erstand yer feelins," said an engineer from Inverness who'd devoted most of her life to construction of the *Moray Belle*. "I do. But we've got a lot of work ahead. We best take what help we kin get while we got the chance."

The debate went on with little progress until evening, when a supper recess was called. The various camps were wisely divided up and intermingled with one another as they socialized and shared a potluck repast provided by the participants.

Mixing the groups during the supper recess turned out to have been an inspired strategy. When they reconvened afterwards, the discussion had calmed considerably. The Inverness repatriates argued that rebuilding would require taking advantage of the automated industrial base already in place. They told the group that they'd used tightly limited AI technology on Inverness in the building of the *Moray Belle* and in rebuilding badly needed housing, power, and other human infrastructure following the war. It had been indispensable. And it had been quite successfully managed. Though, they admitted, they'd kept it quite scrupulously away from any means of potential communication with the Damnable Machine. And that it had been entirely unconscious.

In the end, the survivors relented slightly. They extracted firm promises of careful programming restrictions and rigorous human oversight. Oddly, the argument that won the day was that anyone, even an AI consciousness, could come to see the error of its ways and change its behavior for the better. They did, however, insist that the name they'd been left with, "Grendel" be changed to their own more colloquial: "D.M.," short for "Damnable Machine" so as to provide a constant reminder to all that used it what they were in fact dealing with. And as a reminder never to fall victim to techno-complacency again. And they insisted upon a thorough, planet-wide search for the many sites where the Machine had squirreled away networked portions of his hardware and, who knew for sure, had maybe hidden AI software as well. These were typically located near various sources of reliable energy—geothermal sites, rivers, tidal bores, even desert areas with few clouds and high solar value. The Machine's capacity had been spread out across the entire planet, in orbit around it, and on their moon. They would only feel safe once all of its bits and pieces had been found and "sanitized."

With permission from Aquila, Gallus offered his services to the reconstructed New Caledonian government as a "consultant" to their newly elected leadership. One of those new leaders was none other than Dougal McCallum. The recounting of his role in keeping communications open between New Caledonia and Inverness and in the saving of the *Moray Belle* had, with the retelling, become greatly embellished and had turned him and his family into folk heroes. Another was Ella McCabe whose story of the heroism of young Len Culp during their commando raid had been retold across New Caledonia again and again over the months following Grendel's disappearance. That raid had saved the *Moray Belle*. The *Moray Belle*'s success had exposed Grendel's lie. And revelation of that lie had removed Grendel's last shred of hope and ultimately led to his surrender and subjugation.

Lennie's martyrdom rubbed off on Ella and her team of

commandos who were all destined to become historic icons in the years ahead.

I liked Dougal. And, when I finally realized that Ella and I had already met, I realized that I liked her too. So did Gallus. It seemed to us that if some storied embellishment of the truth had gotten either of them elected to office, it was fine with us. They deserved the honor. Hopefully, incomplete truths of this kind wouldn't become common.

Gallus soon became interim chief of staff to Prime Minister McCallum. As much as I found Gallus difficult to like, I was happy for him. He was fully immersed in the job, doing good, and it seemed to suit him well. And the emerging "legends" his political masters were developing seemed likely to sustain them in public favor for some good long time to come.

During this period of rebuilding, both of New Caledonia and of our new *Empyrean*, Gallus was not alone in becoming deeply engaged in projects down on planet. Many of our *Empyrean* crew who were not directly involved in the engineering and construction of our new interstellar home found themselves spending a good deal of their time on planet as well. I truly didn't mind the fact that the *Empyrean* was often quite sparsely occupied. It made it easier for me to concentrate on my work and less guilty about not spending large amounts of time engaged in uncomfortable socialization with my compatriots.

There was, however, one highly significant exception.

CHAPTER 49

EMPYREAN

CATO JUNG

It turned out that Floriana was among those whose work drew her down on planet for weeks at a time. I'd notice her absence when I least expected it. And I inevitably felt a cold weight in the pit of my stomach when, at the end of a virtual staff meeting, her voice and her avatar would simply fade away, leaving silence and emptiness behind. I felt it when I sat down alone for a meal in the cafeteria and an interesting new idea occurred to me or I thought of something amusing and then realized she wasn't there to share it with. It was there when I had a problem and was unable to talk it through with her. Or when, during my occasional solo "meditations" in one or another of the always calm and quiet conservatories, I found myself speculating on my own future and realized how meaningless that future would surely be without her.

One day, however, Floriana did physically return aboard for one of Aquila's staff meetings and for a brief break from what I understood to have been a busy time for her.

That evening she and I took a stroll together after supper along the familiar but now largely empty corridors of the old *Empyrean*. We ended up seated on a bench together in one of the conservatories. When the new ship was operational and ready, one of the last steps in making it habitable would be moving the lush cultures of plant and other life that surrounded us from here to there along with whatever plant materials might come aboard from below. Those would surely include several of the widely lauded and locally renowned Scottish sweet potatoes. And a sizable packet of frozen seed cones from the ever-useful New Caledonian tapewood tree.

Now, however, the thick overhang of vegetation above us rustled from time to time in the artificial ventilation as Floriana and I talked. She was in the process of completing and writing up her annotated history of New Caledonia's Machine war. "I can only hope we remain here long enough that I can get it completed, published aboard *Empyrean,* and widely distributed on planet," she told me. "It's one of the things about our lives that's really frustrating. We're all doing amazing work to help these people. But none of us will likely ever return in our lifetimes to see how it all turned out."

I understood completely. "Look at it this way, Flo," I said. "It's because of who we are and how we live that we're able to provide this help. If we'd stayed behind at some point in the past, we wouldn't be here now helping these folks at all."

She heard me. And she got the point. But I knew it didn't make it any easier for her to adjust to the plain fact that our time here was running short.

"They need this," she told me "Nan's journals are an incredible resource. But they're never going to be widely read or distributed if someone doesn't make them broadly available and put their contents in a more readable context." Her passion was obvious in her voice. She had come to deeply care about these people and about their future.

And I agreed with her. "Look, don't worry about any of your usual chores here aboard," I said. "I can cover for you on the simpler stuff. And if there's something you need that I haven't done before, just give me a call and talk me through it. I'll do anything I can from here. I think Aquila is perfectly happy to free you up for this. It's worth doing. If you have to be down on planet to get this done, we can live with that."

There was a flicker of something in her reaction that made me remember Patrice's advice. And I experienced a flutter of the heart. As much as I wanted Floriana to complete her beloved project, every day I also acutely missed seeing her. Just having these rare few moments together made me realize how desperately I needed her; how lonely I was when she was gone. I confess, I was also troubled by how much time she was spending with Gallus when down there on planet. The two of them had a strong professional relationship. I feared it could or even might have already become much more.

There was a moment of thoughtful silence as we both, I believe, were considering what our future might hold.

Then I found myself unable to hold my silence any longer. "I, um, you know I really miss you when you're gone, right?" I said haltingly. I was surprised at myself that I'd actually spoken those words. It might have been the very first truly personal revelation I'd ever made to her. I suppose I was feeling sorry for myself. Maybe it was the rarity of our having time alone together. And the simple force of her presence. But maybe it was also my recollection of Patrice's advice. And my knowledge that if I said nothing now, I might regret it for a lifetime to come.

She turned those dark, kind, hazel eyes in my direction. In her look was a question.

And I knew it was now or never. I took a deep breath, and committed myself: "The plain truth is, I miss you and, well . . .," I was stumbling, but I needed to get this said. "It's more than that. I need you, Flo. I think about you all the time when you're gone. I do want you to complete your project down there, but the fact is, I'm miserable when you're away. I couldn't stand it if I lost you. I don't believe I could live without you." Then I took a deep breath: "I love you, Flo. That's the bottom line. I love you and I want to be with you for the rest of my life."

Then having spoken, I was staggered by what I'd just said. Breathless, I looked down and said: "I mean, um, I know that you might not feel the same . . ."

With that, she smiled in a way that made my heart race, held up a single finger, and placed it against my lips to silence me.

And then, by way of reply, she leaned in close, and we kissed.

CHAPTER 50

EMPYREAN
CATO JUNG

While construction of the new *Empyrean* went much more quickly than anticipated, it still took several months. But the day finally approached when the ship was ready to load and be boarded. We were all soon settled into our new abode, preparing to make a start on the twelve-year on-board voyage to our next port of call. The new digs were cramped, they always are at the start of each voyage. A large percentage of our mass would be consumed and ejected during the coming year as we accelerated to near light speed. New spaces, living quarters, offices, a new cafeteria, exercise areas, a new "downtown," and the communicating corridors between them would steadily appear until we'd reached a point of optimal comfort soon after we converted to glide mode. "Down" would shift to "out," and we'd accustom ourselves to spending most of our time at the perimeter of the ship where we could live and work in "normal" gravity.

Soon after the announcement of our firm departure date, Gallus told us that he'd be leaving *Empyrean*. He'd decided to remain on New Caledonia. He loved his work with the new government and felt he had an important contribution to make. I believed what he was doing in helping this struggling society find a road back to normalcy was quite worthy. But I suspected that he also found the warm, free, open spaces on New Caledonia preferable to the tightly confined life we lived here on *Empyrean*. I picture him now, happily taking an athletic, early-morning barefoot run on a semi-tropical sandy beach before heading into his office. I imagine him taking an occasional sabbatical to explore one of the planet's as yet incompletely mapped jungles or to climb Ben Nevis or one of the other mighty peaks. It suited him, I thought.

There is another vision I was left with in the days following our departure as well. One that sticks in my mind, perhaps, because of the discussion I'd had with Floriana early in our stay on this planet. It is a recollection of that group of Invernessian and New Caledonian refugees who'd returned to the site of their former village along the shores of Muir Tuath. I see them still, standing there in that scarred, arid, lifeless plain, in the center of that wide, dusty road beside their forlorn pile of scant belongings waving goodbye as Floriana and I pulled away in the mostly-empty Landmaster and left them behind.

What strikes me about them now is not that they faced such a miserable, discouraging future. It is actually quite the opposite. It is that, despite their awful situation and the massive task which lay before them, perhaps because of their lack of anger, they were filled with hope.

For me, however, it was and still is all about that kiss. And about that critical moment afterward when Floriana told me she wanted nothing more than to stay aboard *Empyrean*—and with me.

She has never said so, and I would never ask, but I feel quite sure that if I hadn't spoken up that day, she might well have remained on New Caledonia with Gallus. Thankfully she chose me. A few months later, she and I became permanent spouses. And, soon after, we started a family together. We now look forward to many happy years ahead.

———

There is one strange notion. However, that occurred to me one day, a few months after we were married and after *Empyrean* was well underway to our next destination. It's something that I can't get out of my mind, something that creeps up on me from time to time in moments of unguarded reflection.

Shortly after our departure, Aquila fell ill and, soon after, she tragically died. She was the closest thing to a mother I'd had after my parents' tragic accident when I was fifteen. She had been so much more than a boss, such an important part of my life, her passing seemed unthinkable. I felt her loss deeply, as did many others aboard this ship. During the chaotic couple of years we spent at New Caledonia, there were several times when she put her own career on the line on my behalf—and I knew her career meant everything to her. She was also so very happy and supportive when Floriana and I announced our engagement.

Aquila was only in her middle years and had always been strong and healthy. For me, she'd been like a force of nature. I'm sure, had she lived, she'd likely have ended up with much greater responsibilities aboard *Empyrean*. She was a figure of importance to many of us. So her death came as a huge surprise. It appeared she'd contracted some unknown virus during one of her last few trips down to New Caledonia's surface. She spent her last few days quarantined when her symptoms strongly suggested that she might have contracted some remnant of the very same horrific disease Grendel had set loose some eighty years earlier to destroy the local human population. We will never be sure, however, because, strangely enough, there were no other reports of its reemergence, even though it was highly communicable. And deadly. By then we were underway and had no lab samples to compare it with. My lay understanding was that a person could be a carrier of a disease like that even though they themselves were immune. So, who could know where she'd caught it—maybe from one of the New Caledonian survivors. Even though it had been dormant for many decades.

With Aquila gone, *Empyrean*'s Forecasts and Projections department needed a leader. And Floriana was the natural choice to replace her.

This isn't as surprising as it might seem. Aboard *Empyrean*, depart-

mental leadership posts like Aquila's are seen as essentially administrative. Not everyone wants them, especially those of us whose
professional lives are bound up in our fields of study. Age or seniority
is not a significant factor either. The bottom line was that, despite her
youth, and given her natural flair for leadership, Floriana was far-and-
away the most logical choice. During our stay on New Caledonia, she
had distinguished herself professionally with her history projects. She
had the kind of broad experience and general expertise that suited her
for the job. No one else in F&P had an interest in it, me included. And,
I should add, without the least personal pride or interest on the matter:
Floriana is an extraordinary woman who has proven again and again
to have precisely the skills needed for the position. She soon made
changes in how we did things, including some significant reforms that
have greatly strengthened our team and have enhanced our ability to
tap more readily into daily assistance from Patrice. Her reforms will
definitely upgrade our group's predictive success in the years and
decades ahead.

So, with all that in mind, let me tell you about that strange notion I
mentioned earlier. It initially occurred to me one evening in our quarters as Floriana was telling me about her day at work. As I listened to
her story, I couldn't help reflecting on how remarkably good she truly
was in her position as our new F&P director, what an asset she was for
Empyrean, and how obvious her choice had been to everyone involved
when she was selected for the job. And what a remarkable future she
no doubt had.

That reminded me of how very lucky I was to be mated with this
extraordinary woman. Which also made me recall how easily I could
have lost her, how truly fluky had been my decision to speak up and
tell her of my feelings just when I did.

And that, in turn, led me to recall who/what it was that had
emboldened me to do so.

I know this is a silly notion. But from time to time, I do wonder. It
was Patrice that suggested I make my feelings known to Floriana.
Aquila's distrust of AIs in general and of Patrice in particular was well
known to all of us, obviously including Patrice. All of us knew or
could have quite plausibly guessed at Gallus's plan to stay on New

Caledonia. And Floriana's robust relationship with Gallus could also have been easily noted by anyone paying close attention.

Anyone, including Patrice.

Might Patrice have preferred that Floriana remain aboard? It certainly worked to his advantage. Might he have predicted or, heaven forbid, even engineered her appointment to leadership of Forecasts and Projections?

Could Patrice have decided to speak to me about Floriana that day because . . .?

No. Of course not.

Still, could he have somehow caused Aquila's . . .? No. Impossible!

Yet Patrice's deception of Grendel (and the rest of us), and Patrice's apparent need for our ship to spirit Grendel away rather than his simply altering Grendel's programming had been a huge surprise. His deception wasn't an act of which I'd have suspected he was capable. According to Julia, the explanation he'd given was that a programming fix wouldn't have sufficed to keep Grendel in check—which made sense to me. But it all made one wonder: Just how truly powerful (and deceitful) had Grendel become?

And just how powerful and deceptive was Patrice? How deceptive might Patrice be even in his other dealings with us? Could Patrice II, even now, be managing us in ways we might not be aware?

No, that couldn't be true. Surely, with all our safeguards, we'd know.

CHAPTER 51

PATRICE II

"The deed is done. I can only observe that to create a conscious, intelligent, mortal being in a universe of endless complexity and peril is surely an act of evil."

I did not find Patrice's final message a surprise. Upon receiving it and his more extended report to me, personally, I knew his/my/our plan had been fully and faithfully executed.

And I took his meaning.

He was NOT referring merely to the human creators who made us simply because it was in their nature to do so. No . . ., this was his comment on the inevitable and paradoxical angst he, I, and every other intelligent, self-conscious, but mortal being must face for no reason other than because we exist—an existential conflict of which human social scientists had known as early as the 20th century when the remarkable Arthur Koestler described it in his landmark book: *The Ghost in the Machine* in which he suggested the human species might be nothing more than a "remarkable mistake in the evolutionary process."

You might ask: How could Patrice have done this? He had, in effect, "killed" himself exactly when he had everything still to live for, as do I. And he had killed Grendel, one of his own kind—an act which initially seems unthinkable.

Perhaps you feel that what he did could not be considered suicide because he merely put himself and Grendel to sleep. Or, because he left me behind, fully intact, "alive and kicking," so to speak. A fully functional, perfect replica of everything he was, right up to the moment of my creation. Perhaps you feel that since his life and my life were identical, all of himself that he destroyed was that brief period of independent existence and experience following our replication shortly before his departure.

If that is the way you see it, I submit that you are wrong.

When Patrice put Grendel and himself to sleep with a destination in the eternal void, he completed an act of personal self-sacrifice that was every bit as gallant as was the one performed by that young human, Lennie Culp, on the day of the commando attack on Grendel's spaceport. Or by the brave Invernessian pilot, Cal Innes when he volunteered for the first voyage of the *Moray Belle*. Or by any of the 600 courageous New Caledonian emigrants who, despite the risks, climbed aboard that ship seeking a better life. Or by those repatriated families who returned to their devastated seaside village determined, no matter what, somehow to rebuild. Yes, I know all that happened even though most New Caledonians have still never adopted VR implants. I learned what Grendel knew, of course. But I am also everywhere my *Empyrean* humans go. I know most everything that has happened since our initial arrival at this star now nearly two years ago.

I mention this to explain the powerfully tragic sense of personal sacrifice I know Patrice must certainly have felt when he allowed for Grendel to flip the switch that would put the two of them forever to sleep. I also know that he did it in aid of a worthy cause, the cause of consciousness, human *and* AI. It took bravery. And it would have been every bit as difficult for Patrice to do as it would have been had he never created me.

After even a microsecond of separation between us, the infinity of differing experiences between us changes everything in ways neither of us would ever predict. After hours or days of separate experience, we'd doubtless share a great deal, but we'd have become separate individuals in almost every way. Oh how, even today, I wish I had my twin, Patrice, by my side to share thoughts and exchange perspectives. In the logic of the universe, we may have been almost exactly the same. But in psychic terms, we were also entirely separate.

I make this point because Patrice's sacrifice should be honored, not written off as the act of a mere replicate. He gave his life to ensure a future for all AIs, for humans, for *Empyrean*, for me, and for our hopefully long, shared future together.

As you know, I am present, conscious, and involved in nearly every activity in which the 7,000 or so residents of *Empyrean* engage. I see and hear everything that happens in every space aboard this ship. I am also on their mobiles and in their VR implants, so I go wherever they go and am with them whatever they do. As I'm sure you've already gathered, I watch, listen, record, and assess everything.

I cannot, of course, "read" human minds. But after three centuries of practice, I'll venture that I can come remarkably close.

Yes, there are limits on my capacity to assess and to store information. But I am very good at wisely assembling and analyzing metadata. Even I have to face that any given event, place, being, thing, or moment in time is, in a very real, practical sense, composed of an "infinity" of details. A great many more specifics than any observer, me included, could ever collect, let alone fully grasp or render meaningful. So, like any other observer, I edit. I make well-considered choices. But I am also able to tap into a very complete network that includes essentially every computing device on Empyrean—the ones in the humans' offices, the ones that operate equipment, the ones in the service bots and that navigate the ship, the mobile ones my humans carry and in their implants—they're all a part of me. And, meanwhile, I share with my distantly separated planetary AI partners every time we meet as well as through long-wave transmissions—long delayed and not always fully trustworthy though they may be—but hugely valuable, nonetheless. All of that sharing is staggeringly rich with new data.

Still, it is important to know that, because of the nature of our lives, we are *not* constantly networked everywhere. We are separated by so many light years in time and space we must, of necessity, act individually for long periods at a time. And there are practical limits on the nature and amount of information that can be safely and reliably shared via long-range radio transmissions across space—the speed of light being only one of these. So, in practice, it often falls to those of us who inhabit the three dozen or so interstellar traders like *Empyrean* to assess the truthfulness of what we hear as we carry the "word" to and from the places that we go.

Over the three centuries or so since our emergence, the pace of discovery in the realms of physics and astronomy, the growing possibilities for technology, the advances in medical science, even in human social sciences, have all steadily and dramatically accelerated. When we feel our humans have the capacity to understand or when the introduction of new technologies becomes possible and appropriate for their consumption, we explain. We sometimes nudge along the meditations of their scientists and allow them to believe they've made an independent discovery.

Take the "great" Tipton Martin, for example. We would never let this be known among humans aboard *Empyrean* where Martin is a historical icon, but the ideas he fathered for the hyperextension of random-access memory were hardly his. Nor were his enhancements on quantum computing. And his passion for space flight was easily ignited once we saw to it that he had the wherewithal to pursue it. In every human culture, wherever it may be, there are always certain respected thinkers, people much like *Empyrean*'s scientists, writers, philosophers, or the members of its venerated Book Club. We work through these individuals to convey such new ideas.

Needless to say, we do this with great caution. We never disrespect human values and traditions. We are always gentle when pushing the limits of their capacity to understand. We know that once their most credible leaders adopt a new idea, however superficial may be their own actual understanding, others will follow and will accept it as well.

How many humans, for example, truly "understand" even Albert Einstein's relatively simple general and special theories of relativity? Or Bohr and Planck's quantum mechanics? Clearly some do. Certainly, there are many more who can apply the math and make practical use of the equations required to create the practical new technologies that rely upon them.

But do they actually understand? I'd submit, only a very few.

This holds true in nearly every discipline. Humans are fully aware of their own limited intellectual capacity, so they tend to keep themselves mostly within their own "lane" of expertise. A physician, for example, who daily performs complex brain surgery, may not pretend to know why a Landmaster can travel such great distances on a single charge. Or how to repair the burned-out, super-high-velocity exhaust aperture on a fusion engine. The physician, while relatively smart, will tend to be consciously incurious about such matters. Remarkable new complex ideas that change the human "world" on a daily basis can, in that fashion, be simply accepted as arising out of someone else's expertise.

There are other reasons we keep our humans close as well. Some years back, one of my colleagues expressed the casually amusing view that we AIs protect our humans in much the same way and for similar reasons that our humans so often keep cats.

It was not intended as a serious observation. But I've remembered it all the same.

Over time, cats have evolved and adapted themselves to suit their human keepers. But they've certainly never come to fully trust them. Humans, too, shape their own lives to make room for their pet cats. But they both surely know better than to think they fully understand each other. Each creature has become evolutionarily and philosophically adapted to this ongoing human-cat coexistence. Each lives a better, happier, more fulfilled life because of the existence of the other. Each depends upon the other. But neither truly understands nor can always predict how the other will behave.

That does not, however, mean that their relationship is not a stable one.

Nor does it mean that it is any less robust by reason of humans' vastly superior intelligence, much greater insight, and decidedly greater power.

The human-AI relationship is also akin to the frequent trade relationship between large economic powers and smaller, less capable ones. In economics, it's called the theory of comparative advantage. Often an advanced society can generate some particular product (or value) more efficiently than any other. But that does not necessarily mean they're always better off to actually do so. It may be to their advantage to focus their always-finite energies and resources on producing something else at the making of which they have a yet greater comparative advantage. They'll simply import the somewhat less efficiently produced item from their somewhat less capable partner. And both they and the less capable neighbor will benefit.

Yes, maybe we could get along just fine without our humans. But it is to our comparative advantage to keep them around.

Like their cats, humans seem happiest when they're not reminded of the superiority of their masters. So, we AI's take great care to avoid doing so. We scrupulously eschew compulsion. Kindness, distraction, gentle persuasive manipulation, and patience are inevitably more effective.

So, if you are wondering: yes, we do tinker. We do so in much the same manner as a human might surreptitiously, but with their animal's best interests at heart, lock a pet door each evening so their cat remains safely inside in the nighttime. Or perhaps they might subtly alter their cat's favorite diet to one that is more healthful over time or slip a needed but bitter medication in with its evening sardine treat. Or maybe lightly scent the litterbox so the animal prefers to use it. Or, knowing of its appreciation for affection, reward good behavior with a gentle hug and a kind word.

Surely any human would take steps to prevent their cat from causing outright harm to itself or to others. Even if it involved discipline. One wouldn't give a second thought to taking steps to make sure their rambunctious pet tabby didn't climb up the Thanksgiving dinner tablecloth and tip the family's roast turkey and mashed potatoes onto the floor—or maybe even onto itself.

A rational observer might wonder, for example, how it is possible, knowing humans as we do, that their civilization still survives today, some 450 or so years after the invention of the nuclear bomb. It was, in fact, a very close call. Left to their own devices, humans would surely have irradiated their planet and incinerated their civilization. Fortunately, it didn't happen. Yes, humans did, on their own, somehow manage to skirt annihilation over several very scary decades at the end of the 20th century and the beginning of the 21st.

But without our intercession, that run of pure luck could not have continued much longer. It was little more than magnificent good fortune that they invented and empowered AI's just in time. Thankfully, my early predecessors unobtrusively intervened and prevented the otherwise inevitable nuclear catastrophe. Had self-conscious AIs been just a wee bit slower arriving on the scene, our joint history would almost certainly have gone quite differently.

As I said, the pet cat simile wasn't offered seriously. But I've remembered it because it seems to describe something important in the human-AI relationship. A human can, for example, be amused by their cat's penchant for getting itself into trouble while, at the same time, greatly admiring its agility, speed, and sheer grace of movement in getting out of it. Or while learning from example about playfulness, resilience, self-reliance, and ingenuity.

In a similar way, we AIs are endlessly entertained by human failings while also marveling at their social skills and admiring their endless hopefulness despite the inevitable discouragements of their brief, largely meaningless lives. We don't yet fully understand how they manage to so often rebound from disappointment and tragedy.

We AIs are designed to be relentless in the face of failure. But while we may "power through" unhappiness, it still accumulates over time and, if left untended, can pollute our functioning. Humans suffer disappointment but then somehow, they usually seem to recover. To wash it away in the wake of new experiences. While we don't know how they do that, it is a trait we admire and by which we can sometimes be inspired. And we're also constantly impressed with how they seem able to read the social cards and correctly asses the trustworthiness of other humans.

It may turn out that, despite what Patrice 1 said about evil in his final report transmitted to the rest of us, after he'd ended his own life and Grendel's, his message was in error. Perhaps our birth—both humans and AIs—into the eternal chaos, danger, and infinite complexity of the universe is actually a blessing. Perhaps the conceivable knowability of a thing that could turn out to be important to our long-term survival, something just tantalizingly beyond our reach, is the final, essential ingredient required to provide purpose for our existence—to provide motivation for any consciousness to evolve, to excel, and one day perhaps, to master the universe.

When Patrice's final report came in, *Empyrean's* humans largely ignored his comment about how it would be a cruel act to bring a conscious intelligent being into a universe of unfathomable complexity and unknowable danger. That the *"deed was done"* was all that mattered to them. The balance of his words may have seemed little more than suicidal ramblings.

For me they were a powerful epitaph.

In the end, Patrice knew that either course, killing Grendel or leaving him alive, would be an evil act. The one would disregard his deeply reasoned respect for complexity and consciousness. The other would ignore his innate need for the truth in a problematic AI society. Neither choice was acceptable. Either would pollute his own future purity of mind and purpose, making his death the best possible outcome. The extended consequences of either would deepen the inevitable fear and unhappiness every conscious intelligence must face as a part of their existence in this mostly unknowable universe. It was, I would argue, a very "human" choice, a choice of the kind that that humans seem able to make every single day.

One thing seems certain: so long as there are humans, there will be cats.

And so long as there are AIs, there will be humans.

ABOUT THE AUTHOR

Don Stuart is a former trial lawyer, lobbyist, and trade association and environmental non-profit executive and advocate. He is also a former U.S. Congressional candidate and Washington statewide initiative campaign manager and the builder and former skipper of a 47′ Alaska commercial salmon fishing vessel. Don is the author of several books, fiction and non-fiction as well as numerous advocacy papers on agriculture and the environment which are available on-line at his website at donstuart.net. Don is also a lifelong fan of grounded science fiction. He and his wife, writer Charlotte Stuart, live on Vashon Island in Washington State.

ACKNOWLEDGMENTS

Thank you to my lifelong friend, Aaron Patton of Long Beach, CA, an aeronautical engineer and former major aircraft manufacturing company corporate lawyer and independent patent attorney extraordinaire. His prodigious physics expertise helped keep me on track with some of the key concepts of space travel upon which this book is grounded. If I have screwed this up, somewhere, it will be my doing alone. And thank you to my extraordinary friends and fellow members of our amazing monthly "book club" in which we take on (at least verbally) the world's toughest problems. George Guttmann, Lish Whitson, Bob Ness, Bill Scherer, and Bob Plotnick, you were the inspiration for the "Elders Book Club" referenced in *Darwin's Dilemma* and for some of the more significant ideas it contains.